"Devon said you had to get married before your thirty-sixth birthday, but she didn't say why."

Cat waited for Luke to tell her it was none of her business, but he shrugged and leaned his head back against the chair, his expression unreadable.

"My grandfather wants me to settle down and breed two or three little Quintains to carry on the dynasty. I made the mistake of telling him I wasn't interested, so he came up with this scheme to force my hand."

Cat told herself that the idea rolling around in her head was insane. It was one thing to think it…but she couldn't actually *say* anything. Could she? She clasped her hands together and pressed them between her knees to hide their nervous shaking. "You could…I mean…it's maybe a little *odd*, but not really any odder than the whole idea of…"

"What could I do that isn't any odder than marrying your not-quite stepsister?" he asked.

"You could marry me instead."

"Schulze delivers a love story that is both heart-warming and steamy."
—Publishers Weekly

Dallas Schulze

The Substitute Wife

MIRA®

ISBN 1-55166-677-4

THE SUBSTITUTE WIFE

Visit us at www.mirabooks.com

Printed in U.S.A.

For Art. Always.

Chapter One

"Let me get this straight. You're eloping to Las Vegas with an old lover and you're asking *me* to break the news to your fiancé that you're dumping him?" Cat stared at her stepsister in disbelief.

"Really, Cat, you don't have to make it sound so... *sordid.*" Devon Kowalski paused in her packing, her neatly plucked brows drawn together in a distressed frown, her lower lip hovering on the edge of a pout. With her big blue eyes and delicate features, she made a heart-tugging picture of hurt innocence. Cat, who knew for a fact that Devon had practiced that particular expression in front of a mirror, was unmoved. She arched her brows and waited, and, after a moment, Devon's expression shifted to a more genuine, if less attractive, pout. "You're the one who likes to read those trashy romance novels," she snapped. "I'd think you'd *understand* me wanting to marry for love."

"I understand wanting to marry for love," Cat said. "What I don't understand is how you can break off your engagement this way. You owe it to Luke to talk to him,

tell him what's going on. You can't just put news like
that in a note and ask me to hand it to the man.''

"Well, I can't *mail* it. I mean, what if it doesn't get
there or something? And it would be *tacky* to just leave
a message on his answering machine,'' she said with a
self-righteous air, as if inviting Cat to congratulate her on
her sensitivity. What Cat really wanted to do was thump
her on the head to see if there was anyone home in there.

Devon folded a blue silk nightie and tucked it along
the side of the suitcase she was packing, then reached for
a handful of panties and bras, all pastels and lace, and
began tucking them into nooks and crannies.

Watching her, Cat racked her brain for what she could
say to make Devon change her mind. Oh, not about breaking the engagement. Frankly, Luke Quintain should drop
to his knees and thank whatever gods he liked that
Devon's high school sweetheart had returned from the
wilds of Minnesota or Michigan or wherever he'd been
just in time to sweep Devon off her dainty size-four feet
and out of Luke's life. Not that Devon was the Wicked
Witch of the West, but she was spoiled and selfish and
unlikely to make anyone a particularly good wife. Luke
was definitely better off without her. Actually, the high
school sweetheart would probably be better off without
her, too, but that was his problem. No, it wasn't the engagement she wanted Devon to change her mind about, it
was the method of breaking it.

Devon might think that leaving a message on the man's
answering machine was tacky, but this wasn't much better. And Cat wasn't all that crazy about being the bearer
of bad tidings. It wasn't that she expected Luke to lop off
her head, but she hated the idea that whenever he thought
of her it would be as the person who'd given him the
news that his fiancée had run off with another man. Not

that he was likely to think of her at all, she admitted wistfully. Once the engagement was broken, he would probably put Devon Kowalski and everyone associated with her right out of his mind. And even if he *did* think of her, it was clear that his taste ran to fragile little blondes with big blue eyes, not tall, leggy redheads with generous curves. *Fragile* was not a word that ever applied to a woman who stood five feet nine inches in her stockinged feet, Cat admitted with a faint sigh.

"Don't you think you owe it to Luke to talk to him, explain about Rick coming back from Michigan and how you realized you were still in love with him?"

"Luke will be *upset*. He might say mean things," Devon said, as if that explained everything, and Cat supposed it did. One of Devon's biggest talents was avoiding unpleasantness of any kind. As far as she was concerned, the thought that Luke might say something "mean" was reason enough to avoid the encounter. It would never occur to her that when a man found himself dumped four weeks before the wedding, he might be entitled to say one or two mean things.

Cat leaned one shoulder against the doorjamb and watched in silence as Devon zipped the suitcase closed and set it on the floor before going to her dressing table, where she began sorting through the rows of bottles, her expression serious as she considered the important question of what makeup to pack for an elopement.

Devon's room always made Cat feel a little like Gulliver entering the land of the Lilliputians, or maybe Dorothy stepping out of the tornado-tumbled farmhouse into Oz. The rest of the rambling old house was filled with mismatched furniture, worn rugs and faded draperies. A handful of nice, if slightly scruffy, antiques sat cheek by jowl with garage sale rejects. It was comfortable, livable, undistinguished. In contrast, Devon's room was all pale, polished wood and thick peach carpeting. Floral drapes in peach and soft, warm green hung at the windows. The overall effect was feminine without being frilly, and it suited Devon perfectly, which was the whole point, of course. Devon's bedroom was designed to complement her the way a black-velvet-lined jewelry box was meant to enhance a strand of pearls. And it succeeded admirably.

The peaches-and-cream prettiness of it always made Cat feel too...everything. She was too tall, her coloring too vivid, her legs too long, her hair too red, too curly. It wasn't so much Devon's bedroom that made her feel that way, Cat thought, as it was Devon herself. When she'd first met Devon, she'd been a gawky thirteen-year-old, all legs and arms and hair. Devon had been twenty, a tiny, blue-eyed blonde, delicate as a china figurine. A brief spell of hero worship had died a natural death under the influence of Devon's benign indifference and unremitting shallowness. Even at thirteen, Cat had known there was more to the world than makeup and boys.

"I really think you should tell Luke yourself that you're breaking off the engagement," she said, giving it one last try. "If you're going to break his heart, you at least ought to do it face-to-face."

Devon shook her head as she selected half a dozen bottles and set them aside. "No. Luke has a *nasty* temper. I'm not going to let him spoil this for me. Besides, I'm *not* breaking his heart. He'll be mad, but it's not like he's *in love* with me or anything." She caught Cat's surprised look in the mirror and huffed a little sigh as she turned to face her. "Look, I didn't tell *anyone* this before, because it wasn't anyone's business, *really,* and I knew people would think it was...well, maybe a little *weird,* but there's nothing *wrong* with it. No one was being hurt or anything." Devon must have seen Cat's total lack of understanding, because she stopped, drew in a deep breath and got to the point. "Luke and I had a...um...a sort of business arrangement."

"Business arrangement? I thought you were getting married."

"We were. That was the business part of it." When Cat stared at her blankly, she laughed, more annoyance than humor in the sound. "*You* shouldn't find it hard to understand. Don't they do that kind of thing all the time in those books you read? What do they call it?" She groped a moment, then smiled when she found the phrase she was looking for. "A marriage of convenience. That's what we were going to have. Only with sex, because, really, how convenient would a marriage be *without* sex?"

A marriage of convenience? Devon and Luke Quintain? The thought made Cat's head spin. That sort of thing didn't happen in real life. Real people didn't make pretend marriages. Except apparently they did, or at least they made pretend engagements, although maybe the engagement had been real, even if the marriage was—would have been—fake. And could you call it a fake marriage if they were sleeping together?

"Why?" It was the only word that managed to slip past her confusion.

"The usual reasons," Devon said, shrugging lightly. Cat's mind boggled at the idea that there were "usual reasons" for a marriage of convenience. Before she could try to sort out what they might be, Devon continued. "Luke's grandfather wants him to get *married* for some reason. Luke didn't tell me why, exactly, but apparently he's got something to hold over Luke's head. He *has* to be married before his thirty-sixth birthday, which is in a couple of months.''

"Okay," Cat said, dragging the word out as she absorbed this new information. "That explains what Luke was getting out of the marriage. What about you?"

"You have to ask?" Devon rolled her eyes, and Cat flushed as a sudden image of Luke popped into her head. No, she supposed she didn't have to ask. The man was not only ridiculously good-looking, but he had that indefinable something that made the muscles tighten low in her belly. It was pretty obvious why Devon would—

"Money," Devon said, cutting through Cat's thoughts.

"Money?" she repeated, trying to shift her thinking from blue, blue eyes and thick dark hair to crinkly green stuff. "Money?"

"Come on, Cat. The man's richer than God." Devon laughed. "His great-grandfather *owned* half the San Fernando Valley back when it was nothing but chicken ranches and orange groves, and his *grandfather* managed to make money even during the Depression. I don't know *details* about his father, but Luke is some sort of real-estate wizard. Every time he draws a *breath,* he's making more money."

"And he was going to...what? Give you money to marry him?"

Devon wrinkled her nose. "It sounds so...*sordid* when you put it that way," she protested. "But, yes, Luke was giving me money to marry him. A whole lot of money, actually." She sounded wistful.

"And you're giving that up to go live on a dairy farm?" Cat asked, then winced at the incredulous tone of her own voice.

The idea of Devon living on a dairy farm had been difficult to grasp even before she knew the truth behind her engagement to Luke Quintain. Now it seemed even more incredible. It wasn't that Devon was mercenary. Not exactly. It wasn't money that Devon loved. It was all the pretty things it could buy. Shopping wasn't a hobby; it was an avocation. It was one of the things that made her good at her chosen career as a decorator—she got to shop for beautiful things *and* get paid for doing it.

"*Money* can't buy happiness," Devon said with the air of someone presenting an original truth. Cat might have been impressed by this new, improved Devon if she hadn't continued, "Besides, I have the engagement ring Luke gave me, and that's worth a *fortune.*" She picked up a small leather jeweler's box from the nightstand and snapped it open to admire the ring inside.

"You can't keep that ring," Cat protested, appalled. Even from several feet away, she could see the way the light caught on the diamonds.

"Why not?" Devon snapped the case shut and closed her hand around it as if afraid Cat might try to snatch it from her. "Luke gave it to me. It's mine."

"Luke gave it to you because you were going to marry him."

"I *was* going to marry him."

"But you're not going to marry him now," Cat pointed out.

"I don't see what that has to do with it." Devon picked up her purse—tan leather, made by Coach and another gift from Luke—and tucked the ring box safely inside. "It's not like I *lied* to Luke. I did plan on marrying him. He gave me the ring, and it's mine. I'm sure he'd want me to keep it."

"Traditionally, you're *supposed* to give the ring back."

"So?" Devon set the purse on the bed and turned back to finish packing her makeup. "Traditionally, you're supposed to be madly in love with each other when you get married. Luke and I had a business arrangement. He gave me the ring for getting engaged to him. We *were* engaged, and the ring is mine. Besides, it's worth a lot of money. It would be *stupid* to give it back.''

That was so typically Devon, that mixture of naiveté and ruthless practicality. With a sigh, Cat gave up any thought of trying to get her stepsister to change her mind. Short of arm wrestling, there was no way Devon was giving that ring back. Realistically, it wasn't as if the value of the ring was going to make a significant impact on Luke Quintain's bottom line. Whatever it was worth, it was probably pocket change to a man who bought and sold Los Angeles real estate like baseball cards.

''So you'll take the letter to Luke?'' Devon asked, focused, as always, on getting what she wanted.

''I don't think—''

Devon picked up the envelope and held it out. ''If you don't take it to him, I'm just going to drop it in a mailbox.''

Cat hesitated, but she knew the other woman well enough to know she would make good on her threat. Even if it hadn't been a love match, Luke deserved better than to have the U.S. Postal Service give him the news that he was being jilted. She crossed the room reluctantly and took the envelope, which was addressed in Devon's childishly round handwriting, with—incredibly—tiny hearts dotting the *i*'s in Quintain.

''Devon, are you sure you—''

''I'm positive.'' Devon zipped shut the tote holding her cosmetics and glanced around the room to see if she'd forgotten anything. Satisfied that she had all the essentials, she looked at Cat. ''I really appreciate you doing this,'' she said, as if she hadn't virtually blackmailed Cat into it. She frowned a little. "I'm sure Luke will remember you. Pretty sure, anyway. I mean, *who* can forget that hair?"

Cat slid the envelope into the back pocket of her jeans and resisted the urge to smooth her hair. It wouldn't do any good, anyway. In her better moments, she fancied the mass of tumbled copper curls had a sort of Botticelli by way of Titian look about it. On a bad hair day—and she'd had more than her share—she thought it was more red mesh scrubber after a trip through the garbage disposal. Either way, she'd learned that there wasn't a whole lot she could do to influence things.

Twenty minutes later, Cat stood on the sagging front porch and watched Devon and her soon-to-be husband drive off down the long gravel driveway, on their way to Minnesota or Michigan by way of Las Vegas. She wished them luck. She was fairly sure Rick was going to need it.

She pulled the letter out of her back pocket and tapped it absently against her thigh. Staring out at the haphazardly landscaped yard, she considered her options. She could wash her hands of the whole thing, pop the letter into a mailbox and never give it another thought. But she wasn't going to do that. Even if it hadn't been a love match, no one should find out they'd been jilted in such an impersonal fashion. She would go to see Luke, give him the letter, tell him how sorry she was that things had worked out this way. It was the right thing to do.

And wasn't it handy that doing the right thing gave her an excuse to see Devon's ex-fiancé again?

There's nothing like falling in love at first sight. That throat-tightening, heart-pounding rush of fear and adrenaline, the sudden knowledge that everything—*every-*

thing—is different now, that your life will never be the same, that *you* will never be the same.

The first time Cat Lang fell in love, she was ten. She and her mother, Naomi, were living in Nevada in a shabby old house that had once been a brothel. Naomi was deep in her oil-painting phase, and the attic apartment had what she claimed was the perfect northern exposure. Cat liked the banisters, which were good for sliding down, and the tangled thicket of shrubs and weeds that masqueraded as a backyard, but best of all was Albert Federman, who lived with his aunt and uncle on the bottom floor. He was fifteen, a tall, thin boy with white-blond hair and pale blue eyes. She saw him for the first time the day she and Naomi moved in.

They moved too often to have accumulated much by way of household goods, but there were half a dozen boxes, as well as an eclectic assortment of tote bags and two plastic laundry baskets, all wedged into the back of a rust-pocked yellow station wagon with fake wood sides. Naomi had carried up one box and a tote before getting distracted by the amazing play of light through the leaves of the big sycamore that dominated the overgrown backyard. Cat left her to her rapt contemplation and went back downstairs to bring up another load. A veteran of more moves than she could count, she knew that the sooner everything was unloaded and put away, the sooner it would start to feel like home. She was on her way up the cracked walkway, arms straining with the weight of one of the laundry baskets, when Albert came out the front door and offered to give her a hand.

She looked up at him, standing there with the sun behind him, creating a halo behind his pale hair, his smile revealing one crooked front tooth, and she felt her heart just fall right at his feet. She knew, in that one instant, that *this* was what true love felt like.

Maybe it had been. It had lasted all that summer, and maybe—if Naomi hadn't decided that oil painting really wasn't what she was meant to do after all, and Nevada was just too crassly commercial to truly nurture her spirit—maybe if they'd stayed, she and Albert Federman would have lived happily ever after. But they'd moved to Sedona, and she'd started school at a commune Naomi had joined. Her broken heart had eventually recovered, and Albert had become a sweet memory.

She'd half forgotten that moment of *knowing,* that sudden understanding that everything was different now. Until Devon brought Lucas Quintain home to meet her father, and Cat was suddenly ten years old again, feeling her heart pound so hard that she was sure it must be visible from the outside, feeling that quick rush of fear and excitement. This was it. This was the moment when her life changed forever. This was the one. But the joy, that odd feeling of recognition, had lasted barely a heartbeat. This was Devon's fiancé. No matter how many times she told herself that she couldn't mourn something that had never been hers, she hadn't been able to shake the feeling of loss.

And now, here she was, on her way to tell Luke that he was a free man again, whether he liked it or not.

Sighing, Cat flipped on the turn signal when she saw the Flintridge exit coming up. Fat lot of good Luke's newly single condition would do her. Just for fun, why not list all the reasons he wouldn't be interested in her? First, his taste clearly ran to petite blondes, not leggy redheads. Second, he was hardly going to look favorably on her after she handed him Devon's letter. Third, even if he could overlook that, he probably couldn't overlook the fact that she was related, in a convoluted fashion, to the woman who'd just unceremoniously dumped him. Fourth, fifth, sixth and on into infinity, she wasn't the kind of woman likely to interest a wealthy real-estate tycoon.

The VW coughed asthmatically as the road narrowed and began to climb into the Flintridge hills. The houses sat back from the road, sheltered amid towering live oaks. Discreet mansions, Cat thought and then wondered if that was a contradiction in terms. Could a mansion be discreet? Maybe, to qualify for the title of mansion, a certain flamboyance was required, which would make these just really, really big, really, really expensive houses.

There wasn't much traffic as the road wound up into the hills. She passed two Mercedes—both black—a silver-gray Rolls and a hunter-green Jaguar convertible. The driver of the Rolls gave her a puzzled look, and Cat giggled as she drove through the intersection. Apparently, tomato-red, thirty-year-old Volkswagen Squarebacks were not exactly a common sight in this neighborhood. She gave the sun-faded dashboard an affectionate pat.

"Don't pay any attention to them, Ruthie. They wouldn't know real class if it bit them on the nose."

The VW chugged its way up the next hill and around a long, sweeping curve, and there was the address Devon had given her, neatly emblazoned on a rustic redwood post that sat to the side of a driveway sheltered by the overhanging branches of an ancient live oak. Cat edged Ruthie up to the top of the driveway and hesitated a moment, contemplating the steep slope that dropped away from the street. All that was visible of the house was an angle of roof and a sharp glint of sunlight reflecting off a window.

Luke was down there, expecting his fiancée to arrive for a quiet dinner. He was probably expecting her to spend the night. Devon hadn't said as much, but Cat assumed she and Luke had been sleeping together. The thought added the acid bite of jealousy to the bevy of butterflies that had taken up residence in her stomach. Really, maybe mailing the letter wasn't such a bad idea. Maybe it was actually a *good* idea. It would allow Luke a certain privacy to deal with the news that he'd been jilted. And would allow Cat to escape like the yellow-bellied coward she apparently was. Muttering under her breath, she turned into the driveway.

The house was not at all what she'd expected. She'd envisioned something starkly modern, all redwood and glass, with lots of eccentric angles. Instead, Luke's home was surprisingly conventional. The lower part of the walls was stone, with white siding above. Multipaned windows, a gray tile roof and a wide front porch with stone pillars and wicker furniture completed a quietly elegant picture. The landscaping was neat if unimaginative, relying heavily on the natural beauty of the big oaks that sheltered the house. It looked like a home rather than the showplace she might have expected from someone who made bundles of money buying and selling real estate.

As soon as Cat shut off Ruthie's engine, the silence pressed in around her. It was the kind of stillness that made it easy to forget that Los Angeles, in all its smoggy glory, lay just over the hill. A mockingbird called a stolen melody and was answered by the raucous cry of a scrub jay. If she hadn't been so painfully aware of the reason she was here, Cat could have savored the quiet beauty. But she wasn't here to enjoy the semibucolic splendor of her surroundings. She was here to tell Luke that he'd been dumped in favor of a dairy farmer from some state beginning with M. According to Devon, the news wasn't going to break his heart, but it seemed unlikely to make his day, either.

The doorbell was a quiet two-toned chime. After ringing it, she shifted uneasily from one foot to the other, fighting the urge to shove Devon's letter under the door and then run like mad. Before she could succumb to temptation, she heard the sound of a dead bolt sliding back. From listening to Devon talk, she knew Luke had a housekeeper, so when the door opened, she was not prepared to find herself looking into Luke's blue eyes.

"Cat?" He sounded surprised, but at least he knew who she was, which was a relief. It would have been embarrassing if her heart was beating double time for a man who didn't even recognize her.

"Luke, I...didn't expect you."

He arched one brow in surprise. "I live here," he pointed out.

Cat felt her face heat and knew he could see the color coming up in her cheeks. There was no hiding a blush with her pale skin. "I was expecting your housekeeper."

"It's her day off." Luke looked past her, and she wondered if he was looking for Devon. If that was the case, he didn't say anything when he saw that she was alone but just stepped back from the door. "Why don't you come in? It's a little chilly for standing in doorways."

Cat hesitated a moment before accepting his invitation. She wanted to tell him that standing in the doorway was just fine with her, but his words had made her aware of the cold air finding its way past the bulky cable-knit sweater she wore with her jeans. Besides, she could hardly just shove the letter at him and run.

"Thanks." He led her across the entryway with its glossy hardwood floors and through an arched doorway into a large but surprisingly cozy room. Soft, blue-green carpeting covered the floor, and the furniture looked both elegant and comfortable, a rare combination in Cat's limited experience. A bank of windows along one wall let in the angled beams of the setting sun, painting everything in gold and red. There was a small fire in the fireplace, and the subdued hiss of the flames added a warm intimacy to the atmosphere.

"Would you like something to drink?" Luke asked, glancing over his shoulder at her.

Cat shook her head. "No, thanks."

"You don't mind if I have something, do you?" He picked up a bottle from the tray that sat on an end table. Amber liquid splashed into the bottom of a snifter. "I was planning on an after-dinner brandy but I have a feeling I'm going to need some fortification earlier in the evening."

He glanced at her, arching his brow in question. Cat flushed and stared at him mutely. This was where she should say something to smooth the way for the bad news yet to come. Something mature and intelligent, something sympathetic but not maudlin, something gentle but not mushy.

"Devon's not coming," she blurted out. *Oh yeah, that was good, Cat. Real sensitive.*

"I kind of figured that." Luke took a swallow of brandy, and Cat couldn't stop herself from staring at the clean lines of his profile. He was wearing jeans and a black V-neck sweater that looked soft and touchable. The thin knit clung to the solid muscles in his shoulders and chest, and Cat's fingers twitched with the urge to put her hands on him, to feel the contrast between the soft knit fabric and the solid muscle beneath.

No matter how many times Cat tried to push her thoughts of Luke aside, she couldn't ignore the awareness that curled in the pit of her stomach. It was more than just attraction, though that was certainly a part of it. This was something else. Something deeper. And it scared her to death.

"So, give it to me straight." Luke turned to look at her, long fingers cradling the snifter. "I take it Devon's absence is permanent?"

Cat nodded reluctantly. He didn't look like a man whose heart was breaking. He looked irritated and… maybe a little relieved. Or was that just wishful thinking on her part?

"She's decided to become a nun? Having a sex change operation? Run off to join the circus?"

"A dairy farm," Cat said, and Luke's brows rose.

"She's joined a dairy farm? I didn't know you could do that."

"Not joined one so much as…well, actually, she's sort of marrying one."

"Marrying a dairy farm?" One corner of his mouth curved up. "She's going to need a pretty big church, isn't she?"

Cat hadn't expected to find any humor in the situation, but there was no resisting that lopsided smile. It only lasted a moment, but it left her feeling a little steadier, a little more in control.

"She's actually just marrying the guy who owns the dairy farm."

"Well, that's a relief. For a minute there, I thought I'd been thrown over for a bunch of Holsteins." Luke took another swallow of brandy and shook his head. "A dairy farmer? I never pictured Devon as the milkmaid type."

"Rick was her high school sweetheart. He lives in Minnesota, or it might be Michigan," she said, frowning.

"Whatever. He came out here to touch base with old friends and…"

"Hit a home run with my fiancée," Luke finished for her, and she nodded.

"He…uh…seems like a nice guy."

"Well, that's a relief. I'd hate to think I'd been dumped for a jerk." Luke's smile faded, and he sighed. "Is there a reason she couldn't do her own dirty work?"

Cat thought about lying, telling him that Devon had wanted to talk to him herself, but she couldn't think of a plausible reason why her stepsister hadn't been able to do just that. Besides, why should she worry about trying to make Devon look better in Luke's eyes?

"She thought you might be upset."

"Upset?" Luke snorted. "Just because my fiancée runs off with another man a month before the wedding?"

He tossed back the last of the brandy and looked at the bottle as if debating the wisdom of pouring another drink. Cat pulled the letter out of her back pocket and crossed to him. "She…left you this."

He stared at the envelope for a long moment before taking it from her. He didn't open it immediately, and Cat shifted uneasily, wondering if this was her cue to leave. Maybe he would prefer to open the letter in private? Before she could decide, he was sliding his finger under the flap, pulling out the single sheet of peach-colored paper. From where she stood, Cat could see that there were only a few lines of writing, and she wondered what Devon had said. As if reading her mind, Luke spoke.

"She says she's sorry to leave me in the lurch like this, knows I'll understand that true love is more important than money, hopes I won't have too much trouble canceling the wedding arrangements, and adds a P.S. that she's keeping the ring." He turned the sheet over to see if there was anything more. There was nothing, and he crumpled both letter and envelope and tossed them into the fireplace. The sharp gesture made Cat flinch.

"I did suggest that maybe she should return the ring," she offered hesitantly.

"I don't give a damn about the ring," Luke snapped. He ran his fingers through his hair, ruffling it into thick dark waves. "Sorry. I didn't mean to snarl at you. It's not your fault your sister ran off with a dairy farmer."

"She's not really. My sister, I mean. She's not my sister." Cat wasn't sure why it mattered. Usually she gave little thought to her rather convoluted family relationships. "She's not even my stepsister, not officially."

"I thought her father and your mother were married."

"No." She shook her head. "My mother and I moved in with Larry when I was thirteen. After a few months, Naomi got a chance to go on this spiritual retreat in Mexico, and she just…didn't come back."

"She abandoned you?" Luke asked, sympathy and surprise mixed in his expression.

"No." Cat's denial was automatic. "Not abandoned. Exactly. I mean, she knew I was with Larry, and she didn't just disappear. After Mexico, she had a chance to study with this healer in Peru, and then there was a gathering of spiritual types in India, and she just sort of…didn't come back." She shrugged, careful not to look at him. *She* understood Naomi, but she knew most people didn't. "So I guess Devon is sort of my unofficial stepsister, but it's not legal or anything."

"I'm sure you'll understand that, at the moment, I'm inclined to think not being related to Devon is probably a good thing," Luke said. "You sure you don't want something to drink?"

It didn't sound like he was in a hurry to get rid of her.

She allowed herself a tentative smile. "Water would be nice."

"With or without carbonation?"

"Without." She wrinkled her nose. "The stuff with bubbles tastes like medicine."

"One water, no bubbles, coming up." He disappeared out the door, presumably on his way to the kitchen.

Cat drew a deep breath and rubbed her palms along the sides of her jeans. Well, she'd given him the bad news, and she was still here. He seemed more irritated than angry, and not at all heartbroken. Apparently Devon had told the truth about her engagement. Which opened up all sort of interesting questions and even more interesting possibilities.

Luke came back in, carrying a glass of water and a tray of hors d'oeuvres.

"Are you hungry? My housekeeper left these for tonight, and it seems a shame to let them go to waste. The shrimp things are terrific."

Definitely not heartbroken, Cat thought, taking the glass from him. He set the tray on the marble-topped coffee table and sank into one of the overstuffed chairs that flanked it, gesturing her toward a seat with one hand and reaching for the brandy with the other. She settled uneasily on the edge of the sofa and took a nervous sip of her water.

"Devon told me about the thing with your grandfather." She hadn't planned on saying anything about it, but Luke didn't seem offended.

"Did she?" He swirled the brandy in his snifter, watching the play of firelight on the amber liquid.

"She said you had to get married before your thirty-sixth birthday, but she didn't say why."

She waited for him to tell her it was none of her business. Or to skip that and go straight for "get out." But he shrugged and leaned his head back against the chair, his eyes fixed on the fire now, his expression unreadable.

"My grandfather wants me to settle down and breed two or three little Quintains to carry on the dynasty. I made the mistake of telling him I wasn't interested in carrying on the dynasty, so he came up with this scheme to force my hand."

"Why thirty-six?" Cat asked. "I mean, why not thirty-five or forty? Thirty-six just seems kind of…arbitrary."

Luke rolled his head to look at her, his mouth twisting in that lopsided smile again. "It doesn't seem arbitrary that he'd blackmail me into marriage, but setting my thirty-sixth birthday as a deadline does?"

Cat shrugged and grinned a little sheepishly. "Well, it does all sound a little…odd."

"Odd. Yeah, you could call it that." Luke took a sip of the brandy and then sat forward abruptly. Setting the snifter on the table, he picked up a shrimp. "As far as I know, the only reason for setting thirty-six as the deadline is that it happens to be my next birthday."

Cat nodded as if that made sense. She took another sip of water and told herself that the idea rolling around in her head was insane. It was one thing to think…but she couldn't actually *say* anything. Could she?

"So you…still have this deadline hanging over your head? He won't give you extra time because Devon canceled the wedding?"

"Maybe." Luke scowled at a slice of prosciutto-wrapped melon. "Hard to say. He wasn't overly impressed with your not-quite stepsister so he may cut me some slack. Or he may not."

"When is your birthday?" Yes, that was good. She

sounded interested, casual. Not at all like someone on the verge of losing her mind.

"Two and a half months." Luke set the melon slice down and reached for the brandy. "Seventy-six days, to be exact."

"That's not very much time." She leaned forward and set her glass on a coaster before clasping her hands together and pressing them between her knees to hide their nervous shaking.

"Not much time," Luke agreed.

"You could…I mean…it's maybe a little *odd* but not really any odder than the whole idea of… Not that there's anything wrong with…" She realized she was babbling and shut her mouth with an audible snap. Luke was looking at her, one brow raised in question, his expression mildly curious.

"What could I do that isn't any odder than marrying your not-quite stepsister?" he asked.

Cat stared at him, thinking that she knew exactly how a deer felt when it was caught in the headlights. Paralyzed, helpless, watching doom rush toward it. Only she *was* her *own* doom, and she was going to do it, going to say it.

"You could marry me instead."

Chapter Two

His housekeeper, Mrs. Bryant, had apparently slipped an hallucinogenic into the shrimp, Luke thought. That would explain what he thought he'd just heard. In fact, it might explain this whole conversation. Maybe Devon's little sister hadn't shown up to tell him that Devon had run off to marry a dairy farmer from some state that began with an *M*. Maybe he hadn't told her about his grandfather's crazy plan to get him married before his thirty-sixth birthday. And definitely she hadn't just said—

"What?" His voice came out as a croak, and he cleared his throat before trying again. "What did you just say?"

"I said…you could marry me instead." From the look in her eyes, he was willing to bet that Cat was almost as shocked by the suggestion as he was.

"That's what I thought you said." Luke downed the last of the brandy and leaned forward to set the snifter on the edge of the coffee table before looking at her again. "You don't *look* deranged," he said conversationally.

"It's not deranged," she protested. "If you think about it, it makes sense."

"On what planet?"

"On this one." Her color rose, but her mouth set in a stubborn line that made Luke uncomfortably aware of the fullness of her lower lip. She had the most amazingly kissable mouth. He hadn't let himself notice it before, on the couple of occasions when Devon had dragged him to her father's house for dinner. His engagement to Devon might not have been the romance of the decade, but it *was* an engagement, and it was just tacky to ogle your fiancée's little sister over the dinner table.

With an effort, he dragged his eyes away from her mouth. "It isn't like trading in a car for a new model," he said, annoyance lending an edge to his voice.

"Actually, it is. Sort of." Cat leaned forward, her expression earnest. "You and Devon had a business arrangement, right?" She didn't wait for him to respond but hurried on as if she had to get it all out at once. "You need to be married before your thirty-sixth birthday, and it apparently doesn't matter *who* you marry so..." She gave him a self-conscious little shrug. "Why not me?"

Why not her? There were so many reasons why not her that Luke didn't know which one to mention first.

"You're too damned young, for one thing," he said, coming up with the first and most obvious problem. "How old are you, anyway?"

"Twenty-one," she said indignantly, then bit her lip. "In five months."

"Twenty? You're twenty?" Luke shot to his feet, snatching up the brandy snifter on the way to the bar. "Do you know how old I am?"

"Is this a test?" Cat turned to watch him as he splashed a healthy dose of brandy into the snifter.

"I'm thirty-five," he said, ignoring her question. "I'm twice your age."

"You're off by five years."

"Don't split hairs." He picked up the brandy snifter and stalked back to the sitting area. He stood in front of the sofa and scowled down at her. "I'm old enough to be your father."

"Technically, I guess, if you were on the precocious side but, since you're *not* my father, I don't see that we have a problem."

Luke pointed the brandy snifter at her. "Thirty-five-year-old men do not marry twenty-year-old girls."

"Sure they do. I could be your trophy wife."

She said it with such bright good cheer that Luke was startled into laughing. But he still shook his head. "No. I'm not in the market for a trophy wife. The whole idea is crazy."

"Not really." Cat rose to her feet, apparently too enthused by this crazy idea to remain still.

Luke told himself that the fact that she had legs a mile long and curves in all the right places was not relevant to the current discussion, but he couldn't help but notice that he would only have to lower his head a few inches to kiss her. Not that he had any intention of kissing her, but still, it was…interesting. His tastes had always run to short, busty blondes, but he had to admit, there was something to be said for a tall, leggy redhead with big green eyes and a mouth that seemed made for temptation.

"It really makes perfect sense." She threw out one hand for emphasis, and Luke found his eyes dropping to her breasts. Was she wearing a bra? It was hard to tell under the bulky knit of her sweater. Funny, how the oversize sweater managed to conceal everything and still be sexy as hell. Or maybe it was just Cat who was sexy as hell. He took a sip of brandy and tried to pay attention to what she was saying.

"I know I'm not as pretty as Devon."

No, but she had something that outshone her not-quite-stepsister's chocolate box prettiness. There was something very real about Cat, an earthiness that made a man think all kinds of things he had no business thinking when he was definitely not going to do anything about what he wasn't thinking about.

"And I'll tell you right up front that I can't do anything about my hair."

Luke could think of lots of things he would like to do with her hair, most of them X-rated.

"It's red and it's curly, and if I cut it short, it just frizzes up like a pot scrubber."

"I like your hair," he said, and caught himself before he could reach for it.

"Really?" Cat looked doubtful, then shrugged, as if to say it took all kinds. "Good, because I'm stuck with it. And I've got to tell you that if you have your heart set on marrying someone with decorating talent, we might as well forget the whole idea right here and now."

Hadn't he already said that? He wasn't actually considering this insane idea, was he? If he wanted a decorator, he could hire one, the way he'd hired Devon to redecorate the company offices. "I don't need a decorator," he said, and was rewarded by Cat's smile.

"Good, because I have the decorating talent of an amoeba. I've flipped through a bunch of Devon's decorating magazines, but unless the room they're showing looks exactly like the room I want to decorate—and it never does—I can't figure out how I'm supposed to translate the ideas in the picture to real life."

A stray beam of late-afternoon sunlight slanted through the window and fell across her hair, turning it to pure fire.

Luke's fingers tingled with the urge to touch, to see if it could possibly feel as warm as it looked.

"But I'm not a total loss as far as traditional wife stuff is concerned," Cat continued, apparently through listing the drawbacks to this insane idea of hers. "I can cook. Actually, I'm a pretty good cook. You know Jack's Place, on Melrose?" She waited until Luke nodded. "Jack Reynolds is a friend of mine, and even he admits I'm no slouch in the kitchen."

Luke didn't really care if she could boil water without help, but he had to admit it was a pretty impressive reference. Since it had opened three years ago, Jack's Place had become one of *the* places to go in L.A. He'd taken clients there a couple of times, and the food was superb. If Jack Reynolds said Cat was a good cook, Luke would take his word for it.

"And I'm good at managing things."

"Managing things?" Despite the fact that he'd already made up his mind that this whole idea was crazy, Luke couldn't resist the urge to pursue that comment.

"Household stuff, mostly," Cat clarified. "My mother wasn't exactly the most practical person in the world, so I sort of watched out for her, made sure she didn't spend all our money on some spiritual quest and forget all about buying food and paying the rent. And Larry is pretty much the classic absentminded professor. If someone didn't look after things, he'd probably cook the cat and put food out for the pot roast." Her smile held affectionate amusement. "So I've been managing things for him pretty much since Naomi dumped me in his lap. Some people just aren't cut out for dealing with day-to-day things."

Funny, how people like that always seemed to find someone else to manage all those tedious little details for them, Luke thought cynically. On the other hand, from

what little he'd seen of his almost father-in-law, he
wouldn't be at all surprised if the man needed help tying
his shoelaces. Cat's description of him as an absentminded professor seemed pretty accurate.

"What about Susan?" he asked. "Can't she manage
things for him?"

Until today, he'd thought Susan was her mother. Maybe
he should have asked Devon for a guidebook to her family
relations.

"Susan is an artist," Cat said, as if that explained everything. When Luke arched one brow in silent question,
she expanded. "She throws pots."

"At anyone in particular?" Luke asked, raising both
brows.

Cat laughed and shook her head. "She's a potter. She
makes vases and urns and stuff." Her hands shaped vague
curves as if to indicate the wide variety of pottery Susan
produced. "She's actually pretty well-known. People col-
lect her stuff, and she's got a couple of pieces in museums
somewhere. She's really very talented."

"So you manage things for Susan, too," Luke guessed.

"Well, not her business stuff. She works through a gal-
lery for that. But she's prone to forget to cash her checks
and return important phone calls. She and Larry are perfect for each other in some ways. They're both very creative, but, unfortunately, they're both prone to forget little
things like eating and picking up the mail and doing laundry."

"Creative? I thought Larry taught anthropology at
UCLA."

"Archeology," Cat corrected. "That's what he does for
a living, and I guess he's pretty good at it. His students
like him, anyway." She grinned suddenly. "Probably be-

cause he's an easy grader. Larry thinks bad grades are discouraging.''

"I always thought so," Luke said dryly, and Cat laughed.

"Me, too." She sat back down on the sofa, and Luke sank into his chair, the brandy snifter cradled, forgotten, in one hand. "Larry earns a living teaching, but his real love is inventing things."

"Anything in particular?" Luke asked.

"All kinds of things, but I think the main goal is to invent something that works." Brow wrinkled, Cat thought about that for a moment. "That's really his main problem, I guess. He has great ideas but the…um… execution leaves something to be desired. My favorite was the garbage disposal/worm composter."

"The what?" Somewhere in the back of his mind, Luke was aware that this was shaping up to be one of the stranger afternoons of his life. He wasn't sure what the protocol was after being dumped by one's fiancée but he was reasonably certain it didn't include sitting down with the bearer of bad tidings—who had already suggested that he could marry her instead—and letting her tell him all about the family he was no longer going to be a part of. Well, at least it was more entertaining than brooding about what he was going to do about his grandfather's ultimatum now that Devon had run off with her dairy farmer.

"The garbage disposal/worm composter," Cat said. She'd nudged her shoes off, and now she curled her legs up under her with a coltish grace that made Luke's thoughts drift in directions he was determined not to let them go. "Vermiculture is a really big business, you know."

"Vermiculture?" Luke raised his brows. "Growing

vermin? I thought the idea was to get rid of them, not cultivate them.''

"Not growing vermin," Cat said, chuckling. "Worms. Growing worms. I guess wormiculture doesn't sound good, or maybe 'verm' is Latin for worm or something.'' She frowned over that possibility for a moment before shaking her head as if physically dismissing the thought. "Anyway, people grow worms and then sell them to bait shops for fishing, but the really big business is dumps, I guess. I'm not sure exactly what they do with them, but apparently they use lots of worms. Supposedly you can make a lot of money that way.''

"And Larry was going to become the Southern California worm king?" Luke asked with lazy interest.

"No, he wasn't going to grow the worms himself. See, you can feed the worms chopped-up leaves and coffee grounds and stuff, so he had this great idea for a garbage disposal that would chop the stuff up and feed it directly into a worm bed under the sink. It was really a great idea, only it had some...problems."

Luke waited, but, when she didn't immediately continue, he prompted her. "Okay, I'll bite. What kind of problems?''

"Well, it chopped up the garbage just fine, but there was something wrong with the way it fed stuff into the worm bed, and instead of feeding the garbage to the worms, it...well, it chopped up the worms, too." She tried to frown at Luke's shout of laughter, but her mouth twitched in sympathy. "You know how, supposedly, if you chop a worm in half, you get two worms? Well, I don't know if that's true, but I can tell you for sure that if you chop them into a bunch of pieces, all you get is chopped-up worms."

"I can see where that would be a problem," Luke said when he could control his laughter enough to speak.

"But the basic idea really *was* good," Cat said, and for some reason that set him off again.

God, he couldn't remember the last time he'd laughed like this. It had been years. It was a shame he couldn't take her up on her insane suggestion that he marry her instead of Devon. He was willing to bet that Cat would make a much more interesting wife.

"So tell me why you'd want to marry me." He hadn't planned on bringing the subject up again, but the words were out before he could stop them. With a shrug, he decided to go with it. "What's in it for you?"

She looked at him, and there was something in those big green eyes that he couldn't read. Some emotion that was there and gone before he could figure out what it had been. Her gaze slid away from his for a moment, and when she looked at him again, there was nothing there but a cautious sort of hope.

"Well, Devon said you guys had a business arrangement, and she mentioned something about a settlement."

Money. Luke felt a surge of cynical satisfaction mixed with a completely illogical twinge of disappointment. In the end, most things came down to money. She and Devon might not be related by blood, but apparently they had quite a bit in common after all.

"How much?"

"What?" The pretty confusion was very well done, he thought cynically. She wasn't as good at it as Devon had been, but the blank surprise was quite effective in its way.

"How much did you have in mind?" He took a swallow of brandy, letting the smoky heat burn the bad taste out of his mouth.

"I...didn't have any particular amount in mind." Cat's

forehead puckered in a slight frown. "Are you very rich?"

The naive question startled him into swallowing too quickly, and the brandy burned all the way down.

"I'm not poor," he rasped, fighting the urge to cough.

"I know that, but I mean, are you *rich?* Devon said you were, but she sometimes gets her facts mixed up. Are you *rich,* rich?"

"I'm rich, rich, *rich,*" Luke told her, amused despite himself.

"Oh, that must be nice," she said, sounding more wistful than envious.

"I've always thought so."

The room was starting to get dark as the sun went down, and he got up, switching on two lamps and drawing the curtains closed against the darkness. The big room immediately took on a greater air of intimacy, warm and cozy, despite its size. When Luke returned to the seating area, he didn't sit down again but chose to stand near the fireplace, leaning back against the mantel as he studied Cat.

"So how much did you have in mind?"

"Are you really thinking about this or just amusing yourself?" she asked shrewdly.

It was a good question. Luke looked at her while he debated with himself. Was he actually considering it? It was crazy. Women weren't like carburetors. You couldn't just swap one for the other—except, in this case, he actually could. It would solve his immediate problem, anyway. His grandfather had given him until his thirty-sixth birthday to get married or he would sell Maiden's Morning to developers. All those acres of carefully tended grapes, all that history and pride, turned into tidy little ranchettes for yuppies commuting to the city. He had to

hand it to Nick Quintain. He was a wily old bastard. He'd
known just where to apply the thumbscrews. Maiden's
Morning was the only part of the Quintain empire Luke
gave a damn about, and his grandfather knew it. Never
mind that the old goat would hate seeing the Napa Valley
vineyard turned into an upscale subdivision nearly as
much as Luke would. He'd said he would sell it, and Luke
knew he would do just that.

Unless Luke got married.

Some might say that asking Devon Kowalski to marry
him had been giving in to his grandfather's blackmail, but
Luke had seen it as another move in the chess game being
played out between the two of them. Nick Quintain
wanted his grandson married and settled, preferably with
a gaggle of great-grandchildren on the way. Luke had proposed to a woman who was everything he knew his grandfather most despised, a featherbrained blonde with a bub-
bly personality, the depth of a mud puddle and the
maternal instincts of a tree stump. She'd been the perfect
means to keep up his end of the bargain while ensuring
that he didn't give his grandfather any of the things he
most wanted. She'd been perfect for his purposes. But she
was gone, and now, here was her not-quite-stepsister, offering herself in her place.

"I'm seriously considering it," he said, aware that the
silence had stretched to uncomfortable lengths. "How
much did you have in mind?"

Cat stared at him wide-eyed, as if, now that he'd said
he was considering her offer, she didn't know how she
felt about it. She uncoiled from the sofa and stood up, as
if she felt better facing him on equal terms.

"I...hadn't really thought about it."

"Well, think about it now," he suggested. "I'm willing
to be generous, but I'm not stupid."

She tilted her head and considered him, a faint smile slipping into her eyes. "No reasonable offer refused?" she suggested softly, and Luke was surprised to hear himself laugh.

"That's pretty much it," he agreed, nodding. He bent to scoop his drink up off the marble topped table, then straightened to lean against the mantel again, the snifter cradled in one hand. "What did you have in mind?"

"Well, a trust fund for Larry, I think. And one for Susan. Separate trust funds in case they split up because, like Naomi always said, you never know where a person's life path is going to lead. I'm not sure just how much. I know they're both grown-ups and should be able to take care of themselves, but I'd like to know that they'll never have to worry about things."

She frowned and chewed on her lower lip while she thought about it. Luke's fingers tightened around the snifter as he forced himself to resist the urge to offer to chew on her lip for her.

When she finally named a figure, it was much lower than he'd expected. She must have seen his surprise and misinterpreted it, because her teeth immediately began to worry her lip again.

"Is that too much, do you think?" she asked anxiously.

Luke took a moment to consider his answer. Either she was incredibly naive or she was one hell of an actress. Devon had driven a shrewd bargain, though he hadn't given her any more than he thought her name on a marriage license was worth. How likely was it that Cat had spent—what? seven, eight years—living with her and could still be as... Well, the only word that came to mind was innocent, which was ridiculous in this day and age, even if she hadn't been living in the same house with

Devon. Which left the possibility that he was being treated to an Oscar-worthy performance.

"No," he said finally. "I think we could work with that number."

"Oh, good." She gave him a bright, relieved smile that lit up her whole face. "I know it probably seems silly, since they're fully functioning adults—well, *mostly* functioning," she corrected with a smile that held a trace of mischief.

"As long as you don't mind roast cat for dinner?" Luke asked, arching one brow, and she laughed, a deep, earthy sound that did things to his gut that had nothing to do with humor.

"Exactly. I just want to know they'll be okay."

"Seems like a lot of concern for two people you aren't even related to," Luke commented.

Something flickered in her eyes, as if the comment had touched a nerve, but she shrugged. "Family isn't always a matter of birth or marriage. They've both been good to me. Larry could have turned me over to Social Services when Naomi didn't come back. No one would have blamed him, but he didn't. He let me stay with him." She frowned slightly. "Of course, it's possible he forgot I was there." She ignored Luke's choked laughter. "Either way, the end result was the same. And when he and Susan got together, she didn't think it was odd that his former girlfriend's daughter was living with him." She paused and then, with scrupulous honesty, added, "I'm not totally sure she's grasped that, actually."

Well, if he married her, he could be reasonably sure he wouldn't be bored, Luke thought, grinning. That certainly hadn't been the case with Devon. Boredom had been a given with her. He'd just decided that was the price he would have to pay—along with a considerable sum of money—for an undemanding wife and a painless divorce when the time came.

"What about you?" he asked. "What do you want?"

"Want?" Cat gave him a confused look.

"You just offered to marry me for my money," he pointed out. "I assume you want something besides a trust fund for your stepparents."

Again there was that flash of emotion he couldn't quite read, a guarded look that was there and gone before he could interpret it.

"I...I'm sure whatever arrangement you had with Devon will be fine," Cat said vaguely.

Luke considered the bargain Devon had driven and thought it would probably be plenty for anyone short of a rock star's ex-wife, but he couldn't resist the urge to prod further. "That's rather trusting of you, don't you think? What if she made a lousy bargain?"

"Devon?" Cat looked surprised. "Devon lives to bargain. I'm sure whatever your agreement with her was, it will be just fine for me."

Interesting that she didn't ask what the agreement was, Luke thought. He contemplated her in silence, one hand idly swirling the last swallow of brandy in the snifter. She looked...uncomfortable with the whole discussion. Cynically he wondered if she thought talking about the settlement might make her look greedy where offering to marry him for money hadn't. It was surprisingly difficult to read what was going on behind those big green eyes. Not that it mattered all that much, he thought. He needed a wife, not a best friend. He already had one of those, and he could trust Keith to see that the prenup protected him.

"A prenup is a given," he said abruptly, and Cat jumped a little, startled.

"A prenup?" she said blankly.

"Prenuptial contract. Everything laid out nice and neat. What you get. What I get in return. What happens when we get a divorce. No surprises. No loopholes."

"*When* we get a divorce?" Cat wrinkled her nose. "Not exactly positive thinking, is it?"

"Realistic thinking," Luke said. "Better than fifty percent of marriages end in divorce, and that's when two people start out pledging eternal devotion. What we're talking about is a business arrangement, not a prelude to romance. You want money. I need to be married for a year. Divorce is pretty much a given, don't you think?"

"Maybe, but Naomi used to say you can only see the path as far as the first curve."

"And that would mean...what, exactly?"

When she frowned, her lower lip stuck out in a slight pout. It was an oddly childlike expression, but the thoughts it engendered were definitely not paternal.

"Well, Naomi tends to prefer obscurity, so I'm not totally sure, but I think it means you can't really predict what the future will bring."

"I think I can safely predict a divorce in my future," Luke said firmly. "So if you have any romantic notions about until death do us part, we'd better call this whole thing off."

"I wasn't sure there was anything *to* call off," Cat said, giving him a direct look. "Are you taking me up on my offer to take Devon's place?"

"I don't know." Luke tossed off the last of the brandy and set the snifter on the mantel. He was far from drunk, but he was aware of a pleasant little buzz, a sort of what-the-hell feeling. Somewhere in the back of his mind, danger signs were flashing, warning him that maybe this wasn't the time to be making life-altering decisions, but it was easy to ignore them.

His grandfather had already made the biggest decision for him, forcing him into a marriage he didn't want. Luke felt a sudden wave of bitter anger at the way the old man was manipulating his life. This wasn't what he wanted, dammit, but it was what he had to do unless he was willing to see a subdivision spring up in place of the vineyards he'd played in as a child. And if he had to do it, he would do it on his terms. The old man had had a bride all picked out for him. Old money, solid family, so well-bred she came with a pedigree. He'd told Nick where he could stick his hand-picked bride and her pedigree, and he'd asked Devon Kowalski to marry him, knowing she was everything his grandfather most despised.

Now, here was Cat, offering to take her place. Even if she hadn't been absurdly young, he'd never gone for redheads, preferring the cool gleam of blondes. But the thought of those fiery curls spread across his pillow made his mouth go dry and other body parts perk up in potentially embarrassing ways.

He wanted her.

It was her eyes that pushed him over the edge. Or maybe it was those legs. God, she had legs all the way up to her neck, and those big green eyes that always looked a little sleepy, as if she'd just crawled out of bed and it might not take too much to persuade her to crawl right back in. If it hadn't been for the eyes and the legs—and the husky little laugh and that wide mouth with its full lower lip—maybe he wouldn't be letting his zipper do quite so much of his thinking.

But, as long as he was thinking with his zipper, he might as well run with it, Luke decided. There were only a few feet between them, leaving just enough time for him to see her eyes widen before he was standing in front of her. She tilted her head to look up at him, but she didn't have to tilt it very much. In heels, she would only be an inch or two shorter than he was. He wanted to see that. Black silk stockings, spike heels and not another damn thing between him and that long, lithe body.

He was going to do it, he realized. He was going to take her up on her crazy suggestion to take her stepsister's place. Maybe he'd even made the decision the minute she made her proposal. Why else would he have sat here talking to her about it? If he hadn't known, deep down, that he was going to do it, then he would have ushered her out after that first stunned moment and gone about the business of finding himself a wife. But he hadn't. Because he wanted this, wanted her.

"Part of the deal with Devon was that this would be a real marriage," he murmured. He lifted one hand and touched just a fingertip to the pulse that was beating wildly at the base of her throat. She swallowed hard, those tilted cat eyes widening endlessly.

"I know." It was hardly more than a whisper. "She told me."

"Do you have a problem with that?" Luke let his fingers curve around her throat. "Do you have a problem with the idea of sharing my bed?"

"N...no."

"Are you sure?" His thumb stroked the sensitive skin under her ear. "Maybe we should see if we're... compatible?"

She stared up at him, her eyes deep and fathomless. "I won't sleep with you tonight."

"Waiting for the papers to be signed?" His smile was sharp and hard. "Want that ring on your finger first?"

"Yes. No." She shuddered as he traced the outer edge of her ear with his fingertip.

"Which is it, Cat?" He leaned down, deliberately using his size to his advantage, crowding her.

"I...don't know you that well," she said. "And I've never...never done that before."

Never done what? Luke pulled back as one possibility hit him. He left his hand where it was, fingers buried in the fire-colored silk of her hair.

"You're telling me you're a virgin?" His tone made his skepticism obvious.

Cat blushed wildly but met his look without flinching. "It's not a crime."

"No, but it's damned unlikely." He eyed her speculatively. Did she think he would get off on the idea of having a virgin bride? Because none of his fantasies of her—and he had a surprising number of them—involved initiating a beginner. Or maybe she thought it would push the price up? But her look was not so much triumphant as faintly embarrassed.

"You don't have to believe me," she said, lifting her chin. "I'm not sleeping with you tonight."

"Who said anything about sleep?" he whispered against her mouth.

This was no gentle, exploratory first kiss. He took her mouth like a conquering warrior, not asking for a response but demanding it. Cat's hands tightened on his arms, as if to push him away, and then she was melting into him, her mouth opening to his, her body curving against his. Luke felt a surge of triumph race through him, and he slid one arm around her waist, pulling her closer, deepening the kiss, his tongue slicking over hers.

The kiss was hungry and carnal, a kiss meant for lovers. She whimpered, a low sound in the back of her throat. It wasn't a protest. It was a plea. She rose on tiptoe, her fingers curling into his dark hair as her mouth opened to his, inviting him to take more, to take her.

Not since he was a randy teenager had he been so instantly, painfully aroused. Luke's hands caught her hips, dragging her close in a quick, convulsive movement, letting her feel the hard press of his erection through the layers of denim and cotton. She caught her breath, her head jerking back, breaking the kiss. Wide green eyes stared up at him, smoky with hunger but holding a new wariness.

"No."

God, she even managed to make "no" sound sexy. Still holding her, Luke bumped his hips into hers, letting her feel his arousal again. Her breath stuttered, and her eyelids seemed suddenly heavy. He could persuade her, he thought. It wouldn't take much. She wanted him. Maybe not quite as much as he wanted her, but if he nudged the heat up a bit, he could have her.

"I'm not going to sleep with you tonight," she said firmly, and his confidence wavered. There was a core of steel in her voice.

Ordinarily he would have let it drop there. It wouldn't be the first time he'd been turned down. Contrary to generations of male whining, no man ever actually died of blue balls. By the time a man reached thirty-five, he'd learned to be gracious about it.

But it had been a bitch of a day. He'd watched a deal on an apartment building in Sherman Oaks go down the tubes because the seller was too stupid to know a good offer when he saw one. His grandfather had called to tell him—for the fifth or sixth time—that he was a damned fool to be marrying that little blond tart when he could have had a fine young woman from a good family, and that Cissy Winslow was still ripe for the plucking. Luke had told him to pluck her himself and hung up. He'd come home, looking forward to a pleasant dinner in Devon's undemanding, if vacuous, company and then ending the evening with some nice, uncomplicated sex.

Instead Cat had shown up to inform him that he was no longer engaged, which would please his grandfather to no end and leave him that much closer to Cissy Winslow's well-bred clutches. As the day's events flashed through his mind, Luke felt the leash on his temper slip several notches. Without taking time to think, he opened his mouth.

"What if I said the deal was off if you didn't sleep with me?"

Cat's spine stiffened so fast, it was a wonder she didn't end up with whiplash. Her eyes went from smoky-green to icy-emerald, and the hands that had been resting on his shoulders were suddenly flat against his chest as she pushed herself back and out of his hold.

"I'd point out that we don't have a deal, and that even if we did, I'm not particularly responsive to blackmail." She looked down as she found her shoes under the edge of the sofa and slid her feet into them.

She was leaving. If he didn't say or do something, she was going to walk out, and while one part of his brain pointed out that that might not be a bad thing, he knew he didn't want her to go.

"I'm sorry. I...that was way out of line."

"Yes, it was." She straightened and gave him a steady look that made it easy to forget that he was older than she was.

"I..." Luke ran his fingers through his hair, searching for some plausible explanation as to why he was behaving like a total bastard. He finally settled on the truth. "It's been a lousy day. A *really* lousy day," he emphasized.

"Finding out I'd been unengaged was just the cherry on the sundae, but that doesn't excuse my taking it out on you." He tried his most ingratiating smile on her. "I'm sorry."

Cat considered him for a moment, her head tilted slightly to one side. Luke resisted the urge to fidget under that steady regard. He'd apologized. She would either accept it or she wouldn't.

"Okay." She nodded, even smiled a little. "According to old wives' tales, men get cranky when they're...um... in extremis."

Against all expectation, Luke heard himself laugh. "In extremis? I think that's the first time I've heard it called that."

On impulse, he reached out, burying his fingers in the heavy red silk of her hair. She stiffened slightly but didn't resist when he pulled her close and lowered his mouth to hers in a long, slow kiss that held both apology and promise. When he lifted his head, he allowed himself a moment of smug pleasure at the dazed look in her eyes. He could still have her tonight, but that would be all he had. He wanted more. More of that sulky lower lip and the husky little laugh. More of those big green eyes that reflected her changing moods like a mirror, and more of that long, lithe body. One night wouldn't be enough.

He released her slowly, keeping her hand in his, rubbing one thumb back and forth over the back of her hand.

"So, what do you think? If I promise not to be a jerk, you think you'd be willing to try this marriage thing?"

Cat's breath caught, and something flared in her eyes, an emotion gone too quickly for him to define. But the smile that followed was warm and open.

"I'd like that," she said.

It wasn't every day that a man traded in one fiancée for another, Luke thought. Instinct told him he was getting a much better deal this time around.

Chapter Three

Jack's Place was neither large nor architecturally impressive. The restaurant was located in a nondescript stucco building on a newly fashionable section of Melrose Boulevard. It had originally been a barbershop, but as the neighborhood declined, so did business, and it became a used-clothing store. When the neighborhood declined further still, it became an adult "toy" store, selling leather goods, body oils and other items for those who preferred sex with accessories. Briefly there was a massage parlor in the back, where massages tended to get very, very hands-on.

A police crackdown closed the shop, and the building sat empty for several years, until the fickle winds of fate and fashion turned Melrose into one of L.A.'s "places to be." Chi-chi shops with whimsical names and stratospheric prices replaced the adult bookstores, used-clothing emporiums and massage parlors. Businesses, legitimate and otherwise, were displaced to make way for valet parking, styling salons and a pet-sitting service that promised to "watch your pets while you shop."

Cat wedged her Volkswagen into a spot between a Mercedes and a Lexus and got out, careful not to bump Ruthie's door against the Lexus's shiny black paint. The hatchback squealed when she lifted it, and she made a mental note to grease the hinges. Maybe this time she would even remember to do it, she thought optimistically.

She opened the flaps of the large cardboard box, checking to make sure her cargo was still in good shape. Lettuce lay in carefully stacked mounds, a riot of soft greens and bronze-toned reds. Bundles of carrots, still dusted with dirt, nestled next to crisp white-and-green shafts of leeks and scallions, and radishes in colors ranging from white to burgundy. The rich scents of earth and green, growing things wafted out, and she inhaled deeply, savoring the scent even more here, in the midst of the traffic smells, than she did when she was actually in the garden.

Satisfied that everything was in good shape, she flipped the box closed and lifted it out, balancing it on her knee until she had the hatchback shut. The huge garden behind Larry's house had been started by his first wife. She'd died when Devon was a child, and it had lain fallow for several years before Naomi and Cat moved in with Larry. Cat had been drawn to the tangled remains of once orderly beds, and had started pulling weeds and tidying things up. Over the years, the garden had become her domain. She planted a few flowers, but her main love was for growing vegetables. At first she'd grown enough to supply the family, but she couldn't resist expanding the garden and trying new varieties, and she was eventually growing more produce than they could possibly use.

She was barely eighteen when she read an article about a chef in Maine who bought much of the fresh produce he used in his restaurant from a home grower. With a feeling that she had nothing to lose, she began calling upscale restaurants. Jack's Place had just been starting to get a reputation as a place to go, and Jack Reynolds's name was beginning to be mentioned when people talked about hot new chefs. At twenty-three, he was a rising young star with a reputation for uncompromising quality. Cat's organically grown produce fit right in with his philosophy. Their relationship had started out as business but had quickly moved into friendship.

The in crowd was apparently busy elsewhere at two o'clock on a Thursday afternoon, and the sidewalk was relatively empty, which made a nice change from Saturdays, when she found herself maneuvering around people who were so busy being seen that they apparently couldn't be bothered to watch where they were going.

The door to Jack's Place was solid wood with a half-round top. Painted bright blue, with the name discreetly displayed in gold lettering, it always made Cat think of the entrance to a hobbit house, as if, once inside, she might find herself taking tea with Bilbo or Frodo. Though the restaurant wouldn't open for a few more hours, Jack generally left the door open for deliveries.

The interior wasn't exactly hobbitlike, but it *was* cozy and comfortable, with dark wood paneling and heavy wooden beams overhead. The flooring was oak and had been rescued from a craftsman-style home in Pasadena that was being torn down to make way for a strip mall, and it showed the scuffs and scars of decades of wear. There was a big fireplace at one end of the room—gas jets and ceramic logs, but, on winter evenings, the effect was almost as nice as a crackling wood fire. Jack cheerfully referred to the decor as fake English manor, but it was warm and comfortable and suited the food he served, which he called upscale, down-home cooking.

Cat pushed the door shut behind her, but her smile

soured when she saw the man crossing the room toward her. He was mincing. She'd read the word in books, but, until she met Phil Douglas, she'd never actually seen a person mince across a room. Still, there was no other word to describe the fussy little steps he was taking. Of course, as tight as his pants were, it was a wonder he could walk at all.

Cat's mouth quirked up on one side as she stood just inside the door and watched him approach. One thing she had to give him, he certainly knew how to make an impression. Not necessarily a *good* impression but definitely an impression.

At five foot seven—if he stretched a bit—and weighing maybe a hundred and forty pounds, soaking wet, nature had not blessed Phil with any striking physical attributes, but he'd made up for it. His hair was bleached nearly white; and he wore it cut short and gelled into a bristly glory. Cat had once suggested it made her think of an albino hedgehog. Phil had not been amused. A row of gold hoops marched along the outer rim of one ear, and two diamond studs decorated the other. He wore a pair of black leather jeans that were so tight Cat wondered if he'd actually had to grease his legs to get them on, but the final touch, the ultimate grace note, was his sweater. Two-inch-wide hot-pink-and-black horizontal stripes encircled his thin frame like a punk version of a barbershop pole.

Phil's expression soured even more when he saw her. "Well, if it isn't our little poster girl for squash growing."

"And if it isn't our poster boy for bad taste." Cat's smile was every bit as nasty as his. "Where did you get that sweater, Phil? Prison wear for the color-blind?"

Phil's mouth tightened into a thin line. He tugged at the bottom of the sweater. "This is a Lucy D. original."

"Really? Where'd she learn clothing design? San Quentin?"

"Not everyone admires the bag-person look," he sneered, giving her black leggings and teal-blue sweater a scathing look.

Cat grinned. "Bag person? That's very p.c. of you, Phil. Wouldn't want to show a gender bias toward the homeless, would we?"

"Are you two fighting again?" Jack asked as he made his way across the dining area. He was tall and lean, with dirty-blond hair that always looked like he'd just run his fingers through it and gray-blue eyes that changed color with his moods.

"He started it," Cat whined, and then spoiled it by grinning.

Jack laughed, but Phil was not amused.

"You know, one thing I *won't* miss is your execrable taste in friends," he spat. Without waiting for a response, he jerked open the door and stalked out, leather pants squeaking with every step.

"I think I've just been insulted," Cat said, frowning at the door.

"Nah. *I'm* the one with bad taste." Jack reached out to take the box from her. "You're just the hapless object of my bad taste."

"What was he doing here?" she asked as she followed him back to the kitchen. "I thought you two broke up."

"We did."

"I didn't say anything when you started dating him."

"You didn't have to. Your expression said it all."

"But he's an annoying little twerp."

"No fair picking on him because he's shorter than you are."

"His twerpiness has nothing to do with his size. Some

people are just born twerps, and Phil would be a twerp even if he were six foot six. And don't try to distract me,'' she added, frowning at him.

"As if anyone could," Jack murmured as they entered the big kitchen. He set the box down on one of the stainless steel counters and turned to look at her, arms crossed, his expression one of deep resignation. "Far be it from me to try to interrupt you when you're in full lecture mode."

"I'm not lecturing." He lifted his brows in mock surprise, and Cat choked on a laugh. "Okay, so maybe I was, but I just don't want to see you get sucked back into a dead-end relationship."

"Yes, Mom." His tone was dry as dust.

"Fine. You can sneer all you want, but just tell me that he's not trying to wiggle his smirky way back into your life."

"My virtue is safe," he assured her. "Phil came by to pick up his favorite whisk and a tart pan he says his grandmother gave him, and to inform me that he's been offered a job in New York, where he plans to create desserts that will be the envy of all Manhattan."

"Good for him," Cat said briskly. "Let him carve the Statue of Liberty in chocolate and float it in a sea of raspberry sauce. That'll wow them."

"Or get him on a TV show about America's tackiest desserts." Jack's smile faded. "Actually, you're right, he really is an annoying little twerp. I'm not sorry he's leaving, but I am sorry it took me six months to figure out how annoying he is. But this does leave me short one hell of a pastry chef." He sighed. "I'm really going to miss his tiramisu."

Cat grimaced. "Please, Jack. I don't want to hear about your sex life."

Jack's sharp bark of laughter banished the faint trace of melancholy from his expression. He turned to open the flaps of the cardboard box. "So, tell me what you brought me today. Is this lettuce the Black Seeded Simpson?"

"Yes and there's a new butter lettuce I think you'll like."

Jack reached into the box to lift out a head of lettuce, looking at the soft green leaves the way another man might have looked at a handful of diamonds. He broke off an outer leaf and tasted it, closing his eyes in bliss.

"Fabulous. I'll serve it with a vinaigrette with just a breath of garlic. Dan Hurley brought in some tomatoes from his greenhouse. He charged the earth for them, and they're not as good as midsummer Brandywines, but they're good, miles above anything else available this time of year."

Cat listened as he detailed possible menu items, exclaiming over the leeks she'd brought in, extolling the virtues of her freshly pulled carrots. She threw in an occasional comment, but her participation was optional when Jack was in what she thought of as his chef mode. She answered questions about what was likely to be available over the next few weeks and told him about the tomato plants she was getting started, so he would have some idea of what would be available in the summer.

They'd established this pattern from the beginning. First they got the business out of the way; then, if they both had time, they would have a cup of coffee, and sit and talk until it was time for Jack to get started on the evening's menus. She gave a small sigh of relief when Jack put away the produce and then reached for a pair of thick white coffee mugs. He arched a brow in her direction, and she nodded. Today, she definitely had time to talk.

She waited until he'd poured coffee for himself and a cup of tea for her and pulled a stool up next to hers at the big work counter.

"So, tell me what you've been up to," he said, pushing a plate of biscotti in her direction.

"Well, actually, I have some news."

"You've won the lottery? A rich uncle you'd never heard of died and left you an estate in Tahiti, and you're anxious to hire a personal chef." He gave her a hopeful look.

She laughed and shook her head. "No, but if I ever happen to have an estate in Tahiti that needs a chef, you're at the top of the list."

"That's something, anyway." Jack picked up a biscotti and dunked it in his coffee. "So what's your news?"

"I'm getting married." She'd planned to lead up to it slowly, maybe draw the suspense out a bit, not blurt it out like that.

"You're what?" Jack's eyes jerked to her face. The biscotti dropped back into the cup, splashing coffee on both his hand and the counter.

"I'm getting married," she repeated, wondering if it sounded as unbelievable to him as it did to her. Two days, and it didn't seem any more real now than it had that night at Luke's house. Maybe, once she saw him again, it would seem like something more than a bizarre dream.

"Marriage as in 'dearly beloved' and 'till death do us part'?"

Cat nodded. She didn't see any reason to tell him that, as far as her fiancé was concerned, the only way the marriage was going to last until 'death do us part' was if one of them was hit by a truck soon after speaking their vows.

"Who is it?" Jack asked. "I didn't even know you were dating anyone. And if you're not only dating someone but on the verge of getting engaged, then why, when Phil stormed out, lock, stock and pastry brush, did we sit right here and commiserate with each other over the difficulties of finding a good man in Los Angeles, straight or otherwise inclined?''

''We weren't dating,'' she told him. ''We're still not, I guess. I mean, do they still call it dating once you're engaged? Or does it just become, you know, seeing each other?''

''You're babbling, and that's a sure sign you're nervous.'' He gave her a stern look. ''Spill it, Cat. Who's the mystery man?''

''Luke Quintain.''

Jack had his mouth open to offer a comment before the name registered. He stared at her for a moment and then shut his mouth with an audible snap. ''You want to run that by me again?''

''I'm engaged to marry Luke Quintain.'' Nope, no matter how she said it, it didn't seem real.

''The same Luke Quintain who's engaged to marry your stepsister?''

''Yes.'' She reached for a biscotti and dunked it nervously. ''They're not engaged anymore, though.''

''What did you do with the body?'' Jack asked.

''What body?''

''Devon's. I don't know your stepsister well, but from what little I've seen, I'm guessing the only way she'd give up all that lovely money, social position and a man who looks like Luke Quintain is if she was dead and buried.''

''Actually, Devon is the one who broke the engagement.'' Cat set the soggy biscotti on a plate and cupped her hands around the mug. ''Her high school sweetheart showed up, and she realized that she was still madly in love with him so she left for Minnesota. Although it might have been Michigan,'' she added in the interest of accuracy.

''What's in Minnesota and/or Michigan?''

''A dairy farm. Rick is a dairy farmer.''

Jack considered that for a moment, then shook his head. ''I don't see Devon as a milkmaid.''

Cat lifted one shoulder in a half shrug. ''I don't, either, but that's what she said she wanted.''

''Well, stranger things have happened,'' Jack said. He frowned. ''I can't think of any, offhand, but I'm sure stranger things have happened. But that doesn't explain how you ended up engaged to your stepsister's fiancé. When did she break the engagement? You didn't say anything about it last week.''

''She only ended it two days ago. She...um...asked me to break it off for her, actually.''

''Two days ago?'' Jack pushed his coffee aside and leaned toward her. ''And you and Luke Quintain are already engaged? Not exactly nursing a broken heart, is he?''

''Not exactly,'' Cat admitted.

''So, tell Uncle Jack the whole story. Start to finish, and don't leave out a single detail. How did you end up engaged to the very wealthy Mr. Quintain?''

''It was my suggestion, actually,'' Cat said for the sheer pleasure of watching his jaw drop.

''If you don't tell me what the hell is going on, I'm going to stuff you in the convection oven.''

She laughed and shook her head. ''Not death by convection! I'll talk, I'll talk!''

And she did. She told him everything. About Devon's engagement being a business matter rather than a love match, about how she'd gone to Luke's house to give him the news and ended up suggesting that she could take Devon's place, help him fulfill his grandfather's terms.

"He thought I was too young at first, but I talked him into it."

"I'm not even going to ask how."

"Not the way you're obviously thinking," Cat said, flushing.

"I don't know what I'm thinking," Jack said. "Except maybe that this sounds like something out of a book." He shook his head. "Okay, I get why Quintain would agree to this. He wants whatever his grandfather is offering if he gets married before his birthday. That's simple. Bizarre but simple. What I don't understand is why you're doing this."

"Money?" Cat had intended it to sound firm and definitive, but Jack knew her too well, and she couldn't manage an authoritative lie, not with him looking right at her, so it came out as a question.

"Try again," he said dryly. "If you cared about money, you'd get yourself a real job instead of growing vegetables for cranky chefs, waiting tables part-time at that greasy spoon in Arcadia, and trying to keep Larry and Susan from getting lost on the way to the supermarket. Have you told them you're engaged?"

Cat nodded.

"And what did they have to say about it?"

"I think they were a little confused. Larry said he was almost sure Devon was already engaged to a Luke Quintain and what were the odds that we should both get engaged to men with that name. Then he said something about a Minoan tradition that men changed their names when they married, or maybe it was in Mesopotamia. I sort of lost track. Susan offered to make us a pot for a wedding gift."

Jack laughed and shook his head. He'd been out to the house many times to see the gardens, and had met both Larry and Susan, so he had no trouble picturing the scene Cat described.

"When it comes to sure things, there's death, taxes and the fact that those two are never going to know what's going on."

"Yeah. It's nice to be able to depend on some things." Cat picked up her lukewarm tea and took a sip.

"So I take it you're not going to tell me why you're doing this?" Jack stood and picked up his cup, carrying it to the sink to dump out the coffee, along with the over-dunked biscotti. He poured himself a fresh cup and glanced at her as he lifted the pot in inquiry. Cat shook her head. She wasn't particularly fond of coffee anyway, and Luke was picking her up here and taking her to see his attorney about the prenup. The last thing she needed was an excess of caffeine zooming through her system. She felt wired enough already.

"It was an impulse," she said, shrugging a little. "I guess maybe I'm more like Naomi than I'd thought, because this just suddenly felt right and I...jumped at it."

It was the truth, just not all of it. If she told Jack the sort of, kind of, maybe love-at-first-sight thing, he would probably think she was nuts and do his best to talk her out of the whole thing. And she didn't want to be talked out of it. The last two days had been an emotional roller coaster—highs filled with visions of her and Luke and happily-ever-after, followed by lows where she wondered if she'd completely lost her mind. But, crazy or not, she wanted this.

"Cat, marriage isn't something you jump into on impulse." Jack looked worried. "I don't want to sound patronizing, but you *are* awfully young to be making a decision like this.''

''You're speaking to me from your vast age advantage?'' she asked, arching one brow. ''Twenty-five doesn't exactly make you the voice of experience.''

''No, but I *do* have more experience than you do.'' Jack saw the stubborn set to her mouth and sighed quietly. Cat was one of the most easygoing people he'd ever known, breaking all clichés about redheads and their temper. But there was a certain look she got when she'd made up her mind, and he knew that arguing further would be a waste of breath. He ran his fingers through his hair, ruffling it into even greater disarray.

''Look, this guy is a lot older than you are, and, if you can believe half of what you read in the gossip rags—''

''Which you can't.''

''—then he's been around the block more than a few times,'' Jack finished, ignoring the interruption. ''Added to that, he's making a marriage that's a business deal, and I *do* believe that not many people get the better of Luke Quintain when it comes to business.''

''I'm not trying to get the better of him.'' Cat picked up her cup, then set it down again without taking a drink. ''I just...I want to do this, Jack. I know it sounds crazy. Okay, it probably *is* crazy,'' she amended in response to his snort. ''But I've been sort of drifting the last couple of years. I chose not to go to college because I didn't have any burning desire to study any particular subject or push for a career. I mean, can you see me working my way up the corporate ladder?'' She leaned back and swept one hand out, indicating her leggings and bulky sweater, the suede half boots.

He smiled and shook his head. ''Maybe not the corporate ladder, but there are other careers, Cat.''

"Sure, but I'm not *pulled* to any of them." She sighed and reached up to push back a lock of hair that had escaped the clips she'd used to pull it back from her face. "I guess what I'm trying to say is that I still don't know what I want to be when I grow up."

"And you think marrying Luke Quintain is going to help you figure it out?" Jack asked skeptically.

"I don't know, but I want to do this," she repeated. "It feels…right. Crazy, but right."

Jack sighed. "Fine. I'll dance at your wedding. Just don't ask me to be matron of honor."

"I think that would be *maid* of honor," Cat said. "I think you'd have to be married to be my matron of honor."

"Maid, matron—I'm not putting on a formal for either one," Jack said firmly.

"Pink satin with a big bow on the back," she coaxed.

His mouth twitched, but he shook his head. "Absolutely not. Pink is *so* not my color."

"Spoilsport."

They grinned at each other, and Cat got up and put her arms around him. "Thanks, Jack."

He knew she was thanking him for not lecturing her more, for accepting her decision. He hugged her back.

"Yeah, yeah, anything for a friend," he muttered, mock-disgusted.

Cat leaned back against his hold. "Except wearing a pink formal. If you were really my friend…"

"I'm only thinking of you. With that hair, you can't possibly be serious about using pink for your wedding." Grinning, he tugged at a loose curl. "Not unless you're going to provide the guests with sunglasses."

"That's it, make fun of my hair, Reynolds." Cat scowled at him. "I'm getting a premonition that chipmunks are going to eat that limestone lettuce I was going to bring you next week.'' Jack's expression of horror made her laugh.

They were standing there, Jack's arms loose around her waist, when Luke spoke from the doorway.

"The door was open."

"Luke!" Cat turned, moving out of Jack's light hold. "I didn't realize it was so late. Or are you early?"

"A few minutes. My meeting wrapped up sooner than expected. Hope my coming by early didn't cause any problems."

"None that I know of," Cat said.

Jack wondered if she was really as oblivious as she seemed to the icy look in Quintain's eyes. No, not ice, he thought a moment later when Luke looked at Cat. Heat. Those cool blue eyes were suddenly laser hot, and Jack was willing to bet it was seeing Cat in his arms that had sparked that look. It was an interesting reaction from a man who was marrying a near total stranger as part of a business deal.

Cat slowed as she approached Luke, suddenly uncertain about how to greet him. He was her fiancé, but, despite that searing kiss they'd shared two days ago, they weren't really on kissing terms. Except maybe she was wrong about that, because Luke took the single step necessary to close the distance between them and reached for her. He buried the fingers of one hand in the thick fall of her hair, tilted her head back and took her mouth in a deep, hungry kiss that left her slightly weak in the knees.

When he lifted his head, she opened her eyes slowly and stared up at him blankly. There was hunger in his eyes, but there was also a look of smug male satisfaction that confused her until his gaze went past her to Jack and the look became edged with subtle challenge. A lightbulb went on over her head, Cat suddenly understood the kiss. He was marking his territory, damn him. Hard on the heels of anger came a primitive little thrill that she did her best to squash. She was *not* going to let herself enjoy the idea that he was feeling possessive of her. It wasn't personal. He probably felt the same way when someone got too close to his car.

"You must be Cat's fiancé," Jack said, stepping forward before she could say any of the things that were hovering on the tip of her tongue. She shot a brief, irritated look at Luke before turning to introduce her incredibly annoying fiancé to her blatantly amused best friend. Obviously Jack had recognized Luke's tactic and thought it was funny.

Tucking her annoyance away for the moment, Cat introduced the two men, explaining to Jack that she'd asked Luke to pick her up here because she wanted to introduce them.

"I've eaten here a couple of times," Luke said as they shook hands. "Your reputation is well deserved. The last time I was here, I had some sort of pork stuffed with vegetables that was incredible."

"Must have been in the summer," Jack said. "I only do that dish when my grower can provide me with baby squash and carrots."

He grinned at Cat. She shook her head. "There's something barbaric about calling them baby vegetables."

"Hey, I'm not the one out clubbing organic free-range zucchini," Jack protested, lifting his hands, palms out, to demonstrate his innocence.

"No, but you profit from the carnage," she said, mock-stern.

"I'm just trying to earn a living."

"Speaking of which, I hate to rush things, but I've got

a meeting later this afternoon that I don't want to miss."
Luke's tone was pleasant, and his touch on Cat's lower
back was light, but she felt herself bristle. For an instant
she was tempted to tell him where he could put his meeting, but she caught the wicked laughter in Jack's eyes and
felt her mouth twitch in a half smile instead. It really *was*
ridiculous, and not just because Jack was gay. They were
friends, and even if he were straight as a ruler, she
couldn't imagine them ever being anything *but* friends,
couldn't imagine ever feeling even a tenth of the electricity she felt when she looked at Luke.

"Actually, I've got to get to work myself," Jack said,
glancing at the big clock that hung on the wall above the
walk-in refrigerator. "We open for dinner in a few hours,
and I've still got to firm up tonight's menu."

A polite exchange of goodbyes with Jack suggesting
that Luke bring Cat to the restaurant for dinner "On the
house" and Luke's teeth bared in a smile that made Cat
think of a *National Geographic* special she'd once seen
on tigers. Jack barely concealed his amusement as he
hugged her goodbye with unnecessary enthusiasm, and
then she and Luke were out of the restaurant.

The clear winter skies and cool temperatures did nothing to cool her temper, but Cat waited until she and Luke
were settled in his car—a disappointingly predictable
Mercedes sedan—and he had pulled out of the parking lot
before speaking.

"Next time, why don't you just pee on me?" she said
conversationally. "It would save time and eliminate any
possibility of misunderstanding."

"What?" Luke's head jerked toward her. Her eyes
were sharp with temper. "What the hell are you talking
about?"

"That ridiculous display in front of Jack."

"What are—"

"Don't pretend you don't know what I mean," Cat snapped, cutting off his denial.

Luke didn't have to look at her to feel the heat of her glare, and he felt his own temper rise to meet hers. His fingers tightened around the steering wheel.

"If you mean the fact that I kissed you, it seemed like the obvious thing to do—as your *fiancé*." There was a subtle sarcasm in the last word, meant to remind her of their bargain. "I don't want people thinking there's anything odd about our engagement."

"I hate to break it to you, but no one is going to think this engagement is anything *but* odd. I mean, look at the situation. On Tuesday, you're engaged to Devon. On Thursday, you're taking me to sign a prenuptial agreement. And then, just look at the two of us." She waved one hand between the two of them. "There's you in your Armani suit and alligator shoes, and here's me in my dress-for-less best. Trust me, you can't slip this engagement in under the radar."

"My shoes are plain old cow, and my suit is not Armani." He refused to think about the Armani suits hanging in his closet at home. "And there's nothing wrong with the way you're dressed. I think you look great." What he actually thought was that the black leggings emphasized those incredible legs and made him want to run his hands up under the bulky sweater to find the generous curves he'd felt pressed against him two nights ago.

"Thank you, but you can take my word for it that no one is going to think this engagement is anything approaching normal, and if you think kissing me like you're a pirate and I'm your latest bit of plunder isn't going to set people wondering, then you've got a strange social circle." Cat's tone was bone-dry. "You were marking territory. It was so obvious that if you'd whipped out a branding iron and heated it over the grill before slapping it on my haunch, I wouldn't have been surprised. And neither would Jack.''

Luke's knuckles gleamed white where he gripped the steering wheel. Had it been that obvious? When he'd walked into the kitchen at Jack's Place and seen Cat in another man's arms, he'd felt a quick surge of something that had translated to one word: *Mine.* The possessiveness was new. If he'd walked in on Devon half-naked in the arms of some buff stud, he would probably have yawned and left them to it. But Cat... There was something different about her. Maybe it was the fact that he wanted her more than he'd ever wanted Devon. More than he could remember ever wanting a woman.

"If you think kissing me like that in public is going to keep people from commenting on our engagement, you're living in a dream world.''

"You didn't seem to object,'' he pointed out. He flipped on the turn signal to make a right onto Beverly Boulevard. A tall man in a tattered suit stood on the corner, preaching to the people walking by, arms waving in frenetic, aimless punctuation.

"No, I didn't object.'' Cat sounded mildly disgusted with herself. "I should have elbowed you in the gut. Or maybe kneed you in the groin.''

Luke flinched. "May I say, on behalf of myself and my groin, that I'm glad you resisted the urge?''

He waited for the small crowd of pedestrians to clear the crosswalk before turning onto Beverly.

"Naomi used to say that violence is never a solution,'' Cat said, then spoiled the pious quote by adding wistfully, "But it certainly would have felt good.''

"Speak for yourself,'' Luke said with feeling. The crisis was apparently over. He could actually feel the tension draining away from her, like a cat with its fur ruffled slowly relaxing.

"Don't do that again," Cat said quietly.

"Kiss you?" he asked, deliberately obtuse.

"No, you can kiss me. I like it when you kiss me. But I don't like being kissed as part of some male dominance ritual," she added before Luke could give in to the urge to pull off onto the next side street and see just how much she liked being kissed.

"I wasn't—" He caught her look of disbelief and shrugged. "Okay, maybe I was, just a little. I... You were wrapped around him like plastic wrap, dammit."

As apologies-slash-explanations went, it wasn't much, but it was the best he could manage when the memory of her pressed against the other man was enough to make his teeth grind together.

Cat sighed. "Jack is my best friend." She caught his surprised look and arched one brow in question. "What? You don't think men and women can be friends?"

"I didn't say that," he protested. They'd reached Century City, and he flipped on the turn signal to enter the garage under Keith's office building.

"You didn't have to say it. Your face said it for you."

"Well, my face was talking without my permission," Luke snapped and then stopped, stunned by the absurdity of the comment. He stopped the car at the entrance to the garage, rolling down the window to take a ticket from the machine, and then glanced at Cat. She was biting her lip, obviously trying to hold back a laugh. Luke sighed as the gate lifted and he pulled into the garage. "You know, I've had more irrational conversations with you in the last two days than I've had in my entire life."

"It's a gift," she said modestly and Luke found himself laughing, something he seemed to do a lot around her.

He pulled into a parking space and shut off the engine before turning to look at her. "Look, I'm sorry I..."

"Acted like a jerk?" Cat filled in when he seemed to be having trouble finding the right words.

Luke's mouth tightened for an instant and then relaxed into a rueful smile. "I wouldn't have put it that way, exactly, but, yeah, I'm sorry I acted like a jerk."

She tilted her head to one side, studying him for a moment before nodding. "Apology accepted. For what it's worth, Jack really is just a friend, and even if I lusted after him, he prefers to date people with more hair on their chests than I have."

"He's gay?" Luke's eyebrows rose.

"Either that or very, very confused about gender." Cat reached out to touch his arm, and Luke felt the heat of her through the fabric of his jacket. "I wouldn't usually mention it, since Jack's sexuality is his business, but I..." She stopped and shook her head. "Look, I know this is a business arrangement and all that, but we *are* going to be married and...living together and everything, and I'd like to think we could be friends. I don't want us to start out on the wrong foot."

It was, Luke admitted, more gracious than he deserved. Finding out that Jack was gay confirmed what he'd grudgingly admitted—that he'd been totally out of line in the way he'd reacted. This unexpected possessiveness made him uneasy. Maybe it was just a sort of delayed reaction to having his fiancée run off with another man. He hadn't thought he'd cared that much, but maybe it had bothered him more than he'd realized.

"I don't want that, either," he said, and was rewarded with a dazzling smile that went straight to his gut. Before he could stop himself, he'd buried the fingers of one hand in the heavy red silk of her hair and tugged her across the seat, taking her mouth in a brief, fiery kiss. When he released her, he felt a surge of pure masculine satisfaction at the dazed look in her eyes, the ragged edge to her breathing. "Just remember, I don't share."

Temper flashed in her eyes, visible even in the dim light of the garage. When Luke started to pull back, she wrapped her fingers around his tie just below the knot and jerked him forward. Her mouth on his was every bit as possessive and demanding as his had been. When she released him, his breathing was as ragged as hers.

"I don't share, either," she said.

They glared at each, the atmosphere in the car thick with lust and temper. For one wild moment Luke was tempted to drag her into the back seat and see if they could burn off the temper by satisfying the lust. Before he could either give in to the urge or firmly decide to resist it, Cat turned away, pushing open her door and sliding out.

It was probably just as well. He wasn't sure how his grandfather would take to the idea of bailing his only grandson out of jail on charges of public indecency.

Chapter Four

Keith Lundquist and Luke Quintain had known each other most of their lives. Their parents had been friends—or at least part of the same social circle. The Quintains were "old" money, which by California standards pretty much meant anything that went back more than one generation. The Lundquists were new money but a very substantial quantity of it. Keith's father was the founder and, as Keith said, the grand pooh-bah of Lundquist Pharmaceuticals. The two couples attended the same charity functions, were invited to the same important parties and belonged to the same country club. Luke and Keith had bonded over a shared indifference to all three.

Their friendship had endured tennis lessons, piano lessons, cotillion, first dates, the divorce of Keith's parents and the death of Luke's father. After high school, Luke went to UCLA to get his business degree, and Keith went to Harvard to study law, breaking the tradition set by his older brother and sister who had, respectively, taken chemistry and business degrees and gone to work for

Lundquist Pharmaceuticals, a move that pleased their father. When Keith opted for law, his father was mildly disappointed, since, as he pointed out to his son, lawyers were a dime a dozen. In a few years the company would be expanding its research facilities, opening a new lab. They would need someone to head it up, someone with a solid background in chemistry. Keith wished him luck in finding such a person and left for law school.

When Keith graduated and it became clear that he had no intention of joining the family business, a family meeting was called. His mother flew in from San Francisco, where she'd established a small, very successful chain of exclusive personal care salons. His father and siblings let the pharmaceutical world spin without them for a few short hours, and they all took it upon themselves to explain to Keith the enormity of the mistake he was making.

As Keith told Luke later over a stiff drink—several of them, in fact—it was like an intervention. All that was missing was a minister or psychiatrist to contribute an officially neutral point of view to the whole proceedings. When Keith proved recalcitrant—stubborn as an ox, was his father's diagnosis—his family retreated to their respective corners—luxury condos, for the most part— shook their heads over his decision and predicted to their respective significant others that he would soon change his mind.

It hadn't happened yet. Instead Keith and his two partners had built a solid practice. He had an office in Century City, a condo in Beverly Hills and plenty of good theater nearby. He had a social life, friends, a reasonably healthy sex life. Aside from the lack of professional football in L.A., life was pretty good.

He counted his friendship with Luke among the good

things in his life. At least he had until recently, when Luke
had apparently gone insane. The first sign had been the
engagement to Devon Kowalski. Admittedly she was a
very attractive woman, but not exactly the type you married. Of course, Luke wasn't looking for true love. He
was looking for a way to meet his grandfather's terms on
his own terms, so to speak. Nick Quintain's big mistake
had been in not specifying a bride. Maybe he'd assumed
that Luke would at least want to marry a woman he liked,
but, if that was the case, he'd underestimated his grandson's stubbornness, a trait that must run in the family,
because Nick was apparently willing to let Luke marry
Devon rather than withdraw his ultimatum.

Keith had talked long and hard against the engagement,
but he might as well have been talking to himself. Luke
had to get married, and Devon was close to hand and
totally unsuitable, which made her the perfect choice. So,
like the good friend and lawyer that he was, Keith had
drawn up the prenuptial agreement, trying to protect Luke
legally, at least. Over the last couple of months, he'd become resigned to the engagement, if not happy about it.
True, Devon was a piranha from the top of her beautifully
bleached hair to the tips of her Ferragamo pumps, but at
least Luke knew what he was getting into. She might take
him to the cleaners, but she wasn't going to break his
heart.

Then, out of the blue, Luke called to tell him the engagement was off. Before Keith had a chance to do more
than heave a sigh of relief, Luke had told him he was
marrying Devon's stepsister. While Keith was still reeling
from that bit of news, Luke had laughed and asked him
if he thought he was too young to have a trophy wife, and
then he'd refused to offer any explanations, the bastard,

saying that he wanted Keith to form his own opinions when he met Cat. Keith had, of course, already formed quite a few opinions, starting with his best friend's apparent insanity.

He had a pretty good idea of what Cat Lang would be like. Small, blond and grasping. The sort of woman who looked helpless even while she was helping herself to everything she could get her hands on. When his secretary buzzed to tell him Mr. Quintain and his fiancée had arrived, he could hear the stifled curiosity under the professional indifference, and he knew what she was thinking. Hadn't Mr. Quintain and a completely different fiancée been here just a month or so ago?

Sighing, Keith told her to send them in. He thought he knew what to expect but the woman who walked in with Luke didn't look anything like the image in his head. Luke had always had a weakness for little blondes, but Cat Lang was tall, and her hair was a thick, copper-colored tumble of curls that looked like they might at any moment escape the confinement of the plain gold clips she'd used to pull them back.

Devon had been pretty, like the girl on an old-fashioned box of chocolates. Cat's features were too strong to be called pretty. Her mouth was too wide, her nose too long, her cheekbones too defined. Her eyes were her best feature. They were wide set, thickly lashed and deep green, with a faint tilt to the outer edge that gave her a vaguely exotic look. She wasn't pretty, but there was something about her... He couldn't define it, but once you looked at her, you wanted to keep looking. She was...maybe "striking" was the word.

And young. Definitely young, which explained Luke's comment about a trophy wife.

Good God, what the hell had Luke gotten himself into this time?

Half an hour later, he was no closer to having an answer to that question. Cat Lang was nothing like he'd expected. It wasn't just her looks. Everything about her was a surprise. First of all, she was warm and friendly and—although it hardly seemed possible—genuine. She didn't cast adoring looks at Luke to try to make it seem like a love match, but neither did she approach the situation like a hard-nosed businesswoman. She seemed to view the whole thing with a mixture of rueful amusement, as if acknowledging exactly how odd this arrangement was, and lively interest, as if she were embarking on an adventure.

Even her name was unexpected. Luke had called her Cat, and Keith had assumed that was either a meant-to-be-cute nickname or a diminutive for Cathy or Catriona or something. He hadn't expected:

"Catherine Willow Rain Skywalker Lang." Cat caught their startled looks and shrugged. "Naomi was sort of a hippie, a decade or two too late. When she had me, she was in a back-to-the-roots phase—her spiritual roots, not her genetic ones." Receiving nothing but a blank look from Keith and a raised eyebrow from Luke, she continued. "See, when Naomi did a past-life regression, it turned out that she'd been a Native American back, oh, maybe a couple hundred years ago. She wasn't sure what tribe, but it didn't really matter, and the whole thing ended badly when she was trampled by a buffalo. But she liked that a whole lot better than the life where she worked in a sweatshop in London and died in a fire, or the one where she—well, that's not important. The thing is, she wanted to give me names that celebrated nature and growing things, so that's why Willow and Rain.''

"And what about Catherine and Skywalker?'' Keith asked, compelled to know the whole story. "Was her Native American name Skywalker?''

Cat grinned, and the expression took her from striking to breathtaking in a heartbeat, so that Keith actually felt momentarily dazzled.

"Naomi saw *Star Wars* twenty-eight times when it first came out. I'm just lucky she didn't name me C-3PO or R2-D2.''

"And the Catherine?'' Keith asked weakly.

"Well, I think Naomi was actually a little embarrassed by that.''

"Embarrassed that she'd named you Catherine but not that she'd named you after a tree, a weather phenomenon and a Jedi knight?'' Luke asked.

"Yes. You see, I was named Catherine after Naomi's godmother. Her very wealthy godmother,'' Cat clarified. "It was a moment of pure worldly greed, and I think she spent a lot of time meditating to try to cleanse her spirit after she did it.''

"Yeah, I can see where that would leave a big old spot on your spirit,'' Luke said dryly.

"Well, Naomi thought so. I think she was a little disappointed, though, when her godmother died and all she left me was a very ugly pearl necklace. She left everything else to the Nature Conservancy, so they could purchase a pond full of some sort of endangered frog, and to the University of Colorado to fund a scholarship for the study of amphibians. Really, when you think about it, it's a good thing Naomi didn't know her godmother had a thing for frogs, because she might have named me Kermit instead of Catherine.''

It was the first time Keith could remember laughing at a prenup meeting.

Luke had wondered what Keith would have to say about his new fiancée. He hadn't made any secret of his opinion of Devon. "Shallow" had been the kindest thing he'd had to say. He also made his opinion of the whole ''marriage of convenience'' thing very clear, at the same time asking why, if Luke insisted on doing something that made no sense at all, personally or legally, couldn't he at least do it in better company? While it would be going too far to say that Cat had changed Keith's mind about the arrangement, half an hour after meeting her, he seemed at least reconciled to the idea.

Luke felt pretty much the same way. He'd been resigned to the idea of marrying Devon, but he hadn't been looking forward to having her living in his home, sitting across the breakfast table from him every morning. Her idea of an interesting conversation was discussing the latest who was doing whom Hollywood gossip. She'd been a responsive, if unimaginative, lover and a mediocre conversationalist, but her biggest selling point had been that she was so completely the opposite of what his grandfather had had in mind for his bride.

He wasn't sure what the old man was going to think of his new fiancée, and this time around, he didn't care. At least he wasn't going to be bored with Cat half an hour after the wedding, which made her a significant improvement over her sort-of stepsister. If his grandfather thought she was unsuitable, he would count that as a bonus.

He listened with half an ear as Keith went over the

prenup agreement with her. It was the same agreement he'd had with Devon, with the additional provisions Cat had requested for her stepparents. Interesting that it hadn't occurred to Devon to insure her father's future. A more charitable man might assume that she'd planned to take care of him with the money she was getting herself but Luke was not feeling particularly charitable toward his erstwhile fiancée, and he was willing to bet that the idea of providing for anyone besides herself had never crossed her mind.

In contrast, Cat seemed more interested in that part of the settlement than in finding out what her own take might be. Could be an act, Luke thought, watching her as she listened to Keith explain the provisions for the trust funds. She might think that her generosity would inspire him to open his wallet wider for her. If that was the case, she was in for a major disappointment. Hell, for all he knew, this was part of some elaborate plot she and Devon had cooked up. Except he couldn't figure out what the angle would be.

Lord, he was starting to sound like something out of an Oliver Stone movie, seeing conspiracies in every shadow.

Luke stood abruptly. Keith and Cat both looked at him, and he jerked his head toward the coffeepot that sat on a maple credenza near the door. "Is that actual coffee or the swill you usually drink?"

Keith grinned. "You're safe. Molly made a fresh pot after lunch."

"Give the woman a raise." Luke arched his brow at Cat, but she shook her head.

"My body is a temple," she said with suspicious primness. "I don't put things in it that aren't good for it. Unless it has chocolate in it." She paused to consider. "Or coconut. Or pecans. Or caramel. And I do like steak and a baked potato with sour cream. And vanilla—''

"Stop," Keith said, laughing as he raised one hand, as if pushing away temptation. "You're making me hungry."

"Don't like coffee, I take it?" Luke asked as he poured himself a cup.

"Not particularly," Cat admitted. "But the whole body-is-a-temple thing sounds so much better than if I just said it tastes awful. I mean, saying it tastes awful might come across as a comment on a person's taste. Or lack thereof."

Luke's mouth twitched and then was sternly controlled. "That's very tactful of you."

"I thought so."

If they'd been alone, he might have given in to the urge to kiss the mischief from her smile. Instead, he turned away, putting a spoonful of sugar in his coffee and stirring it as if the task required his full concentration. He wasn't sure what bothered him most—that he'd had the urge, or that, for one crazy moment, he'd actually considered following through on it and kissing her with Keith looking on.

Luke turned back to the conference table, grimacing a little as he sipped his oversweetened coffee. This was a business arrangement, he reminded himself. The fact that he found her desirable was a bonus, like the possibility that his grandfather would find this engagement as offensive as the last one, but he couldn't lose sight of the main purpose of marrying her. Despite what *some* body parts might think, the main purpose was *not* to get Cat in his bed, though he was starting to think that might be an even better bonus than infuriating his grandfather.

Keith was explaining some clause in the agreement to Cat, part of the provision for her stepmother. Feeling restless, Luke carried his too-sweet coffee over to the window, where he could stand and watch the traffic on the street. He'd never noticed it before, but from twenty stories up, it was hard to tell a Lexus from a Chevy. There was probably some profound life lesson to be drawn from that, Luke thought. No doubt Cat's mother, the missing Naomi, would have an appropriate quote about cars and the meaning of life. The woman sounded like a fruitcake. Interesting that her spirituality hadn't gotten in the way of her dumping her child on her boyfriend while she took off for parts unknown.

Of course, maybe she'd done Cat a favor. God knows, the kindest thing his own mother could have done would have been to walk out on her family, though the idea of Lily Quintain trekking off to some ashram to improve her spiritual side fell well outside the realm of possibility. Taking off to improve her wardrobe or her social standing—now *that* he could imagine, but, while Luke was vague on just what went on at an ashram, he was fairly sure it didn't involve either designer originals or cocktail parties.

"But that's ridiculous." Cat's raised voice made him turn from the window, his fingers tightening around the cup. He was behind her, and he could see the light catching in the heavy red curls of her hair as she shook her head. Obviously she'd found something in the agreement she didn't like.

"That was the amount in the original agreement with your sister," Keith said firmly. There was a shift in his expression that Luke thought of as his lawyer face, a subtle hardening, his eyes taking on a slight chill. "You said the original agreement would be acceptable."

"Stepsister. Sort of," Cat corrected automatically "And I didn't know *that* was the original agreement. That's just…ridiculous."

Money, Luke thought. It was always money. His mouth twisted cynically. He wondered how much more she thought she was worth.

"It's too much," Cat said, leaning back in her chair and shaking her head again. "I mean, look at those numbers. They're absurd."

There was a moment's silence. Keith shot Luke a quick look over Cat's head, and Luke saw the same wary surprise he felt reflected in his friend's eyes. Neither one of them could quite believe what they were hearing.

"Too much?" Keith repeated carefully.

"Yes." Cat flicked her fingers at the documents and laughed. "Honestly, I can't believe anyone would pay—" She shifted sideways in her seat to look at Luke. "Did Devon honestly talk you into paying her that much? Because I don't mean to sound bitchy, but, honestly, I think you were getting ripped off."

"Do you?" Luke came forward, leaning one hip against the table as he looked down at her, his expression unreadable. "She asked for more."

"Really?" Cat's eyes widened in surprise. "Well, I knew Devon had a healthy opinion of herself, but I didn't realize just how healthy it was. You know, I think she'd have settled for a lot less," she said confidingly.

"Maybe." Luke had thought so, too, but had decided it was worth paying extra to cut the negotiations short.

"You know, if this is the way you handle your real-estate investments, you must get ripped off a lot." Cat sounded both concerned and disapproving. Keith stifled a laugh, ignoring Luke's warning glance.

"I'm generally a bit tougher when it comes to real estate," Luke assured her.

"You'd have to be, or you'd be broke by now."

Luke set his coffee cup aside and crossed his arms over his chest. "So what do you think would be a fair settlement?" he asked curiously. "Three quarters that amount? Half?"

"Even half is an awful lot of money." Cat frowned at the papers.

"So how much do you want? The deal was that you marry me and I pay you a lot of money, so you must have had a dollar figure in mind."

Cat stared at him blankly for a moment and then looked away. Luke was shocked to find himself fighting the urge to reach out and smooth the little frown lines between her eyebrows.

"I guess I didn't think of a specific number," she admitted. "I thought Devon would have…but I never *dreamed* she would have asked for this much."

"You don't think you're worth as much as Devon?" he asked, then regretted the faintly mocking tone when he saw the color run up under her fair skin.

"I don't think *anyone* is worth this much," she said. "And look at this clause." She tapped her fingers on the agreements. "It says I get another five million for every additional year or portion thereof that we're married. What if we split up five days after an anniversary? That would cost you a million a day."

He'd been a bit sloppy there, Luke admitted. Keith had argued against that clause, saying the money should be prorated, but Devon had been yammering at him, and he'd been seized by the conviction that he would be lucky to make it to the end of the one year that his grandfather required without killing her, so the extra money wasn't going to be an issue. It was too soon to tell whether Cat was going to drive him to consider murder, but somehow, a year or maybe even more didn't sound completely impossible, which meant this marriage could become even more expensive. A sane man would accept her obvious willingness to drop the clause as the blessing it was, but the last few months of his life had not exactly been benchmarks for sanity, and Luke felt a quick, irrational little surge of anger that put an edge to his voice.

"I guess I'll just have to make sure we get divorced *before* an anniversary, then, won't I?"

Something flashed in Cat's eyes that could have been hurt. She looked away, and Luke caught Keith's look of disapproval. Great, now his lawyer was on her side. Except, the way she made it sound, maybe it wasn't quite as much of a his side/her side thing as it had been with Devon. Not when it came to money, anyway, which led him to the question of why the hell was she marrying him? If she wasn't out to gouge him for every penny she could, what did she want? A small voice inside suggested that it might be a good idea to find out, but he ignored it in favor of the bigger voice that pointed out that he only had six weeks to get married and the part of him that wasn't thinking in words at all but just knew how much he wanted her.

"So what *did* you have in mind, Cat?" Keith asked, warmth back in his voice and expression.

"Well, I guess I'd want enough to get training of some sort, although I don't know in what, exactly, since I can't seem to decide what I want to be when I grow up." Her smile invited them to share the joke. Keith laughed. Luke managed a half smile.

Dammit, she couldn't be for real. This was all part of some plan, some scheme. She was after something. No one complained about getting *too much* money.

"And I know I'll need a wardrobe, because my clothes aren't going to be the right sort of clothes. Not unless you're planning on passing me off as a poor relative with eccentric taste," she said, glancing at Luke. "I know from watching Devon that a new wardrobe is going to cost a lot." She frowned a little, and when she continued, she seemed to be thinking out loud. "I'm pretty sure Ruthie's engine is going to need to be rebuilt."

"Ruthie?" Keith asked.

"My car. She's old, but she's solid."

"That hunk of scrap metal you drove to my house the other day?" Luke asked. He shrugged. "Just get rid of it and buy something new."

"Get rid of Ruthie?" Cat looked at him as if he'd suggested she sell her child. "I worked like a dog to earn the money to buy her when I turned sixteen. She's a classic."

"Ignore him," Keith cut in before Luke could question her definition of classic. "When it comes to cars, his taste is all in his mouth. What kind of car is…ah…Ruthie?"

"She's a 1971 VW Squareback."

Luke allowed himself a smirk at Keith's expression. Maybe he wasn't a car buff, but he knew that the tomato-red heap of junk that had been parked in his driveway two nights ago was not on any list of "classics."

"Really?" Keith managed to look…well, not exactly impressed, but not appalled, either. "You…um…don't see many of those around."

"No. I couldn't replace her."

Luke resisted the urge to suggest that a donkey cart would probably have about the same amount of power. Obviously, when it came to Ruthie—God, he couldn't believe she'd actually named that thing—Cat was not likely to have much sense of humor.

"Actually, this money isn't to cover your expenses while you and Luke are married," Keith said, tapping his fingers on the agreement. "You'll have a monthly allowance to use however you want. And things like wardrobe and...transportation will be covered elsewhere. The settlement is separate from that and makes sure you're taken care of in the event of a divorce."

"In the event of a divorce?" Cat repeated, and Luke could hear the laughter in her voice even before she looked at him. "Sounds like a weather condition." When Keith continued to look concerned, she sighed. "Okay, I'm not dumb, and it's not that I'd *mind* having some money. I mean, who wouldn't like to be rich, right? But this is just way, way beyond what I need, and I—"

"The agreement stands," Luke said abruptly and then nearly looked around to see who had used his voice to say something so stupid. The woman was asking for *less* money, and he was going to refuse?

"Luke." Keith's voice had that cautionary I'm-your-lawyer-and-you-should-listen-to-me tone.

"You agreed to take whatever Devon had arranged," Luke reminded her, ignoring Keith.

"But it's too much." She seemed genuinely distressed, which, for some reason he couldn't quite define, torqued his temper up a few more notches.

"That was the agreement," he said flatly, and he felt a surge of satisfaction at the quick flair of temper in her eyes.

"I don't need that much." She pushed back her chair and stood up, putting them on more equal footing. "I don't want that much."

"Cat. Luke." Keith rose, too, but neither of them paid any attention to him.

"We agreed that you'd take whatever Devon had arranged." Luke moved closer, glaring down at her. Cat tilted her chin and glared right back.

"I. Don't. Want. It."

She was wearing some light floral scent that teased at his senses. He wondered where she'd applied it. Had she dabbed it on the soft skin behind her ears? On the pulse he could see beating at the base of her throat? Maybe on the delicate skin at her wrists?

"You agreed—" he began, only to have Cat cut him off with an impatient gesture.

"You keep saying that, but I didn't know what I was agreeing to, and I don't see any reason why we can't just—"

Pigheaded didn't even begin to describe her, Luke thought irritably. Why didn't she just take the damned money? It was what she was marrying him for, after all. Why couldn't she just…? It suddenly occurred to him that this was the most ridiculous argument he'd ever had. No wonder Keith was looking at the pair of them as if they were both candidates for a padded cell. They were fighting about her wanting *less* money?

He interrupted her without apology. "If you don't sign the papers, I'm going to double the settlement."

He put every bit of this-is-my-final-offer menace in his tone, learned over the last ten years of buying and selling real estate in one of the most volatile markets in the country. Cat reacted to the tone first, temper flaring in her eyes, that lush mouth firming with anger.

"Fine," she snapped. "Go ahead and…" She trailed off and looked at him. "You're going to do what?"

"I'll double it," he threatened.

She would make a lousy poker player, he thought, watching a succession of emotions flicker across her face. Indignation—*how dare he?* Confusion—*did he really say what I think he said?* Uncertainty—*he's kidding, right?* And finally an irrepressible twinge of humor.

Cat bit her lip and shot him a look from under her lashes. "Do you…uh…close a lot of deals by threatening to double the amount you're offering?"

"This is a first," Luke admitted.

"Well, I can see where you get your reputation for being ruthless in business."

"Yeah, people all over the L.A. basin know not to mess with Luke Quintain for fear he'll pay you twice as much," Keith said dryly.

Cat turned her head to look at the papers on the table. She frowned. "It just seems like too much. I really don't need—"

"You can always give it to charity," Keith said hastily, trying to prevent an argument from starting up again. God alone knew what Luke would offer next. "Think of all the good things you could do with that much money."

"I suppose." She reached for the papers reluctantly, gathering them in a neat stack before looking at Luke again. "You're sure you won't reconsider?"

He shook his head. "It's this or twice as much."

Cat's mouth twitched in a quick smile that was at odds with her put-upon expression. "Well, if you're going to be that way about it…"

Keith noticed that neither of them mentioned the possibility of pulling out of the deal altogether. Maybe because that really *wasn't* a possibility. Looking from one to the other, he thought it was almost possible to see actual sparks flying between them. You could practically taste the pheromones in the air.

He'd thought Luke was more than slightly cracked when he got engaged to Devon. He'd upgraded the diagnosis to certifiably insane with the announcement that one engagement had ended and another had begun in the space of an hour. After meeting Cat, he'd revised his opinion marginally. He still thought this whole marriage idea was nuts but Cat…Cat was an altogether different proposition from her stepsister.

Then again, seeing the way Luke was looking at her, Keith felt a sudden uneasy twinge and wondered if maybe Devon would have been a safer bet after all.

Chapter Five

Luke parked the Mercedes next to his grandfather's ancient but impeccably maintained Rolls-Royce. He'd suggested once that a new car might be a good idea. It had sparked a lecture on the evils of a throwaway society and the absurdity of getting rid of a perfectly good car just to buy something newer and not nearly as well built. Thinking about it now, Luke heard an echo of Cat's voice in Keith's office this afternoon, telling them that the ridiculous heap of scrap metal she drove was old but solid. He grinned. Maybe, just for fun, he would point out that the two of them shared an appreciation for older cars. He would love to see Nick's face when he got a glimpse of Ruthie.

His mood considerably improved by the thought, Luke was still smiling as he got out of the car. He circled around the back of the Rolls to reach the neat brick walkway that led to the kitchen door. When he was growing up, the rambling old house in an exclusive area of Pasadena had been home, far more so than the redwood-and-glass collection of boxes and angles where he'd lived with his parents. This was where he'd come to show off good report cards, his new driver's license and the black eye he'd gotten playing hockey. His parents were generally too absorbed in their own lives to pay much attention to what was happening in his, but he could always count on his grandparents to be there and to be interested.

It was only in the last few years, since his grandmother's death, that he and Nick had begun to butt heads so often. He hadn't realized how much she'd acted as a buffer until she was gone. Or maybe it was just that her death had left a gap in his grandfather's life, a gap he felt compelled to fill by trying to run his grandson's life. Or maybe he was just getting cranky in his old age. Whatever it was, this crazy marriage thing was only the latest and most spectacular of their conflicts.

He let himself into the big kitchen and was immediately enveloped in a rich amalgam of cooking smells. Steam drifted upward from a cast-iron pot on the stove, filling the room with the scent of beef and chilis. A short, swarthy man with thick coal-black hair liberally sprinkled with gray stood at the butcher-block table, using two forks to shred a mound of tender beef. He looked up as Luke opened the door, his nearly black eyes lighting, a welcoming smile creasing his weathered face.

"Señor Luke."

"Luis." Luke made a show of inhaling. "Is that your green chili?"

"*Sí.*" Luis's grin widened. "You want to taste it?"

Luke shook his head. "No, thanks, I'd like to keep my stomach lining intact this week."

"You need to toughen up that tender stomach of yours. My chili will put hair on your chest."

"Or put me in the hospital," Luke said dryly. It was an old argument, one they'd been having since Luke was young enough to half believe that eating Luis's incendiary cooking might really put hair on his chest.

Luis grinned and shook his head. "Your grandfather, he eats my chili and he's eighty-five years old. You should be embarrassed, a man your age."

"My grandfather has a cast-iron stomach to go with his granite head."

Luis sighed as he scooped up the pile of shredded beef and dropped it into the simmering chili. "You two. Always butting heads. You are too much alike."

"I'd be insulted if I didn't know you actually like the old goat."

Luke reached up to loosen his tie and undo the top button of his shirt as he leaned back against the door frame. In a few minutes he would go find his grandfather and they would continue the chess game that was their relationship these days. Today, for the first time, he was almost looking forward to it, but it still felt good to relax a little before gearing up for another round.

Luis Ramirez had been born in Guadalajara, but he'd crossed the border as a teenager, spending nearly four years as a migrant farm worker before being hired by Luke's grandfather to work in the gardens. In the forty years since then, he'd moved from gardening to driving the Rolls and, for the last decade or so, had been a combination of chauffeur, cook, butler and household manager. He had never been intimidated by either Nick Quintain's reputation or his temper, which was a source of both admiration and frustration to his employer.

To Luke, Luis had been almost an adoptive uncle, the sort of relative you had by choice rather than an accident of birth. Luis had taught him to drive, taking over the task when it became obvious that Nick's attempts were likely to end in double homicide.

"You are both goats," Luis informed him. He picked up a wooden spoon and pointed it in Luke's direction. "Both stubborn and hardheaded. Too stubborn and too hardheaded to admit when you're wrong. Your grandfather, he lays down the ultimatum. That's bad. Then you— you pick it up and ask that girl to marry you." He shook his head in disgust before turning to plunge the spoon in the pot, stirring with more vigor than seemed necessary. "I wash my hands of the both of you but I will tell you this, Señor Luke, do not marry that one. She makes me remember a mule my grandfather once had. Too narrow between the eyes." He laid the spoon back on the counter and shook his head. "You'll have trouble with that one."

Luke allowed himself a moment to savor the thought of Devon's reaction to hearing herself compared to a mule.

"I'm not marrying her."

"No?" Luis gave him a sharp look, and Luke had to fight the urge to shuffle his feet like a grubby ten-year-old with a frog in his pocket.

"No. I'm...there's someone else. Another girl. Woman. Another woman." It was more explanation than he would have given anyone else. "I...think you'll like her," he added, surprising himself. But it was true. He could easily picture Cat and Luis sitting at the butcher-block work island, swapping recipes. She would probably offer him some of the vegetables she apparently grew to sell— something he'd learned courtesy of Keith, who'd thought to ask her what she did for a living. It hadn't occurred to him to wonder about that, but then, he had a hard time getting his thoughts to move above belt level where Cat was concerned.

Luis cocked his head to one side, his dark eyes intent. "This woman, you love her?"

"No." It came out more forcefully than he'd intended, and Luke said it again, more quietly. "No. But I like her. She's...different." He smiled suddenly, tightening his grip on the briefcase as he straightened away from the door frame. "And she's not at all narrow between the eyes."

Luis grinned. "Then she is an improvement over the other one, at least."

"Yes, she is," Luke said confidently. He didn't know what he was getting into, but he knew, whatever marriage with Cat would be like, it was bound to be an improvement over marrying Devon.

"Is my grandfather in the den?"

"*Sí.* Like a bear with a sore paw all day. Grumbling, complaining." Luis picked up the spoon and jabbed it into the pot of chili again. "I put extra jalapeños in the chili." He said it with such satisfaction that Luke laughed out loud.

"Maybe I should have brought a fire extinguisher." He left the kitchen to the sound of Luis's deep laughter.

When he was a boy, his grandfather's den had been one of his favorite places. In the winter, especially, he loved to lie on the rug in front of the fireplace and watch the flames twist and leap, casting ever-changing patterns of light and shadow over the book-lined walls and the soft leather furniture. His grandfather would be sitting at the big polished mahogany desk, doing paperwork. His grandmother, who taught freshman English at UCLA, would be sitting on the sofa, a stack of essays beside her, waiting to be graded. Periodically she would read some passage aloud, either because it was exceptionally good or because it contained some comic error of grammar or syntax. Before too long his grandfather would abandon his paperwork and go sit in the big, high-backed leather chair that no one else ever sat in. He would light a cigar, ignoring his wife's mild chiding about the possible health risks and "Good heavens, Nicholas, I don't see how you can smoke something that smells that bad." Secretly, Luke agreed with her, though he would never admit as much.

Those had been the times when his parents were away on a trip and he'd stayed with his grandparents. Occasionally it was business that took them away, but more often it was his mother's constant, restless need to be *seen*, to be where the important people were or, more often in the years before his father's death, to be near her latest lover. Luke hadn't really cared what the reasons were. He'd just enjoyed the fact that his parents' absence meant he got to stay with his grandparents.

Now, as he stood in the doorway and looked at his grandfather, he felt a mixture of love and a deep, cold anger. One thing you could say about Nick Quintain, he was not a man to inspire indifference. At eighty-five, he still had the ramrod-straight posture he'd gained during his stint in the military during World War II. His hair was still thick, though it was no longer dark. Instead it was a distinguished-looking silvery-gray. The blue of his eyes had faded, but they were still sharp and piercing, leaving whoever he was looking at with the impression that he could see beneath the surface and drag out their deepest secrets. Sitting behind the big desk, wearing a pale blue shirt with the sleeves rolled up and the gold-framed glasses he despised needing, Nick looked like exactly

what he was—an aging but still powerful man, a man
accustomed to being in control.

Looking at him, Luke knew that he was probably looking at himself fifty years from now. He'd seen photos of
his grandfather as a young man, and they looked enough
alike to pass for twins. It was logical to assume that they
would age alike. He wondered suddenly what it would
feel like to look back on eighty-five years of life.

"Waiting for a written invitation?" Nick asked.

"Should I be?" Luke moved into the room. It smelled
of leather and lemon polish, the tang of woodsmoke and
the faint, almost dusty smell that he associated with li-
braries.

"I expected you an hour or more ago." Nick frowned,
his dark brows nearly meeting over the bridge of his nose.

"We didn't set a time, and I had other things to do,"
Luke said easily. He set his briefcase on the desk and
popped the latches. He chose to ignore the comfortable
chair that had been pulled up to the desk. Sitting down
across the desk from where Nick sat in his high-backed
chair would put him at a psychological disadvantage. It
put the person on the other side of the desk in a position
of authority. He didn't doubt that Nick had thought of that
when he set the chair there, but Luke had learned his
business skills from a master. Maybe Nick had forgotten
teaching him that little trick.

"I've got the papers on the VanValkenburg property,"
he said, pulling a stack of documents out of the briefcase.
"They've agreed to the price we wanted, and we've
agreed to take the building as is."

"As is? What's wrong with it?" Nick reached for the
paperwork.

"The plumbing is shot, and, according to Dickerson,

the wiring was probably put in by Edison.'' Anticipating his grandfather's request, Luke pulled out the estimates from the contractor. ''Also paint, new carpets and drapes, and some landscaping.''

''Why not just tear the place down and put up a new building?'' Nick asked irritably. ''It would be cheaper.''

''That area of Venice is starting to increase in value, and the people moving there like the old buildings, makes them feel in touch with their roots, I guess. The work is going to cost us, but once it's done, we'll be able to sell the units for enough to more than make back our investment.''

''If the market doesn't shift,'' Nick grumbled. ''If buyers don't decide they don't give a damn about their roots. If—''

''If California doesn't break off into the Pacific,'' Luke interrupted. ''If the sky doesn't fall. Someone once told me that real estate is always a gamble but research can even the odds a bit.''

Nick scowled, annoyed at having his own words turned against him but he reached for a pen, muttering as he scrawled his name on the documents. ''I never did like Venice. Bunch of artsy types pretending it's 1930 and they're Scott and Zelda, and those damned, smelly canals.''

''The canals don't smell anymore, and the artsy types are willing to pay some fairly substantial sums of money in support of their pretense.'' Luke gathered up the signed papers and tapped them on the desk to straighten them before setting them back in his briefcase and taking out another set of contracts.

He had repeatedly refused his grandfather's offer to take over Quintain Inc. It might have been twenty years ago, but he hadn't forgotten the driving lessons. Maybe, as Luis said, they were too much alike. Whatever it was, working too closely together was a bad idea, and, while Nick might believe himself when he said he would leave things in Luke's hands, Luke knew better. The day Nick Quintain retired would be the day they buried him. He would never be able to hand his company over to someone else. But once Luke had his own Quintain Properties established, it turned out that, where their business overlapped, the two of them worked surprisingly well together.

When the second set of documents were signed, Luke paper-clipped them together and dropped them back in his briefcase. Was the sudden silence as obvious to Nick as it was to him? A few months ago they would have had plenty to say to each other. Potential new business, or politics, or just the latest news about who was getting divorced or married or buried. Nick would have invited him to stay for dinner, and, unless he had other plans, Luke would have taken him up on it. Tonight, though, just the thought of Luis's green chili was enough to give him heartburn. He wondered if Nick missed that sense of camaraderie as much as he did, wondered if it had occurred to him that blackmail wasn't exactly the best way to foster feelings of warmth and fuzziness between them.

Luke shut the briefcase with a soft thunk that sounded too loud in the quiet room.

"I'll see you next Saturday, then?" Nick said, his tone making the words a question.

"Saturday?" Luke asked absently as he snapped shut the latches on the case and reached for the handle.

"Your engagement party?" One dark eyebrow lifted. "You *are* still engaged, aren't you?"

The engagement party. *Shit.* It had been Devon's idea,

a compromise when he refused to agree to a huge wedding with half of Los Angeles on the invitation list and the other half invited to the reception he wouldn't consider, either. He should have canceled it when Devon ran off with her dairy farmer, but he'd had other things on his mind. Things like acquiring a new fiancée less than an hour after losing the old.

"I'm still engaged," Luke said slowly. He lifted the briefcase off the desk, feeling a sudden wicked twinge of amusement. This wasn't the way he'd planned to tell his grandfather about Cat, but what the hell. It served him right for being such an interfering old goat. "Actually, the plans have changed slightly. There may be a few names to add to the guest list." Cat was bound to have friends she would want to invite, after all.

"Doesn't have anything to do with me," Nick said, looking both puzzled and irritated. "Tell your secretary if you want to invite more people. Though why you'd want to invite more than the bare minimum to watch you make a damned fool of yourself, I can't imagine."

"And my secretary will be sending out a…revision to the invitation," Luke said, ignoring the interruption.

"Revision?" Nick frowned. "What kind of revision?"

"To change the bride's name." Luke gave that a moment to soak in. "I'm not marrying Devon Kowalski."

"Well, thank God for that." Nick caught himself and gave his grandson a suspicious look. "You're changing the bride's name but not canceling the party? You're already engaged to someone else? Who is she?"

"Catherine Willow Rain Skywalker Lang," Luke said with real satisfaction, not all of it caused by the pleasure of watching his grandfather's eyebrows climb almost high enough to meet his hairline.

"How many women are you marrying?" he demanded.

Luke smiled, the first genuine smile he'd given his grandfather in months. Nick looked even more uneasy.

"Just one." He turned toward the door, ignoring Nick's spluttered protests. It wasn't often he got to see the old man speechless. Might as well leave on a high note. "You'll meet her at the party."

He was at the door before Nick found his voice again. "At least you're not marrying that tart," he said, snatching the last word.

"No, I'm marrying the tart's sister," Luke said, snatching it right back before closing the door on his grandfather's dropped jaw.

Cat had been to a lot of parties in her time. Naomi had loved any sort of gathering of people, whether it was a protest rally or a funeral. *Gatherings create such energy, baby. You can just feel it wash right over you, filling up your own well of psychic energy.* At seven, Cat had conjured up a vague image of parties as a kind of psychic gas station.

Naomi's parties, whether she was giving them or just attending them, tended to be full of people with wire-rimmed glasses, colorful clothing and indeterminate gender, jug wine, and smoke from incense and funny little hand-rolled cigarettes with a cloying sweet scent. Conversations about the importance of cleansing one's aura and the need for embracing positive energy were commonplace.

There were parties at Larry's house, too but they always seemed to happen *to* Larry, like something he'd tripped over or fallen into. He would wander through the gathering of graduate students, faculty and artists with a faintly bewildered expression on his face, as if he couldn't quite place who all these people were and how they'd come to be in his house.

There were still plenty of wire-rimmed glasses but the clothing was less colorful at Larry's parties, running heavily to blue jeans and T-shirts, once again making gender a matter of guesswork. Jug wine and beer were the beverages of choice, and no one smoked anything at all because this was Southern California, after all, where the citizens were willing to breathe the smog but blanched at the thought of cigarette smoke. Conversation tended toward the miserliness of the stipends given to struggling grad students or the latest faculty affairs, though, one time, a near fistfight had broken out between two archeology professors over the question of when and how humans arrived in North America. Cries of "Twenty thousand years is a crock" and "Why don't *you* try crossing the Pacific in a canoe?" had rung out over the sun-dried tomato dip and white wine spritzers.

Aside from the occasional professorial fistfight, though, there wasn't that much difference between the parties she'd gone to when she lived with Naomi and the ones that happened to Larry. Cheap food, cheap booze and lots of conversation.

But this…this…gathering… *This* was a horse of an entirely different color, Cat thought as she looked around the country club. And that color was green, as in money, lots and lots of money. Not that anyone was so crude as to display any of the crisp green stuff. They didn't have to. The setting screamed money with every wood-paneled, plush-carpeted inch. Waiters in white jackets moved deftly among the guests, offering delicate bites of smoked trout, asparagus wrapped in prosciutto, tiny bite-size crab cakes and something wrapped in pastry that tasted vaguely like pizza. A long table of dark, polished wood was set up in front of a bank of huge windows that looked out over an artfully lit koi pond. On the table were more appetizers, including silver bowls nestled in snowy-white ice and filled with mounds of caviar. Cat thought there was a certain irony in displaying caviar in front of a fishpond but suspected she was the only one who noticed.

If the room itself hadn't gotten across the point that she'd stepped into a whole new world, the guests would have. Luke had told her they were mostly business acquaintances. People he was friendly with, people he'd done business with, but not necessarily personal friends. She recognized a number of the guests—the hostess of a syndicated talk show, a local news anchor, all shiny teeth and shiny hair, a judge who had presided over a high-profile trial a year or so ago, and a movie critic who made it a point to hate any movie that didn't have subtitles.

Her own guest list had hardly been long enough to qualify as a list. She'd invited Jack, who'd promised to turn the restaurant kitchen over to his assistant chef for a couple of hours. Larry and Susan had been invited by Devon, of course, but Cat felt she could reasonably call them her guests now.

She'd been concerned that they would feel out of place, but, if she'd thought about it, she would have realized that she didn't need to worry. One advantage of being oblivious to the world was...well, being oblivious. She didn't have to worry about them fitting in because *they* didn't worry about it. They were sitting at a table near the window now, talking to a short rotund man who, if Cat remembered correctly from Luke's introduction, made documentaries for public television. No doubt one or both of them would turn up on a PBS special on making pottery or digging up the past or digging up pottery of the past.

Cat had been surprised when Luke had told her that Devon hadn't invited anyone else. She would have assumed that her stepsister would be eager to show off her new status, but, when she thought about it, it actually made sense. Devon had been stepping into a new social circle, and she wasn't the sort to try to hold on to old ties when the new ones were so much more interesting.

Ouch. The cattiness of the thought made her wince. Devon wasn't her rival, she reminded herself. She was the one marrying Luke in three weeks, which was a panic-inducing thought.

She smiled and shook hands as Luke introduced her to a tall, rail-thin woman whose skin was so taut and wrinkle-free that you could almost see the gleam of bone underneath. She was apparently president of something or other and obviously on *very* good terms with her plastic surgeon. The woman's eyes swept her up and down with a barely veiled curiosity that had become very familiar during the last hour. She'd received variations of the same look from every one of the more than sixty guests, except for one older woman who had stared at her vaguely for a moment before ordering a vodka martini, straight up and no vegetable matter. The woman's son had looked horrified as he shepherded his mother off. It had been the one genuine moment of the evening.

This was her engagement party, Cat reminded herself, and then had to swallow an hysterical giggle. Did that sound as absurd to Luke as it did to her? She slid a sideways glance at him, half expecting to see him vanish in a puff of smoke, proving all this was a figment of her overheated imagination. But he was there, solid and real.

She could feel the heat of him along her arm, smell the faint spice of his cologne. He was wearing a dark blue suit that did amazing things for his eyes. She'd always thought she preferred a man in jeans, but that was before she'd seen Luke Quintain in a suit. There was something about that thin veneer of civilization over coiled strength that was very sexy.

"You holding up okay?" Luke asked as the woman with the tight face moved off in response to a languid wave from a painfully thin young man with a receding chin and oversize glasses that made him look like a praying mantis.

"I'm okay," Cat said, warmed by the fact that he'd thought to ask. "I feel a little like a bug under a microscope, but I expected that. At least no one's thrown any rotten fruit."

Luke's mouth curved in a smile. "If that's your definition of a successful evening, I think you need to raise your expectations a little."

She shrugged. "What can I say? I'm easy to please."

"Really?" Luke's eyes warmed in a way that made her breath catch. "That sounds...promising."

Cat felt her skin heat and knew he had to be able to see the sudden color in her cheeks—the curse of a redhead's pale complexion. It wasn't the first time she'd seen hunger in a man's eyes, but it was the first time it had made her stomach tighten with an answering hunger. She wanted to give him a snappy comeback, something witty and sophisticated to show how...well, how sophisticated and witty she was, but her tongue seemed to be glued to the roof of her mouth, so she had to settle for a blush and looking away. Oh yeah, that was the way to impress a man—tongue-tied and stoplight-red. She hid behind her water glass.

Luke allowed himself a small, smug smile. One thing he'd learned in his short acquaintance with Cat was that not much threw her off balance. Broken engagements, sudden engagements, displays of jealousy and prenuptial agreements—she'd taken them all in stride. But this…this heat between them, that made her stumble. It made him wonder if there was some truth to her claim of inexperience.

Hard to believe that any woman made it to almost twenty-one these days still pure as the driven snow, and maybe it was politically incorrect to think so, but it was particularly hard to believe with a woman who looked like Cat. Sex on a stick. He couldn't remember where he'd heard the phrase, but it certainly fit. Though not as well as that dress, he thought, feeling a potentially embarrassing twinge of pure lust. He'd wondered what she would look like in something besides the bulky sweaters she seemed to favor, but the reality was even better than he'd imagined.

It was a classic little black dress. There was nothing about the dress that caught the eye except what it did for the woman who wore it. The V-neckline was just low enough to reveal a tantalizing glimpse of cleavage emphasized by the simple gold chain she wore around her neck, the end dipping into the shadowed cleft between her breasts. His fingers twitched with the urge to trace the path of that chain. If the neckline was a tease, the skirt was pure temptation. The thin fabric clung to the soft curve of her hips and ended at midthigh to display approximately a mile of legs. Simple black pumps with a tall, narrow heel brought her almost eye to eye with him, and it was suddenly impossible to imagine that he'd ever thought he preferred fragile little blondes to tall, leggy redheads.

It was an effort to drag his eyes back up to her face. Judging by the hectic color in her cheeks, she'd noticed his distraction and Luke felt his own face warm. What was it about this girl—woman, dammit!—that made him behave like a hormone raddled sixteen-year-old? Acting like a jealous idiot when he met Jack Reynolds and now gaping at her cleavage in the middle of their engagement party. All that was left was groping her in the back seat of his car, and he'd already come closer to that than he liked to remember.

Luke was aware that they were receiving a lot of discreet and some not-so-discreet glances from the guests. So far, no one had come right out and asked him how he'd shed one fiancée and picked up another one so quickly, but he could feel the buzz of curiosity. Not that he could really blame them. If he'd wanted to be discreet, he should have canceled the party. Sending out revised invitations, announcing that the party was still on but the bride-to-be's name had been changed, had been a bit like throwing down a gauntlet, inviting everyone to speculate until their brain cells overloaded. Maybe, just maybe, he'd let his annoyance with his grandfather get the best of him, he admitted.

"What are you two doing over here in the corner?" Keith asked as he joined them. "Aren't you supposed to be mingling?"

"I'd rather tie a slab of raw bacon around my neck and go swimming in a pool of underfed piranhas," Cat said cheerfully.

Luke inhaled his Cabernet and wheezed for a moment

until he got his breath back. Keith's laughter drew still more openly curious looks from the guests.

"You'd probably be safer with the piranhas," Keith said, still grinning.

"Most guests at the country club make it out alive," Luke said dryly.

"Not if they're eating those crab cakes," Jack said, joining them in midconversation. "If that's crab, I'm Tom Cruise. And the quiche is not only a cliché, it's pedestrian. But the shrimp puffs are actually quite decent."

Cat laughed and slid her arm through Jack's. "You have the manners of a rabid wolverine," she said lightly. "Jack, this is Keith Lundquist, Luke's friend and attorney. Keith, this is Jack Reynolds. Jack owns a restaurant, which makes it okay for him to bitch about the food. If he was just an ordinary civilian, it would be terribly rude."

Jack had the grace to look embarrassed as he shook Keith's hand. "Sorry. I don't get much chance to eat someone else's cooking. Guess I got carried away."

"It's okay," Keith said. "I didn't cook any of it, and actually, I didn't care for the quiche, either."

"I thought you hated quiche." Luke's fingers curved around Cat's upper arm, tugging her against his side. For show, he told himself. It had nothing to do with not liking the way she was all but plastered to Jack's side. She shot him a warning look, and he returned it with a look of such bland innocence that her eyes brightened with sudden laughter. When she let her body curve into his, it took more willpower than he would have believed to keep from dragging her behind the nearest potted ficus and kissing her senseless.

"Every right-thinking American hates quiche," Keith said firmly.

"Just Americans?" Jack asked.

"Well, Europeans are so…European when it comes to food." Keith frowned and shook his head. "I mean, think about it. They eat snails, for God's sake. I don't care how many biologists trot out excuses, the damned things are bugs. And then there's sauerbraten. What the hell is a sauerbraten, and why would anyone eat it? Even the English have bangers and mash, and toad in a hole. Can you honestly trust the judgment of people who eat something called toad in a hole?"

"And pigs in a blanket isn't suspect?" Jack asked as he snagged a wineglass from a passing waiter.

"Of course not. It's a simple descriptive term. It's a pig in a blanket. What else would you call it?"

Luke let his fingers splay across Cat's hip and heard her draw a quick sharp breath. She was wearing a soft floral perfume, something light that teased at his senses, made him want to lean down and see if he could find all the places she'd brushed it, see if she tasted as good as she smelled. It made it difficult to keep his mind on the conversation but he made an effort.

"Keith thinks Tommy burgers are the height of culinary accomplishment," Luke said.

"Tommy's is a Los Angeles icon," Jack said.

That sparked an immediate and enthusiastic discussion about the relative merits of double and triple burgers, and whether cheese masked the flavor of the chili or enhanced it. Luke tuned most of it out. He wondered what the patrons of Jack's Place would think if they knew the chef harbored a not-so-secret lust for chili burgers and fries.

"Warning, Will Robinson." Keith's murmur dragged

Luke's attention back to the conversation. ''The eagle has landed.''

Following the direction of Keith's gaze, Luke saw his grandfather entering the room. Cat must have felt the sudden tightness he couldn't control. He felt her look at him, and then her hand came to rest over his. Offering support, he realized, both amused and a little touched.

''Is that your grandfather?'' she asked.

''In the flesh.'' He let his arm drop from her waist and took her hand instead. For show, he told himself. Because that was what he would do if they were madly in love. He led her forward, preferring to meet his grandfather halfway rather than waiting for his approach like a guilty child afraid of punishment.

''That the grandfather who's making him get married?'' Jack asked.

Keith thought of pretending ignorance, then shrugged. Obviously Cat had told him the real reason behind her marriage to Luke. ''That's the one. Nick Quintain, real-estate tycoon and marriage broker.''

Jack grinned. ''I've got ten bucks says Cat can take him.''

Keith opened his mouth to take the bet and then shook his head, remembering Luke threatening to double the prenup settlement. One thing he'd learned in his brief acquaintance with Cat Lang was that she was a wild card.

''I've seen her in action,'' he said. ''I wouldn't bet against her.''

''No smart man would,'' Jack said, edging closer to hear the conversation.

''Grandfather, I'd like you to meet my fiancée, Catherine Lang. Cat, this is my grandfather, Nick Quintain.''

Luke's tone was neutral as he made the introductions but Cat could feel the tension humming through him where his arm pressed against hers. She wondered if he was worried about his grandfather's reaction or hers.

Cat studied the man standing in front of her. She'd been curious about him ever since Devon told her the reasons behind her engagement to Luke. Her curiosity had intensified when she found herself taking Devon's place. If it wasn't for this man, she wouldn't be standing next to Luke right now. In fact, since he'd only asked Devon to marry him to fulfill the terms his grandfather had set, they would probably never even have met. So, in a sense, she supposed she should be grateful to him. But when she thought about the way he was manipulating his grandson's life, gratitude wasn't the first emotion she felt.

This was what Luke would look like someday, she thought. Tall, silvery hair, blue eyes faded by time, but his gaze still sharp and piercing, Nicholas Quintain was an imposing man. He wore an impeccably tailored suit and leaned lightly on a carved ebony walking stick.

"Cat?" Nick's mouth curved in a chilly smile. "That's an unusual name."

She felt Luke's fingers tighten over hers and spoke before he could say anything. "It's short for Catherine, Mr. Quintain. My friends call me Cat." She gave him a friendly smile. "You can call me Catherine." She let a beat go by, saw the barb strike and widened her smile. "Or Cat, if you prefer."

"I don't," he said shortly.

His eyes skimmed over her, seeking faults. Cat refused to give in to the urge to tug at her hemline or pat a stray curl into place.

"So you're going to marry my grandson." The words were a statement, but the tone made them a challenge.

"That's the plan," she said easily. Her hand tightened around Luke's.

Nick caught the subtle movement, and his lip curled. Luke had seen CEOs of major corporations wilt under the patented Quintain sneer, but Cat didn't seem bothered by it. She gave him an almost sleepy smile and leaned a little closer to Luke, until they were pressed together from shoulder to hip. The contact was enough to distract him for a moment so that he almost missed her next words.

"You know, Mr. Quintain, blackmailing your grandson into marriage is really bad karma. Too much of that sort of thing and you could end up as a cockroach in your next life."

Luke let out a startled snort of laughter as Nick's glare grew ferocious.

"I beg your pardon."

"Oh, you don't need to beg my pardon. It's not a twelve-step kind of thing, where you need to apologize to people or anything. You just try to live your life in a more positive fashion. And it never hurts to do a good deed or two."

"Are you offering me advice on how to live my life?" Nick's voice was so cold, Luke wouldn't have been surprised to see icicles form on the nearest guests. Out of the corner of his eye, he could see Keith listening to the exchange with open fascination, Jack a half step behind him, his eyes bright with suppressed laughter.

"No." Cat widened her eyes in surprise. "My mother always said that everyone has to choose which path they'll take. Maybe you *want* to come back as a cockroach. I mean, there's probably a lot to learn from a life spent as

a cockroach. When you think about it, they're real sur-
vivors, and they've got the whole group-living thing down
pat.''

Watching his grandfather try to process the gentle flow
of words, Luke almost felt sorry for him. He was nearly
positive he was being insulted, but there was nothing in
Cat's tone or expression to support that theory. It wasn't
the first time someone had objected to Nick's occasionally
overbearing tactics, but it was a safe bet that it was the
first time he'd been threatened with karmic retribution.

"I am certainly not going to spend time as a cockroach," he snapped.

"Well, I hope not, because really, even if you could
learn a lot that way, it doesn't sound very comfortable,
does it?" Cat gave him another of those friendly smiles.

Nick opened his mouth, then closed it again without
speaking. The muscles in his jaw twitched. He glared at
Cat, but she had turned to give her empty glass to a waiter
and missed the searing look. Frustrated, Nick turned the
glare on his grandson. Luke raised his eyebrows a little
and let his mouth curve in a faint smile. He wanted to
laugh out loud.

It was worth every penny in the prenup settlement to
see his grandfather left speechless by the threat of life as
a cockroach.

"I still don't see why you couldn't have parked at the
club," Luke said, flipping on the turn signal and turning
right onto Foothill Boulevard. It was almost one o'clock
in the morning, and there wasn't much traffic, so he had
plenty of time to shoot his fiancée an exasperated look.

"Valet parking," she said simply. "I don't trust Ruthie
to valet parking."

"You don't *trust* them?" His voice rose in disbelief. "What? You think they're going to steal that thing?"

"Of course not. I'm fond of Ruthie, but I'm not delusional." The look she gave him said she wasn't sure the same could be said about him. "Thirty-year-old Volkswagens aren't exactly on anyone's list of top-ten most-stealable cars. The problem with valet parking is that they don't know how to treat her."

"Don't tell me. You have to sing 'Feelings' while you turn the key? Or maybe offer up an incantation to the spirits who watch over people who drive old cars?"

Cat laughed and shook her head. In the intermittent glow from the streetlights, Luke could see that a few curls had escaped the soft knot she'd used to tame her hair. His hands tightened on the steering wheel. He'd spent the entire evening resisting the urge to slide the pins from her hair so he could watch it tumble around her face and spill down her back in a heavy wave of flame-colored silk.

"Ruthie has a few quirks," Cat said, and he made an effort to drag his mind back to the conversation. "Last time I used valet parking, I explained how to put her in gear, but it was apparently too confusing for them, because they ended up putting her in neutral and pushing her into a parking place." She gave him a mock scowl when he laughed. "It was very embarrassing for Ruthie."

"Probably pretty damned embarrassing for the parking valets, too."

He turned into the mall parking lot, empty at this late hour, an acre of cracked black pavement divided by faded white lines. Forty years ago this had all been new and shiny and exciting, the latest in modern convenience shopping. Over the years, malls like this had slowly lost ground to the sleek, enclosed Gallerias with multilevel parking and everything under one roof. Mail order and Internet shopping had also taken a toll. Luke gave this particular mall another ten years before it succumbed to old age and changing tastes, and completed the slide from mildly shabby to outright eyesore. Something would take its place. Office buildings, a new, shiny mall with lots of glass and a cappuccino bar at either end.

"Is there a reason you had me pick you up at a mall?" he asked as he parked the Mercedes next to Ruthie, sitting in solitary splendor beneath one of the pink-tinted lamps that marched along the rows of empty parking spaces.

"I had to buy hose," she said, stretching out one leg, pointing her toe and making his mouth go dry with lust.

"I could have picked you up at your stepfather's house," he said absently, his eyes tracing the long, long line from the toe of her sleek black pump to the hem of her skirt. Stockings or panty hose? he wondered, and then wished he hadn't. The thought of her in a lacy black garter belt and sheer silk stockings was not exactly what he needed right now.

"But I'd still have had to stop somewhere and buy hose," she pointed out, sounding a little puzzled at having to state the obvious.

Luke blinked and looked at her blankly for a moment, replaying the conversation in his head. "Yeah. Right. Sorry. I was…thinking about something else." Like how those long legs might feel wrapped around his waist.

He shoved open the driver's door and stepped out into the parking lot, drawing a deep breath of chill night air. Where was a little ice storm when you needed it? he thought. Something guaranteed to cool the most overactive libido, which his seemed to be lately.

He circled around the back of the car, arriving on the

passenger side just as Cat pushed open her door and slid out. Those damned legs were going to be the death of him, he thought, half amused, half angry. Hunger and need had him closing the gap between them, had him reaching for her. As if it belonged to someone else, he saw his hand slide around her waist, under the soft wool of her coat, felt the indentation of her waist, let his fingers settle on the curve of her hip.

Cat tilted her head back, looking up at him. The street lamp leeched the color from everything it touched, painting her in shades of dark and light. Dark hair, pale skin, her eyes deep mysterious pools, the almost-bruised darkness of her mouth. She didn't say anything, didn't pull back as he lifted his free hand and slid his fingers into the soft knot of her hair, searching out the pins that held it and pulling them loose, letting them scatter on the pavement. Her hair tumbled around her shoulders, and Luke curled his hand into it, letting it slide through his fingers. He felt a nearly painful surge of need. Hunger. Anger that he wanted her so much, that he had so little control where she was concerned.

Cat shivered as his fingers brushed against her nape. He hadn't said anything, had barely touched her, but she could feel the weight of his eyes on her, feel the intensity of his hunger. It pressed against her in a soft, warm weight, sliding over her skin, making her need, making her want. His head lowered, and she let her eyes flutter shut, her lips parting in anticipation of his.

The first touch was light, fleeting, a promise and a tease. When Luke lifted his head, Cat sighed with regret. Her eyelids felt weighted, too heavy to lift. Her head tilted, lips parted in an unconscious plea, asking for more. She heard Luke's breath hiss between his teeth, and then his mouth was on hers again, warm and hungry and demanding.

It was just like the first time. That same surge of hunger and need spilling through her, heating her skin, weakening her knees. She brought her hands up, fingers curling around the edges of his jacket, clinging to him as the world rocked and spun around them. His tongue slid along her lower lip, both invitation and demand. She gave in, opening her mouth to him, taking him inside, meeting his need with a matching hunger.

Luke made a sound in the back of his throat and shifted forward, crowding her back against the side of the Mercedes, holding her there as he took his time ravaging her mouth, melting every bone in her body in the process. Cat was helpless to do anything but respond. This was what she'd been dreaming about since the first time he'd kissed her.

When he finally lifted his head, she was trembling, not with cold but with need. Her fingers were wrapped tight around the edges of his coat, and if she hadn't been trapped between the solid weight of his body and the smooth steel of his car, she would probably simply have melted onto the blacktop. His legs were braced on either side of hers, and she could feel the rigid length of his erection through the layers of clothing. The knowledge that he was hard for her, that he wanted her that much, sent a quick shiver up her spine.

"Come home with me," he whispered, pressing damp kisses against her temple, over both eyelids, against her already kiss-bruised mouth.

Cat was tempted. Why not go home with him? Why not let him take her to bed, show her where all this heat could lead? They were engaged, going to be married soon.

Why wait? It would be so easy. She closed her eyes against temptation and shook her head.

"I'm not going to sleep with you tonight," she whispered, and wondered at the husky sound of her own voice.

"Why not?" Temper edged out seduction, and she felt his hands tighten on her, stopping just short of bruising strength. "You've got a ring on your finger now. Isn't that enough? Or does it have to be the right ring?"

The sneer in his tone touched off her own temper, making her feel dizzy with the abrupt change of mood. Cat stiffened, releasing her grip on his coat as she pulled away from his hold.

"It's not about the damned ring," she snapped. "My life has taken a hundred-and-eighty-degree turn from where it was a week ago. I just spent several hours being stared at, weighed, judged and probably found wanting by all your friends—and I use the word lightly. I had two people offer to represent me when we get a divorce, some guy groped me so hard, I think I still have his handprint on my butt, and one of your old girlfriends cornered me in the ladies' room and in a spurt of vodka-fueled nostalgia, wanted to compare notes on your technique in bed. I'm tired, I'm nervous, and I don't know you that well. I'm flattered that you want me enough to be a jerk about it, but you can damned well wait a couple more weeks."

In the dead silence that followed her outburst, the sound of a car driving past on the street was painfully loud. Cat leaned back against the solid support of Luke's car and closed her eyes. Maybe she should just take off the ring now and save him the trouble of asking for it. Then she could drive herself to a sanitarium somewhere and check herself into a nice padded cell for a month or two.

"Who groped you?"

Luke's voice held anger, but it didn't seem to be directed at her, and Cat cautiously opened her eyes.

"What?"

"Who put his hands on you?"

Possessive much? she thought, and told herself that she was not, absolutely not, going to feel any sort of thrill over that sort of male— Oh, who was she kidding? She liked hearing that tone in his voice, liked that he felt possessive. It wasn't love, but it wasn't indifference. For the moment she would take what she could get.

"It doesn't matter," she said. "I dealt with him."

"It does matter. I don't like the idea that some idiot thought he could put his hands on you."

"No? I notice you're not worried about what your old girlfriend had to say about your bedroom technique."

"I don't have anything to worry about in that department," Luke said, grinning wickedly.

Cat's laugh was startled and breathless. It was arrogant as hell, but she had to admit that there was something very seductive about that kind of confidence. She was willing to bet his arrogance was justified, and that thought was just a little more than she could take. She was standing in an empty parking lot at one o'clock in the morning. She was tired and wired and more than a little confused. A few more minutes of this conversation, of being so close to him, close enough to feel the heat of him in contrast to the cold night air, and she was going to do something she would... Well, maybe she *wouldn't* regret it, but that didn't mean it would be smart.

With an effort, she forced herself to straighten, giving up the support of the car, careful to step sideways, away from Luke's tall frame.

"I'm going home." It came out a little more defiant

than she'd intended, sounding more like a challenge than a statement, as if she expected him to try to stop her.

His hand came up, and she watched it warily, not sure if she should dodge or throw herself at him. All he did was brush his fingers over the curve of one cheekbone.

"You okay to drive home?"

She nodded, her voice stolen by the gentleness of the touch, the unexpected concern in the question.

Luke's fingers trailed down her cheek, drifted over her jaw and settled finally on the pulse that fluttered at the base of her throat. Cat felt that light touch all the way to her toes. He leaned toward her.

"Get lots of sleep between now and the wedding," he whispered, close enough for her to feel his breath warm against her mouth. "You're going to need it."

His lips covered hers in a quick, hard kiss that was over before she could respond, assuming she could have summoned any coherent response. Taking the keys from her hand, Luke unlocked Ruthie's door. A firm hand on her shoulder steered her into the driver's seat, pushed down the lock button and shut the door again. Moving on autopilot, Cat slid the key into the ignition and started the car, offering up a brief prayer of thanks when Ruthie's engine cranked over immediately, because if Luke had had to give her a ride, she knew she would have ended up in his bed—at her own request. And it was too soon for that. Wasn't it?

Chapter Six

Like most little girls, Cat had fantasized about her wedding. She'd pictured herself sweeping down the aisle in a long white dress, a faceless but handsome bridegroom awaiting her at the altar, rows of elegantly clad family and friends watching her exchange vows with the love of her life. She would be the most beautiful bride ever.

Unlike most little girls, her mother hadn't shared her fantasy.

When Naomi found her putting a pillowcase on her head and prancing around the room pretending it was a veil, she shook her head sadly and sat her daughter down to have a serious talk. Not the one about the birds and the bees. At eight, Cat already had a pretty good idea of where babies came from. Six months living in a commune had done more for that aspect of her education than any sex education class could ever have hoped to accomplish.

No, this was the talk about how she should never let cultural biases get in the way of her empowerment as a woman.

"You have to remember, baby, that the traditional

Western marriage ceremony is a ritual that encourages thinking of a woman as a chattel. I'm sure most people don't think of it that way, but just the idea of having her father give a woman away like she's a bale of hay or a draft horse, and phrases like 'I take this woman'—though, of course, it also says 'I take this man,' which suggests that the two of them are actually owning each other, which isn't really a good thing for either of them. But that's not my point. My point is, baby, that you have to always be careful not to let yourself get sucked into the dominant social paradigm and end up sacrificing your individuality, letting 'I' become lost in 'we.' Do you understand what I'm saying, baby?''

Cat had nodded, trying to look as though she understood what putting a pillowcase on her head and pretending she was wearing a pretty dress had to do with sacrificing things and owning people. If she said she didn't understand, her mother was sure to try to explain it to her, because Naomi was a big believer in answering every question, but the answers were frequently more confusing than the original question had been.

Now, a dozen years later, her own wedding less than an hour away, Cat wondered what Naomi would think about what she was doing. What would Naomi say if she knew her daughter was marrying a man she barely knew, a man who already had their divorce planned, if not actually scheduled? Cat grinned suddenly. Naomi wouldn't be bothered as much by the idea that Luke was planning to divorce her as by the idea that he was planning anything so far ahead. *You never know where the road might go, baby. If you're too focused on a particular destination, you may miss the really important turns.*

If Cat told her she was halfway in love with a man who was marrying her as a means to an end—well, that and to get her in bed—Naomi would probably murmur some tangled comments about the importance of following one's heart and the need to embrace whatever fate had to offer, possibly wrapped in a metaphor involving rocks and water flowing around them, or maybe something to do with trees bending in the wind or standing firm against it. Then she might offer a few vague words about Luke's aura, his birth sign, the current alignment of the planets, and a quote from Thoreau or Shakespeare or Confucius that might or might not be relevant.

Cat sighed and smoothed her hand over the full skirt of her dress, enjoying the way the ivory silk felt against her skin. If she was looking for someone to tell her that she was doing the right thing, Naomi wasn't really the person she wanted, because, aside from drive-by shootings and animal sacrifice, Naomi always thought that everyone was doing the right thing. Everything was part of some amorphous *plan,* a grand design that was unscripted and yet would eventually come to some marvelous conclusion, like one of those mystery parties where the guests ''solved'' a crime that was, by its very nature, already solved.

Not that she really needed anyone to tell her she was doing the right thing. She knew she was. Well, she knew it wasn't a totally *wrong* thing, anyway. Or to put a more positive spin on things, it was potentially a very right thing and the only way to find out for certain was to dive straight in. It would just be nice to know if there was enough water in the pool.

Maybe it was this room, this house, that was making her suddenly doubt herself, she thought, looking around the quietly elegant bedroom. Luke's home was beautiful, and it obviously belonged to someone with plenty of money, but his grandfather's house was in a whole new category. There was a refined elegance about it that made her suddenly aware of her youth, of her total lack of social sophistication, of the fact that she'd eaten more Hamburger Helper than she had filet mignon.

Cat wandered over to the window and looked out on the formal rose garden with its neat brick pathways. The roses had just been given their annual pruning, and stood bare and rather cranky looking. If she were closer, she would probably be able to see the faint swelling of leaf buds. In a few weeks, new foliage in shades of bronze and green would cloak the bare canes, and, by May, the air would be heavy with the scent of new blossoms. Behind the rose beds, discreetly screened by a tall boxwood hedge, were an Olympic-size swimming pool, tennis courts and a guest cottage that was bigger than anywhere she'd lived when she was growing up. The main house had an eight-car garage, a "viewing" room with a widescreen television bigger than the screen in her local multiplex, two dining rooms, a breakfast room, six bedrooms and an uncounted number of bathrooms.

A short, stocky Hispanic man had answered the front door and introduced himself as Luis, then said Luke had not yet arrived and Mr. Quintain had said that she was to be shown to the blue bedroom if she wished to freshen up. She hadn't felt any particular need to freshen anything but was afraid that the alternative might be time spent alone with her future grandfather-in-law. The blue bedroom was suddenly very appealing.

So here she was, in the blue bedroom, trying to figure out what she was doing in a house where the bedrooms actually had names and wondering if she was about to make a huge mistake. Maybe it was silly to be so intimidated by a house, but what did she know about this sort of lifestyle? She was a waitress and a gardener, not a debutante. She knew just what to do about tomato horn worms or how to handle obnoxious customers, not the correct way to crook her little finger while drinking tea or the precise angle at which to cross her ankles.

"Hey, you decent?"

Breath catching on the edge of panic, Cat turned as Jack poked his head past the partly open door. One hand pressed against the knot in her stomach, she couldn't hold back a quick, startled laugh when she saw that his eyes were squinched shut.

"No, I'm naked except for a feather boa and a cigar."

He laughed and opened his eyes, pushing the door the rest of the way open and stepping into the room. He was wearing a dark blue suit, and a gray shirt with a conservative gray-and-blue-striped tie. She'd never seen him dressed up, and for a moment it made him seem like a stranger. Then he grinned, and the sense of unfamiliarity disappeared. "You know I'm never going to believe that. I know you don't smoke."

"I suppose the naked with a feather boa part is believable?"

"More than the cigar."

He stopped a few feet away and tilted his head to give her a long, considering look. Cat resisted the urge to fidget. She'd found the dress in a vintage-clothing store, and she knew it suited her. Ivory silk, cut off the shoulders, with a simple scoop neck, nipped in waist and an extravagantly full skirt that fell to midcalf and whispered faintly when she walked. It was feminine without being fussy, romantic without being froufrou and just wedding-y enough to fulfill some of those childhood fantasies without giving her bridegroom the idea that she was...well, that *she* was getting ideas.

"You look incredible." The simple sincerity in Jack's

voice made Cat release a breath she hadn't even known she was holding. She gave him a shaky smile.

"Well, you wouldn't let me do pink satin."

He laughed and reached out to pull her into a quick, tight hug. "Hey, what's the point of having a gay friend if you don't take my fashion advice?"

"I don't think that's very politically correct of you," she said, giving him a mock disapproving look as he stepped back.

"It's okay. I'm allowed to make queer jokes. It's one of the perks of being part of a minority. We get a special dispensation on things like that. But I could be doing every woman in greater Los Angeles and I'd still know that you look incredible. Luke isn't going to know what hit him."

"I didn't buy the dress for Luke," Cat said firmly, and then flushed when Jack raised one eyebrow in silent disbelief. "Who asked you, anyway?" she muttered.

Before he could answer, there was a tap on the half-open door. "I heard a rumor someone was getting married," Susan said, pushing the door the rest of the way open as she came into the room. She was wearing a long, floaty dress in an abstract raspberry-and-yellow print that shouldn't have suited her short, plump figure but did anyway.

Cat bit back the urge to say that no one *she* knew was getting married. She could go out the window. It was only two stories. How many bones could she possibly break? Swallowing the bubble of panic that threatened to choke her, she smiled at the older woman. She'd come this far, and she wasn't backing out now.

"Did Larry find his cuff links?" she asked. When she'd left the house, a massive search had been underway. Well, as massive as was possible when Larry kept forgetting what he was looking for and Susan was more interested in the sketch she was working on for a new vase.

"Yes, they were in that wooden jewelry box on top of his dresser, exactly where they should have been and the last place he thought to look."

Susan gave Jack a vague, sweet smile, as if she knew she'd seen him somewhere before but couldn't quite place where. Cat saw Jack's eyes spark with sudden humor and gave him a quelling look. He'd met both Larry and Susan several times when he came out to the house to look over the gardens. After the third or fourth introduction, he had begun using different names, introducing himself as Pablo Marconi, a semiprecious gem dealer from Belize, or Billy Joe Bob Dooley, come up from Alabama to visit a fellow pigeon-raising enthusiast in Cucamonga. Each ridiculous name and occupation had been greeted with a polite acknowledgment, an invitation to make himself at home and total amnesia when he next appeared.

"You remember Jack, don't you?" Cat said before he could open his mouth. "My friend who owns a restaurant and buys most of my vegetables?"

"Of course." Susan shook his hand and smiled. "Would you mind terribly if I asked you to go away? I'd like to talk to Cat."

Jack glanced at Cat and, when she didn't offer any objection, he nodded.

"Sure. I want to get a front-row seat for the wedding, anyway."

"With only five guests, I think they're pretty much all front-row seats," Cat pointed out dryly.

"Can't be too careful." He leaned down to brush a kiss across her cheek. "Break a leg, kid."

Susan frowned faintly as she watched him leave. "Owns a restaurant? I thought he raised some sort of livestock,'' she murmured. She shook her head, dismissing the question, and turned to look at Cat. "I feel like I should say something maternal right about now, since your mother isn't here to do the job. I assume we can skip the lecture about the birds and the bees?"

Cat gave a choked laugh and nodded. "I think I'm pretty well up to speed on the birds and the bees."

"Good." Susan looked relieved. "I don't know what on earth I'd say, anyway. I never did figure out why it was called the birds and the bees in the first place. Sounds downright kinky, when you think about it. Mixing species that way."

She smiled when Cat laughed. "You know, I didn't have children, which is a very good thing, because I'd probably have forgotten them or let them fall in the kiln, but since I've married Larry, I've come to think of you as the daughter I never could have managed to raise myself. I hope you don't mind that."

"No." Cat stopped, fought to get control of her voice. "I don't mind. You and Larry have been…well…you're family."

"Exactly." Susan seemed relieved that she understood. "I've always thought family should be a matter of heart rather than blood. Take my brother, Henry, for example. He was a whiny brat when we were children, and he grew into a whiny adult. Not a single likable characteristic, and the fact that we happen to share a few genetic markers doesn't make him any more tolerable." She reached up and patted Cat's cheek. "So, since we've agreed we're family, I'll tell you that I don't know what's going on with you and Luke. I don't know why he was engaged to Devon, then suddenly engaged to you. I'm not asking for an explanation," she said, holding up one hand when Cat started to speak. "It's none of my business. I just wanted

to tell you that he's getting a much better deal with you
than he ever would have had with Devon. I love Larry
dearly, and I suppose, if I were a better person, I'd love
his daughter just because she *is* his daughter, but the girl's
got the emotional depth of a mannequin.''

"But she's very pretty,'' Cat said, startled by the wistful tone of her own voice.

"She is for now,'' Susan agreed comfortably. "But she
won't age well. Those fat-cheeked blondes never do. By
the time she's forty, she'll look like a candle that's been
left sitting in the sun too long.'' She smiled at Cat's startled laugh. "You've got good bones. When you're forty,
you're still going to look good. Trust me on this.''

"So if I wait twenty years, I'll be able to compete with
Devon?'' Cat asked, trying for humor and managing
something that wavered uncomfortably close to plaintive.

"You're more competition than she could possibly handle right now,'' Susan said firmly. "Only a complete idiot
would think anything else, and I don't think your Luke is
a complete idiot.''

While Cat was wondering if that meant the other
woman thought Luke might be a partial idiot, Susan was
fumbling under one fluttering panel that drifted down the
side of her dress. She murmured in triumph when she
found what she was looking for as her hand disappeared
into a concealed pocket for a moment.

"This belonged to my grandmother. I've never worn it,
because it doesn't really suit me, but it will look lovely
on you, and I want you to have it.''

Cat gasped as Susan opened her hand to show a pretty
heart-shaped pendant. Small diamonds glittered in the
bright winter sunlight spilling in through the window. The
setting had the rich, soft gleam of gold, the warm patina
of age.

"Don't say you can't take it," Susan ordered, and Cat shut her mouth with a snap. "Now, come sit in this chair so I can fasten it. I think it's going to look very nice with that dress."

Cat did as she was told, sitting on the dainty chair in front of the vanity, watching in the mirror as Susan lifted the necklace over her head. The older woman was still talking, something about how lucky Cat had been to find such a pretty dress and how well it suited her. Cat let the words flow over her along with a tentative feeling of confidence.

Susan didn't seem to think she was crazy to marry Luke. Of course, that didn't mean it wouldn't turn out to be a mistake of colossal proportions, but it was nice to know. Maybe she was going to end up with a broken heart. But maybe not. And if she backed out now, she would always wonder what might have happened if she'd gone through with it.

Keith had been to quite a few weddings in his time. His brother and sister were both working on their second marriages. His father was currently split from wife number three, and his mother was still married to husband number two. He'd been there for every promise of love and eternal devotion. Add in friends, friends of the family and business associates, and he'd seen perhaps more than his share of weddings. He'd been to huge, splashy affairs and small intimate ones, and, during one hazy, drunken spring break spent in Las Vegas, he'd stood up—well, leaned a little—as best man for a friend who was marrying a stripper he'd met two days before. Last he'd heard, they had three kids and were living a life of suburban bliss outside Chicago.

But even with all those weddings under his belt, this

one stood out from the pack, and not just because it was his best friend tying the knot. The same best friend who'd once said he would rather be drawn and quartered than say "I do." Keith wasn't sure what it was. There weren't many people, but he'd been to smaller weddings. When his buddy married the stripper, the only other witness had been an Elvis impersonator who worked in a club next door to the neon-lit chapel.

The setting wasn't traditional, but his sister's first husband had been an oceanographer with connections at Sea World, and their wedding had been held next to the orca tank, with a bored killer whale looking on. By comparison, the elegantly decorated living room, with its polished hardwood floors and muted upholstery, was a paradigm of traditionalism.

No, it wasn't the setting or the lack of guests that put this wedding in a class by itself. Maybe it was knowing that Luke and Cat were going into this marriage without even the illusion of happily-ever-after in mind that made it seem so unique. Luke, at least, had no illusions. He wasn't so sure about Cat, he thought uneasily.

Keith looked at the two of them, standing next to the French doors that led out toward the rose gardens, talking to Larry and Susan. The dull gleam of gold and diamonds on Cat's left hand caught the clear winter sunlight that spilled in through the glass. In her soft ivory dress, with her hair caught back from her face and then left to spill down her back, she was a study in contrasts. Ice and fire, innocence and temptation.

There was blatant possession in the hand Luke rested on the small of her back. Keith had known him too long to mistake the way he was looking at his bride. His grandfather might have pushed him into getting married, but he'd obviously decided that the arrangement was not entirely without benefits.

He knew Luke well enough to read him, but Cat was more difficult. Despite her seeming openness, he got the feeling she played her cards close to the vest, revealing less of herself than it seemed she was showing. Most of the time she seemed to view the world—and herself—with a kind of sleepy amusement, but once in a while, when she looked at Luke, there was something in her eyes that made Keith wonder if she was marrying him for all the wrong reasons—like because she was in love with him.

"So what do you think?" Jack asked, settling into the chair next to Keith.

Keith glanced at him, caught his nod toward Cat and Luke.

"Think about what?" he asked cautiously.

"Very cautious and lawyerlike." Jack sounded more amused than annoyed. "Don't admit anything until you find out what the other guy's thinking. My father would approve."

"Your father's a lawyer?"

"Blood and bone. Big Boston law firm. You may have heard of them, Reynolds, Martin, Stewart and Reynolds? The first Reynolds is my father. The second one is my older brother."

"I've heard of them." Keith nodded, impressed. "They handled the Ardmore-Smith case last year. Managed to keep the government from throwing the CEO in jail for fraud. That took some pretty impressive footwork. They've got a solid reputation."

"So I've heard." Jack's dry tone held a thread of bitter humor that made Keith wonder what the story was behind it. Sounded like it was more than a preference for warm weather that had him living a continent away from his family.

"So what do you think?" Jack asked again, nodding toward the newlyweds. He caught Keith's cautious look and grinned. "Cat told me about the whole deal. Quintain needs to get married. She gets a fat settlement. Yadda, yadda, yadda. Everyone lives happily ever after, more or less. Not hard to guess there was something going on, what with Quintain being engaged to Devon one day and Cat the next."

"It could have been love at first sight," Keith pointed out.

"For Cat, maybe. She's inclined to lead with her heart. But Quintain?" Jack arched his brows in disbelief. "I don't think so. He doesn't strike me as the love-at-first-sight type."

Keith wondered if that was an insult, and if it was, shouldn't he say something in defense of his best friend? But Jack's tone was more matter-of-fact than critical, and besides, he was right. Luke was about as likely to dive headfirst into love as he was to suddenly flap his arms and take off flying. He wasn't even a good candidate for a gradual approach to the whole falling in love thing. He caught Jack's eye and realized he hadn't answered the original question. What did he think of this whole setup?

"It's a very...practical arrangement for both of them," he said.

"Sure it is," Jack agreed easily. "Quintain needs to be married for...what? A year? So a year out of their lives and Cat walks away a rich woman, and he gets whatever it is his grandfather's dangling in front of his nose. Practical all the way."

"But?"

"Nothing, really." Jack caught Keith's eye and

shrugged. "I just never thought of practicality as Cat's driving force."

That summed it up, Keith thought, looking at the newlyweds. He understood why Luke was doing this. It still seemed more than a little crazy, but he knew exactly what Luke was getting out of it. He wasn't sure what Cat was after. Money was the obvious answer, but if that was all she wanted, it didn't seem likely that she would have argued that the settlement was too generous. He'd worried then that Luke might be getting more than he'd bargained for. Now he wondered if Cat might be getting a lot less than she hoped for.

It was a good thing she'd gone into this marriage with low expectations, Cat thought, slanting a sideways glance at her new husband. He hadn't changed out of the suit he'd worn for the wedding, but he'd taken off the jacket and rolled up the sleeves of his white shirt. It was a surprisingly sexy look, but it was a little hard to appreciate it when he was so completely absorbed in the paperwork spread out on the tray table in front of him. He'd pulled a stack of papers out of his briefcase the moment the plane was airborne, muttering something that might have been an apology before losing himself in his work.

Cat sipped her orange juice—freshly squeezed and perfectly chilled—and wondered if he would have brought work along on the honeymoon if he'd married Devon. And what would Devon have done if he had? Pouted prettily, no doubt. Coaxed him into paying attention to her.

She sighed and looked out the window, but there was nothing to see but clouds and really, once you'd seen the top of one cloud, you'd seen them all. It was something of a disappointment, but once she was past the novelty of actually having room for her legs, flying first class was just as boring as flying coach. She reached for her drink again, then stopped, staring at the unfamiliar glint of gold and diamonds on her ring finger. Sunlight angled through the small window, making the diamond in her engagement ring glitter with icy fire.

She was married. She was married to Luke. She and Luke were married. Wed. Hitched. Joined together in holy matrimony. A package deal. A couple. No matter how she phrased it, it didn't seem real.

It had only been a few hours, but the ceremony had already taken on a hazy edge, like something she'd dreamed. A few words spoken by a judge who was also a friend of the family, a ring sliding on her finger, a surprisingly chaste kiss from Luke, and it was done. She was a married woman. After all the buildup and worry and doubt, the actual ceremony had seemed almost anticlimactic.

Now, here she was, off on her honeymoon. That was something she hadn't expected. A honeymoon seemed too...romantic for the business arrangement their marriage was supposed to be, but Luke probably wanted everything to look normal. Which, when she thought about it, was a really depressing reason for going on a honeymoon. So she wouldn't think about it, Cat decided. She would just enjoy the idea of spending five days at a vineyard in Napa Valley.

She'd never been to Napa Valley, though she and Naomi had lived only an hour or so away in Berkeley for almost a year right before they moved to Los Angeles. They hadn't spent much time outside the city. For all that she liked to talk about her deep connection to nature and Mother Earth, Naomi was a city girl through and through, and generally limited any actual contact with nature to neatly mowed parks and pretty little wildflowers in tidy beds.

Cat glanced at Luke, who was scribbling notes in the margins of the contract he was reading. Her breath escaped in a quiet sigh. So far, this wasn't exactly shaping up to be the sort of honeymoon most girls dreamed of, but even if Luke worked through the whole five days, at least she would get a chance to see one of the most beautiful areas in California.

Luke worked until their plane touched down in San Francisco, reading through the papers even after the tray table was locked back in place for landing. Cat entertained herself by mentally planting the summer garden, trying to remember exactly where she'd planted which crops so she could rotate them among the beds. She debated ordering a new load of mulch, trying to decide if the benefits outweighed the cost and then realized that she really didn't have to worry about that anymore. She was, by virtue of the ring on her finger, a wealthy woman. Or she would be in a year and a day. In the meantime, she had a monthly allowance that was more than the budget of most third-world nations. A few cubic yards of mulch wouldn't even put a dent in her checking account.

Oddly enough, it was not a comforting thought. She'd worked hard to make her little garden patch profitable. It was disconcerting to think that she no longer needed to worry about the cost of mulch or water, or whether or not she could afford to build a cold frame this year or had to wait until next. It took some of the fun out of things and made her realize how much of her pleasure came from the challenge of it.

Apparently this whole having-money thing was not as

easy as it looked from the outside. Cat sighed and gripped the armrests as the plane began its descent.

Luke's fingers closed over hers, making her jump, her head jerking toward his.

"Don't worry," he said, leaning close and pitching his voice to be heard under the whine of the engines. "I have it on the best authority that this pilot hasn't crashed a plane yet."

Cat laughed, feeling her mood lift. She wasn't particularly afraid of crashing, but she turned her hand anyway, let her fingers slide between his. Having money and being married were going to take some major adjustments, but there were definite compensations.

Cat's first impression of Napa Valley was of a myriad of greens and golds. The setting sun angled across the rolling hills, casting long shadows broken by streaks of light filled with deep emerald and the brilliant gleam of wild-mustard flowers. Luke had rented a car at the airport, and he drove with the easy familiarity of someone who knew the roads well. Obviously this wasn't his first trip up here. Cat filed that away as something to ask him about later, and let herself sit back and enjoy the scenery.

Maiden's Morning Winery was at the top of a long road that wound through rows of grapevines. It was nearly dark when they arrived, but she caught glimpses of neatly trimmed vines stretching along wire trellises in the car's headlights. Luke stopped the car in front of a big house that looked like a movie set version of a Mediterranean villa. Off-white stucco walls were shadowed by rustic peeled post trellises. There wasn't enough light for Cat to identify their leafy covering, but the golden glow of outdoor lighting spilled over colorful baskets of impatiens that hung underneath the trellises and beds of pansies that nestled up against the base of the porch, sheltered from wind and frost. The L-shaped house cradled a courtyard paved in worn brick, laid in a herringbone pattern. A shallow, rectangular pool stretched along one side of the courtyard, and when Luke pushed open the door, Cat caught the musical splash of water from the tiled fountain at one end.

She slid out of the rental car and looked around in delight. If she'd been asked to design the perfect house to sit in the middle of a vineyard, this was exactly what she would have come up with. It practically oozed old-world charm and character. The door opened before Luke reached the shallow steps that led up to the porch, and warm, honey-colored light spilled out into the courtyard.

"Luke! It's been ages since we've seen you. You don't have to be on your honeymoon before you come see us, you know." The woman who hurried down the steps was small, fair-haired and apparently didn't need to breathe, if Cat could judge by the nonstop stream of words. "Of course, this *is* the perfect place for a honeymoon. Cold this time of year, but that's good, because it's so much more interesting if you have to bundle up. Where's the fun in spending all day on a beach wearing next to nothing and then going back to a hotel room and wearing nothing? No excitement in that."

Without slowing, she gave Luke a quick hug, then released him and darted over to Cat, who was standing near the front of the rental car. She reached for Cat's hands, her grip surprisingly strong for a woman of such delicate build. "You must be Luke's wife. We're so glad to meet you. I'm Lucy, and that's my husband, Charlie." She waved one small hand in the direction of the house, where Cat could see the silhouette of a very large man just stepping onto the porch. "Welcome to Maiden's Morning."

Cat waited a moment to be sure the flood of words had stopped before responding. "Thank you. What I saw of it as we drove up looks lovely."

"The most beautiful place on earth," Lucy said.

"Now there's an unbiased opinion for you." Charlie spoke for the first time, his voice as deep and slow as his wife's was light and quick. His chuckle reverberated in the courtyard as he stepped off the porch to shake hands with Luke. "Good to see you, Luke. Lucy's right, it's been too long."

"Charlie." Cat could see the gleam of Luke's smile in the near dark. "Pining for my help with the pruning, are you?"

This was apparently a private joke between them, because Charlie threw back his head and laughed, a big booming laugh that made Cat smile. "I hid the shears when I heard you were coming," he said, still chuckling. Turning, he smiled at Cat and held out his hand. "Welcome to Maiden's Morning."

"Thank you." His hand enveloped hers, and she had to tilt her head back to meet his eyes. He was older than she'd thought at first. The light spilling off the porch revealed the network of lines around his eyes and the gray streaks in his full beard. Now that her eyes were adjusted to the light, she could see that Lucy's hair wasn't blond, as she'd thought at first, but a pretty silvery-gray. Her face, like her husband's, showed the marks of time.

"There's coffee on," Charlie said as he released Cat's hand. "And I've got a bottle of the '96 Cab I was going to open after dinner. We can—"

"Charlie." Lucy shook her head at him. "They're on their honeymoon. They have better things to do than drink coffee and talk wine."

Cat wondered if Luke wanted to stay and have coffee

and drink wine, if maybe she should say something about not minding, but Luke had moved to stand next to her, putting his hand on the small of her back, and he was reaching for the keys Lucy pulled from the pocket of her jeans.

"Maybe tomorrow," he told Charlie. "I'd like to try the '96."

"The guest house is all ready for you," Lucy said. "I aired the place out, put fresh linens on the bed and stocked the kitchen. You don't have to come out for days."

Cat was grateful for the darkness that hid her flush. Funny, how with everything that had been going on, she hadn't really given as much thought as she might have expected to the fact that this was her wedding night. She'd been focused on the engagement and then on the wedding, not really expecting it to happen. Once it had, she'd been so amazed that she hadn't really thought beyond the basic fact that they were married to what was going to happen next.

Next. On her wedding night. *Their* wedding night. Her stomach fluttered with something that could have been panic.

Luke's hand shifted, turning her back toward the car. She heard him telling Lucy and Charlie good-night, promising to drop by the house tomorrow, heard Lucy tell him to watch his priorities. She thought maybe she laughed when the others did, but she wasn't sure. Her mind was filled with thoughts, images, and she suddenly felt simultaneously hot and cold.

The guest cottage was not that far from the main house, but a curve in the road hid the two buildings from each other, giving the illusion of isolation. In the darkness, the cottage was only a vague outline—only one story, a steep roofline, the pale gleam of stucco punctuated by wide windows. There was a low picket fence, with a trellis that arched over the open gate. Cat caught a glimpse of bare canes as she followed Luke up the brick walkway and guessed that, in summer, roses would cover the archway. She wondered what color they were and imagined their sweet scent.

The porch light was on, a warm pool of light spilling over the brick flooring, catching the edge of a wrought-iron table and the two chairs sitting beside it. In the summer, the view would be lovely, past the rose-covered arbor, out over the tidy rows of grapes and down into the valley. Even now, in the dark, with the winter-cold air making her wish she'd brought a heavier coat, the promise of it drew her, made her wonder if she would get a chance to see it in summer.

The key snicked in the lock, and Luke pushed open the door, gesturing for her to go in ahead of him. The floor of the entryway was red tile, the color softened by years of wear. Cat had a vague impression of soft-white plaster walls, graceful archways and warm wood furnishings. She noted it all with the ten percent of her brain that wasn't squeaking in terror over the fact that she was alone with Luke for the first time since they'd said "I do."

Chapter Seven

When he was in his twenties, Luke had been driving over the Angeles Crest one night and had come around a corner to find himself nearly nose to bumper with a deer. He'd hit the brakes, swerved and, with a little skill and a lot of luck, managed to avoid hitting the deer, smashing into the mountain on one side of the road or careening off into the canyon on the other. Two things had stuck with him from that incident: the incredible adrenaline rush of brushing that close to death and coming away a winner, and the look of frozen fear in the doe's eyes as she stood pinned in his headlights.

The way Cat was looking at him right now was remarkably similar.

The dress she'd worn for the wedding had been elegant, chaste. It had made him want to messy her up, pull the pins from her hair, kiss the primness from her mouth, and find the heat and passion beneath the ivory silk and lace. Before Luis drove them to the airport, she'd changed into a pair of trim charcoal-gray slacks and a mossy-green cowl-neck sweater that clung just enough to fuel a man's imagination. He'd actually been grateful for the last-minute contract that had come in before he left the office that morning. It had given him something to occupy his mind other than thinking up ways to lure her into the dubious privacy of the airplane bathroom.

All during the drive from San Francisco, he'd kept his hands on the wheel and his eyes on the road. It hadn't been easy. He couldn't remember ever wanting a woman the way he wanted Cat. Somewhere in the back of his mind he knew that should probably worry him. It was dangerous to want anyone that much. He'd watched his father panting after his mother, so hungry for any crumb of attention that he'd been willing to ignore the succession of lovers she hadn't even bothered to try to hide. But there wasn't any real comparison. His father had been desperately in love with his wife.

He liked Cat, but he wasn't in love with her. In lust, maybe, but not in love.

When he shut the door, she twitched like a nervous cat. Her eyes slid toward him and then away, and her knuckles showed white where she gripped the overnight case she'd carried in from the car. A more sensitive man might have been offended by his bride's obvious nervousness. A kinder man would have offered reassurance. A better man might have offered to sleep on the sofa. It probably said something terrible about him that having her look at him like he was about to tie her to the railroad tracks sparked a wicked sense of humor.

''So why don't we just do it right here?'' he asked conversationally.

Cat's eyes widened into huge green pools. ''Why don't we do what right here?''

''You know.'' Luke waggled his eyebrows up and

down. "The horizontal mambo. Play hide the salami. Boff like bunnies. Make the beast with two—"

Cat's giggle cut him off. Well, he hadn't really envisioned his wedding night as a laugh fest, but it was better than having her looking at him with those big, scared eyes that made him feel like the villain in a bad melodrama. Besides, she looked damned cute with her eyes sparkling and her teeth biting her lower lip, trying to hold back another laugh.

"What?" He widened his eyes in shocked amazement. "You mean you don't want to roll around on the tile floor?"

"It's…tempting." Her voice was almost steady, but her eyes sparked with humor. "And ordinarily I'd…um… take you up on the offer, but it's… Actually, I'm allergic to tile."

"To tile?" Luke arched his brows and looked doubtful. "I've never heard of an allergy involving tile."

"It's very rare." She looked regretful.

Luke sighed. "Well, if I'm not going to get to fulfill my lifelong fantasy of having sex on a cold, hard tile floor, we might as well see what Lucy left us for dinner."

It had been silly to let herself get so worked up, Cat thought two hours later. A warm shower, half a glass of wine and a good meal, and she was having a hard time remembering why she'd nearly flipped out at the thought of being alone with Luke. Too many changes, she decided. Too many changes too quickly. She'd thought that growing up with Naomi, who changed her life the way most people changed their socks, had made her pretty good at dealing with major life changes. But apparently, following her mother's endless quest for spiritual enlightenment hadn't prepared her for finding her own life sud-

denly turned upside down, and the fact that she'd been
the one to do the turning didn't make it any easier.

Still, shocking as it was to realize that she was married
to the man sitting across the table from her, she didn't
regret making the choices that had brought her here. Now
that she'd recovered from the mini panic attack that had
gripped her when they first arrived at the cottage, she
could feel a little flutter of excitement, the same excitement that had led her to suggest he could marry her instead of Devon. It was more than desire, though that was
certainly a part of it. Maybe it wasn't quite love yet, but
it was edging that way, maybe faster than was safe. Then
again, if safety had been her main goal in life, she would
have gone from high school to college and would now be
halfway to a degree in something useful. Dabbling her
fork in the scattering of crumbs left from a slice of truly
exceptional chocolate cream pie, Cat smiled a little.
Maybe there was more of her mother in her than she'd
realized.

Luke watched the expressions flicker across her face
and wondered what she was thinking. For someone who
seemed so completely open, he found her surprisingly
hard to read. Or maybe he was just looking for hidden
meanings that weren't there.

"Get enough to eat?" he asked, edging his plate away
and leaning back in his chair.

Cat started a little, as if she'd forgotten she wasn't
alone. Luke wondered if maybe he should be offended
that his bride of less than twelve hours had apparently
forgotten his existence, but after a meal of Lucy's excel-
lent stuffed flank steak and two glasses of a Cabernet—
not the '96, but a very nice vintage—taking offense just
took more energy than he was willing to expend. Besides,
she was giving him a half-shy little smile that made him

want to jump her bones. Then again, just about everything she did made him want to jump her bones, so maybe the smile wasn't to blame.

"I couldn't eat another bite," she said, setting her fork down on her plate and pushing both away. "It was a wonderful meal."

"Lucy does a mean flank steak." Luke looked at the bottle of wine, debated with himself and decided another half glass wouldn't be out of line. He wasn't sure Cabernet was really the wine of choice to follow chocolate cream pie, but he was willing to chance it. He lifted the bottle and arched a brow at Cat. She shook her head, her mouth twisting in a slightly apologetic smile.

"I know it's probably a capital crime to say this when I'm sitting in the middle of a vineyard, but all wine pretty much tastes like grape juice gone bad to me."

Luke shuddered as he tipped the bottle over his own glass and watched the wine splash out, ruby-red with a hint of fire. "God, I've married a peasant."

"Sorry." Cat shrugged apologetically.

"Just don't tell anyone. Lucy and Charlie would run us out of town on a rail."

Cat bit her lip, almost managing to look ashamed if you ignored the laughter sparkling in her eyes. "It can be our little secret."

He gripped the stem of his glass between thumb and fingers, turning the glass slowly on the table, in no hurry to drink. Cat toyed with her fork, keeping her eyes down. It was a pity she didn't drink. A little more wine might have relaxed that last bit of tension he could see humming through her. He'd never had to get a woman drunk to get her into bed and he didn't plan on starting now, but it might be easier on both of them if she were more relaxed.

Luke dropped his eyes to his glass, watching the light

play through the wine as he turned it idly between his fingers. He knew there were men who found innocence erotic, but virginity had never held any particular appeal for him. He'd certainly shed his own at the first opportunity, courtesy of the girl who cleaned his parents' pool. He'd been fifteen to her seventeen, and grateful that at least one of them knew what they were doing. Since then, he'd always preferred women of experience, women who knew what they wanted and how to give him what he wanted. But, looking at Cat, he had to admit—reluctantly—that there was something very appealing about the idea that he would be the first to touch her, the first to see desire spill into her eyes, the first to smooth his hands over the pale satin of her skin.

Luke shifted uncomfortably in his chair and picked up his wineglass. Might be safer to think of something else. Unless he could persuade her to start their honeymoon on the dining table. And that was a bad image to have drifting through his head. That fiery hair spilling across the polished wood, her body laid out— He took a swallow of wine and forced his thoughts in another direction. Or tried to. Seemed like his thoughts only had one direction tonight.

Desperate for a distraction, Luke was just about to comment on the weather when Cat spoke.

''You know—'' she slanted him a look from under her lashes, her expression both uncertain and curious ''—considering the fact that he was the one who wanted you to get married, your grandfather didn't seem all that happy at the wedding.''

Obviously he was the only one having a hard time keeping his thoughts above waist level. While he'd been fantasizing about ravishing her in assorted places and interesting ways, she'd been thinking about his grandfather.

Sighing, he looked across the table at her, debated briefly how to answer the question she hadn't quite asked and decided that there was no reason not to be honest.

"He had someone else in mind," he said. His glass clicked against the polished wood as he set it down. "Cissy Winslow. Old family friends, old money." He glanced at her, arched one brow. "Winslow Department Stores?"

"Wow." Cat's eyes widened, and she pursed her lips in an impressed little moue. If he kissed her now, would she taste of chocolate? "That's not just old money, it's a *lot* of money," she said, and he dragged his eyes away from her mouth.

"Well, old money's not all that impressive unless there's a lot of it." He started to reach for the wine bottle to top off his glass but changed his mind. Getting drunk and passing out on his wedding night was not part of the plan.

"I suppose not." Cat pleated the edge of her celadon-colored linen napkin. "So how come you didn't marry her? I mean, why not marry the woman your grandfather had picked out? Wouldn't that have been easier?"

"Because I was damned if I'd let him control everything." Luke's tone was sharper than he'd intended, revealing more than he liked.

"So you gave in on the marriage but made sure to pick someone he'd dislike."

She didn't look upset, just mildly curious. Interested. Was she really so indifferent to his grandfather's opinion? To his? The thought stung, made his answer blunter than it might have been.

"Pretty much." He pushed his empty plate back. The conversation was nudging aside the lazy anticipation he'd been feeling. "Devon was about as far from what he had in mind as I could find, short of trolling for a hooker on Sepulveda. Shallow, not too bright, grasping and social climbing, with about as much maternal instinct as a tree stump.''

Cat winced at the description, opened her mouth to say something in Devon's defense, then closed it without speaking. It was a little harsh, maybe, but basically pretty accurate. ''And you were going to marry her when you thought of her that way?''

''Why not?'' Luke shrugged. ''I wasn't looking for happily-ever-after, just looking to meet my grandfather's terms.''

Cat toyed with her fork, resting it on its side, then turning it right side up. Some questions were probably better not asked, she reminded herself. And curiosity killed the cat, which was so ridiculously apropos that she felt her mouth curve. ''So if Devon got an F on your grandfather's grading curve, where do I fall?''

Luke debated for a moment before deciding to stick with the truth. ''I don't know. I had…other things in mind when I agreed to marry you.''

He had the satisfaction of seeing Cat's eyes widen and a quick rush of color tint her cheeks. She looked away for a moment, regained her composure. When she looked at him again, her expression was serious.

''Why *did* you do this? Why did you marry me? Or marry anyone, for that matter? What is your grandfather offering that you want so much that you'd marry a woman you don't even like? You've got plenty of money. It can't be that.''

''Can't it?'' Luke picked up his glass and downed the last swallow of wine. ''People will do some odd things for money,'' he said, looking at her over the rim.

She flushed again, darker this time, and looked away uncomfortably.

"I guess they will."

Guilt pinched at him. He hadn't meant to make her uncomfortable. No, that wasn't quite true. Her questions had stung, for some reason, sharper than they should have. It wasn't unreasonable that she would want to know why he'd entered into this bargain between them. He should have been expecting her to ask. Devon hadn't, but Devon hadn't been interested in anything that didn't pertain directly to money—how much? How soon? How quickly could she spend it? Cat was different. The money didn't seem to interest her as much as it should have. For a moment Luke was tempted to ask her why *she* was doing this, but he wasn't sure he would like the answer.

"This vineyard belongs to my grandfather," he said, offering an answer to her questions rather than the apology she probably deserved. "I spent every summer here from the time I was eight until I left college.

"Charlie's great-grandfather started Maiden's Morning in the late 1800s. His grandfather did pretty well with it, managed to hold things together through prohibition and the depression. Charlie's father..." Luke glanced across the table, met Cat's eyes and shrugged. "He knew wine, but he didn't know business. My grandfather bought the winery more or less by accident in the early sixties."

"How do you buy a winery by accident?" Cat had leaned her elbows on the table and propped her chin on her folded hands.

"It was part of a package deal. He bought several properties at once, and Maiden's Morning was one of them. The winery was on its last legs, hadn't made a profit in years, and wine wasn't the hot ticket it is now. Not American wine, anyway. Charlie was just out of college, and he was convinced he could make the winery a paying proposition. His father was ill—dying—so Charlie put on a suit and tie and took the bus to L.A. to talk to my grandfather.'' Luke's mouth curved. ''Granddad says he was a tall, skinny kid with a bad haircut and Coke-bottle glasses. He had all these charts and graphs and plans for expanding the winery—new vines, a bigger operation all around.''

''And your grandfather saw that he knew what he was doing?''

''No, he thought Charlie was crazy as hell.''

''But he obviously kept the winery, so he must have thought it was a good investment.''

''He figured it was a sink hole, bound to lose money as fast as it was pumped in, but he thought Charlie had a lot of balls to approach him with an idea for expansion when it was obvious the place should be shut down, and he liked the fact that Charlie didn't try to play the pity card, didn't say anything about his father's health or whine about how long the winery had been in the family. He just presented Granddad with this insane idea to throw more money into a dying venture.''

''So, he gave him the money because he thought Charlie had guts?''

''Pretty much.''

Cat's mouth curved in a delighted smile. ''That's a wonderful story.''

''Well, he also knew it would be a good tax deduction,'' Luke added, but she brushed that off.

''Don't spoil it with practicalities,'' she said, sitting back in her chair and waving one hand. ''I like the unpractical side better.''

''It was definitely unpractical. Charlie knew wine, but if Americans hadn't started drinking more of it and then discovered that California wines could hold their own against the French, the winery would have gone belly-up anyway.''

''But it didn't, and everybody ended up living happily ever after,'' Cat concluded with a satisfied smile. She seemed to remember where the conversation had begun and frowned. ''So what does this have to do with why you married me?''

''I spent summers here,'' Luke repeated, coming at the question from the side. ''Charlie and Lucy were like another set of parents to me, only more interested than mine ever were. Charlie tried to teach me the wine business, but I don't have the nose for it.''

''Or the pruning skills?'' she asked, remembering Charlie's laughing comment earlier.

''Or the pruning skills,'' Luke agreed, grinning. ''Though the incident in question happened when I was eleven, so I think he should cut me some slack.'' His smile faded. ''I love this place. My grandfather owns a lot of property. Some of it's worth a lot more than this. Some of it's probably as beautiful, but this is the one place that matters to me. And the old goat knows it. He'd been after me to get married for a couple of years, but a while back I was...involved with a woman he particularly disapproved of.''

Cat didn't even try to hide her curiosity, lifting her eyebrows in silent question, and he found himself expanding on that statement. ''She was an...exotic dancer.''

Her eyes widened, and her mouth dropped open a little. Luke waited for the shocked exclamation or maybe a lecture on the exploitation of women.

''You dated a stripper? Wow, that's so neat.'' Cat dropped her hands flat on the table and leaned forward, eyes sparkling with interest. ''Did she have tassels?''

"Tassels?" Her unexpected reaction left his mind blank.

"On her...um...breasts. I saw this movie once, about a stripper who had tassels, and she could make one twirl left and one twirl right at the same time. I thought that showed an amazing amount of muscle control." She sounded faintly envious.

Luke stared at her. Did she stay up nights thinking of ways to *not* react like other people?

"She didn't have any tassels as far as I know."

"Oh." Cat didn't let this minor setback weigh her down for long. "I've never seen an exotic dancer in person. Is she still working in L.A.?"

"I don't know," Luke lied, suddenly afraid she was going to ask him to take her to see Billie dance. For just a minute he had a nightmare vision of taking Cat into The Blue Parrot Lounge to watch his former lover dance. God help him, she would probably ask for twirling lessons, and *that* was an image he did *not* need in his head.

"We lost touch," he added, wanting to make sure that door was firmly closed. "She might even have moved back to Atlanta." It wasn't a lie. Just because Billie had said she would rather eat dirt than ever set foot south of the Mason-Dixon line again, that didn't mean she hadn't changed her mind.

Cat sat back in her chair, looking disappointed. Luke drew a shallow breath, feeling as if he'd just skirted a potential disaster.

"So your grandfather didn't like the fact that you were dating a stripper." Cat frowned. "That seems a little narrow-minded. I mean, just because she was a stripper, that doesn't mean she couldn't also be a Rhodes scholar."

The thought of Billie Dubois as a Rhodes scholar was enough to boggle the mind and make him choke back a laugh. Billie had been a walking, talking, nontassel twirl-ing cliché. A body to make a man's mouth go dry and not much of a brain. Thinking about it now, Luke was vaguely ashamed that he'd spent as much time as he had dating a woman he hadn't really liked or respected.

"Billie wasn't really Rhodes scholar material," he said finally. "And Granddad had heard…rumors about her that made him less than enthused about the fact that I was seeing her. He was afraid I was going to marry her. I wasn't. Not even close."

"But you were too pigheaded to tell him that," Cat guessed.

Luke nodded, thinking that piece of pigheadedness had cost him dearly. Not that he had any complaints at the moment, he admitted, looking at her. He was surprisingly content with where his stubbornness had gotten him. For now, anyway.

"After Billie and I broke up, he started pushing Cissy Winslow on me as the perfect wife. I probably should have done more to make it clear that I wasn't interested, no matter how great a match he thought it was." Luke sighed and reached for his empty glass, sliding it in idle patterns on the polished table. "He got it in his head that if he just gave me a shove, I'd fall into holy matrimony with her, so he came up with the idea that if I didn't get married before my birthday, he'd sell Maiden's Morning, lock, stock and—literally—barrel, but if I got married and stayed married for at least a year, the winery would be mine."

Cat frowned. "But he wouldn't really sell the winery, would he? Put Charlie and Lucy out of their home?"

"He knew he wouldn't have to follow through on the threat, because he knew I'd do damned near anything to stop him, but yeah, if I didn't get married, he'd have sold the place. He'd have hated it almost as much as I would, but he'd have done it. Nick Quintain never makes idle threats."

"Well, I think that's just…stupid," Cat said. "For him to do something like that just because he said he would. That's just dumb. And it seems like he should have known you well enough to know that if he gave you an ultimatum like that, you were going to do something to thumb your nose at him. I've only known you a few weeks, and *I* figured that out."

"Apparently he underestimated my capacity for stupidity. That's what he told me when I told him I was going to marry Devon. He was sure that once he'd forced the issue, I'd pluck Cissy Winslow like a ripe plum."

"Was Cissy eager to be plucked?" Cat asked.

"Not particularly. Last I heard, she was having a torrid affair with a ski instructor."

"How tawdry." Cat looked down her nose, haughtiness spoiled by the laughter in her eyes.

"Yes, isn't it?" Luke said, dry as dust. "And aren't you sorry you asked why I'd jumped into this marriage?"

"No." Cat ran her finger around the rim of her glass, making the wine shiver. "It seemed so odd—that you'd let him force you into something you didn't want to do, I mean. And, for what it's worth, I think you did the right thing. It would be awful if Charlie and Lucy lost their home."

Would it seem quite so much the right thing if it hadn't also happened to make her a rich woman? But it was hard to hang on to his cynicism when she was looking at him as if he'd just done a good deed.

The mellow chime of the mantel clock in the living room seemed overly loud, and they both started. Cat looked away.

"It...it's getting late, isn't it?" She picked up her plate, reached for his as she stood up. "I'll just rinse these off."

The kitchen, like the rest of the house, had an old-world charm. A rustic tile floor and maple counters, plain muslin curtains over the window above the sink. There was a breakfast nook with a gently scarred maple table, and cheerful blue-and-white-checked cushions on the chairs.

Cat set the plates next to the sink and turned on the water. Did Luke like to sit down to a real breakfast, or did he prefer to get by on a cup of coffee and a bagel? Maybe she would try an omelette in the morning. Tomorrow morning, when they woke up after...tonight.

She fumbled, knocked against a plate and sent a fork skittering across its surface to land with a clatter on the counter. Silly to be nervous, she told herself, drawing a deep breath. She might not have much by way of hands-on experience, so to speak, but she certainly knew what was involved. Picking up a plate with a hand that was steady—almost—she held it under the running water to rinse it. She wanted Luke. He made her stomach go tight and her skin feel all tingly. It was either an allergy or lust.

"Leave the dishes until morning."

She hadn't heard him come in, and the sound of his voice startled her. Her fingers tightened on the plate.

"There're just a few. I can—oh."

His hands settled on her hips, and she could feel the heat of him behind her. His lips touched the back of her neck, left bare by the soft knot she'd swept her hair into, and she shuddered with the pleasure of it. The plate clattered against the sink as she set it down, freeing her hands to grip the edge of the counter, holding on to it as his hand slid beneath the hem of her sweater, palm flattening against her stomach. She felt the imprint of each finger on her skin, heat radiating from that single touch.

"We can do them in the morning," he said, and she nodded without having the faintest idea what she was agreeing to.

She could feel his erection, hard and solid against her bottom, imagine the heat of it even through the layers of cloth separating them. It was hard to breathe, and her head was suddenly too heavy to hold up, so she let it fall back against the solid support of his shoulder. Eyes closed against the light, which had been a gentle glow a moment ago but now seemed dazzling, Cat could only feel. Feel the slow slide of his hand moving upward, across her midriff. Feel the heat of his breath on the side of her throat. Blind with the sudden surge of need, she turned her head toward him, breath escaping on a soft moan as his mouth covered hers.

He tasted of chocolate and wine, sweet and sharp. When he turned her in his arms, she went willingly, eagerly. His mouth devoured hers, hunger feeding hunger, need building need, until she trembled with it, hands fisting in his hair, body arching closer to his. It was impossible to believe that she'd been frightened of this. Of him. This was what she wanted, what she needed, what she had to have. She'd been waiting her whole life for this moment, this man.

When he circled her to the door, she linked her arms around his neck, her body swaying into his as they left the kitchen, drifted down the hallway. Slow, deep kisses delayed them. Luke pressed her back against the wall next to the kitchen door and tasted the soft skin under her left ear. When they were halfway down the hall, his fingers flicked open the clasp of her bra, and she shuddered, head dropping back against the wall as his palm cupped her breast beneath the softness of her sweater. It was like a dance, slow and sensual, melting her bones, making her skin tingle with awareness, arousal swelling up in a thick, warm tide. The quiet snick of the bedroom door closing behind them was superfluous, because the rest of the world had ceased to exist the moment he put his hands on her.

When Luke had been very small, he remembered he had gone into a bakery with his grandmother. She'd told him he could have one cookie, whichever one he wanted. It had been a tantalizing glimpse of grown-up freedom. He could remember standing there, breathing in the scents of sugar and butter and baked things, and staring in the display cases at the dazzling array of treats, any one of which could be his, and not being able to choose among so many wonderful things. He felt much the same way now and wondered how Cat would feel about being compared to a bunch of pastries. She would probably laugh, that husky little laugh that made him think dark and lustful thoughts.

Right now he was past the point of thinking and well into doing. There was irony in the fact that, now that he finally had her in his hands, he didn't know where to start. He wanted to bury his hands in the heavy red silk of her hair, and he wanted to slide them over the soft warmth of her skin. He didn't want to give up her mouth, but he wanted to taste the pulse that beat at the base of her throat and the satiny hollow between her breasts. He wanted to touch and taste every inch of her. He wanted all of it, right here and now. Wanted the heat and rush and mindless pleasure of it, wanted to bury himself in her, feel her close, hot and wet around him, feel her shudder with need, with pleasure.

Slow, he reminded himself. She was new to this—and there was no point in trying to convince himself any longer that the idea didn't appeal to him on some atavistic level. He liked knowing that he would be the first and—for the next year, at least—the only. Gentle, he thought. Slow and gentle.

"Luke, please," she whispered against his throat. Her fingers tugged at his belt buckle, and slow and gentle went out the window. He reached for her sweater, the word *now* pounding in his head like a drumbeat.

Afterward, Cat couldn't remember how he got her clothes off. One minute she was rumpled but fully clothed; the next she was naked as the day she was born, and he was lifting her, easing her back against the cool linen sheets. In some distant part of her mind, she thought she should feel self-conscious. After all, it was the first time she'd been completely naked in front of someone else since…well, since forever, really, unless you counted her mother bathing her when she was a child. Shouldn't there be awkwardness and uncertainty and maybe just a touch of fear?

But it wasn't fear that had her trembling as she watched Luke toe off his shoes and kick them aside. And it wasn't cool air that made her nipples tighten when he pulled his shirt off over his head, too impatient to deal with buttons. His eyes never left her, and she thought she could feel the heat of that gaze like an actual touch on her skin, stroking over her body. When his hands dropped to his belt, Cat felt the color come up in her cheeks, but she didn't look away. She didn't want to miss anything.

He was beautiful, she thought. Broad shoulders, a solidly muscled chest covered by a light dusting of dark, curling hair that narrowed to a thin, dark line that cut across the taut muscles of his stomach. The rasp of his zipper sounded loud in the quiet room, and Cat fought the urge to close her eyes as he stripped his pants and shorts down at the same time.

Oh, my.

Luke had plenty of experience in the bedroom, perhaps more than his fair share. Once past his hormone-riddled youth, when all sex seemed wonderful, he'd chosen his lovers carefully, preferring experience and skill. If pressed, he would have said that he'd had—and been had by—the best. But he'd never, in twenty years of bedroom play, experienced anything more erotic than having Cat watch him undress.

Lying back against the plain white linen sheets, her fiery hair scattered across the pillows, she was everything he'd imagined—and more. Her skin was creamy white, with a scattering of freckles across her shoulders and the upper curves of her breasts. Pretty pink nipples that made his mouth water with the need to taste. He couldn't remember ever *wanting* this much. And having her eyes on him, full of curiosity and desire... If he wasn't careful, this was going to be the shortest wedding night in history.

His hands were not quite steady as he stripped off his pants and shorts, letting them fall to the floor as he straightened. He saw Cat's eyes widen, her mouth dropping open a little as she stared at him.

"Don't tell me you've never seen a naked man before," he said, irritated at finding himself suddenly self-conscious.

"Only in magazines," she said, dragging her eyes up to his face with an obvious effort. "This is a lot more...three-dimensional."

Laughter was something he hadn't expected, but he should be getting used to the unexpected around her. Still smiling, he slid onto the bed, bracing himself above her.

"Is that a complaint?" he asked, easing downward until only a breath lay between them.

"N…no." Cat's hands came up, hovered uncertainly and then settled against his ribs, a tentative touch that made his skin twitch with the need for more. "No complaints."

"Good." He lowered his head until his breath ghosted across her mouth. "Because I plan on being three-dimensional as often as possible for the next few days."

Her breath hitched, and her eyes widened for a moment; then a quick spark of laughter turned them to emerald green. Her mouth curved in an irrepressible smile. "Is that a threat or a promise?"

"You decide," he said against her mouth, tasting that smile.

Her mouth softened beneath his, her tongue offering a quick, teasing touch that left him wanting more. He doubted he would ever get enough of her—the taste of her mouth, the silken feel of her skin against his body, the ripe weight of her breast in his palm. She shivered, her breath escaping on a soft moan when he teased her nipple to aching hardness with lips and tongue.

"Luke!" She gasped his name as his hand slid downward.

"Let me," he whispered, kissing away any protest she might have made.

He'd told himself slow, gentle, ease her along. He would take his time, make it last, draw it out all night. It was a pretty good plan, as plans went. And it flew right out the window the minute he cupped her, felt her arch into his touch. She was already damp for him, her body welcoming him and slow and gentle were drowned out by the insistent beat of now, now, *now*.

Next time he would make it last forever, drag it out

until they were both half-mad with needs but not this time. He had to have her now or explode.

Some last remnant of sanity and longtime habit had him dragging his hand from her, rolling half away to scrabble in the drawer of the nightstand for the package of Trojans he'd put there when he unpacked earlier. He rolled back toward her, already ripping open the packet.

"No." Cat put her hand on his, stopping him. When Luke looked at her, she was flushed, her eyes focused somewhere around his collarbone. "You don't have to.... It's safe to...I'm taking the pill," she finally got out in an embarrassed mutter. "It seemed like the best idea, what with...everything that was going on."

"Pregnancy isn't the only thing to worry about," he said, even as the thought of having her without barriers cranked his arousal up another notch. "You may be pure as the driven snow, but I'm not."

She looked at him, her eyes steady. "If you tell me it's safe, I'll believe you."

Luke hesitated and then nodded. Safe sex was one of the few rules he'd never broken, not even during his hormone-driven teenage years. He probably shouldn't be breaking it now. She was on the pill. Good. Fine. Great. But when it came to sex, he'd always been a belt-and-suspenders kind of guy. You could never have too much protection. Then again, he'd never in his life wanted a woman the way he wanted this one. And having her like this...with nothing between them...

Watching him, Cat saw his decision in his eyes even before he dropped the half-open condom package over the side of the bed. It hit the floor with a soft tick, hardly audible over the drum of her pulse. He shifted, and her stomach jumped as she felt the drag of his erection, rock hard and already damp. Instinct had her opening for him, welcoming him, sighing at the first heated brush of him.

His fingers curled into her hair, his eyes holding hers, fierce and hot, as he entered her. Dimly, she thought there should be pain, discomfort, some last virginal twitch of fear and uncertainty. Instead there was an aching sense of fullness, of completion. This was what she'd been waiting for.

Cat had thought she'd known what to expect. She'd read books, seen movies. She figured the real-life experience would lie somewhere between the shooting stars and fireworks of her favorite novels, and the dry, clinical descriptions of high school health classes.

Then Luke began to move, and she forgot everything she thought she knew. It wasn't fireworks. It was fire and heat and power. Electricity crackling through every inch of her, making her burn with need and hunger.

She arched to take him deeper, wanting more. Luke shuddered, groaned, muttered something that might have been prayer or imprecation. Cat couldn't tell the difference, not with this need filling her, driving her.

"Please," she whispered against the sweat damp skin of his throat. She wanted, had to have, needed. Her nails bit into his flanks, her body twisting restlessly. "Please."

And Luke answered her plea—filled his own need— with the hard, driving rhythm of his body against hers. It wasn't slow or gentle. It might even have been a little rough. Tomorrow she would have bruises where his fingers gripped her hips; his back would show the marks of her nails. Tonight, all that mattered was the relentless drive toward satisfaction.

Cat gasped, her body arching beneath him, her eyes going blind as she clung to the edge of the precipice for a taut instant. Luke felt her tighten like a fist around him.

A sharp oath escaped between his gritted teeth as she tumbled over the edge, dragging him with her into the spinning pleasure.

He was going to move. As soon as he remembered how. Luke pressed his face into the cool linen pillow next to Cat's head and made an effort to slow his breathing to something less than a pant. Vaguely, he thought maybe he was too heavy for her, that he had to be crushing her, but when he gathered enough energy to try to move, she muttered a protest that was more sound than word and tightened her arms around him. Okay. So he could just stay where he was for a while. A few minutes. An hour or two. Whatever it took.

He could smell them with every breath he took. Shampoo and flowers and sweat and sex. It was a heady combination. Ordinarily it might have been enough to make him consider the possibility of a second round—something a little slower this time—but he was fairly sure that he'd just come hard enough to lose brain cells, and he wasn't as young as he used to be.

Cat shifted beneath him, long legs sliding up alongside his, fingers tracing down the length of his spine. Her head turned, breath brushing his ear. He felt a definite stir of interest.

On the other hand, the night was still young, and he wasn't all *that* old, Luke decided, turning to catch her mouth with his.

Chapter Eight

Luke woke to an empty bed and the smell of coffee. The latter almost made up for the former. Almost. Rolling over, he stared blearily at the rough-textured plaster on the ceiling and tried to decide whether he should get up and seek out the coffee, which would probably also lead him to Cat, or if he should stay where he was and hope Cat might bring the coffee to him. After a few minutes, when neither his bride nor a cup of coffee appeared, he rolled out of bed. His pants were crumpled on the floor near the foot of the bed. His shirt seemed to have vanished, but, after last night, he didn't think the sight of him bare-chested was likely to shock Cat.

The thought of last night sent a tingle of interest to body parts that should, by rights, be too damned tired to be interested in anything. He allowed himself a smug smile.

Luke pulled on his pants, standing to zip them, and then arched his back in a bone-popping stretch. There was nothing like a night of incredible sex to make the world seem like a better place.

The kitchen was warm with the scent of coffee and the muffins that were cooling on a rack on the counter. Cat was standing in front of the sink, her hands wrapped around a thick white china mug as she looked out the window. Luke spared a glance for the spectacular view of hillsides covered in grapevines and the vivid yellow of wild mustard, tattered remnants of morning fog still clinging to the ground. Beautiful as it was, it couldn't compete with the view inside.

Cat was wearing his missing shirt. Just the shirt and nothing but the shirt. The sight of those long legs beneath the plain white cotton made Luke's mouth go dry. Caffeine deprivation and blueberry muffins took an immediate back seat to another kind of hunger.

He must have made some noise—possibly a whimper of lust—because Cat turned from the window and smiled at him. Her face was gently flushed, and there was a new awareness in her eyes.

"Hi." She looked away, cleared her throat and gestured to the counter. "I…made coffee and muffins. I wasn't sure what you'd want for breakfast, but I found a box of muffin mix, and I thought, since Lucy said she'd stocked the kitchen, it was probably okay to use it. The mix, I mean, not the kitchen."

She had pulled her hair back with a pair of bright yellow clips, and her face was bare of makeup. The top two buttons of the shirt were undone, exposing a wedge of pale skin, the hollow at the base of her throat and, when she turned to reach for a cup for him, the inner curve of one breast. There was an innocent sensuality about it that had him as hard and aching as if they hadn't already tangled the sheets together three times the night before.

"I can make omelettes, if you like," Cat said as she poured coffee for him. "Jack says my omelettes are passable. One of his assistants told me that's pretty high praise.''

Luke took the cup from her, his eyes on the tantalizing sway of her breasts beneath the thin fabric of his shirt. She obviously hadn't bothered with a bra. He wondered if she'd taken any other lingerie shortcuts. The thought of her, naked under his shirt, was…distracting.

She nudged the sugar bowl down the counter a bit. ''There's sugar, and the cream's in the fridge, if you want it. I made tea for myself. I hope the coffee's okay.''

Luke took a sip of coffee and fought to keep his eyes from crossing as his taste buds cringed. It was strong enough to strip paint and maybe dissolve the wood underneath. Cat gave him a hopeful look, and with a mental apology to his stomach lining, he swallowed.

''It's fine,'' he told her, and was rewarded with a wide smile, proving that the truth might set you free, but lying sometimes had its own rewards. Bravely he took another swallow and then set the cup on the counter.

''That's my shirt.''

Cat blinked in surprise and then looked down at herself. ''Yes. I didn't think you'd mind. I forgot to pack a robe, and I didn't want to…''

''I mind.''

''What?'' Startled, she looked at him.

''I mind a lot.'' He slid two fingers between the buttons over her belly button and tugged her a half step closer. Cat's eyes widened, and one corner of her mouth kicked up in a half smile.

''Gee, I'm sorry. If I'd known it would upset you, I wouldn't have borrowed it.'' Her lower lip thrust out ever so slightly, and she twisted her fingers around one button. ''I guess I should take it off.''

''Good idea.'' Luke tugged sharply on the shirt, and

she stumbled up against him. "I'll help you. The buttons can be tricky," he whispered against her mouth.

Luckily the muffins reheated quite nicely in the microwave.

Luke hadn't planned on taking a honeymoon with Devon. The thought of spending several days in her exclusive company ranked right up there with root canals and opera recitals on his personal list of things best avoided. Once out of bed, he'd never had much to say to Devon, whose conversation had run the full gamut from *A* to *B*—and sometimes didn't make it past *A*.

Cat's conversation, on the other hand, ran from *A* to *Z*, with detours into a few alphabets he didn't recognize. If there was a topic that didn't interest her, it was going to take more than a five-day honeymoon to find it. He'd planned the honeymoon with purely carnal intent. The thought of spending five days in bed with her had led him to clear his schedule with a ruthlessness that had left his assistant reeling and had probably cost him a lucrative deal or two, but a man had to set his priorities, and given a choice between money and sex, he knew where his lay.

It had been worth losing a deal or two, he admitted three days into their honeymoon. Not just the sex, though that was more phenomenal than it had any business being, considering her lack of her experience. Apparently sex, like baseball or higher math, was something some people just had an aptitude for. Or maybe she'd studied it the way she apparently studied anything that caught her attention. The idea of Cat poring over sex manuals brought an equal mix of amusement and arousal, a feeling that was becoming all too familiar.

He wasn't surprised that they were good in bed together. Grateful, occasionally astonished by just how good it was, but not really surprised. It was the electricity between them that had made him agree to her crazy suggestion that they should get married. He would have been surprised if they *hadn't* been good together. What did surprise him was how much he enjoyed her, even out of bed.

Where Devon had been interested in little that didn't directly affect her, Cat was interested in anything and everything. She'd pumped him for information on the real-estate business until he was sure she could have run Quintain Inc. herself if he should suffer a head injury that caused temporary amnesia.

As near as he could tell, her education before she and her mother had come to live with Larry Kowalski had been…well, *eclectic* would be a kind word. *Hit-or-miss* might be more accurate. Frequent moves in pursuit of Naomi's spiritual enlightenment had limited Cat's opportunities to attend conventional schools.

"Naomi said she thought formal education would be too confining, too establishment, but actually, I think it would have been pretty inconvenient for her. Yanking me out of public school every few months would have involved paperwork and explanations, and Naomi preferred to avoid both."

It was said without resentment. They were sitting in the living room on the evening of their first full day in the cottage. Luke had laid a fire in the fireplace, and gold and orange tongues of flame were licking at the logs, the faint crackle and hiss a backdrop for their conversation.

Luke sat in one of the two wing chairs that flanked the fireplace, a glass of brandy cradled in one hand. Sex, sightseeing, more sex, a good meal and the promise of yet more sex to come had left him feeling lazy and more relaxed than he could remember feeling in a very long time. Cat had started out sitting in the other wing chair but slid out of her seat to curl up on the floor, watching the flames. Luke watched her.

"Officially, I was homeschooled," Cat said.

"Officially?" He hadn't expected to enjoy her conversation almost as much as the sex. Almost. He was a man, after all. "What was it unofficially?"

"Unofficially, I spent a great deal of time in the library wherever we happened to be living, reading everything I could get my grubby little mitts on. Naomi encouraged me to read whatever I wanted." She paused and flashed him a look from under her lashes as her mouth curved in a quick little smile. "Well, it was really more a case of she didn't pay much attention to what I was reading, but it would never have occurred to her to censor it if she had, so I guess it was pretty much the same thing as encouraging me."

"So what did you read?" Balancing the snifter on his thigh, Luke let his head fall back against the chair, watching her from under half-closed lids.

"Everything," she said immediately. Her smile took on a mischievous edge. "My favorite thing was to read books that had been banned somewhere."

"The thrill of forbidden fruit?"

"Exactly." She grinned suddenly, eyes dancing with laughter. "We lived in Minneapolis for a few months when I was eleven or so. Naomi was working at a Wiccan bookstore. It was summer, so I didn't have to worry about anyone wondering why I wasn't in school, and I practically lived at the library. Naomi came to get me one evening, and one of the librarians pulled her aside and asked if she knew what I was reading."

Cat pursed her mouth primly and raised the pitch of her voice a little, and somehow managed to project the image of a much older woman. "'Some things just aren't appropriate for children, Ms. Lang.' Naomi blinked at her, and then looked all confused and concerned and asked if the library carried pornographic materials. The librarian— Miss Fleck, I think her name was—puffed up like a pouter pigeon and said that while there was certainly nothing of a pornographic nature in *her* library, she didn't think it was appropriate for a child of my age to be reading Nabokov or even Plato, because I couldn't possibly *understand*.''

Cat laughed suddenly, remembering. ''Naomi smiled this sweet, vague little smile and said that a man's reach must always exceed his grasp, or, in this case, a child's reach must exceed her grasp, or did she really mean that there were more things in heaven and earth, Horatio? Although, when you thought about it, saying Horatio really seemed to limit the effectiveness of that particular quote, because how often did you meet someone named Horatio? Maybe Shakespeare should have chosen a more common name, like Bob or Mary, except the quote just didn't sound quite the same that way, did it?''

Picturing the scene, Luke grinned. ''What did Miss Fleck do?''

''Ran like a rabbit,'' Cat said, laughter dancing in her eyes. ''By the time Naomi finished, poor Miss Fleck looked like a frightened horse, eyes rolling in their sockets, skin twitching. I actually felt sorry for her.''

''Sorry enough to confine your reading to Nancy Drew?''

''I said I felt sorry for her, not that I feared for her life,'' Cat said dryly. ''Besides, it wouldn't have mattered if I had. She avoided me like the plague the rest of the summer. I think she ran whenever she saw me coming up to the desk to check out books, so she wouldn't have known the difference.''

"*Did* you understand what you were reading?"

Luke swirled the last of the brandy in the snifter with an absent twist of his hand, watching her face, letting hunger drift through him in a slow, lazy tide. The firelight cast bright, dancing shadows over her face, those long legs, now stretched out in front of her. Her hair was brighter than the flames, and he had the fanciful thought that it would warm his hands if he touched it.

"Well, I didn't really understand *Lolita* so Miss Fleck was more or less right. But since I didn't understand it, I don't think it did me any serious harm. I sort of enjoyed Plato, but I suspect I missed a lot of the deeper meaning. I think I enjoyed the *idea* that I was reading Plato more than anything else. That was the summer I decided I was going to be an intellectual, read all the great books, maybe become the youngest *Jeopardy* champion in the history of the world."

Luke tried to remember what his fantasies had been when he was eleven. Pitching for the Dodgers, quarterback for the Rams. He'd had vague thoughts of becoming an astronaut, or maybe a fireman. He doubted if he'd even known what an intellectual was, let alone thought about being one.

"You were a seriously weird kid," he said, and Cat laughed.

"Probably. I spent a lot of time alone or with adults. I never quite knew what to say to other kids when I was around them. Not much common ground, I guess."

"They didn't want to have a scholarly discussion of *Plutarch's Lives*?" he guessed.

Cat wrinkled her nose. "No, and neither did I. It's a really boring book."

Luke laughed. He'd thrown the name out because it sounded obscure and dull. He should have known she would have read the damned thing. ''Expect the unexpected'' seemed to be the rule with her. It was going to make the next year more interesting than he could have anticipated when he'd agreed to marry a near-total stranger.

After tossing back the last of the brandy, he set the snifter on the marble-topped coffee table. The click as glass met marble brought Cat's head toward him. Her eyes were deep, dark green, fathomless. A man could lose himself in her eyes, Luke thought, reaching for her, pulling her up with him as he stood. If he were the sort of man inclined to lose himself in a woman's eyes. Lucky for him, he wasn't.

On the third full day of their honeymoon, when Charlie offered to give them a complete tour of Maiden's Morning, Luke opened his mouth to politely refuse, thinking that Cat wouldn't be interested in learning how to make something she didn't like to drink. Besides, he wasn't sure he wanted to spend that much time out of reach of a bed. But before he could politely turn down Charlie's offer, Cat was accepting with obvious enthusiasm.

Which was why the third day of his honeymoon was spent as a threesome—four, if you counted Charlie's dog, Brumley, a large creature of uncertain pedigree who sneered at Luke from beneath a cascade of shaggy gray fur and then attached himself firmly to Cat's side, to her evident delight. Luke told himself it would be immature to be jealous of a dog. Besides, he got to take her home when the tour was over. Take *that,* furball.

Cat wanted to know every detail of wine making, from planting the vines to putting labels on the bottles. At the end of a day spent touring the vineyards, from fields to cellar, Charlie clapped Luke on the back and told him

he'd made a damned fine choice and presented them with
a bottle of '68 Cabernet as a wedding present. It was a
near-legendary vintage for Maiden's Morning, and Luke
accepted it with the proper appreciation, resisting the
temptation to tell Charlie what Cat thought of wine in
general. No sense in spoiling what was obviously the beginning of a beautiful friendship.

That night he built a fire in the living-room fireplace
and made love to her on the sofa, lifting her to sit astride
his hips, watching the graceful lines of her body as she
arched above him, filling his hands with the soft weight
of her breasts, losing himself in the sounds of her pleasure.

"Luke. Luke, wake up."

He came awake too quickly, heart pounding with a rush
of fight or flight triggered adrenaline. Cat was bending
over the bed, one hand on his shoulder, her hair falling
around her face, shadowing her face.

"What?" He sat up, shoving the covers back as one
possible crisis after another flashed through his mind.
Armed robbers, rabid animals and appendicitis bounced
around in his sleep fogged brain. "What's wrong?" He
swung his legs out of bed and reached for his robe, trying
to look as if he was alert enough to fend off any dangers
or drive to the nearest hospital.

"Nothing's wrong. You've just got to see this." Cat
tugged on his arm, pulling him to his feet. "It's incredible."

What was incredible was that she was not only awake
but alert, Luke thought as he stumbled after her. They
hadn't gotten much sleep last night—or the night before,
for that matter. Three days—and nights—and the heat between them showed no signs of cooling. He distinctly re-

membered looking at the clock after their last bout and
seeing that it was four o'clock. So why was she awake
at—oh, God—six-thirty, and what could she possibly
need to show him?

"Look!"

Luke barely managed to avoid stumbling into her when
she stopped in front of the living-room window. He focused bleary eyes out the window, looking for the alien
spacecraft. There *had* to be an alien spacecraft.

"What am I looking at?"

"The balloon!" Cat pointed out the window at the hot
air balloon drifting over the valley. Painted in gradated
shades of blue, ranging from midnight to summer-sky
pale, it floated gracefully above the rows of vines. "Isn't
it amazing?" Cat asked, bracing her hands on the deep
window embrasure and leaning forward until her nose was
almost pressed against the glass.

She was wearing one of his shirts again, a blue chambray that provided a nice contrast to the fiery tumble of
her hair. Long, bare legs and bare feet, eyes sparkling with
delight. Despite lack of sleep and a near surfeit of sex,
Luke felt a twinge of lust. She was going to kill him, he
thought. But it was certainly a hell of a way to go.

"Isn't it incredible?" she asked, never taking her eyes
from the balloon.

"They're pretty common around here, actually," Luke
said, resigning himself to the fact that he wasn't getting
back to bed—for sleep or any other activity—as long as
the balloon was visible. "Hot air ballooning is popular in
the valley. It's a big tourist attraction. If you lived here,
you'd barely even notice them after a while."

"I don't think I'd ever stop noticing something so
beautiful," Cat said, sighing with pleasure as the sun

edged out from behind a cloud and light slid across the balloon in a warm, golden flow.

No, she probably wouldn't stop noticing, Luke thought, watching her face. She would be just as excited at seeing her hundredth hot air balloon as she was at seeing her first. He didn't think he'd ever seen anyone who enjoyed life as thoroughly. Clichéd as it was, he suspected that, if life handed Cat a roomful of lemons, she would learn to live on lemonade.

It was disgustingly early, he was short on sleep, and he'd seen enough hot air balloons in his time to know this one was nothing special. The polished oak floor was cold beneath his bare feet, and he needed at least four more hours of sleep to feel human. And if he was too jaded to be thrilled by the balloon and the fog-wreathed grapevines and the rising sun painting everything with thin, golden light, then he was certainly too jaded to... Oh, the hell with it. He wasn't jaded enough to hold out against her obvious pleasure in the moment.

Luke slid his arms around Cat's waist from behind. She immediately leaned back against his chest, bringing her hands up to rest on his forearms.

"Beautiful, isn't it?" she said on a sigh.

"Beautiful," he agreed.

Chapter Nine

When Cat had decided to make the leap into marriage with Luke, she hadn't thought much beyond that single astonishing concept. Looking back on it from the vantage point of three whole weeks as a married woman, she wondered if maybe a part of her had believed it wouldn't actually happen, that they wouldn't really tie the knot, so why waste time thinking of what might come afterward?

Not that it would have made any difference, she thought, looking at one of the flower arrangements that had been delivered earlier in the day. She couldn't possibly have imagined what her life would be like once she said "I do." Growing up with Naomi had given her more practice in adapting to change than most people got in a lifetime, but spending her childhood as an incidental passenger on her mother's unending journey toward spiritual enlightenment hadn't been quite enough to prepare her for the shock of suddenly becoming Mrs. Lucas Quintain.

She felt like Dorothy in *The Wizard of Oz*, snatched up by a tornado, tumbled around and set down in a whole new world. Only, instead of Technicolor, Munchkins and a yellow-brick road, she got a new bedmate, more money than any sane person could spend and a driveway that was a serious challenge to Ruthie's transmission. Of the three, it was the money she was finding most difficult to adjust to.

Ruthie's transmission could always be replaced, and sharing a bed with Luke was…well, it was definitely a change, but not the sort one complained about. Her mouth curved in a smug little smile. No complaints about that at all. But the money was something else.

Cat's smile faded. It seemed ridiculous to complain about having too much money, and she wasn't complaining. Not really. It was just that it added a whole new layer of complications to her life, complications she felt ill equipped to handle. There was more money in her checking account right now than she'd ever seen in her life, and that was just for one month. She had no idea what Luke expected her to spend it on. A small island nation, perhaps? She'd started leaving the checkbook in the bedroom, hidden in her underwear drawer, because she felt conspicuous carrying it around, like somehow people were going to take one look at it and just *know* what her bank balance was.

It wasn't just the money itself. It was all the stuff that went with it. To start with, there was the house. She and Naomi had once spent the winter living in a house nearly this big—them and three other families. Now, here she was, just her and Luke and all this space. Maybe she'd picked up more of her mother's philosophy than she'd thought, but she felt faintly guilty about having all this room for just the two of them.

And servants. What was she, the daughter of a hippie wanna-be, doing with servants? Well, one less servant now, which was why she was hovering in the entryway, contemplating the changes in her life. Maybe preparing a few excuses to give Luke?

Except she didn't need excuses, dammit, she thought with just a touch of defiance. He'd told her to do whatever she wanted as far as the house was concerned.

But he hadn't told her to fire his housekeeper.

Mrs. Bryant is a treasure, he'd said. *Mrs. Bryant has been with me for five years. She keeps everything running like clockwork,* he'd said. *You can count on her,* he'd said.

What he hadn't said was, *Why don't you fire the woman a couple of hours before our first dinner party, Cat?* A dinner party that included the VP of a bank and someone else who was terrifically important for some reason that escaped her at the moment.

Her very first business dinner, a sort of public debut as Luke's wife. She'd bought a new outfit, paying a truly astonishing amount of money for a pair of soft black pants and a matching jacket that looked like an architectural experiment gone bad on the hanger but did all sorts of interesting drapey things once she had it on. An ivory silk blouse and black pumps with tall spikey heels completed the outfit. When she put it on, she felt cool and sophisticated, like Myrna Loy in some witty movie from the '30s. Too bad she felt more like Lucy about to face Ricky with her latest disaster.

Luke flipped on his turn signal and edged the Mercedes toward the freeway off-ramp, grateful to be exiting before the traffic started to back up through the tunnel going into Pasadena. It had been a good day. He'd nearly closed a deal to unload an apartment house in Santa Monica this afternoon. It wasn't a firm commitment yet, but instinct told him it would be, and he trusted his instincts.

Instinct had made him take a chance on marrying Cat—

that and a healthy amount of lust—and look how well that was working out. She'd fit seamlessly into his life, not disarranging things. Devon would never have been able to resist rearranging things—his closet, the furniture, his life—but Cat just slid in and made herself at home, much like her feline namesake.

Really, he should track down Devon and her dairy farmer and buy them a great wedding present. He wondered if you could gift wrap a Holstein.

Turning up into the Flintridge Hills, he allowed himself to feel slightly smug. He still bitterly resented Nick's medieval interference in his life, but he had to admit that things had actually worked out pretty well. In a little less than a year, Maiden's Morning would be his, safe from Nick's meddling. In the meantime, he was married to a beautiful, sensual woman. Not only was the sex great— better than great—but he actually enjoyed her company. He liked her, dammit. She was…fun. Quirky. Nothing about her was what he expected.

She'd married him for his money, but she didn't seem to care all that much about the things money could buy. She drove a car that was older than God and wore no jewelry other than the wedding ring he'd given her. She was more comfortable in faded denim than silk, and when she went shopping, she brought home books rather than clothes or jewelry.

She hadn't rearranged the furniture or moved anything as far as he could tell, but the house looked more lived-in somehow. There were books stacked on side tables. Magazines on gardening, archeology and the latest Hollywood gossip were scattered wherever Cat happened to have settled to read them. Battered tennis shoes sat next to the fireplace, and yesterday he'd found a pair of worn leather gloves and a trowel sitting on the table in the foyer next to his briefcase.

The sudden clutter in his previously immaculate home could have been annoying, but he found it oddly appealing. He tried to imagine how he would have felt if it had been Devon leaving decorating magazines and makeup brushes lying around and shuddered.

Maybe he owed the dairy farmer a couple of Holsteins.

Turning down the steep driveway, he shook his head at the sight of Ruthie, in all her tomato-red glory, sitting in front of the garage. He hadn't believed Cat was serious about keeping that ridiculous hunk of scrap metal, but she'd refused all offers to replace it.

After parking the Mercedes next to it, he slid out, arching his back in a long, luxurious stretch before reaching back in the car for his jacket and briefcase. It had been a long day, and it wasn't over yet. The dinner party tonight was part business, part pleasure, and would provide a low-stress way of introducing Cat into his world.

The engagement party had been too big and impersonal. This was a small gathering. Porter and Dania Westheim were old friends. He'd done a lot of business with both Dania's bank and Porter's construction firm. He hadn't known the Southerlands as long, but Roger had bought two properties from his company over the last five years, and he'd seen them socially a few times. Laura Southerland was an attorney with a practice that focused on social issues. Most of her work was pro bono. Luckily for Laura and her clients, Roger's work was not.

Keith finished out the guest list, making it an odd number, unless he brought a date. Keith's presence would give Cat at least one familiar, friendly face. Not that she would need it. Cat could probably strike up a conversation with a wooden post, he thought, grinning.

She'd been nervous about tonight, but once the guests arrived, she would be fine. Luckily she wouldn't have any real responsibilities. Mrs. Bryant would see that everything was running smoothly. All Cat had to do was enjoy herself.

"You did what?"

Cat shifted uneasily under Luke's stunned gaze. She'd planned to lead up to her announcement slowly, maybe offer him a glass of sherry or possibly a full body massage to get him nice and relaxed before delivering the bad news. But he'd barely managed to set his briefcase down before she blurted it out. Now she repeated it again, speaking slowly and distinctly.

"I let Mrs. Bryant go."

It didn't make any more sense the second time she said it.

"Let her go?" He repeated it blankly, trying to absorb the meaning. "Let her go where?"

"Let. Her. Go." Cat's tone took on an edge of impatience. "Fired her, canned her, showed her the door, gave her the boot, terminated her. Choose your euphemism. She's gone."

Luke reached up to loosen his tie, his eyes skimming over the entryway, half expecting to see chaos already creeping out of the woodwork. Margaret Bryant had taken care of the house with wonderful efficiency for the last five years. She was the perfect housekeeper—invisible. She was, as any number of people had told him, a gem, a very well-paid, irreplaceable gem. And she was gone.

Cat shifted from one foot to the other, curling her toes against the cool tile floor. Her new shoes were about as comfortable as one could expect shoes with a three-inch heel to be, which was why they were currently tumbled in a heap next to the living-room doorway, where she could admire their sleek, sexy lines without actually having to endure cramped toes and an altitude-induced nosebleed. She wished now that she'd put them on before talking to Luke, because she felt at a disadvantage in her elegant suit with her feet bare except for silky hose.

"Okay." Luke drew a deep breath and then released it slowly. "Okay. I'm sure this makes perfect sense." He didn't sound like he believed it, but Cat gave him an A for effort.

"She was a nasty old bat."

"I didn't hire her for her award-winning personality." Luke reached for his tie again, wrenching it loose with a quick gesture that made Cat wince. "I hired her because she was good at her job. Really, really good at it," he added with heavy-handed sarcasm.

"She made Consuela cry."

"Who's Consuela?" Luke asked, bewildered.

"The maid. *Your* maid," she added with obvious disapproval. "She comes in three days a week. She's eighteen, and she's helping to support her mother and four younger brothers. Her father was in a car accident, and now he's in a wheelchair. He does wood carvings, but, let's face it, that's not exactly going to pay the rent. Her mother works at a restaurant called El Toro Loco in Hollywood, making minimum wage, which isn't nearly enough to support a family. Consuela wants to be a fashion designer, but there's no money for school, and no time, either, because she helps with her brothers. And they are *not* in the country illegally."

"I didn't say they were," Luke protested. There was a vague throb starting in his temples. Too much information, he thought. There was just too damned much information. All he wanted to know was what had happened

to his gem of a housekeeper, and instead he was being
bombarded with the family history of someone he
couldn't even remember seeing.

"No, but Mrs. Bryant did," Cat said. Her hands, which
she'd been trying to keep still so that she would look calm
and collected, flew out in a quick, angry gesture. "Well,
she implied it when she threatened to have Consuela deported. She can't, of course, but Tomas has the flu, and
Guillermo got in trouble at school, and Consuela was already upset."

Tomas and Guillermo must be two of the fabled
younger brothers, Luke decided. The throb in his temples
was moving from vague to definite. Very definite.

"She was half an hour late. Half an hour! And
that...witch threatened to call INS and have her whole
family deported. Even if they were here illegally, it would
have been appalling."

"Yes, but maybe she didn't really *mean* it," Luke protested in the faint hope that there might be some way to
reverse the damage.

"She meant it. She said it was a shame foreigners were
allowed to take jobs that should belong to *real* Americans,
which shows that she's not only a nasty old bat but she's
stupid. Consuela is a fifth-generation Californian. I doubt
if Mrs. Bryant can say the same about *her* family."

For one brief moment Luke considered the possibility
of suggesting that if Mrs. Bryant were informed of Consuela's extreme nonimmigrant status, all might be made
right, but, catching the militant look in Cat's eye, he re-
frained from saying it out loud.

She must have sensed that his indignation on Consuela's behalf was less than overwhelming, because she
crossed her arms over her chest and looked at him. "Besides, she called me a tart. And an upstart. Not at the same

time," she added in the interest of accuracy, and then grinned suddenly, a quick flash of real amusement banishing the unfamiliar sternness from her face. "Upstart tart sounds like an all-girl rock band."

"Has she been giving you trouble right along?" Luke asked, anger threading through his voice.

"Nothing I couldn't handle." She said it with such assurance that he had to believe it. "She apparently thought I trapped you into marriage, though I can hardly blame her for that," Cat added fairly. "When you swap fiancées in less than an hour, you've got to expect people to think there's something a little flaky about the whole thing. And she was afraid I was going to step on her toes, which I guess I did when I fired her."

"That's about as thorough as toe stepping gets," Luke agreed, mentally waving goodbye to five years of a flawlessly run house.

"Actually, I don't think she believed that I *could* fire her. She said she'd talk to you about it. Well, actually, what she said was that we'd see what Mr. Quintain had to say about it, which I guess means she thinks you'll override me."

It wasn't quite a question, but Luke caught the edge of doubt in her eyes.

"I guess she's in for a surprise," he said, and was rewarded with a brilliant smile.

"That's what I thought. Who needs her, anyway?"

Luke took that to be a rhetorical question and gave her a smile he hoped would be taken as agreement.

"We'll manage just fine," Cat continued, oblivious to his incipient panic. "I've got everything all arranged for the dinner tonight. We can—"

"Dinner?" Luke groaned. In the first panicked realization that he was now housekeeperless, he'd forgotten about the dinner. "We can cancel," he said, glancing at the clock and then shoving one hand through his hair as he tried to figure out whether or not it was too late for that. "Or maybe we can get reservations somewhere. There's that new place that opened up in LaCañada a couple of months ago."

"Not to worry." Cat grabbed his hand and pulled him out of the entryway. Feeling a little like Alice down the rabbit hole, Luke let himself be led into the kitchen.

"I told you I had everything taken care of," Cat said, smiling happily at the tall, blond-haired man who stood next to the kitchen island. "Jack's going to cook dinner for us tonight."

If Jack's expression was anything to go by, he didn't share her joy over that prospect. He'd just pulled a large chef's knife from the knife block when they walked in, and now he pointed it in Cat's direction, glowering at her over the gleaming blade.

"You owe me. Big time. Big, big, *big* time."

Ignoring his hostile stare, Cat nearly bounced with pleasure as she looked at him. "Isn't it lucky Jack's Place is closed tonight?"

"Lucky?" Jack snarled. He was wearing a pair of faded jeans with a hole in one knee and a black T-shirt that had seen better days. A blue-and-white-checked towel was tucked into the waist of his jeans, dangling down his right leg. "My one night off and *you* want me to cook dinner." He looked at the knife and curled his lip in a sneer. "What do you sharpen your knives with? A nail file? I've seen better edges on a roll of toilet paper."

"Think of it as a busman's holiday," Cat said cheerfully, ignoring his bad temper. "Or a busperson's holiday, if you want to be politically correct."

"I'll just think of it as incredibly bad luck that I hadn't made it out of the house before you called."

Before Cat could say anything, the kitchen door opened and Keith staggered in, overloaded with grocery bags. "Hope I got everything," he puffed breathlessly as he heaved the sacks onto the counter next to the refrigerator. "I knew there was a reason I avoided supermarkets. Man, those places are like a war zone." He started unloading items from the bags as he spoke. "I got the last package of chicken thighs in the meat case, possibly the last package on the planet, from the way some old lady in a purple sweatsuit glared at me when I put it in the cart.

"You said small leeks, but I don't know what's small and what's large in the land of leeks, so I bought some of every size they had." He tossed several bundles of leeks on the counter, looked up, saw Luke and grinned. "Hey, Luke. You're home."

Luke was glad one of them was sure that was where he was. He was fairly sure *his* home was calm and organized and didn't come stocked with hostile chefs wielding large knives.

"I was nearly killed by a five-year-old pushing a shopping cart," Keith continued, reaching into the next bag. "I think she achieved warp nine by the time she hit the end of the aisle. Who knew those things could go that fast? They didn't have fresh crimini mushrooms, so I bought some portobellos. I figured a fungus is a fungus, and they both sounded Italian, so you could probably substitute."

Jack made a noise somewhere between a moan and a snarl and snatched up the bag of mushrooms. "I'm going to start monitoring my calls all the time," he said, dumping them out on the counter. "*All* the time." He glared at Cat. When she was not visibly shriveled, he turned his attention to the mushrooms, glowering down at them. "Portobellos. Might as well have brought back a bunch of bananas," he muttered.

"Just for that, you can do your own shopping next time," Keith told him without heat. "I risked life and limb for this stuff. You want more than one kind of Italian mushroom, go to Italy."

Jack hunched one shoulder and continued to scowl at the mushrooms.

Keith grinned and reached into the next bag. "They didn't have crème fraîche, and when I asked a kid who worked there about it, he said all their cream was fresh and seemed offended that I'd asked, so I bought one of every kind of cream they had. I figured you could fake it."

Jack watched, apparently in too much pain to comment, as Keith set containers of sour cream, half-and-half, nondairy cream, heavy cream and cream cheese on the counter.

"And just in case, I got a couple cans of cream of mushroom soup." Two cans with familiar red-and-white labels joined the dairy display. "And when I was looking for your pink peppercorns—which they didn't have either, by the way—I saw this. I didn't think it was what you had in mind, but I figured better safe than sorry." Keith set a small container on the counter next to the soup.

"Cream of tartar?" Jack said faintly. He gave a sudden demonic smile and nodded. "Yes, that will be very useful. No problem." His voice began to rise. "I can just whip up a gourmet meal out of cream of mushroom soup and nondairy creamer. Maybe I'll bake the portobellos in the sour cream. I can do a side dish of leeks and..." His eyes were a little wild as he looked around. "I know, more leeks. I'll probably start a trend—redundancy in food."

He snatched up a thick leek and shook it. "And for dessert I'll serve the cream cheese, lightly whipped and sprinkled with cream of tartar. And right after that, my reputation in ruins, I'll just go drown myself in the nearest large body of water."

"What about the chicken thighs?" Keith asked, undisturbed by the sight of an apparently deranged man armed with a large vegetable. "That's the last package they had."

Jack's fingers knotted around the leek, and Luke noticed that a little vein had begun to throb in his temple. He sympathized. He was fairly sure his veins would be throbbing, too, if one too many shocks hadn't pretty much congealed his blood.

"This is really very exciting," Cat said, squeezing Luke's arm. "I hardly ever get to see Jack in his obnoxious chef mode. Usually he's much friendlier and not nearly as much fun to watch."

Jack turned a searing look on her.

Her smile didn't waver. Luke wasn't sure if he should commend her courage or deplore her lack of survival instincts.

Jack lifted the battered leek and pointed it at her like a sword. "You." He put an impressive amount of loathing into the word. "Get out of my kitchen," he said between gritted teeth.

"Okay." She grinned at him. "Let me know if I can help."

With images of vegetable-powered mayhem flashing through his mind, Luke pulled her toward the door.

Reminding Keith of a junkyard dog guarding his territory, Jack watched until they disappeared through the door. There was a moment of silence, and then he sighed abruptly and tossed the abused leek onto the counter, watching as it knocked over the cream of tartar container.

"As an attorney, I should probably warn you that the last time someone committed murder with a vegetable in the state of California, they got life in prison. We take our agricultural products seriously in this state."

"It's hard to stay really pissed at someone who's so fucking pleased with herself," Jack said, sounding more resigned than irritated.

Keith laughed. "Well, she's got one of the hottest chefs in L.A. to cook dinner for her. She has reason to be pleased with herself."

"Don't forget the chump part. Hot chef and chump. I know better." Jack shook his head in disbelief at his own foolishness. "As soon as she said she wanted a favor, I should have just hung up the phone and started packing. Oregon is nice this time of year."

"Does Cat ask for a lot of favors?" Keith reached for one of the carrots Jack had already cleaned.

"No. But when she does, you should run as fast and as far as you can. Last year she asked me to do her a favor and I ended up catering a lunch for five hundred grubby children at some charity event."

"Five hundred?" Keith stared at him over the carrot.

"Fifty," Jack admitted grudgingly. "It was hellish."

Keith bit off the end of the carrot and chewed thoughtfully. "So what did you make for fifty kids? I don't see them being really big on braised duck breasts on a bed of arugula with pine nuts and feta."

Jack grimaced. "Who can blame them?" He sighed and began opening cupboard doors until he found the coffee. "I made pigs in a blanket, macaroni and cheese, and hamburgers." He grinned reluctantly when Keith choked on a laugh. "I cooked with a bag over my head, of course, to protect my increasingly tattered reputation and tried not to hear the no-taste little monster who whined about not having any SpaghettiOs.''

"Upstaged by Chef Boyardee." Laughing, Keith fell back against the counter.

Jack measured coffee into the filter and punched the button to start the coffeemaker. "It was a humbling experience, to put it mildly. And now she's got me acting as her personal chef. My humiliation is complete."

"Do you really mind?"

Jack paused in his search for cups and glanced at Keith. "Well, I won't say that I dream of cooking on my night off, but it won't kill me. Or I thought it wouldn't until I got here and found out the late, unlamented housekeeper apparently took most of the food with her when she took off on her broomstick. I'm good, but there's a limit to what I can do with a can opener."

"No one expects you to compete with Chef Boyardee," Keith murmured, and Jack laughed.

"Good thing, too." His smile faded, and he sighed. "Besides, I was really looking forward to seeing the new Schwarzenegger movie."

"Schwarzenegger? You like Schwarzenegger?" So much for stereotypes, Keith thought. He would have guessed Jack was a subtitle kind of guy.

"Guilty pleasure." Jack shrugged sheepishly. "Besides, a friend of mine did some of the stunts in this one. He gets blown through a plate-glass window and plunges fifty stories to his death."

"Cool."

"I thought so. Oh well, guess I'll try to catch it next week." He gave Keith a considering look. "You know anything about cooking?"

"I know how to boil water," Keith admitted cautiously. "And I'm hell on wheels with a frozen dinner."

Jack sighed. "You'll do." He picked up a dish towel and tossed it in Keith's direction. "Take off your jacket and wash your hands. You've just become a sous chef."

"A who?"

"My assistant."

"Oh, good. Now I'll have something to fall back on if I'm ever disbarred."

Jack grinned. "Don't knock it. There are people who would kill for a chance to work with me."

"Yeah? Got their phone numbers?" Keith asked, already moving to the sink to wash his hands.

Luke shut the front door and leaned back against it, listening to the sound of the Southerlands' Jaguar moving up the driveway. He arched one brow at Cat, who was standing in the living-room doorway.

"So."

"So." She bounced lightly on her heels, her mouth curving in an irrepressible smile. "I told you there was nothing to worry about."

Her tone of blatant self-congratulation made Luke's mouth twitch. "So you did. How could I have doubted it?"

"That will teach you to be pessimistic."

"Realistic," he countered. "The housekeeper was gone and an apparently homicidal chef was in the kitchen—not exactly on Martha Stewart's list of dinner party preparations."

"But it all worked out. I think everyone had a good time."

"Everyone had a great time." He shook his head in

amused disbelief. "It would never have occurred to me to put everyone to work in the kitchen."

"I didn't exactly plan it that way." Cat reached up to pull the pins from her hair. It tumbled around her shoulders, a flood of copper against the heavy black silk of her jacket.

Luke's mouth went dry, but he stayed where he was, enjoying the pleasant buzz of anticipation building in his gut.

"If Laura hadn't recognized Keith when he served the hors d'oeuvres, no one would have known anything unusual was going on."

It had been one of those unforgettable moments—Laura Southerland, fingers poised over the hors d'oeuvres tray, mouth dropping open as she realized who her waiter was.

Explanations had followed, and he still wasn't clear on how everyone had ended up in the kitchen. Remembering his last glimpse of Jack, armed with a leek and looking ready to use it, he'd wondered if their dinner party was likely to make the ten-o'clock news as the scene of murder by vegetable. But Jack's bad mood had apparently vanished, and he'd accepted the sudden invasion in good spirits. How introductions had led to everyone being put to work was still a little vague, but since no one had seemed to mind, it probably didn't matter.

"Do you think Laura really will look into Mr. Gutierrez's case?" Cat asked. She slid off her shoes, sighing with pleasure as her feet came into contact with the cool tile.

"If she said she will, she will." Luke wondered if he should worry that the sight of her bare feet was enough to crank his arousal up a notch. "From what I know of her law firm, it's exactly the kind of thing they handle."

"Well, it would be nice if she could get him some kind

of settlement. From what Consuela says, the accident was the other driver's fault. If that's the case, then his insurance company should do something to help her father at least get some kind of training so he can earn a living."

She shrugged off her jacket. The silky little ivory shell she wore under it looked soft and touchable, but not as soft and touchable as her skin.

"The kitchen looks like a tornado struck it," Cat said. "I wouldn't put it past Jack to have used twice as many pots as he really needed just to pay me back for interrupting his evening." She curled her toes against the tile for the sheer pleasure of watching Luke notice the small movement. Knowing he was so focused on her was making it difficult to keep her mind on the conversation, but she wasn't quite ready to end the game yet. "He really should thank me. He was going to see some cheesy action movie, which would probably have rotted out his brain and ruined his hearing."

Luke pushed himself away from the door, and she felt a little flutter of excitement in the pit of her stomach. He'd been watching her, standing there by the door with a sort of lean and hungry look that made her skin feel all hot and sensitive even before he touched her.

"I should probably get started on cleaning up the kitchen," she said, knowing it wasn't going to happen.

Luke shook his head and started toward her.

"The pans will be a lot harder to clean if they're left." Pulse skittering, she edged away.

"We'll buy a new set."

"That's a rich-boy approach to the problem. Just buy a new set instead of cleaning the perfectly good set we already have." She debated the possibility of darting past him into the kitchen and decided she would never make it. Fleeing up the stairs seemed a bit pointless, since it was pretty obvious that was where he wanted her to go. The living room was a possibility.

"I *am* a rich boy. I get to use rich-boy solutions." He shifted the angle of his approach, cutting her off from the living room.

Cat took a cautious step backward, feeling for the bottom step. Ridiculous to feel this wild mix of excitement and just a little fear. There was no question where this was going to end. No question where they both wanted it to end, but that didn't make the game any less exciting.

Luke was almost within arm's reach, blue eyes hot enough to burn. Or melt, which might explain why her knees suddenly felt all quivery.

"You know, a stitch in time saves nine." Her voice was amazingly steady, considering the fact that she was in danger of hyperventilating. "Or a scrubbed pot in the hand is better than an unscrubbed one in the kitchen."

Her fixation on dirty dishes might have been irritating if he hadn't been able see the need in her eyes. He set one hand on the newel post, his arm brushing hers, a few inches of air all that separated his body from hers.

"Go upstairs." There was a definite satisfaction in hearing her breath hitch, in seeing those big green eyes widen and darken even as her chin lifted in automatic response to his order.

"Why should I?"

He leaned closer, spoke with his mouth a scant inch from her ear. "I'll give you two choices. We can spend the next couple of hours scrubbing dirty dishes, or you can go up those stairs like a good little girl and we can spend the rest of the night naked and sweaty."

Cat's knees went from Jell-O to water, and she wrapped her fingers around the lapels of Luke's jacket, purely for support.

"N...naked and sweaty?"

Luke's teeth scraped the delicate skin under her ear. "Completely naked and very sweaty."

"W...well, that's a...very difficult...oh, my...choice." She couldn't quite manage to sound casual, but, considering how talented his tongue was, it was a miracle she could talk at all. "I suppose, as your wife, it's my...duty to..."

He slid both hands up under the thin silk of her shell, flicking open the front hook of her bra with the ease of practice, and cupped her breasts. Cat forgot how to talk, how to breathe. Her head fell back as she arched into his touch, wanting more, needing more.

"Luke, please." She wasn't sure what she was asking. For him to stop or for him to take more. It still scared her just a little, the way he could take her up so quickly, have her shaking and needy and clinging to him with just a touch.

"Yes. Yes." He whispered it against her ear, against the pulse that beat frantically at the base of her throat, against the line of her jaw, against the delicate skin of her eyelids. And all the time, his hands—those wickedly clever hands—were teasing her, stroking her, building the fire higher and higher until it was like being burned from the inside out.

When he lifted his head and looked down at her, she felt drugged with the weight of the hunger he'd built in her. But not so drugged that she couldn't read the glint of very male satisfaction in his eyes. That look of smug pleasure was enough to put a little of the stiffening back into her knees.

"It's a tough choice," she murmured, smoothing one hand over the fine cotton of his shirt, feeling a little smug herself at the rapid thud of his heartbeat under her fingers.

"Choice?" His blank look made it obvious that conversation was the furthest thing from his mind.

"Cleaning the kitchen or getting naked and sweaty in bed with you." She eased back until his hands slid out from under her top, then leaned forward to catch his lower lip between her teeth. "Completely naked and very sweaty, I think you said."

"Uh." It was the best he could manage, with all the blood in his body heading south. He reached for her again, surprised when she sidestepped neatly.

"But, after giving it due consideration, I think duty must come first," she said with bright good cheer. "Do you want to wash or dry?"

Wash or— Luke felt his mouth drop open. She was kidding. Wasn't she? He was about to ask when she suddenly laughed and turned to dart up the stairs. Surprise— and a lack of blood available for brain function—kept him frozen in place, but only for an instant.

He caught her halfway up the stairs, one hand wrapping around her wrist to yank her to a halt as he crowded her up against the railing. "Nice girls don't tease," he whispered against her mouth.

He kissed her until she was weak and clinging to him, then kissed her again for the pleasure of hearing her moan in surrender. Satisfied that she was properly chastised, he bent and slid his arm under her knees, enjoying her little gasp of surprise when he scooped her up.

"Who said I was a nice girl?" she murmured against his throat.

Chapter Ten

Being single in his twenties had been good, Keith thought. Life had been full of possibilities, most of them female and enough of them willing that it would have been ridiculous to think about settling down with just one. School, then getting his practice off the ground, had occupied most of his time, leaving little left over for things like building relationships. He had as much social life as he could manage and plenty of friends of both sexes.

Life was good.

Then his friends started getting married. Suddenly it seemed like he was attending more weddings than parties. That was okay. He was sentimental enough to like the idea of happily-ever-after, even when he knew the odds were that "ever after" only lasted a few years. For the most part he approved of his friends' taste in significant others, and he didn't mind being the single guy at dinner parties. He didn't even mind the occasional attempt at matchmaking, though he'd learned that the words *She's perfect for you* could be the prelude to both a pleasant evening and the date from hell.

Life was interesting.

But he'd noticed lately, now that he was creeping toward forty, that things were changing yet again. His friends had kids or were divorced or both. Some of them were working on second marriages, and Chuck Vincente, that overachiever, was on wife number three. Conversations tended to center around diapers, finding good day care or visitation rights, none of which had any personal relevance to him. He was starting to feel less like the token single guy and more like the odd man out.

Natural progression, he told himself. So he was something of a slow starter. He would get there eventually. Meet a woman he could picture sharing a life with, buy a house in Pasadena or the Foothills or maybe Santa Monica. Have a kid or two and start worrying about retirement accounts, life insurance and finding the best private school, just like everyone else he knew.

Besides, it wasn't like he was the last bachelor around. There was always Luke, and he could pretty much count on Luke to remain single. Even when Luke had planned on marrying Devon, Keith had known things wouldn't really change. Then Devon took off for the land of milk and...well, more milk, and Luke made a fast switch and married Cat. In theory, things still shouldn't have changed. It wasn't a real marriage. Hadn't he drawn up the papers making sure it would end neatly?

Funny, but six weeks after the wedding, Luke's marriage looked pretty real from the outside. And there it was in a nutshell. Outside. Luke's marriage had an outside, and he was there. Not so much on the outside looking in. That implied a degree of wistfulness that made him want to gag. He didn't feel wistful. Much as he liked Cat, he wasn't envious of Luke's marriage to her. No, it wasn't that he wanted what Luke had. It was just that Luke's marriage had made him aware that maybe there were some gaps in his own life, which was pretty ironic, under the circumstances.

Which was why he was driving aimlessly around on a Sunday afternoon, trying to decide what to do with himself. A street sign caught his eye, and he made an abrupt right turn, earning him an annoyed honk from the driver in the station wagon behind him. Keith waved his hand in a gesture that could either be taken as apology or brushoff and began scouting for a parking place.

Fifteen minutes later, he was pushing open a bright blue door with Jack's Place written in discreet gold lettering. He hadn't seen Jack Reynolds since the night of the dinner party, the night he'd discovered that he would rather argue a case before the Supreme Court while wearing nothing but his underwear than cook for a living. But despite Jack's slave-driving tendencies, Keith had liked him, and he was at loose ends and maybe even a little lonely.

The interior of the restaurant was dark after the sharp winter sunshine outside. Keith stopped just inside, waiting for his eyes to adjust. He'd known of the restaurant even before he met Jack, but this was the first time he'd been there. The decor was comfortable, with a vaguely old English feel to it—lots of dark, scarred wood and a big fireplace at one end. The room was empty, which surprised him. Either no one in L.A. was hungry or—

"Sorry, we're closed." Jack's voice came from near the fireplace, and Keith squinted in that direction.

"How about if I come bearing chicken thighs?"

A quick snort of laughter told him that Jack had recognized him. "And here I am, fresh out of cream of tartar."

"That's okay. I don't really have chicken thighs."

Keith made his way between the empty tables. When

he got closer, he saw that Jack was not alone. His companion was a short, slender man wearing a pair of white pants that were so tight they looked as if they'd been painted on and a mesh shirt in a virulent shade of yellow-green that made his skin look as if he were in the last stages of yellow fever. His hair was bleached nearly white, and he wore it short and moussed into bristling spikes that reminded Keith irresistibly of a hedgehog.

"Sorry if I interrupted," Keith said, wondering if maybe Jack's companion was an actor still in costume or just had really bad taste.

"You're not interrupting," Jack told him. "Phil was just leaving."

Now that he was close enough, Keith could see that Jack's mouth was tight with anger, his eyes more gray than blue. Whoever Phil was, it didn't look as if Jack was particularly happy to see him.

"Who is this?" Phil demanded, looking Keith up and down. His mouth curved in a tight little sneer. "Is this your new bitch?"

Keith had read about someone's jaw dropping open but had never actually experienced that particular reaction himself. Until now. He was fairly sure his eyes bulged, too.

"Oh, for God's sake, Phil." Jack sounded more weary than angry. "You give a bad name to the word *fag*."

"Well, is he?" Phil shot an angry glance at Jack and then looked at Keith again, his dark eyes bright with malice. "I suppose you think things will be different with you?"

"I...uh..."

"Well, they won't be. Jacky isn't going to take you home to meet mom and dad, no matter how *GQ* you look."

"Phil, go away." Jack straightened away from the table he'd been leaning against. "You're embarrassing yourself. Worse, you're making me think being straight might not be such a bad thing."

"Ha." Phil tossed his head, a gesture rendered less than effective by his short, spiky hair. "Don't blame me for your hang-ups. Some of us aren't ashamed to embrace our sexuality."

"Go away, Phil," Jack said tiredly. "Or I'm going to have my attorney—" a jerk of his head to indicate Keith "—sue you for—" He looked at Keith for possibilities.

"Harassment and trespassing, just for starters," Keith said promptly. "And if this sort of behavior is habitual, my client would be within his rights to request a restraining order to be filed against you."

"Fine." Phil spat the word out. "Just…" He caught Keith's raised eyebrow and apparently thought better of whatever he'd planned to say. Spinning on his heel, he stalked out, not an easy thing to do in pants that tight, Keith noted.

The door thudded shut behind him, and in the sudden silence Keith could hear the muted clank of dishes and the sound of voices coming from behind the swinging door beside the fireplace. Apparently they weren't completely alone.

"Business always this light on Sunday?" he asked, looking around the empty restaurant.

"We're only open for lunch on Sundays. We closed an hour ago. We were just finishing cleanup when Phil showed up." Jack ran his fingers through his dark blond hair, rumpling it into careless waves. "If I'd known he was going to drop in, I'd have locked and barred the door." He caught Keith's eye and hunched one shoulder in a half shrug. "Sorry about the scene. Phil is sort of in-your-face about being gay."

Keith's eyes widened in shock. "He's gay?"

Jack stared at him for a moment and then started to laugh helplessly. "Yeah, I guess it is pretty subtle, isn't it?" His laughter faded. "You know, the most embarrassing thing is that I have to admit we used to be involved."

"Don't feel bad. When I was in college, I dated a girl whose main ambition in life was to moon Clint Eastwood."

Jack snorted, choked and laughed again. "And you gave her up?"

"Well, it occurred to me that, if I kept dating her and, through some freak circumstance, she actually stumbled over Dirty Harry himself, I might find myself an accessory to the mooning, and I really didn't want to hear the words 'Go ahead, kid, make my day' up close and personal."

Laughter eased Jack's embarrassment, and he relaxed back onto the support of the table, stretching his legs out in front of him. The left knee of his jeans was starting to wear through, he noticed with a twinge of real regret. These were his favorite jeans, nicely broken in and butter soft.

Keith moved to lean against the table opposite, mirroring his pose. Jack tilted his head, looked at him.

"Did you come by for lunch? I could probably be persuaded to rustle up something."

"Well, if you felt compelled to cook something, I could eat, but I actually just happened to find myself in the neighborhood and decided to drop in."

"Just in time for the floor show," Jack said, sighing.

"Well, it was educational, in a way. I mean, I found out that I look very *GQ and* that I shouldn't expect to meet your parents anytime soon.'' Keith frowned, considering. "I think I should be flattered on the one and offended on the other."

"When you consider the way Phil dresses, I wouldn't be so sure that saying you look like something out of *GQ* is a compliment," Jack pointed out dryly. "And, trust me, if I wanted to impress my parents, you'd be tops on the list. You're not only straight but you're an actual, honest-to-God lawyer. They'd probably adopt you on the spot."

He heard the unexpected bitter note in his own voice and flushed. God, Phil's visit must have gotten to him more than he'd realized. He straightened away from the table, waving one hand to dismiss his words.

"Never mind. Old news."

"I take it your family didn't encourage you to embrace your sexuality?" Keith asked conversationally.

"The only things they wanted me to embrace were a law degree and pretty much anything in a skirt." He narrowed his eyes suddenly. "Come to think of it, Phil has this little red plaid number...."

Keith's sharp bark of laughter made Jack grin. He didn't think he'd ever met a straight guy who was so completely at ease with the fact that he was gay. Even the ones who had no problem with it preferred not to mention it.

"It's not really a problem. Frankly, they're an uptight bunch. Besides, when I told them I was moving to L.A., they were so thrilled with the idea of having a whole continent between them and any potential embarrassment that they gave me the money to start this place. I thought about telling them to stuff it, but practicality won out over pride."

"From what I've heard of the place, I think it's safe to say that Los Angeles restaurant goers are grateful."

"Flattery will get you a meal," Jack said, smiling, feeling the last of the tension from Phil's unexpected visit drain away.

"Sounds good." Keith pushed himself away from the table, starting to follow him into the kitchen. "One thing I've got to tell you, though. No matter what you feed me, I'm not going to be your bitch."

The year before Cat's mother met Larry and moved in with him, she and Cat had spent several months living with "Aunt" Maureen, an elderly woman who lived in a rambling old house in San Francisco who, as far as Cat knew, was not related to her by any blood ties. Naomi had actually met her in the supermarket and helped her carry her groceries to the car, and next thing Cat knew, she and Naomi were living in the cramped servants' quarters at the back of the older woman's house.

If Maureen was a little confused by her sudden acquisition of relatives, she didn't seem to have any actual objections to the new arrangement. Cat liked the fog that rolled in from the bay and the way the houses elbowed each other for room on the narrow lots, yet somehow managed to look comfortable in their close quarters. She liked the big old house with its winding staircases and multipaned windows, and didn't mind that Maureen had a tendency to forget her name or sometimes left out food for a cat named Myrtle who had been dead for several years.

They'd lived there for two months when an old friend invited Naomi to spend some time at a nudist colony. *Clothing optional, really,* Naomi had explained to Cat. *It's a chance to truly experience one's physical self without the societally imposed constrictions of clothing, to really connect with nature in a way primitive man once took for granted.*

Cat thought of pointing out that primitive man had also eaten grubs and small rodents and had generally lived a short, brutal life, but she knew that her mother wasn't really interested in such a heavy dose of reality. She murmured something she hoped would sound supportive and tried to find a tactful way to tell Naomi that she had no intention of spending time around a bunch of naked strangers, clothing optional or not. But she didn't have to worry. Naomi had looked up from the small bag she was packing, her green eyes a little worried.

I think you should stay here with Aunt Maureen, sweetheart. Not because there's anything at all wrong *or improper about the whole thing but I just think you're a little young to be making this sort of decision, and I don't want you to feel pressured into something you may not be ready for. Do you understand what I'm saying?*

Cat understood that she wasn't going to have to make up an excuse to keep her clothes on, and that was all she cared about. She nodded, tried to look as if she were looking forward to the day when she was old enough to decide to run around naked with a bunch of strangers and waved Naomi off without regret. She'd stayed with Maureen, put out food for the deceased Myrtle and tried not to think of her mother tiptoeing naked through the tulips.

When Naomi returned three weeks later, she spoke at length of how wonderful it had been to experience the world as nature had intended, without the artificial shield of clothing to interfere with true communication with the natural world and other people. Cat had listened, nodded and put it all in the mental file marked ''Naomi's experiments.'' She hadn't really thought much about it since.

But she was thinking about it now.

She tugged nervously at the knotted belt that held her coat closed. It was ridiculous to feel so…naked. She was modestly covered from throat to midcalf. She tugged at a lapel and then forced herself to lower her hand to her side. If she would just stop twitching, no one would look twice at her. She was just one of several people in the elevator. Nothing to notice. Nothing out of the ordinary.

Was this elevator always this slow? As she watched the row of numbers over the door, it seemed to take forever for them to change. She'd only been to Luke's office once before, but she didn't remember it taking this long to get to the twentieth floor. What if there was something wrong, some malfunction that caused the elevator to move slower and slower and then finally stop—between floors, of course? Cat's breath caught on a panicked little hitch. Just her, the UPS driver with his hand truck stacked with boxes, an older woman with steel-gray hair and a pinched mouth, and a young man in an expensive suit who had *budding executive* practically tattooed on his forehead. There they would be, the four of them, trapped, and, for reasons that weren't immediately obvious, she would have to take off her coat. How would she explain what she was—or, actually, what she *wasn't*—wearing under it?

The ping of the bell startled her, and her eyes jerked back to the display. Tenth floor. Only halfway there. The UPS driver exited, and the doors slid shut. Cat practiced yoga breathing and tried to remember why this had seemed like such a good idea. So it was Luke's birthday. Why couldn't she just have baked him a cake?

The elevator stopped again on the twelfth floor, and the other two occupants got out, leaving Cat alone. She sighed as the doors slid shut. Eight more floors. There was still time to change her mind.

She shifted slightly until she could see her reflection in

one of the narrow mirrors that flanked the doors. Other than a slight trace of panic around the eyes, she looked normal. No one looking at her would know she'd lost her mind. At least when they hauled her off to the funny farm or arrested her for indecent exposure, she would be looking her best.

This time, when she smoothed her hand over the coat, she wasn't testing its coverage. She was simply enjoying the feel of it. She'd never owned anything so blatantly luxurious in her life. The coat had cost more than the rest of her wardrobe combined. Two days later, she was still suffering from sticker shock, but she had to admit that she'd gotten her money's worth. The classic duster style suited her, made her height a thing of elegance. The sand-washed silk was so soft and rich, it felt like woven sin, and the warm hunter-green color made her eyes look huge and dark and full of mysteries.

Cat had never thought of a coat as a sensual garment until she slid her arms into the sleeves for the first time and felt the weight of it fall around her. She'd been half-way to talking herself out of her crazy idea for surprising Luke until she looked in the fitting room mirror and saw a stranger looking back—a tall, sophisticated woman, a confident woman, the sort of woman who could look the world dead in the eye and dare it to notice she was practically naked.

So she bought the coat, but the stranger had apparently been left behind at Nordstrom's, because the woman who was here right now was giving serious thought to hitting the stop button and then making her escape through the emergency hatch on top of the elevator.

A cheerful little ping announced her arrival on the twentieth floor. Her heart beating somewhere in her throat, Cat stepped off the elevator.

Grateful for well-oiled hinges and secretaries with a weakness for romance, Cat eased open Luke's office door. He was sitting at his desk, eyes on the stack of documents in front of him. His charcoal-gray suit jacket was tossed over the arm of the sofa, his white shirtsleeves rolled up to bare his forearms. His hair was tousled, as if he'd run his fingers through it, one heavy dark wave falling onto his forehead. He was the most impossibly beautiful man she'd ever seen, and he was hers.

For a few more months, anyway.

Cat rubbed her thumb over the inside of her wedding ring and tried not to wonder if she would still be wearing it a year from now. One day at a time, she reminded herself. There was no sense in thinking too far ahead, worrying about the future. That was one bit of Naomi's philosophy that she believed absolutely. If you spent too much time worrying about the future, you were likely to miss out on the present, and whatever the future might bring, her present was pretty good.

She pushed the door shut with a deliberate click, leaning back against the solid wood panel, posing just a little as Luke looked up. His irritated expression shifted with gratifying speed when he saw her.

"Cat."

Hard to worry about the future when he smiled at her like that. Hard to believe there was anything *to* worry about.

"I hope I'm not interrupting anything wildly important." She couldn't quite stop herself from twitching the belt a little tighter. "I wanted to wish you a happy birthday."

"You wished me a happy birthday this morning," Luke said, resisting the urge to glance at the clock on his desk. He had a meeting in half an hour, and he still had some paperwork to go over before Chandler got here.

"That didn't really seem like enough." Cat moved away from the door and wandered closer to the desk. "You only get one thirty-sixth birthday, after all. Do you have a few minutes?"

"Not really." Luke glanced at the stack of papers waiting to be read. "I've got a meeting in half an hour, and I still need to go over some things before then." There was a faint edge of impatience to his voice, and Cat's lower lip thrust out in a hint of a pout.

"That's too bad, because I really wanted to get your opinion on something."

He raised his brows in inquiry and tried not to notice how the storm-gray light spilling in through the windows made her hair look like pure copper.

"I wanted to know what you thought of my shoes," Cat said, circling the desk.

Shoes? She'd driven to his office and was interrupting him in the middle of a work day to show him a pair of shoes?

Luke opened his mouth to say something caustic, then forgot to close it when she put her foot up on the edge of his desk. The shoe in question was black, open-toed and backless, with a heel so tall and thin it probably qualified as a lethal weapon. He'd once dated a woman who'd referred to a similar pair of shoes as her fuck-me pumps. He hadn't needed to ask why.

But it wasn't the shoe—which screamed sex—that dried up all the spit in his mouth. When she put her foot on the desk, Cat's coat fell back—way, way back—baring about a mile of slender leg clad in a sheer black stocking.

And nothing else. Not so much as a whisper of a hemline. The shoe—and his meeting—was forgotten as his entire being focused on what she might be wearing under that coat. Because she couldn't possibly be— Sure, it was something you read about someone doing or saw in the movies, but she couldn't really be... But if she was...

"What do you think?" Cat asked.

What did he think? He thought getting hard that fast might be dangerous. He thought office sex had never been one of his fantasies and maybe he'd been missing out on something. He thought this was starting to look like the best birthday of his life.

"What are you wearing under that?" His voice rasped in his throat.

"Under this?" Cat let her foot drop to the floor and the coat swung shut, covering her modestly from throat to midcalf. But it was too late. He already knew the modesty was a sham, and his imagination was working overtime, presenting him with possibilities. She fingered the lapel, eyes wide and not quite innocent. "Why would you ask that?"

Her hand slid down the lapel, tracing the edge of the coat until she reached the belt. There were no buttons on the coat, Luke realized. Which meant that if the belt was loosened...

Without taking his eyes from her, he hit the intercom button.

"Sharon, I don't want to be disturbed until further notice."

"Yes, Mr. Quintain. What about your appointment with Mr. Chandler at two-thirty?"

"Call him and tell him something came up."

Cat's eyes lit with wicked laughter as she looked at his lap. Luke gave her a threatening look and reached up to pull his tie loose. "What else do I have scheduled?" he asked.

"Nothing until Ms. Lubinski at four."

Luke ran his eyes over his wife. The coat covered everything interesting but when he thought about what might be under it…or what he suspected *wasn't* under it…

"Give Mr. Chandler the file on the Harmony Gardens project, and ask him to go over it and then take the meeting with Ms. Lubinski. See if he can schedule lunch tomorrow to discuss it." He ran his eyes over Cat again and let arousal nudge up a few notches to just short of a full boil. "You can go home early, Sharon. I'm going to be busy for the rest of the afternoon."

He barely waited for his secretary's acknowledgment before breaking off the connection.

"The rest of the afternoon?" Cat asked, raising her brows. "Are you sure you can afford the time? I mean, you're such a busy man and all. I wouldn't want to interrupt your work."

Luke didn't bother to answer. He got up and went to the door, then snapped the lock shut with a quiet click. He leaned back against the door, crossed his arms over his chest and looked at her.

"Take it off."

"Take what off?" It was thin as rotten ice, foolish to think he would buy it for a moment, but now that she was here and he was here and they were both here, her stomach was jittery with nerves and she was almost sure this was a really bad idea.

"Take the coat off, Cat." The quiet order melted her knees and several important synapses in her brain.

"Your secretary probably heard you lock the door," she pointed out. "She's going to think we're…um… engaged in unbusinesslike activities."

"I plan on being extremely unbusinesslike for the rest of the afternoon." His tone made it a promise, and Cat's heart was suddenly beating so hard, she felt breathless, which seemed a medical contradiction, since if her heart was pumping that much faster, shouldn't she be getting *more* oxygen? Luke pushed himself away from the door, and scientific inquiry took a back seat to panicked arousal.

"Shouldn't we close the curtains?" She glanced over her shoulder at the bank of windows that looked west over the Los Angeles basin.

"The only way anyone can see in is if they're in a helicopter, and I promise to throw myself in front of you at the first sound of rotors." His voice was dark as honey, laced with amusement and...affection?

Cat drew a deep breath and loosened the belt, hesitating another instant before slowly drawing the coat open and letting it slip from her shoulders to fall in a dark pool at her feet.

Luke felt hunger spike through him, sharp as a lance, almost painful in its intensity. The images that had been dancing in his head hadn't even come close to the reality.

A black silk teddy skimmed over milk-white skin, the lacy edge just barely covering her nipples, the high-cut style making the most of those endless legs. Sheer black thigh-high stockings ended a few inches below the teddy, and that glimpse of pale skin on her upper thigh was somehow more erotic than if she'd been stark naked.

"I just wanted to wish you a happy birthday," Cat said, and he dragged his gaze back up to her face. "But if it's too much of an interruption, I could just get you a pair of cuff links or something."

"I don't wear cuff links." Luke tugged his shirt open with an impatience that cost him a button. It pinged as it hit the desk, spinning across the polished surface. "And I don't mind the interruption." The shirt drifted to the floor, and his fingers went to work on his belt buckle. "In fact, don't ever hesitate to interrupt me at work." His zipper rasped down. "Consider this a permanent invitation to interrupt me any time at all."

Cat's giggle ended on a breathless little sound of surprise as Luke's hands closed over her hips, sliding under the thin silk to cup her bottom. He tugged her closer, and she lifted her hands to his shoulders, not sure if it was the high heels or the way he was looking at her that was making her feel unsteady.

"I usually just tear the paper off my birthday presents." Luke's mouth brushed over hers, barely touching before moving away, tasting the curve of one cheekbone, the delicate skin at the corner of her eye, the line of her jaw. "But I think I'm going to unwrap you very, very, very slowly."

It could have been a threat or a promise, and either way, Cat wasn't sure she would survive. But it was bound to be a hell of a ride.

"You're going to kill me." The muffled complaint came from somewhere around her collarbone.

It took an amazing amount of effort to lift her hand and put it on Luke's head, sinking her fingers into the silky darkness of his hair.

"Maybe I *should* have gotten you those cuff links."

Using his last ounce of strength, Luke managed to lift his head enough to look into Cat's face. Her smile was more replete than apologetic. She looked rumpled and tousled and very pleased with herself. Despite the activities of the last half hour—activities that he was nearly sure had caused permanent damage to several important motor functions—Luke felt a twinge of interest. Groaning, he dropped his head back down on her shoulder and sent a stern mental reminder to certain body parts that he wasn't as young as he used to be.

Cat shifted, curling toward him, and his arm tightened around her waist, his knee sliding higher across her hips as he drew her a tiny bit closer. They were sprawled on the floor next to the sofa. He'd actually been aiming for the sofa when he steered them in this direction, but it proved to be too narrow, so they'd ended up on the floor, along with two cushions and a throw pillow. The narrow black lacquer coffee table lay on its side somewhere above their heads, and Luke had a vague memory of shoving it out of the way, hearing it tip, followed by the secondary thud as the lapis-colored art glass vase that had been on the table tumbled to the floor.

His shirt was on the floor near the desk, along with one of Cat's shoes. The other shoe had fallen behind the sofa. His pants and briefs were lying under his desk chair. One sock was on the desk, and the other hung drunkenly across the front of his flat-screen monitor.

The whereabouts of Cat's clothing was easier to pinpoint, since she'd been wearing so little. One long black stocking dangled from the shade of the floor lamp that sat near the sofa. He wasn't sure about the other one but had vague memories of tossing it over his shoulder. The black silk teddy was lying under one of the sofa cushions. It hadn't survived the encounter intact. He could see the end of one strap trailing across the floor, and he distinctly remembered hearing something tear while he was trying to get Cat out of it. So much for unwrapping presents slowly, he thought.

"That garment is an invention of the devil, you know."

His conversational tone made Cat grin.

"Well, if this was a test to see if you could avoid temptation, I think you failed."

"I don't remember you complaining."

"No complaints," she agreed in a dreamy voice.

She kept her eyes closed, the better to enjoy the warm weight of Luke's body draped half over hers, the pleasant lethargy that filled her. The carpet was a little scratchy against her back, and she could feel bruises coming up on her hips where he'd gripped her, held her as he filled her. Her throat was dry, probably a result of all the gasping and panting she'd done. She would have given the entire balance in that ridiculous checking account for a glass of cool water, but she couldn't seem to gather up the energy to do anything about it. Crawling to the minibar in the corner seemed like too much effort, and walking was out of the question. The way her legs felt, she wasn't sure she would ever walk again. It didn't seem important at the moment.

"How did you get past Sharon?" Luke asked suddenly. "She doesn't generally let people just wander into my office."

"I told her I wanted to surprise you. Apparently she has a romantic streak."

Luke pictured his secretary, who was short, stocky and uncompromisingly gray in hair color, clothing and personality, and tried to imagine her with a romantic streak. The image wouldn't come clear, and he lifted his head and gave Cat a suspicious look.

"You didn't fire her, did you?"

"Of course not." She frowned at him. "Just because I fired the housekeeper, it doesn't mean that I go around firing people right and left. I don't think I *could* fire your secretary."

"You could try," he muttered, letting his head drop back down. It was just too much of an effort to hold it up.

"Besides, things worked out okay after I fired Mrs.

Bryant, didn't they? I think Merry is working out very well."

Luke confined himself to a noncommittal grunt. His replacement housekeeper was a tall, lanky young woman who wore head-to-toe black, including her lipstick and eye shadow. The only relief from her monochromatic fashion statement was the glint of gold and silver from assorted piercings—eyebrow, nose, ears and lower lip were all visible. He didn't want to think about what might be concealed under the layers of unrelieved black. He had to admit—grudgingly—that the house hadn't fallen apart. Merry—a singularly inappropriate name—did her job with a quiet efficiency that was at odds with her peculiar appearance.

"I vote we stay here for another year or two," Luke said without lifting his head from where it was pillowed against her shoulder. "I think I can snag my cell phone from here. We can order pizza when we get hungry."

"I think I'd get pretty tired of pizza after a couple of years." Cat stroked her fingers through his hair.

"We'll switch off with Chinese," he suggested, proving that his reputation as a problem solver was not unfounded.

"Sounds good, but what do we tell your grandfather?"

"Tell him to get his own pizza delivery." Luke's mutter was taking on a thick, sleepy edge. Cat tightened her fingers in his hair, tugging gently.

"We're going to his house for dinner tonight, remember?"

"Tonight?" Luke's voice descended perilously close to a whine. "Do I have to?"

"Yes," Cat said firmly. "It's your birthday, and your grandfather wants to celebrate it with you."

"I could call and tell him something came up." His

hand slid upward to cup her breast. "And then I could make sure something did come up."

Cat shivered as his thumb brushed across her nipple, teasing already sensitized flesh to life. But she was made of sterner stuff than that.

"No matter what comes up or how often it comes up, we have to go to your grandfather's house for dinner. It would be rude to cancel at the last minute."

"He wouldn't care."

"Yes, he would." She tugged at his hair until he lifted his head and looked at her. "The two of you are behaving like a couple of four-year-olds. It's obvious you love each other, but as soon as you get in a room together, you both start bristling and posturing like a pair of gorillas, beating your chests and grunting. Maybe it's an excess of testosterone."

"He started it," Luke muttered, and Cat laughed out loud.

"Oooh, that's very mature. Want to throw in a nanny-nanny-boo-boo?"

He glared at her. It was a look that had been known to make junior executives and belligerent building managers quake in their boots. Cat was not visibly impressed, and he had to consider the possibility that the glare was less effective when he was lying on his office floor, stark naked, and smelling of sweat and sex. Which reminded him that he really had better things to do than discuss his relationship with his grandfather.

"Fine. We'll go to dinner. But I'm going to need fortification to get through the evening."

Cat laughed in startled pleasure as he rolled onto his back, pulling her with him so that she lay sprawled across his body. His obviously interested body, she realized, feeling the heat of his erection against her belly.

"Fortification, huh?" Her voice was husky with the quick rush of arousal. "Is that what they're calling it these days?"

Cat had been to some unique birthday parties in her time. Naomi's twenty-fifth birthday, for example, had included a specialist in past life regression, a palm reader and a young man who claimed to be a werewolf. Cat had been mildly disappointed that it was only a quarter moon, since a werewolf on the hoof, as it were, sounded rather exciting.

A couple of times, when they'd been settled in one place for long enough for her to attend a regular school and make friends, she'd had a chance to attend a more traditional celebration. After werewolves, tofu and turbans, a clown, sticky sweet cake and paper hats seemed rather tame, but the novelty of it had been entertaining.

She hadn't expected palm readers or clowns at Luke's birthday party, and Nick Quintain just didn't seem like a party-hat kind of guy. She'd been prepared for dinner to be quiet, dignified even. No dancing on the table, no balancing spoons on her nose, no wearing a lampshade as a hat—she could do dignified.

But there was dignified and then there was…this thing. This three-people-sitting-at-a-table-big-enough-for-twenty thing. This not-talking thing or, even worse, this talking-about-the-weather thing. Cat had been to funerals where the conversation was more lively.

She looked across the table at Luke, but he was studying his plate as if the answer to world peace could be found lurking in his bowl of vichyssoise. At the head of the table, Nick was glaring at his wine as if its presence was a threat to national security. Once past the social niceties, they'd hardly spoken to each other.

Cat barely restrained the urge to cluck her tongue in exasperation. Honestly, the two of them were like a pair of three-year-olds, although that was really unfair to three-year-olds since they probably would have just slugged each other and then gotten on with life. If she could just get them to talk to each other...

"Luke just bought an apartment building in Pasadena," she said, breaking a silence that threatened to grow to epic proportions. If anything could get the two of them talking, it should be real estate.

Nick switched his glare from the wine to his grandson. "That place on Green? I thought we agreed it was a money pit."

"You agreed," Luke said, leaning back in his chair and meeting his grandfather's gaze. "I think it's a pretty good investment."

Nick snorted. "Only if you've got money to burn. Most of those tenants have been there since Roosevelt was in office and the rent hasn't gone up in forty years. Worse, that one old bat has a nephew who's a reporter, thinks he's Woodward and Bernstein all rolled into one. If you'd done your research, you'd know that. You try to raise the rent or convert to condos and he's going to turn you into Simon Legree in the press. If you're smart, you'll dump the place as fast as you can, take the loss and count it as a lesson learned."

"The lesson being that I should listen to you?" Luke's arched brow added sarcastic emphasis to the question.

"Well, you certainly could do worse," Nick snapped.

Cat sighed. Apparently, real estate hadn't been such a good topic after all. "Actually, I thought it was a really good idea for Luke to buy the building," she jumped in before Luke could say anything. "Most of the tenants have been there practically forever. We met with them a couple of days ago and they were so grateful when Luke told them that he wasn't going to raise the rents or throw them out so he could turn the place into condos.''

"He's not...." Nick's eyes shot from Cat to Luke and back again. "Just what is he going to do? Let the place sit while he loses money?"

Cat let the heavy sarcasm wash past her and answered the question as simply as possible. "Yes."

She took a sip of vichyssoise. It really was delicious. Maybe she could talk Luis into giving her the recipe.

"You're going to..." Nick was having a hard time getting the words out. "You bought the place knowing you'd..."

"Lose money," Luke supplied the words his grandfather couldn't quite manage. "That's right. Cat met Mrs. Gilberstein while they were both doing volunteer work at Descanso Gardens and when Mrs. Gilberstein told her how worried she was about what would happen to the tenants when the building was sold, Cat thought it would be a nice idea if I bought it. I've already signed an agreement with the tenants that they can live there as long as they like and, when they move—or die—I'll start converting individual apartments into condos and selling them."

"That could take years," Nick said, appalled.

"Probably."

"Why on earth would you do something that stupid?" Nick asked, sounding genuinely curious.

"It's not stupid," Cat said. "It's kind and generous and it's not like Luke can't afford the loss. He's got more than enough money."

"More than enough money?" Nick stared at her in disbelief. "What does that have to do with anything? I know the value of supporting charities, give a damned tidy sum to them every year, but there's a difference between that and just…just…''

"Losing money," Luke supplied helpfully.

"Losing money," Nick snapped. "If you want to do a good deed, why not find those people another place to live, pay their moving expenses?"

"But that wouldn't make up for them losing their homes," Cat said.

"Is this more of that karmic nonsense you were spouting at the engagement party? People turning into cockroaches if they don't do enough good deeds?"

Nick turned the full weight of his glare on her. Cat was not visibly impressed. She took a last spoonful of her soup before pushing the bowl back a little. "More or less. It's all a matter of balancing the wheel. If you prefer the Judeo-Christian version, I suppose you could interpret it as the whole doing-unto-others thing."

"Funny, how doing unto others usually seems to translate into the rich giving something to the poor," Nick said with heavy sarcasm.

"It makes sense when you think about it. The rich are the ones with something to give, after all. Besides, it's not as if Luke isn't getting something out of this deal. Mrs. McKenna made him a plate of her special Swedish dream cookies and Mrs. Gilberstein is going to crochet him an afghan."

"And Mr. Silberman has promised us pick of the litter when his cat has kittens," Luke murmured helpfully.

"I wouldn't count on that," Cat warned him. "According to Mrs. Gilberstein, Fluffy is not only a tomcat but Mr. Silberman's wife had him fixed two years ago."

Since Nick had turned a rather alarming shade of purple, Cat thought it was just as well that Luis entered the dining room then to take away the soup plates and bring in the main course.

By the time dessert was served, Cat wasn't sure who she most wanted to smack. After the real-estate debacle, she'd chosen her topics more carefully, but there apparently wasn't anything that Luke and his grandfather didn't disagree on. A mention of the possibility of bringing a pro football team to Los Angeles sparked an argument over whether or not tax dollars should be used to pay for building a new stadium. That degenerated into a testy exchange about the decline of modern sports. Since she knew for a fact that Luke's interest in football was virtually nil, he had to be arguing purely for the sake of argument. If she could have reached him, she would have kicked him under the table.

From there, the conversation—and she used the term lightly—shifted to politics and, as she watched them square off over the proper use of state taxes, she decided that enough was enough. They both looked up as she pushed back her chair.

"I'm going to go see if I can talk Luis out of some of his recipes. When you two are done squabbling, I'll be in the kitchen."

Without waiting for a response, Cat picked up her dessert and left the dining room, leaving the two men staring after her.

Nick recovered first. "Squabbling?"

"That's what she said." Luke pushed his plate away and reached for his coffee. "According to Cat, we act like four-year-olds, though she also suggested gorillas," he added thoughtfully. "Either way, she seems to think we're ridiculous."

"Ridiculous?" Nick's chest swelled with indignation.

''Cat pretty much calls them as she sees them,'' Luke said.

Nick shoved his plate away and, for an instant, Luke was reminded irresistibly of the four-year-old Cat had called him—called them both. He bit back a smile, knowing his grandfather wouldn't appreciate the comparison. The sound of Cat's laughter drifted through the door and Nick's scowl deepened.

''She's not easily intimidated.'' There was grudging approval in the comment.

''I haven't seen anything intimidate her yet,'' Luke said. ''I think she'd tackle hell with a hand basket if the mood struck her.''

''Not much like her stepsister.'' Nick slanted him a look that held a hint of challenge, but Luke wasn't in the mood to pick up the bait.

''Not a thing like her,'' he agreed. And he was damned glad of that.

Chapter Eleven

"This is a bad idea." Luis glanced at his employer, who was sitting in the passenger seat of the big Rolls. "Señor Luke won't like it if you harass his wife."

"Who said anything about harassing her?" Nick snapped, shooting him an irritated look. "I just want to get to know the girl. No crime in that, is there? She's married to my only grandson. I don't think it's unreasonable that I'd want to get to know her."

Luis snorted. "Get to know her? You want to pry and to interfere. *That's* what you want to do. A smart man would have learned his lesson already. If you want to know what I think—"

"I don't," Nick snapped.

"—I think you should leave well enough alone. Señor Luke did a good thing when he married Señorita Cat. If you keep your nose out of their business, maybe they can work things out. Maybe you would even get those great-grandchildren you want so much."

"I didn't ask for your opinion, and I am *not* interfering. Miss Cat." It was Nick's turn to snort. "Sounds like a character in a children's book. *Catherine*—'' he put a heavy emphasis on the name ''—is part of the family. For now, anyway,'' he added under his breath.

The rest of the drive was made in silence, unless you counted the occasional muttered comment from the driver's seat, comments Nick ignored. He might be a stubborn old man, but he didn't have to dignify the accusation by responding. He sat staring straight ahead until Luis halted the Rolls in front of a rambling house that looked as if it had seen better decades. The paint was faded and worn, the porch roof sagged like an old lady's stockings, and the front yard was... Well, actually, there wasn't really a front yard, just packed dirt and a few rather tattered-looking shrubs.

There were two partially dismantled cars parked to one side, and as Nick got out of the car, Larry Kowalski appeared from behind one of them. He was wearing a pair of what looked like suit trousers and a faded black T-shirt. On his right foot he wore a battered running shoe and on his left a brown dress loafer. He looked as if he'd been halfway through changing clothes when he got distracted and wandered outside. Grease streaked one cheek, the front of the T-shirt and the knee of his slacks.

''Mr. Kowalski, I hope you don't mind me dropping in like this.'' Nick held out his hand.

''Not at all.'' Larry gave him a vague smile as they shook hands. ''Haven't we met?''

''At your stepdaughter's wedding. I'm Luke's grandfather.''

''Oh, yes.'' There was nothing in Larry's slightly protuberant brown eyes to suggest that he had any recollection of meeting Nick, but it didn't seem to bother him. ''Do you know anything about internal combustion engines?''

"Not really."

"Too bad." Larry looked disappointed. "I had an idea for improving fuel efficiency, but I'm afraid I don't really know enough about them to be sure it will work."

Apparently losing interest, he half turned as if to wander back to the cars. Nick gaped at him for a moment. Luke had mentioned that the man was absentminded, but he hadn't said that he was actually mentally deficient.

"I was hoping to see your stepdaughter, Mr. Kowalski. Luke's housekeeper said she was here."

Larry turned his head, looking at him blankly for a moment. "Cat? Why would you want to see Cat?"

"She married my grandson," Nick reminded him.

"Oh, yes, that's right. You said that already, didn't you?" Larry gave him a friendly smile. "She's probably around back, in the gardens. She spends a good part of the day there, watering and weeding and such. You can go around the side." He gestured to a dirt path. "I'm sure she'll be glad to see you."

Nick wasn't nearly as sure, but he didn't see any reason to say so. He turned away, then stopped, struck by inspiration. Turning back to his host, he smiled in a way that would have struck terror into the hearts of anyone who knew him well.

"You know, if you have questions about engines, I'm sure my chauffeur would be happy to talk to you."

"Really?" Larry looked as if he'd just been offered a treat.

"Oh, yes." Nick glanced at the Rolls, where he knew Luis was settled down with the newest Grisham book, and his smile widened to sharklike proportions. "Luis loves to talk about engines. Just be sure to tell him I suggested he talk to you."

The thought of Luis dealing with the terminally absentminded professor put a bit of a spring in Nick's step as he walked around the side of the house, walking stick tapping the ground more for effect than actual support. Maybe next time Luis would think twice about lecturing him.

The rear of the house was as tidy as the front was disorganized and untended. Garden beds were arranged in neat rows, each filled with a dizzying assortment of plants. When he was a boy, his grandparents had gardened on a ranchette in the San Fernando Valley but this bore no resemblance to the long, skinny rows of vegetables he remembered. This looked more like a tropical jungle.

He was debating the wisdom of plunging into that jungle in search of his grandson's wife when she appeared from between two of the beds. She was wearing a pair of jeans, old and faded to white at the knees and along the side seams. A worn chambray shirt hung open over a hot-pink T-shirt that just managed to avoid clashing with her hair, which was bundled up in an untidy knot on top of her head. A dented galvanized bucket dangled from one hand, and she had a plastic tray full of plants balanced in the other.

For just an instant Nick felt a sharp pang of envy. She looked so young and vibrant. It made him painfully aware of his own age, of the fact that often as not he needed the walking stick for more than show, of the aches and pains he'd learned to accept as part of growing older, of the way the clock was ticking down. He shook his head, irritated by the maudlin turn of his thoughts. There were more important things to focus on at the moment.

Maybe he *was* an interfering old s.o.b., but Luke was the only family he had left, and he had a right to do what he could to see that he was happy. The plan to force the boy into marriage might have been poorly thought out, but that didn't mean he should just wash his hands of the whole thing. If anything, since this was more or less his fault, he was obligated to make sure Luke didn't get hurt.

Nick had been appalled when Luke told him he was going to marry Devon Kowalski, but he'd understood his grandson's motivations, just as he'd understood Devon's. Luke had been using his choice of bride to thumb his nose at him, and Devon had wanted both money and social position. Neither had been difficult to understand. He wasn't so sure about Miss Catherine Willow Rain Skywalker Lang. Money, of course. It had to be about money. The question was, how much and what was their agreement? And if she'd married his grandson for his money, why was she still working in this garden? Selling vegetables, for God's sake!

He knew Luke had been deliberately keeping them apart. Aside from meeting Cat at the engagement party and again at the wedding, Nick had only seen her once, at dinner a week ago, on Luke's birthday. On that occasion Luke had made sure his wife and his grandfather were never alone. It was obvious that he'd entered into this marriage to fulfill the terms Nick had set down, but if that was the case, why did he seem almost…protective of the girl?

Nick was just about to make his presence known when Cat looked up and saw him.

"Mr. Quintain?" She made it a question.

"Catherine." Nick moved forward, stepping carefully as he moved off the dirt path and onto the mulched pathways between the vegetable beds. "I hope you don't mind my dropping in."

"Of course not."

Her smile was welcoming, but he noticed that her eyes

remained watchful. He smiled his best harmless-old-man smile. "The gardens are beautiful."

"Thank you." Cat returned the smile, but the caution remained.

Not as stupid as her stepsister, he decided. Devon had been embarrassingly eager to see the smallest courtesy as a sign of open-armed welcome.

"My grandparents had a big vegetable garden," he said conversationally. He planted the walking stick on the ground and rested both hands on top of it. "They lived in the San Fernando Valley, back in the twenties and thirties, when the Valley was still full of orange groves and chicken ranches. Seemed to me like the weeds grew faster than the vegetables, but maybe that was because my grandmother was inclined to dragoon me into helping her pull them out."

Cat's smile grew a little warmer, her posture relaxing a bit. "My theory is that weeds grow faster because they know someone's likely to come along and yank them up." She bent to set down the bucket and the flat of plants. "I garden intensively—plant things close together. It creates a sort of living mulch that helps shade out the weeds, but I still spend quite a bit of time crawling around pulling them up."

Nick nodded, gave the garden a thoughtful look. "I imagine you could afford to hire someone to do the weeding for you," he said casually. "Luke must have settled quite a bit of money on you."

"Must he?"

He glanced at Cat and was surprised to see a twinkle of genuine amusement in her eyes. It gave him the disconcerting feeling that she was laughing at him.

"I know my grandson well enough to know he'd be

generous," he said, sounding more defensive than he would have liked.

Cat hooked her thumbs in the front pockets of her jeans and cocked her head a bit, still watching him with that hint of laughter.

"You know, it would save us both a lot of time if you'd just spit out whatever you came here to say, Mr. Quintain. I've got tomatoes to get in the ground." She nodded to the flat of plants. "And I'm fairly sure you didn't drive all the way out here to chitchat about gardens."

Nick felt a grudging twinge of respect for her bluntness and nodded. "You're right. I wanted to talk to you."

"Would you like to sit down?" Cat offered politely. "Maybe have a glass of lemonade? The lemons are from our own tree."

"No, thank you. I'm fine right here."

She didn't push but simply waited for him to state his business. She was too damned calm, he thought, suddenly irritated. As if she'd already made up her mind that nothing he said would bother her.

"Why did you marry my grandson?" If she wanted to bypass all the polite rigmarole, that was fine with him.

"That's none of your business." Cat's tone was as polite as if she were turning down an invitation to tea. She didn't look offended or annoyed or even surprised. "I won't discuss my relationship with Luke with you."

"He's my grandson," Nick began, temper sharpening his voice.

"And my husband," she interrupted without apology. "Our marriage is none of your business. I *will* tell you one thing, though. If you really wanted him to marry Cissy Winslow, you went about the whole thing completely wrong."

Luke had told her about that? Nick barely kept his jaw from dropping open.

"I did, did I?" His tone was dark with anger, but Cat didn't seem to notice.

"Completely wrong." She shook her head as if she couldn't believe he'd handled it so poorly. "You should have told him you *didn't* want him to marry her, maybe have said you'd rather he married anyone *but* her. I can't believe you've known him all his life and haven't figured out that, when you push him, he's going to do the opposite of what you want him to do."

Nick opened his mouth to tell her exactly what she could do with her opinions and then shut it again without speaking. She was right, dammit. He'd known he was making a mistake trying to shove Cissy Winslow down Luke's throat, and he'd done it anyway. And here was this…this…girl, barely old enough to vote, figuring it out after knowing Luke for just a few months, telling him where he'd gone wrong. It was damned irritating.

"He's stubborn as an ox," he muttered. It was as close as he was willing to get to admitting she was right.

"And I suppose you can't imagine where he gets that?"

"Maybe he did get a bit of it from me," he admitted reluctantly. He tapped his cane on the ground, pride warring with concern in his expression. "And maybe I shouldn't have pushed Cissy Winslow on him—or pushed marriage on him at all, for that matter."

She raised her brows. "You think?"

Her dry-as-dust tone had Nick hovering between anger and a sudden unexpected urge to laugh. This visit wasn't going at all the way he'd thought it would. He couldn't remember the last time someone had been so completely indifferent to his opinion. It was refreshing. And annoying.

"Didn't your parents teach you to respect your elders?" he growled finally.

"Only when they're right," Cat said, giving him a bright smile.

This time, Nick did laugh. "I'm not sure whether I should envy Luke or be afraid for him."

Cat's expression softened, gentled somehow. "I won't discuss my marriage with you, but I will tell you that I won't hurt him."

Nick looked at her, saw the emotion in her eyes, and suddenly he knew the answer to his original question. He didn't know what, if anything, the money had had to do with her marriage to his grandson, but he knew it hadn't been her primary motivation. She was in love with Luke.

And his first thought wasn't relief but a quick, unexpected pinch of concern, not for his grandson but for Cat. He'd been worried that Luke would get hurt, but maybe it wasn't Luke who was at risk.

Lucky's Bar & Grill had blue-collar pretensions. The floor was wooden, scarred, and covered with an atmospheric layer of sawdust and peanut shells. The tables were as battered as the floor; the napkins were plain white paper; two pool tables sat on one side of the room; and a jukebox offered a selection of country and light rock. The bartender was big, bald and had a colorful assortment of tattoos ranging up each heavily muscled arm.

But the working-class atmosphere was somewhat muted by the lack of an actual working-class clientele. The customers were mostly white-collar computer geeks and managers from the nearby industrial park. Orders for white wine spritzers and Chivas on the rocks outnumbered the calls for draft beer, and happy hour snacks included California rolls, tiny meatballs and a low-fat chili that had gotten a rave review in the *Los Angeles Times*. On Fridays and Saturdays the small stage in one corner became a karaoke lover's paradise.

Luke was profoundly grateful that this was Thursday. The perky boy band currently assaulting his ears—and his digestion—was bad enough. He didn't want to think about listening to an endless stream of Michael Bolton and Celine Dion wanna-bes chirping into a microphone.

It had been Cat's idea to come here after she read an article that claimed the hamburgers at Lucky's were among the five best in Los Angeles. He had a sneaking suspicion he was going to end up tasting the other four. For someone who'd grown up with a vegetarian hippie for a mother, his wife was quite the carnivore. The fact that she also considered tofu edible was a mystery.

A broken water pipe had closed Jack's Place overnight, leaving Jack with unexpected free time. Luke wasn't sure if it was friendship or a desire to share the misery that had led him to ask Keith to join them, but here they all were.

"If the hamburgers aren't really the best I've ever eaten, I'm going to sue the restaurant critic for false advertising," Luke said, looking around the bar. "I don't know why we had to drive to Long Beach for burgers. Jack's supposed to be some sort of wunderkind chef, isn't he? Can't he make a decent hamburger?"

Keith shrugged and plucked a tortilla chip from the basket in the center of the table. "Maybe making a hamburger is too simple. You know, like a surgeon who can do a brain transplant but can't figure out what to do about a paper cut."

"Brain transplants?" Luke raised his eyebrows.

"Somebody's got to be doing them." Keith dipped the chip into the bowl of salsa and popped it in his mouth, talking around it. "Hey, if they can clone a sheep, they can move a brain."

"I'm not sure the two things are related, and how did we get from hamburgers to cloned sheep?"

"You were whining that Jack should be able to make a good hamburger," Keith said helpfully.

Luke thought about taking issue with the word *whining* but decided to let it go. Maybe he *was* whining. He reached for a chip and tried not to grimace when the boy band gave way to a twangy male voice complaining about the lack of love in his life. *Take the clothespin off your nose, buddy. You might get lucky.*

"I'm just surprised he wants to go out at all," Luke said, scooping up some salsa on the chip. "He spends all his time in a restaurant. I'd think he'd want to eat at home once in a while."

"He does the cooking either way," Keith pointed out, shrugging. "So maybe there's not much difference. At least this way, someone else is doing the work."

"I suppose."

Luke reached for another chip, his attention shifting across the room to the pool tables. Jack was standing at the end of one, watching Cat as she leaned over the table to set up a shot. She was wearing a pair of black jeans, and a blue-and-black-striped sweater that was cropped at the waist. From where he was sitting, he had a nice view of those long legs in snug denim and maybe an inch of bare back showing where the sweater had ridden up a little.

Desire was a warm, familiar weight in his gut. He kept thinking the heat would burn off, that he would wake up one morning and look at her and *not* want her but it hadn't happened yet. More than four months of marriage, four months of incredible, mind-blowing sex on a steady basis, and he still felt as randy as a sixteen-year-old around her. It bothered him a little, but it seemed kind of stupid to worry because he was getting too much sex.

Jack said something to her, and she laughed suddenly, sounding young and happy. Despite himself, Luke smiled, feeling his bad mood slide away. The drive across L.A. at rush hour, the hunt for a parking place, the godawful music, none of it seemed quite as irritating as it had a moment ago. And that worried him more than anything else. Sex was one thing, but this warm, fuzzy feeling…that made him uneasy.

"So things are working out pretty well, I guess," Keith said, and Luke dragged his attention back to his best friend.

"What's working out?" He reached for another chip. The salsa was actually pretty good. If the burgers measured up to it, maybe it would even be worth the trip.

"You and Cat. The whole marriage thing. It looks like it's working out okay. You guys seem pretty comfortable with each other."

Luke shrugged. He preferred not to think about how "comfortable" they were. "If I have to have a wife for a year, I couldn't do better."

Keith winced, thinking of the way Cat looked at Luke. She was in love with him, he was nearly sure of it, and it didn't sound like Luke was thinking beyond the one-year deadline.

"I like Cat."

"So do I," Luke said easily and then grinned. "I should probably send Devon and her dairy farmer a thank-you present."

Keith wondered if he should say something like *Wake up and smell the coffee, you dope. Your wife is in love with you.* But he had a natural male dislike of stepping into an emotional minefield, and he wasn't sure Cat would appreciate his interference, anyway. Feeling vaguely guilty, he chose a more neutral topic.

"Have you heard from Devon since she took off? Does she know you and Cat are married?"

"I think Cat wrote and told her about it." Luke didn't sound particularly interested in how his former fiancée might have reacted to the news that he'd married her step-sister.

Keith had to admit to a twinge of curiosity. From what he'd seen of Devon, he couldn't picture her smiling and giving her blessing. He would be willing to bet that there was a healthy streak of dog-in-the-manger under that art-fully streaked blond hair. Just because she'd been the one to break the engagement, it didn't mean she was going to smile benevolently when someone else married Luke and all his money.

Luke frowned as he watched Jack sling his arm around Cat's shoulders and drag her against his side in a quick, affectionate hug. Why couldn't she have a normal best friend? Someone to share all those girl things women did—shopping and getting their nails done and going to the bathroom together. Someone *female*. Then again, the inaptly named Merry had been a waitress at the last café Cat had worked at, and the word *normal* didn't really seem to apply.

At least Jack didn't dress like something out of central casting for a low-budget vampire movie. So, he was tall, blond and good-looking. And male. And had a great sense of humor. And was male. At least he didn't wear black lipstick and dye his hair purple.

"You and Jack have been hanging out together quite a bit, haven't you?" he asked suddenly.

Keith choked rather spectacularly on a tortilla chip. By

the time he'd coughed and wheezed and Luke had slapped him on the back and he'd gulped down some water, Luke seemed to have forgotten asking the question.

"You okay?" Luke asked, looking ready to perform the Heimlich at a moment's notice.

"Yeah." Keith nodded. His voice was raspy and his face was flushed, but he was okay, unless you counted the possibility that he was losing his mind.

Luke's question had made him suddenly aware that he'd been watching Jack as he leaned over the pool table. Specifically, he'd been staring at Jack's butt. Not in an absent not-really-knowing-where-his-eyes-were-focused kind of way but in an admiring Jack's-got-a-really-great-tight-butt kind of way.

Where the hell was that coming from?

Keith reached for his glass and gulped down half his beer. Looking up, he caught Jack watching him, brows raised in concern. Keith waved one hand to indicate he was okay. Jack would probably be more concerned if he knew what was going through his head. Or maybe not. Presumably Jack had no major objection to having another guy ogling his butt, but Keith wasn't used to finding himself the ogler.

Not that he'd been ogling. Looking wasn't ogling. Looking was just…looking. He couldn't control where his eyes were every minute, or even what direction his thoughts were taking.

Luke was right. He'd been spending a lot of time with Jack lately. They'd gone to some Lakers games together. Jack had season tickets and, while Keith had never been a basketball fan, he had admitted that it was more interesting live than it was on television. When a client gave him a pair of tickets to see *The Lion King*, he'd called Jack to see if he wanted to go. A few months ago, he would have called Luke, but these days, inviting Luke meant inviting Cat and, while he had no objection to that, he only had two tickets.

So, yes, he was spending time with Jack, but it didn't mean anything. *And the fact that he'd been staring at Jack's ass?* That didn't mean anything, either. Not a damned thing. Jack had a great ass. Nothing wrong with noticing that. Just because he was a guy, it didn't mean he couldn't notice when another guy had a great ass. That was what equal rights were all about, wasn't it?

''Hey, Reynolds, don't try to fake a 9-1-1 call to avoid the ugly reality that you're about to lose this game.''

Jack turned back to the table and arched his brows at her. ''Who says I'm about to lose?''

''I do. Along with the fact that you're a lousy player.'' Cat's grin was taunting. ''That's what you get for growing up a rich boy. Now, if we were playing polo, I bet you'd beat the pants off me.''

''Sometimes I think you miss the whole point of me being gay,'' Jack said plaintively. ''What would I do with your pants once I had them?'' He looked at the table and sighed. ''And for the record, I'm not any better at polo. The only thing I know how to do with a horse is fall off.''

''Sad.'' Cat shook her head in mock sympathy.

''Yeah, well, we can't all have your advantages. Learning pool from Michigan Lardbutt himself and all.'' Jack lined up his cue and took a shot. The cue ball spun madly across the table, striking two balls, neither of them his.

''Alabama Slim,'' Cat corrected, trying to sound disapproving, not an easy thing to do through a giggle. ''Naomi dated his son.''

''And let you hang out in a pool hall while she was off canoodling on the bayou.''

"Actually, we were living in Spokane at the time, and I don't think there *are* any bayous there." She knocked the ten ball into a pocket and looked up to see Jack looking across the room at their table. There was something in his eyes that... Oh dear. She missed the next shot. "So is he still breathing?" she asked, straightening up from the pool table.

"What?" Jack started as if he'd forgotten she was there.

"Keith. Is he still breathing? Because I read an article once on how to perform a tracheotomy. All I need is a penknife and a clean straw, and we're in business."

"I don't think that will be necessary," Jack said, grinning. "But I'm sure Keith would appreciate knowing you were prepared to leap into the breach."

Cat watched him lean over the table, lining up his shot. He was going to miss again, she noted absently. It was amazing that a man who could use a chef's knife to mince a carrot at lightning speed couldn't grasp the essentials of holding a pool cue.

"So you and Keith are spending a lot of time together lately," she said casually.

"Some. Gives me something to do with the other half of the Lakers season tickets Phil gave me for my birthday." Jack looked up, grinning at her over the table. "I suppose a better man would have given them back to him."

"Or a stupider one."

He missed the shot, which surprised neither of them. Straightening, he gave the table a resigned look. "Good thing I don't have to earn a living this way."

"Good thing," Cat agreed, grinning.

"Have you spent much time with Keith?" Jack asked

as she leaned over the table. "I know he and Luke are tight."

Not at all fooled by the casual tone, Cat straightened and looked at him. "Are you making conversation, or is there something you want to know?"

"I..." Jack shrugged and smiled a little sheepishly. "We've had a lot fun together, and once in a while, I get the idea that he might— But it's probably my imagination."

"As far as I know, Keith is straight as an arrow," she said, deciding this was one occasion where it was definitely kinder to be blunt.

Jack shrugged again, one corner of his mouth kicking up in a rueful half smile. "That's the problem with living in California. All the good men are either married or straight." He caught her eye, read the concern there and shook his head. "No big deal. I just thought... Guess my gaydar is on the fritz."

Cat laughed, but the worry was still there. She leaned back over the table to knock the last few balls into the pockets. She would hate to see Jack set his sights on someone he couldn't have, though she was hardly in a position to throw stones when it came to that, she admitted ruefully.

More than four months into her marriage to Luke, and the only real change was that she no longer thought she might be in love with him. She knew she was. The only thing she was absolutely sure Luke felt for her was desire. And maybe that he liked her. Affection, if she wanted to stretch a point, which she did. Desperately. Liking could become love, she reminded herself.

However, the question was could it happen in the next eight months.

Chapter Twelve

The calendar said it was June, the month when summer made its formal arrival, picnic season was officially declared, and everyone broke out their shorts and tank tops. Except that, in a climate where eighty-degree weather was possible year round, no one ever put away their shorts and tank tops, and picnics were as likely in January as in June. More likely, Luke thought, since the sun was a more reliable visitor in January.

Throwing one last, disgusted look at the gray weather outside, he hit the button to close the garage door and then tossed the opener onto the passenger seat of the Mercedes before slamming the door shut. He'd been born and raised in Los Angeles, and the annual bout of June gloom still managed to surprise him every year. Subliminal conditioning, he decided, as he walked around the nose of the Mercedes. It was all those calendars showing graceful yachts sailing along under beautiful blue skies and happy children running through the sprinklers. Thirty-six years of June being an almost guaranteed dead loss in terms of sunshine and warmth, and he was still caught off guard.

Luke patted Ruthie's hood as he walked past, grinning a little as he realized that he thought of the ridiculous little car by name now. Cat had finally taken Ruthie in to have her engine rebuilt the month before. The VW had been gone for almost two weeks, and Luke had been surprised to find he actually missed seeing the tomato-red absurdity parked in the garage next to his car. The rented replacement had seemed hopelessly dull.

Merry was standing at the stove when he let himself in from the garage. As usual, she was wearing head-to-toe black. Today's monochromatic ensemble consisted of an ankle-length skirt, a black knit crop top and what appeared to be combat boots. She'd changed her hair color, veering from last week's purple to blood-red with two black streaks framing her thin face. Heavy black eyeliner gave her the look of a sleep-deprived raccoon.

For just a moment Luke felt a pang of nostalgia for the days when his housekeeper hadn't looked like an extra from a slasher movie. He'd never given any thought to what Mrs. Bryant wore, but, in retrospect, her neat, tailored dresses and gently graying hair seemed wonderfully soothing.

He let the door shut behind him, and Merry turned to look at him. As far as he could tell, she had only two expressions: gloomy and gloomier. He wasn't sure if this indicated a depressive personality or if she thought a smile would clash with her image.

"Cat's sick," she said by way of greeting.

"What's wrong?" Frowning, Luke set his briefcase on the counter. "She was fine this morning."

"Well, she's not fine now. She's got this flu that's been going around. My sister had it a couple of weeks ago. Couldn't get out of bed for four days." Merry didn't sound entirely unhappy about this, which probably said something about her relationship with her sister.

"Where is she?" he asked, walking across the kitchen.

"Upstairs." Merry turned back to the stove, picking up a wooden spoon to stir the pot she had simmering. For just an instant Luke had a flashback to a high school production of *Macbeth,* and the three witches stirring their big cauldron and muttering incantations. Merry would have blended right in.

"I've made some chicken soup," she said, banging the spoon against the side of the pan before setting it on the spoon rest. "My mother's recipe. Plenty of garlic and black pepper." She turned the burner down and set a lid on the pot. "Be sure she at least takes a little broth. She's been puking her guts up all afternoon, and you have to watch out, make sure she doesn't get dehydrated. There's juice in the fridge. See if you can get some of that down her."

Merry lifted her jacket—big surprise, it was black—off one of the hooks near the back door and shrugged into it. "I wasn't scheduled to come in tomorrow, but call if you need me. I don't have any classes I can't make up later."

"Thanks."

Merry nodded briskly and disappeared out the back door without another word. Luke stared after her for a moment and wondered if there was some adage about not judging a vampire by her clothes.

If he'd given it any thought, Luke would have guessed that Cat would be a good patient. He would have been wrong.

The first sign that he should abandon all hope of rational behavior was when he went upstairs to find her in one of the guest bedrooms, lying fully clothed on top of the unmade bed, wrapped in the bedspread and shivering.

"I'm fine," she said as soon as he pushed open the door.

"Merry says you've got the flu."

"I never get sick."

So denial really wasn't just a river in Egypt, Luke thought, studying her ashen complexion and red-rimmed eyes.

"Why are you in here?"

"I didn't want to expose you to this bug."

"The bug you don't have because you never get sick?" he asked politely.

"Yes." Her lower lip stuck out in something that an unkind person might have called a pout.

"That's very nice of you, but unless you think you caught this thing this morning, I was probably pretty well exposed to whatever it is last night, don't you think?"

Illness had slowed her thinking, so it took her a minute, but he figured the faint wash of color that came up in her cheeks meant her memory was still working.

"Well, you might not have gotten it," she insisted.

"Honey, I think I can safely say that if either of us has anything that can be caught, we've passed it along by now." Without bothering to argue the point any further, Luke crossed the room and scooped her up off the bed, bedspread and all.

"What are you doing?" She would have flung her arms around his neck but they were trapped in the bedspread.

"I'm carrying you."

"Why?"

"Because you're sick and you should be in bed."

"I can walk." Cat was torn between indignation—she didn't need him to cart her around like a sack of laundry—and taking a slightly guilty delight in feeling small and helpless, not a sensation she was accustomed to.

"Sure you can, but I've already got you, and it would be silly to put you down in the middle of the hall just so you could walk ten feet to get back in bed again."

She was nearly sure there was a flaw in his logic, but her head was throbbing and her stomach felt tender to the touch, and there was a godawful taste in her mouth and the light in the hall made her eyes hurt, so she just closed them and let her head rest on his shoulder. She would feel better in a minute. In the meantime, if Luke wanted to carry her around, she couldn't really conjure up the energy to protest.

The next three days passed in a blur. Luke had never nursed anyone through an illness. As a child, when he got a cold or flu, either the housekeeper took care of him, or, once he was a little older, his grandmother would swoop down on whatever house his parents were currently not really sharing and carry him off to stay with her and his grandfather. He'd been a disgustingly healthy child, so it hadn't happened often, but he could remember bowls of soup served in bed, his grandfather teaching him to play chess, and his grandmother reading to him from *The Jungle Book*, the story interspersed with her commentary on what a shame it was that a fine writer like Kipling was so neglected in schools these days.

It was only now that he realized what a perfect patient he had been.

Cat didn't want to eat soup or juice or nibble on dry toast. Not that he could really blame her, when whatever she ate had a nasty tendency to come back up again. His offer to teach her to play chess was met with a moan. Ditto checkers, poker and, in desperation, Old Maid, though that did at least elicit a comment that that was an incredibly un-PC name for a card game, and how would he like it if the game was called Old Unwanted Guy?

So much for entertainment.

She fretted about being sick, about him missing work to take care of her, about her gardens. When Luke made the mistake of saying he thought the gardens could probably survive a few days on their own, she asked him where he'd gotten his degree in agriculture. A few minutes later she was nearly in tears as she apologized for being so hard to get along with.

Luke's reassurance that she wasn't difficult at all didn't exactly ring with sincerity, but he did put in a call to the teenager who lived next door to Larry and Susan and gave Cat occasional help in the garden, and hired the boy to patrol the vegetables twice a day armed with a weeding fork and a bucket of soapy water for dealing with any sudden bug invasions. Short of a plague of locusts, he thought that should be enough to stave off horticultural tragedy.

Cat seemed to ricochet between the conviction that she was going to be completely well any minute now and an equally powerful certainty that death was imminent—and welcome. Holding her hair back while she threw up at three in the morning, Luke couldn't really blame her.

When the bout was finally over, he got her a glass of water to rinse her mouth, then dampened a washcloth with cool water. Cat sighed with relief as he bathed her fever-flushed face and neck. They were both sitting on the bathroom floor, and she leaned her head against his shoulder, giving herself up to the unfamiliar pleasure of having someone take care of her.

"I'm never sick," she mumbled, half-asleep.

Luke's hand cupped her nape, tilting her head back. Cat opened her eyes to find him looking intently at her nose.

"What are you doing?" Her tone hovered between crabby and whiny.

"This disproves the Pinocchio theory," Luke said, looking solemn. "You just told a huge lie, and your nose didn't grow at all."

Laughter rasped at her throat and made her already pounding head throb even more.

"I'm sorry to be so much trouble," she sighed, letting her head rest against his shoulder again. Having him hold her made her feel a little less achy. This time she didn't offer any objection when Luke stood and scooped her up off the floor to carry her to bed.

For Cat, the first two days passed in a haze of throwing up and sleeping, sipping broth and sleeping, and then throwing up some more. On the third day there was more sleeping and less throwing up, and the cup of broth Luke brought her actually tasted like food. She kept down all the broth he gave her for lunch, and as a reward, he brought her a bowl of the *albondigas* soup Consuela's mother had made for her and sent with her daughter.

"I'll even let you have a meatball," he offered.

"Oh, goody."

"What do you think you're doing?"

The sharp question made Cat jump. She grabbed for the doorjamb to stabilize her wobbly balance and turned cautiously to look at Luke. He was standing just inside the bedroom doorway, arms crossed over his chest, brows drawn together in a stern frown as he looked at her.

"I thought you were going to stay in bed?"

It was a measure of her weakened condition that the

first thing that came to mind was *you're not the boss of me*. Luckily illness hadn't completed destroyed her brain.

"I was…ah…just going to take a little shower?" Despite herself, her voice rose at the end, making it a question rather than the firm statement she'd intended. His expression didn't warm, and Cat decided that a good offense might be the best defense. "You're home early," she said accusingly.

"I told you I was going into the office for a few hours. I didn't realize I needed to keep a strict schedule so you'd have time to sneak around doing things you're not strong enough to do."

"I want a shower." It was perilously close to a whine, and she saw Luke's mouth twitch. Okay, so maybe being pathetic was going to get her further than being mature. "I feel absolutely disgusting, Luke." She reached up to tug at her hair, which was bundled up in a loose knot on top of her head. "I can't stand it another minute."

Luke wavered. He should probably bundle her back to bed. She was already wavering on her feet, knuckles white where she gripped the doorjamb. And she'd planned on taking a shower? Talk about an accident waiting to happen.

This was the fourth day since she'd come down with what she referred to as the plague. She'd been doing well enough that he'd decided to spend a few hours in the office, tidying up some of the loose ends he'd left dangling when she got sick. He'd left her with a stack of magazines, a deck of cards and the remote to the television, along with strict instructions that she was not to try to do anything more strenuous than lifting a glass of juice.

Cat saw the muscle in his jaw flex and decided to pull out the big guns. To hell with being an independent woman. If she didn't get clean soon, she was going to go batty, and though she would never say it out loud, she probably *had* bitten off more than she could chew. Without the support of the door, she just might collapse in an undignified heap. All that was keeping her upright was the siren call of hot water and shampoo. In pursuit of a higher goal, there was nothing wrong with a little judicious begging now and again.

"Please."

Luke tried to hold on to his stern disapproval, but it just wasn't possible when she was standing there, practically wobbling on her feet, big green eyes all pleading and hopeful.

"Okay, but I don't think it's a good idea to wash your hair. That can wait until you're completely over this bug." He said it firmly, making it clear that it would be a waste of time to try to coax him into changing his mind.

He'd obviously gone wrong somewhere, Luke decided ten minutes later. Maybe he should have stayed firm about it being too soon for a shower. Maybe agreeing to that had put them on the slippery slope that had led…here. He flexed his fingers against Cat's scalp, and she sighed with pleasure as she leaned into his touch. Maybe his mistake had been in deciding that the best way to make sure she didn't hurt herself was to climb in the shower with her. It was difficult to remain stern when you were buck naked.

Or maybe it was just that once she was in the shower, naked and wet and hopeful, he didn't have the willpower to say no. She was, she'd pointed out, already wet. Would it really be so much worse if her hair got wet, too? And, distracted by the way the water glistened on her skin and the sudden flash of memory that reminded him of what they'd been doing the *last* time they were in this shower together, Luke had found himself nodding and agreeing that it probably wouldn't make any real difference. Next thing he knew, he had his hands full of suds and wet hair.

The shampoo smelled of apples and wildflowers, sweet and tart. Wet, her hair looked almost black, and it slid through his fingers like heavy silk. The weight of the water pulled the curl out of it, and it fell in a glistening dark curtain almost to her waist.

He felt a definite twinge of interest in things beyond cleanliness, but he could see the faint tremor in her arm where she had it braced against the smoke-colored tiles, and he suspected her legs were just as wobbly. Stubborn as an ox, Luke thought with a mixture of irritation and affection.

Affection? The word gave him pause. This wasn't real, he reminded himself, turning her under the spray to rinse her hair. This was a temporary arrangement. Yes, it had turned out better than he'd had any right to expect, but it was still just smoke and mirrors, a legal bow to his grandfather's demands. Almost half of the required year was gone. Another six months or so and they would go their separate ways. Friends, hopefully, but definitely separate.

He wasn't suited to a long-term relationship. Not with Cat or anyone else. It would be stupid to lose sight of that. He didn't *want* to lose sight of that.

"Is that a gun in your pocket, or are you happy to see me?"

"Jesus!" Luke jolted back as her hand closed around his half-formed erection. "Cat. Don't…. You don't have to…"

His protest trailed off on a groan as she stroked him to full hardness. God, this was what getting regular sex did to him—four days and he felt like he'd been celibate for a year. With an effort, he forced his eyes open and looked down at her. She looked like something out of a book of mythology—if it came in a porn version, maybe. The water darkened her hair to a deep, deep red-black. Moisture beaded on her shoulders and arms, on the soft thrust of her breasts, caught in the thatch of curls at the top of her thighs.

Luke was fairly sure that, if he didn't have her in the next minute, he would be the first man on record to actually die from unsatisfied lust. Generations of adolescent boys would suddenly be proven right. But some dim remnant of civilization insisted on being heard over the testosterone pumping through his veins. She might look like a wet dream, but she was barely over a nasty bout with the flu.

"Cat, it's a nice thought." He caught his breath as she slid her hand down to cradle the aching weight of his testicles. "A really, *really* nice thought," he groaned. "But I don't think you're quite well enough for... Ah, God, you're killing me."

"Shh." She kept one hand on his erection and brought the other up to slide into his hair, tugging his face down to hers in a kiss that was pure sex. If he hadn't already been rock hard, he would have been by the time she broke the kiss off. "You've taken such good care of me, Luke. Let me take care of you now."

Luke watched in dazed disbelief as she dropped to her knees in front of him. His fingers clenched in her hair as she took him in her mouth. The fine spray from the shower gilded everything, gave everything a hazy, otherworldly look. But there was nothing otherworldly about the feel of her mouth on him, the sweet hunger in the way she took him in. He should stop her. He hadn't even thought she was well enough to take a shower, let alone...this. He should definitely stop her. For her own good.

Groaning, he let his head fall back, eyes dropping shut as he gave in to the pleasure, the need, letting it pulse out of him, letting her take it, take him.

For a little while there was nothing but the patter of water against tile and the ragged sound of his own breathing. It was all Luke could do not to collapse in a heap. With a supreme effort of will, he lifted his head away from the wall, looked down at Cat. She was still kneeling, the water a sparkling veil around her, her eyes, those big green eyes with their exotic tilt, bright with a look that was a little smug, a little uncertain and all woman. And then, as if that wasn't enough, as if she hadn't already just about killed him, she let her tongue come out, stroking slowly across her lower lip. Tasting him, Luke realized, and felt his heart slam against his chest, new arousal beating hard and fast in his blood.

It wasn't enough. It was never enough with her. The thought made him almost angry. His fingers tightened against her scalp, and she let him draw her to her feet, her eyes never leaving his, letting him read the hunger, the need. Luke's mouth crushed hers, tongue sweeping inside. He'd never known anything as erotic as the ocean-hot taste of himself on her tongue. Without taking his mouth from hers, he leaned down, one hand catching her knees, the other behind her shoulder, as he lifted her in his arms. Nudging the shower door open with his foot, he carried her out of the bathroom and into the bedroom, ignoring her breathless little protest about getting the sheets wet as he dropped her on the bed, following her down, his body covering hers, making her his.

Chapter Thirteen

When Cat was growing up, *birthday* had been two words, as in *birth* day, a day to celebrate, not just one's arrival on the planet earth but one's place in the grand scheme of the universe. Candles were sometimes lit, but they weren't on a cake. They were to encourage meditation or draw good spirits, or maybe keep away the bad ones. Cat had always been a little unclear on the details. Naomi would tell her how welcome her birth had been, make vague allusions to the father Cat had never met and rarely gave any thought to, and express her hopes that Cat would find her spiritual center and live a balanced life.

If there was cake, it was likely to be made out of carrots and honey and whole wheat flour, and taste like a sweetened hockey puck. There were usually presents, but they tended to be socially responsible or of a spiritual nature—a doll, handmade by some endangered native people in some part of the world she'd never heard of, her very own gazing ball to help her see into her inner spirit, a book of cleansing prayers. She'd often thought it was a shame Mattel didn't make a Maharishi Barbie or maybe G.I. Joe the Pacifist, complete with his own flower-bedecked machine gun.

She didn't remember missing normal birthday parties, with cake and presents and screaming children who ate too much and then threw up, but she had to admit that she was looking forward to finally having a real one of her own, complete with cake and presents, hold the screaming children and the throwing up.

Especially hold the throwing up, Cat thought, shuddering at the thought. Even after a month, *that* memory was still vivid. But if anything illustrated the old adage about every cloud having a silver lining, it was her bout with the flu last month. Painful as it had been, it had almost been worth it to have Luke take care of her so sweetly.

It had to mean something. No one nursed someone through a stomach flu unless they were being paid large sums of money or had an emotional connection to the victim. Luke had to care for her to do that, didn't he? The woman in the mirror looked hopeful but unconvinced, and after a moment Cat turned away from her reflection. She refused to drive herself crazy worrying about it. As Naomi would say, worrying about the future wasn't going to change it. It was a little scary to find herself agreeing with her mother, but this was one time when she was absolutely right. Marrying Luke was the biggest gamble she'd ever taken. Only time would tell whether or not it was going to pay off. It was just a little scary to see the year rushing by so quickly. Less than six months to go now.

Cat deliberately pushed the thought aside as she left the bedroom and went downstairs. She could worry about the future any time, but she was only going to get one twenty-first birthday and she intended to enjoy every minute of it.

* * *

Some years, the June gloom lingered all summer, disappointing hordes of tourists and annoying the native Angelenos, but this year, when the calendar page turned, so did the weather. June's hazy skies and cool temperatures gave way to July's pale blue, nearly cloudless skies and heat. Those who had been complaining about the dreary weather promptly switched to complaining about the rising thermometers. The beaches filled up with surfers and sunseekers, and the weather reports routinely listed the air quality as unhealthy. Not that it did much good, since most people insisted on breathing anyway.

Aside from breathing, Keith didn't intend to move for several more hours. Maybe a couple of days. Eyes closed against the sun sparkling off the water in the pool, he reminded himself forcefully that groaning wasn't manly. It was okay to stuff yourself full of kebabs and roasted-in-the-husk corn and top it off with really good cake and ice cream, but a real man would suffer in silence.

"I think I'm going to die," Jack groaned as he dropped onto the redwood lounger next to Keith's. "I haven't eaten that much in years."

"Isn't that breaking some rule in the chef's handbook—eating too much of your own cooking?"

"Not when it tastes that good," Jack said.

Keith opened his eyes and turned his head to look at him, and couldn't help but grin at Jack's smug smile. Not that Keith could blame him. Jack had managed to take traditional barbecue fare—chicken kebabs, corn on the cob, grilled vegetables and good old potato salad—and turn out something extraordinary.

"I thought New Englanders were supposed to be taciturn and modest."

"They are, but Californians are talkative and boastful. The conflict is just tearing me apart." Since he was currently stretched out, looking the picture of relaxed contentment, Keith took that statement with a grain of salt.

A metallic clang and a muttered curse drifted from the other side of the pool. Keith winced in sympathy and then reminded himself that it was Luke's own fault for giving Cat a present that had to be put together. You didn't have to be a parent to know that the two most terrifying words in the English language were *assembly required.*

If he squinted, he could just make out Luke and Cat where they sat in the shade on the opposite pool deck. Next to them was a box the size of a small pony, an assortment of tools he was willing to bet Luke hadn't used in a decade and a scattering of metal parts that were supposed to go together. Even from here, he could see Cat leaning forward, all but vibrating with delight.

Weird, he decided. She was just plain weird. He'd once given a girlfriend a diamond pendant, and she hadn't been nearly as excited as Cat was over getting a shredder. In Keith's world, shredders were small appliances into which one fed unwanted documents too sensitive to simply toss in the trash. This shredder apparently ate plants—redwoods, from the size of it.

Another clang and a more pungent curse drifted across the water.

"He should have bought it already assembled," Jack said without opening his eyes.

"It didn't come assembled."

"Then he should have hired a mechanical engineer to put it together in the dead of night or something. Did you *see* those diagrams?"

"Yeah." Keith shuddered and gave up any thought of doing the best friend thing and offering to help. His mechanical skill pretty much began and ended with figuring out how to plug in an appliance.

"He made major points with Cat, though," Jack commented. "She wouldn't have been nearly as excited if he'd bought her the Hope Diamond."

"Not unless it could go in the compost pile. What the hell *is* a compost pile, anyway?"

"Vegetable waste, soil, maybe some manure, all layered together and left to rot. The finished compost does great things for the soil."

"I'm sorry I asked," Keith muttered.

"Just think of it this way: those three ears of corn that you ate owe their flavor, at least in part, to compost."

"I'm not sure that helps, especially since you reminded me that I ate three ears of corn."

"Just try not to think about it," Jack said soothingly.

Maybe he could just add it to the list of things he was trying not to think about these days, Keith thought. Like the fact that he was way too aware of how good Jack looked in those faded denim cutoffs and tank top. Really good. Like the fact that he thought about that sort of thing a lot more than any guy should be thinking about it. More than any straight guy would think about it, anyway, and if there was one thing he was sure of, it was that he was straight. Definitely straight. Always had been, unless you wanted to count a couple of experiments in college, but he'd never counted them before and saw no reason to start counting them now except...

He couldn't quite shrug off this uneasy feeling in the pit of his stomach whenever he was around Jack, or when he thought of him—which he did a great deal more often than he should. It was a familiar feeling. He'd had it a couple of times before, but it had always been for someone with more curves and less hair on their chest.

"Did I spill something?" Jack asked, and Keith jerked

his eyes up, suddenly aware that he'd been staring at the other man's chest.

"I...uh..." He groped for a plausible explanation, something that didn't involve...anything. Like the truth. "I was just noticing the...uh...ring," he said finally, trying for casual. He nodded at the outline of a ring just visible through the thin knit of the tank top. Jack obviously had his nipple pierced, which was no big deal, nothing to make his mouth go dry.

"This?" Jack flicked his finger against the ring. "Youthful indiscretion."

"Didn't it...hurt?"

"Hurt like hell." Jack grinned. "I was seventeen, and drunk as a skunk. I'd come out to my parents the week before. My father told me not to be ridiculous, it was a phase I was going through, and my mother, bless her clueless soul, asked if I thought a session with her shrink might make me feel better." His laughter held a trace of old bitterness. "And then they never mentioned it again. I don't know if I thought getting my nipple pierced was going to punish them or make them suddenly realize that their youngest son really, truly was gay. I'd never have had the guts to do it sober, but once I did it, I figured I might as well keep it."

He flicked his finger against the ring again, and Keith was suddenly remembering a long-ago girlfriend telling him how much more sensitive her nipple was after she'd had it pierced, and then all the spit was gone from his mouth, and the air felt thick and hard to breathe.

"Keith?"

He dragged his gaze up to Jack's face and saw... everything he was thinking reflected in the clear blue of Jack's eyes. Jack raised one eyebrow, asking the question Keith didn't even want to ask himself.

Around them the air was still and hot; the rest of the world faded away to nothing. Keith felt his life hanging in the balance. All he had to do was reach out. Just a touch and he would be...what? He would be gay? Bisexual? Suddenly waving the rainbow flag and marching in parades? That wasn't who he was, who he wanted to be. He was...he was confused as hell, that was what he was.

Sucking in a sharp breath, he leaned back. Not far, not dramatically, but he leaned back. And saw comprehension spill into Jack's eyes, saw something that might have been hurt or maybe disappointment flash across his face, and then Jack looked away, looked across the pool to where Luke and Cat were still doing battle with the shredder.

"Hey, looks like they've made some progress," he said.

The moment, whatever it had been, was gone, and Keith told himself he was relieved. Of course he was relieved, because that wasn't who he was, who he wanted to be. He didn't really feel whatever it was he thought he'd felt. It was just that he'd been putting in too many hours at work, spending too much time alone. Or maybe he needed more exercise, something that would release plenty of endorphins. That was what he needed. Lots of endorphins. Maybe he would start running again. A lot.

"Did Jack seem okay to you?" Cat asked.

With an effort, Luke pulled his attention from the slow stroke of the brush through her hair. There was something intensely erotic about watching her brush her hair, the slow drag of the brush, the way her hair rippled beneath each stroke. The first time, he'd half suspected she was doing it deliberately, but it had been obvious that she had no idea the simple bedtime ritual made his mouth water, and he hadn't enlightened her. In some odd way, the fact that she *wasn't* trying to entice him added to his enjoyment.

"Jack seemed okay to me," he said, trying to focus on something besides the way the lacy black nightgown clung to every curve. It had been a private birthday gift from him, and now that he saw her in it, he wondered if maybe he had masochistic tendencies.

"I probably imagined it." She lifted her arms as she began brushing the back of her hair. Her breasts lifted, pressed against the thin silk, and Luke swallowed a whimper. "I wonder if maybe this sort of thing, you know, birthdays and holidays and things like that, makes him think about his family."

"What about his family?" It was difficult to keep track of the conversation when he was fighting the urge to leap off the bed and throw her to the floor and have his wicked way with her. The knowledge that she would almost certainly respond with enthusiasm made it even harder, made *him* even harder. But there was pleasure in anticipation, too, and he stayed where he was.

"The way they don't accept him. His being gay, I mean." Cat set down the brush and turned to look at him, leaning back against the edge of the dresser. "I don't get that. I mean, I can see worrying about your kid because you know it's going to make things tougher for him, but I don't see why it should make such a huge difference otherwise who they love."

"Not everyone is as progressive as your mother," Luke said dryly. "Some people have a hard time coping with anything outside the norm."

"I suppose, but it doesn't really make much sense. I mean, think about it, it's not like they're going to watch their kids having sex one way or the other, so what difference does it make what sort of equipment their partner comes...equipped with?''

"Most people don't see it that way."

"I guess." Cat sighed at the injustice of it.

Luke was just rethinking the whole pounce and ravish scenario when she tilted her head to one side and looked at him. "You know, I don't think I've ever heard you mention either of your parents."

Talk about a way to really kill a mood. Luke barely stopped himself from physically flinching back, a reaction she would be sure to notice and file away in that surprisingly sharp brain of hers.

"Not much to say," he said, pleased that he sounded perfectly casual. "My father had a heart attack when I was sixteen. We were never particularly close, so it wasn't as much of a tragedy for me as it might have been."

"What about your mother?"

Trust Cat to home right in on the thing he least wanted to discuss. "Last I heard, she was living in Paris. We aren't close, either."

And that was a masterpiece of understatement. A fucking Michelangelo of understatement, Luke thought. Suddenly too restless to sit still, he pushed himself up off the bed.

Hit a sore spot, Cat thought, watching him prowl to the window and twitch aside the curtain to look out into the darkness. Obviously he wasn't as indifferent to his parents as he liked to think. Well, if anyone knew about difficult parents, she did. Not that Naomi had been difficult, exactly, but she'd certainly presented a unique set of challenges, and there were times when Cat had to admit to feeling a certain amount of ambivalence when it came to her mother. Luke hadn't sounded ambivalent. He'd sounded cold as ice. For a moment she was tempted to probe a little, to see if she could find out more about his parents. But something in the set of his shoulders told her it was unlikely to be a pleasant conversation.

It was still her birthday, at least for a couple more hours, and she didn't want anything to spoil what had been a perfectly lovely day and what she hoped would be an even lovelier night. If she'd known mentioning his parents would put a crimp in the mood, she wouldn't have said anything.

It had been such a nice mood, she thought, sighing a little. She'd taken extra time brushing her hair, enjoying the feeling of having Luke's eyes devouring her, watching her every move. She didn't know what it was about seeing her brush her hair that got his motor running, but it worked every time. She wasn't sure he even realized how it affected him, but his eyes would get that sleepy, heavy-lidded look that made her go a little weak in the knees. He didn't say anything, just watched her, and she would instinctively slow the brush, dragging out the anticipation, waiting for that moment when he would come stand behind her, setting his hands on her hips and pulling her back until she could feel the hard length of him pressed against her bottom, feel the heat radiating from him, the hunger.

Unfortunately the only thing he was radiating at the moment was tension. He was staring out the window as if the fate of nations could be seen in the darkness outside. He was wearing only a pair of black silk pajama bottoms, and she could see the tightness in the long muscles of his back.

Cat sighed and moved away from the dresser, curling her toes into the plush blue carpeting as she crossed the room to stand behind him. Deciding that a good offense was the best way to go, she set her hands against his sides just above the waist of the pajama bottoms.

"You know, I was really hoping you had another present for me." She leaned forward to place a soft kiss on his spine, right between his shoulder blades, feeling him shudder a little.

"You were, huh?" His voice was husky, aroused, and she felt hunger slide through her, warm and liquid. "What did you have in mind?"

"Something really...personal." Without warning, she slipped one hand under the silky fabric to cup his erection.

"Holy—" Luke jolted at the touch, feeling his arousal, which had faded a bit, roar back to life, scorching several potentially important areas of his brain to ash. Not that he cared. Hadn't he read somewhere that most people only used ten percent of their brain anyway? So if he'd just burned out a few million cells, then he would just have to switch over to that auxiliary ninety percent.

"I was thinking of the kind of gift that keeps on giving," she whispered against his back, and Luke found himself laughing, despite the fact that he was hard enough to pound nails.

He turned slowly, feeling real regret when her hand slid from him. Still, the view more than made up for that loss. She was standing inches away, her head tilted as she looked at him through her lashes, her mouth curved in a positively lascivious smile. It was a good look for her. A really, really good look.

Luke slid his palms down her arms from shoulder to wrist, catching her hands in his and rubbing his thumbs lightly over the thin skin of her inner wrists, feeling the rapid beat of her pulse.

"The gift that keeps on giving, huh?"

"Sure, like planting a tree in someone's name, or

maybe...'' She paused and let her eyes flick down his body and then back up. She ran her tongue over her bottom lip, a slow, damp stroke that made every cell in his body sit up and take notice. ''Maybe like an all-day sucker.''

He wasn't sure how she managed to look both innocent and wickedly knowing at the same time, but she did it, and the combination sent most of his blood supply heading south.

Cat squeaked in surprise when his hands closed around her waist. He lifted her and practically threw her onto the bed. It was more rough-and-tumble than romantic, but the impatience of it, the *need*, made her so hot, she was half-surprised her skin didn't burn Luke when he touched her.

He stripped the negligee from her with more efficiency than finesse. His hands were not quite steady, and that was more erotic than any smooth, practiced touch. Not that Luke didn't have plenty of those, she thought, whimpering as he slid his hand down her belly to cup the soft thatch of curls. He'd definitely had practice, and he was living, breathing proof that practice made perfect.

Luke watched hungrily as Cat arched into his touch. Her legs parted, long, sleek thighs trembling as she opened to him, offered herself to him. She was so incredibly giving. He didn't think he'd ever had a lover who gave of herself so generously. There was no artifice in her response, nothing studied. The blatant honesty was more erotic than any practiced bedroom skills.

She never pretended in bed. Even at the beginning, he'd never had to guess what she wanted. He'd had more experienced lovers, but he'd never had a lover who was so completely truthful. Would she learn to lie when she had more experience? Other lovers? The lovers she would surely take when this marriage of theirs ended, when they'd gone their separate, no-hard-feelings ways? Would those other men teach her the games most people seemed to know instinctively?

"Luke. Please."

With an effort, he pushed the thought of those phantom lovers out of his mind. The future wasn't his concern. It was the present that mattered.

"Shh," he whispered against her mouth as he lifted himself over her, hips sliding into the welcoming cradle of her thighs. He shuddered as she reached between them, slender fingers gripping him, guiding him. And then she was yielding to him, her body gloving him, taking him even as he took her. Her soft sigh of pleasure was lost in his groan as he filled her, made her his.

Holding his weight braced on his arms, he began to move, slowly at first, waiting for her to pick up the rhythm and echo it, push it faster, take what she needed from him, even as she gave him everything he wanted. Her fingers wrapped around his arms, holding on as if he was the only solid thing in the universe.

Luke watched her face, saw the sexual flush warm her cheeks, loved the way she caught her lower lip between her teeth as if trying to hold back her soft moans. Her fingers tightened on his arms, short nails biting into his skin as she arched suddenly, shuddering beneath him as the peak rushed at her. He wanted to hold on, hold out, watch her go over the edge, then push her up again, watch her eyes go all dazed and heavy with the force of it.

As if she knew what he was thinking, Cat opened her eyes and looked up at him, and suddenly he was seeing things he'd never seen before, reading what was in her heart and, oh God, she loved him. *She loved him.*

The sudden shock of knowledge burst over him at the same moment he felt her tighten around him, heard her cry out as the pleasure took her. Groaning, he let her take him over the edge, his arms all but collapsing, his body blanketing hers as his climax was wrenched out of him. Luke buried his face in her hair, shuddering out his pleasure.

She loved him.

What the hell was he supposed to do with that?

Luke tossed the environmental impact report for a proposed new industrial park down in disgust and shoved his chair back from the desk. He'd been staring at the damned paperwork for twenty minutes and hadn't made it past the first paragraph. He was well-known for his ability to concentrate under less than ideal conditions—crowded airports, construction sites, the back of a limo in rush-hour traffic—he could work through any distraction. Or so he'd thought.

He stood in front of the big picture window and looked out over the Los Angeles basin. Smog gave everything a hazy look. From the foothills to the north, looking down on the city, he would be able to see a brown layer of crud, but closer up, the smog simply gave everything an out-of-focus look. It was almost romantic, like vaseline smeared on a camera lens to hide the reality and wrinkles of an aging star.

Luke shoved his hands into his pockets and focused his gaze on a faint glint in the distance that might or might not be the Pacific. He really had to get a handle on this...problem. The last couple of weeks, his attention span had been roughly that of a two-year-old. He'd faded out in the middle of a meeting with a very wealthy gentleman from Belgium who seemed to think that owning a large piece of Los Angeles real estate would be a good thing. Luckily the ever-efficient Ms. Sinclair had covered for him with a skill that was going to substantially increase her year-end bonus, but he couldn't count on his assistant to pick up the slack every time his brain went on vacation.

He just had to deal with the...situation.

Luke nearly rolled his eyes at the thought. *The situation. Don't be a wuss, Quintain. What you have to deal with is the idea that your wife—your* temporary *wife—might be in love with you.*

Even articulating the thought made him uneasy. For two weeks he'd been trying to stuff the idea back down, out of sight, and for two weeks it had been popping up at unexpected moments, derailing his concentration. So maybe if he acknowledged it, thought about it, maybe he would be able to dismiss it and get on with his life.

Was Cat in love with him? It would explain why she'd married him when she didn't seem to care much about money and the things it could buy. Except that was crazy, because they'd barely known each other when she'd offered to marry him. She couldn't have been in love with him then—unless you believed in love at first sight, which he didn't. He barely believed in love at tenth or twelfth sight. But just because he didn't believe in it, that didn't mean Cat didn't.

Restless, Luke turned away from the window. Love wasn't part of their bargain, dammit. He didn't want her to love him any more than he wanted to be in love with her. And maybe she wasn't in love with him. Maybe he'd imagined what he thought he saw in her eyes the night of her birthday. Maybe he was imagining the things he'd seen since then, the caring, the softness in her eyes, the confusion when he pulled back—and he'd been pulling back a lot lately. He couldn't help it. The thought that she loved him scared the hell out of him. He liked her, didn't want to see her hurt. He especially didn't want to be the one to hurt her.

"It was supposed to be a business deal," he muttered, glaring at the fish swimming lethargically across his monitor.

Even if she wasn't in love with him, even if that was just his imagination running amok, he'd realized that they were building connections between themselves, ties that would be hard to break. Invitations now automatically included the two of them; people who'd met Cat asked about his wife.

Somehow, when he hadn't been looking, they'd become a couple. It had been stupid of him not to see that coming. Even his parents, as dysfunctional a pair as he'd ever seen, had, in their own peculiar way, been a couple. They'd gone places together, been a unit.

If he hadn't been so hell-bent on thumbing his nose at his grandfather, he would have thought things through a little better, figured out that you didn't exchange vows with someone, slide a ring on her finger, live with her, *sleep* with her for God's sake—share your life with her for a year, and then walk away without leaving a few scars on both sides.

When Cat had suggested that he could marry her in Devon's place, he'd pretty much turned off his brain and let his zipper do all the thinking. He'd wanted her, wanted her badly enough to ignore the little voice that had suggested there was more to this than he knew. He should have turned her down when he found out how old she was—or rather, how old she *wasn't*. Not that her age was really the problem. Chronologically she might be fifteen years younger than he was, but he had an uneasy feeling that she was older than he was in every way that mattered. And there'd been that whole business with her complaining about the settlement being too large. Why the hell hadn't *that* set off alarm bells? Because he hadn't wanted it to. He hadn't wanted there to be any reason why he shouldn't marry her.

Halfway back to the window, Luke stopped. Maybe he was looking at this the wrong way. Say Cat *was* in love with him. Did that really make any difference to anything? If she'd somehow gotten it into her head that she loved him—or thought she did—it wasn't really his problem, was it? In fact, since she hadn't said anything about it, it wasn't really even his business.

God, that sounds cold, he thought, frowning out the window. But he didn't mean it that way. Still, he didn't have to take on some huge load of guilt for whatever she might feel for him. He wasn't responsible for her emotions, which sounded so much like New Age psychobabble that it made him wince.

Yet it was more or less true. If he asked Cat if she was in love with him—and he would rather have a root canal without Novocain—and she said yes, what the hell was he supposed to do? Bringing it out in the open would only make them both feel uncomfortable. If she said no, then he was going to feel like an egomaniacal jerk, and either way it was going to make things awkward between them. Better to just ignore it, push it out of his mind. He was probably imagining things, anyway.

Feeling vaguely dissatisfied but unable to think of a better plan of action, Luke pulled out his desk chair and sat down again, but he didn't immediately reach for the neglected paperwork. She couldn't be in love with him. He didn't *want* her to be in love with him. He felt a sharp twinge of anger. Love wasn't part of their bargain, dammit.

The quiet buzz of the intercom was a welcome distraction. He hit the button, half-hoping there was some disaster in the offing—something to take his mind off the soap opera his life was threatening to become.

"Ms. Kowalski is here, Mr. Quintain."

Kowalski? Luke stared at the intercom, mind blank as he tried to place the name. It only took a moment. Devon? Devon was here in Los Angeles, not milking cows in Minnesota or Michigan or wherever? Well, wasn't life just full of surprises?

Luke glanced at his watch. He had an appointment, but not for another hour. The environmental impact report had waited this long. It could wait another few hours.

"Send her in, Ms. Sinclair."

He barely had time to stand up and move out from behind the desk before the door was pushed open and Devon floated in on a cloud of Chanel. She was wearing pale gray linen slacks and a powder-blue silk blouse that made the most of her eyes. She'd cut her hair, and the pale gold cap of soft curls suited her, giving her a rounded features a winsome appeal.

"Luke." She put a wealth of feeling into the single word, her pretty blue eyes filling up with pretty tears as she held out her beautifully manicured hands. "It's *so* good to see you."

"Devon." It was obvious that she expected him to take her hands, so he obliged, thinking that they felt small and insubstantial compared to Cat's. He squeezed her hands and then released them. Had she always been so...little? He could already feel a crick forming in his neck as he looked down at her. "I thought you were happily married and living in Michigan."

"Minnesota, it was *not* happy, and I am thankful to say I am *not* married anymore."

"Divorced?" Luke asked. She looked so slight. It was

hard to believe he'd made love to her without crushing her.

"Yes, thank heavens." Devon shuddered, her eyes filling with tears again. He wondered how she did that—let her eyes fill with tears and then got them to go away again without any spilling over. "Oh, Luke, I made such a *huge* mistake. I don't know what I was *thinking*. I just…I guess I got caught up in the fantasy of my first love coming back to me, but it was *ridiculous* to think we could go back. I mean, he had *cows,* for God's sake."

"Dairy farmers usually do," Luke murmured. Had she always spoken in italics?

"The *worst* thing is that I let you down." Devon put her hand on his sleeve and looked up at him with an earnest expression. "I just *hate* myself for leaving you in the *lurch* like that."

"That's okay. Everything worked out all right."

"So I *heard,*" Devon said and something hard and angry flashed in her eyes. "You married *Cat?*" She gave a tinkling, insincere little laugh. "Honestly, Luke, *what* were you *thinking?*"

He didn't really think she would appreciate hearing that he'd been thinking how much he wanted to get her stepsister into bed, so he settled for a noncommittal smile.

"Why don't we sit down and you can tell me what you're doing back in L.A."

Always willing to talk about herself, Devon let him settle her on the big sofa, accepted the glass of white wine he poured her and rattled on happily about her plans for picking up her decorating business again. Luke nursed a half glass of wine and wondered if he would be breaking any important rules of etiquette if he sent the dairy farmer a thank-you gift for preventing him from making the biggest mistake of his life.

Chapter Fourteen

Cat was lying on the sofa in the living room when she heard the doorbell ring. She groaned a protest but sat up. Merry and Consuela were both gone for the day. Luke wasn't home yet, and she was constitutionally incapable of ignoring doorbells and phones.

She was going to have to work on her constitution, she thought a minute later when she peered through the peephole. Devon. It had to be an hallucination brought on by lack of sleep and the nausea that had had her lying down in the first place. In fact maybe she was still lying down and she was dreaming this. Because Devon was in Michigan or Minnesota or one of those other multisyllable states in the middle of the country. But the tile floor felt convincingly cold under her bare feet, and her stomach did a nasty little roll that felt very real.

Cat was tempted to pretend no one was home, but that would be childish. With a wistful thought that children had all the fun, she drew a deep breath and pulled open the door.

* * *

Half an hour later, Cat was nursing a headache, a glass of iced tea and a profound wish that she hadn't let good manners override her better judgment. She was also both sympathetic to and deeply envious of Rick, Devon's former true love and now her former husband. Picking through the italics and exclamation points of Devon's conversation, it was apparent that Rick had expected her to actually contribute something besides her charming presence to their life together. Devon's vision of her life hadn't included housework, cooking, living more than ten miles from a mall, winter temperatures below sixty degrees or a husband who had anything to occupy his time besides making sure she was happy, and it certainly hadn't included having anything to do with large smelly animals.

Cat couldn't help but pity Rick for the disappointment he must have felt when it became obvious that Devon was ill suited to her new life, but she also envied him, because he was, after all, a couple thousand miles away, while she was trapped here, listening to Devon.

She was only half tuned in to what Devon was saying, so she nearly missed the abrupt change of topic.

"So…you and Luke?" Devon's voice was arch to match her neatly plucked brows. "You could have just knocked me over with a *feather* when I found out the two of you were *married.*"

"I wrote and told you myself," Cat reminded her.

"Of *course* you did." Devon looked at her tea glass, pulling her pretty features into a pensive expression. "You know, I think *that* was the beginning of the end of my marriage, really."

Cat knew she didn't want to hear where this was going, but, short of gagging the other woman, there was no way to stop her. Barely restraining a sigh, she settled back against the soft leather of her chair. Devon was sitting on the sofa. Late-afternoon sunshine filtered through the branches of the huge live oak that sheltered the west side of the house and spilled through the bank of windows into the living room.

Cat had read once that sunlight was the most merciless light, showing up any flaw. But if Devon had a flaw, she couldn't find it. Her peaches-and-cream skin looked like…well, peaches and cream. She'd not only cut her hair but she'd gone a couple of shades lighter with the color, so that it teetered just short of platinum. On most women it would have looked cheap and hard. On Devon it just emphasized the fragile, dainty, incredibly annoying petiteness of her.

That familiar sense of being tall and gangly crept over her. She fought the urge to pat her hair, as if a hand pat could somehow transform it from tumbled to sleek. She'd spent the morning working in the garden, and she'd showered and changed when she got home. Now the peach-colored shorts and T-shirt she'd put on after her shower seemed too short, too tight, too obvious. She hadn't bothered with makeup, and she knew Devon could probably count every one of the freckles the summer sun had sprinkled across her nose.

It had been a very long day even before Devon showed up. This morning she'd discovered the limp remains of half a dozen summer squash plants that had succumbed to squash vine borers overnight. Bobby Kincaid, the neighbor's sixteen-year-old son, who was usually a reliable source of labor, had, in a moment of testosterone-driven madness—and strictly against her orders—tried to run a stack of Mexican fan palm fronds through her birthday shredder. It had taken her almost two hours to take the shredder apart and peel the fibrous mass off the blades. The thermometer was hovering in the mid-nineties, and people could chirp all they wanted about it being a *dry* heat, but ninety-five degrees was damned hot, no matter how dry it was.

Having Devon sitting on her sofa, looking perfect, with not a single bleached-blond hair out of place and her whole I'm-petite-and-pretty shtick just oozing out of her, was just the icing on the cake. It reminded her that this was the sort of woman Luke had dated. He might not have been in love with Devon, but he'd dated her, slept with her, and not because some fake marriage thing had thrown her into his bed.

It was probably ridiculous to worry about it, but she was just so damned tired. She'd been tired for days now. It was starting to worry her, but not as much as the sense that Luke was pulling back, trying to put some distance between them. It could be her imagination, but she didn't think so. And now, here was Devon, parked on the sofa and looking just too, too beautiful.

Some days, life just sucked.

It took a conscious effort to focus on what Devon was saying.

"When I read your note saying that you and Luke had gotten *married,* I felt the bottom just *drop* out of my stomach. It was a real *epiphany,* and I knew, I just *knew,* that I'd made a terrible mistake. But of course I was married to Rick, and I *had* to try to make things work."

"So you tried for six whole months?" Cat couldn't resist saying, but sarcasm was wasted on Devon.

"Yes, and I can't *tell* you how hard it was. I mean, I already *knew* it was *never* going to work out, so I was just *wasting* my time."

Cat thought of pointing out that she'd been wasting Rick's time, too, but doubted it would have any impact.

Trying to get Devon to think of someone else's point of view would probably only confuse her.

"It's not like Luke and I were in *love,* of course." Devon's mouth curved in a smile that managed to look both wistful and secretive. It was an interesting trick, and Cat wished it didn't make her stomach knot. "You of *all* people *know* why we were getting married."

"He needed to meet his grandfather's terms, and you wanted his money."

Devon looked momentarily pained by this blunt summation, but she moved gamely past it. "That's the *basic* reason but...well, with a man like Luke, it's never going to be the *only* reason. I'm sure *you* understand that." She gave a tinkling little laugh and threw Cat a knowing look. "I mean, you've been *married* to him for, what? Four or five months now?"

"Seven and a half," Cat murmured. Which left her with four and a half months to convince Luke that he couldn't live without her.

"I was just so *surprised* that Luke married *you.* I mean, you're *hardly* his type." Devon laughed again, inviting Cat to share the joke. "No offense intended, Cat, but I mean, *you?* And *Luke?*" She hardly seemed able to contain her mirth at the very idea. "Don't think I *blame* you or anything."

Don't think I care *or anything,* Cat barely resisted saying.

"He is *filthy* rich, after all, and well, I know I don't have to tell *you* that *no* woman is going to marry Luke *just* for his money. I stopped to see him before coming here. *Not* because I was trying to stir up old *feelings* or anything," she said with another of those tinkling little laughs that grated on Cat's nerves like fingernails on a chalkboard.

Or maybe it was the idea of Devon going to see Luke that grated on her. Not that she was jealous. That would be stupid. Because she knew Luke didn't have any romantic feelings for Devon. If she was sure of anything, she was sure of that. Practically.

"I just thought we should clear the air. We *are* family, after all. In-laws." Devon laughed again, and Cat allowed herself to fantasize about stuffing her stepsister's perky blond head up the chimney. "It was so *good* to see him. Not to be indelicate or anything, but he really is quite... *magnificent,* isn't he?"

Cat looked at her, sitting there like a bleached-blond cat contemplating a particularly fat and juicy canary. Well, the canary in question was already spoken for, at least for the next four and a half months.

"You mean, isn't he magnificent in bed?" She said it casually, enjoying the way Devon's eyes widened in surprise. "Well, I think so." Cat allowed herself a little laugh, pleased when it came out sounding throaty rather than choked. "Of course, my experience isn't *nearly* as...extensive as yours." She gave her stepsister a friendly smile. "I guess that's one disadvantage of being *so* much younger. I just haven't had time to accumulate all *your* experience."

Naomi would say she'd just put a big old dent in her karmic wheel, but Cat thought a little wobbling in the afterlife might be worth it for the sheer pleasure of watching Devon's expression. It was obvious that she was trying to decide on the appropriate response. She started to frown, hesitated, thought about smiling, then frowned a little more as she attempted to parse the sentence. Had she just been insulted? Had Cat suggested that she slept around, or that she was old, or both? But Cat was smiling, so maybe it was a compliment? Maybe she should say thank-you?

"Mmm. Yes. *Of course,* I…" Devon stopped, cleared her throat and gave Cat a very bright and completely insincere smile. "Do you think I could get another glass of iced tea? The weather is just so *hot* today. Of course, it is a *dry* heat, so it's not nearly as bad. You wouldn't *believe* the weather in Minnesota."

Cat tuned out the words as Devon followed her out to the kitchen.

A psychiatrist could probably write a book analyzing the dynamics going on at this table, Keith thought, looking at his companions. Five people, at least four of them faking having a good time. He wasn't sure about his own date. Maureen might be genuinely enjoying herself, which said less about him as a date than it did about her ignorance of the undercurrents going on at the table.

Luke was pretending to be interested in what Devon was saying. Cat was pretending she didn't mind that Luke was pretending to be interested in what her stepsister was saying. Devon was pretending that she *wasn't* practically throwing herself at Luke, but, if she got any closer to him, she was going to be in his lap. As for himself, he was pretending that he was actually interested in his date, that he wasn't wondering what the hell was going on between Luke and Cat and Devon. And he was pretending really, really hard that he didn't have one eye on the door to the kitchen, wondering if Jack was going to come out and say hello.

Come to think of it, what they had was a soap opera writer's fantasy. All it needed was for someone to turn out to be someone else's long lost child or sibling, and maybe a touch of amnesia, demonic possession and a snappy theme song, and they would be the hit of day-time TV.

"I've heard nothing but good things about the food here," Maureen said, looking around the restaurant.

On a Friday night, the tables at Jack's Place were all filled. The waitstaff wove their way among them with unobtrusive efficiency. The low-level hum of conversation was punctuated by the discreet clatter of silverware on china. The clientele was eclectic—locals wearing the Southern California casual version of dress-up, tourists dressed in their best designer knockoffs, the star of a popular action show, wearing diamonds, about three pounds of gold chains and combat fatigues to match the Humvee currently intimidating lesser cars in the parking lot.

"Jack's Place is supposed to be one of the hottest restaurants in L.A.," Maureen added.

"Jack has worked really hard to put it on the map," Cat said, and Keith wondered if he was the only one who noticed that her smile was strained.

"I've heard he's very young," Maureen commented.

"Well, that all depends on your perspective," Devon said. "He's in his mid-twenties, which probably seems quite old to you, Cat, but rather young to the rest of us."

She threw a laughing look in Luke's direction. His lips twitched, but only a real optimist would have called it a smile. Keith thought it was a measure of Devon's determination to build ties with Luke that she was willing to play the age card.

"Yeah, Jack's four years older than I am," Cat said dryly. "Practically old enough to be my grandfather in some cultures."

Maureen laughed, Devon looked confused, and Luke looked as if he wanted to be somewhere else—anywhere else. Cat glanced at him and then looked away. Her care-

fully controlled expression revealed a great deal to someone who knew her. Keith wondered what was going on
with his best friend, not to mention his best friend's marriage.

He hadn't seen much of the two of them since Cat's
birthday party last month. He'd been busy with work, and
he'd been picking up the threads of his neglected social
life. This was his first date with Maureen, who worked
for a law firm on the floor below his, but last week he'd
gone out with Penny, who had turned out to be even more
painfully perky on a date than she was at the health club
where they'd met. The week before that had been a double
header—two different women, neither of whom he remembered with any clarity.

He'd also started running again, dragging himself out
of bed at six o'clock in the morning and pounding the
pavement for forty-five minutes before staggering back to
his condo to collapse in a heap of aching feet and twitching muscles. Twice a week he hit the gym, which was
where he'd met perky Penny. He was getting buns of
steel, iron abs and biceps like rock, and he was fairly sure
he'd permanently restructured his spinal column. A couple
more months like this and he was going to end up either
in terrific shape or crippled for life.

He hadn't had time to think about his own life, let alone
worry about what was going on in his friend's marriage.
And hadn't that been the point? he asked himself. No time
to think, no time to think about anything, especially not
about—

"Jack!" Cat's voice held real enthusiasm for the first
time. "Aren't you afraid the kitchen will collapse without
you there to keep things going?"

"I figure the troops can manage without me for ten
minutes." He reached out to tug one copper red curl that

had escaped the soft knot that confined her hair. "Try the fresh tomato linguine. Those Brandywines you brought in this afternoon are incredible."

"Of course they are. I wouldn't waste my time growing anything but incredible tomatoes." Cat gave him a bright smile, and Keith noticed Luke watching her, his expression unreadable. "You remember my stepsister, Devon," Cat said, her smile tightening a little.

"Sure." Jack gave Devon a friendly nod, but his eyes were cool, watchful. "Is your husband visiting L.A. with you?"

"No husband." Devon's laugh was tight and a little shrill. "Just me. I've moved back to L.A. all by myself."

"And this is Maureen," Cat said quickly, covering up the awkward pause. "Keith's...friend."

She seemed to stumble a bit over the introduction, but Keith wasn't really paying much attention. Jack was smiling at Maureen, accepting her compliments on the appetizer, every inch the friendly host. Over her head, his eyes met Keith's. His smile twisted slightly, and his eyes held a wry acceptance. Keith suddenly felt about an inch high. He'd been avoiding Jack, like he expected Jack to...to what? Suddenly jump his bones? God, wasn't that the classic heterosexual male reaction? The conviction that every gay man was secretly lusting after him?

"You missed a great game last week," Jack said. "The Lakers were really on a roll. It's too bad you couldn't go."

"Yeah." Keith nodded, trying to look as if he hadn't lied about having other plans and then spent the evening sweating over a hot Nautilus machine.

Jack looked away, his smile widening to include the others. "You guys do know that it's house policy that friends pay double, right?"

He lingered a few more minutes before moving away to talk to other diners. "Gotta keep up my celebrity chef image," he said, laughing.

Keith reached for his wine and wondered when he'd become so uptight. So damned hypocritical. He experienced a momentary sexual identity crisis and started avoiding a friend? Whatever he felt—and he wasn't ready to admit he felt anything—Jack would never have pushed for more. He'd missed Jack, dammit. They'd had fun together, laughed, argued, talked. He missed that. He even missed the damned basketball games.

No matter how he looked at it, he couldn't escape the conviction that he'd acted like an idiot.

"So what's going on?" Jack asked, pushing the door shut behind him and leaning back against it.

Cat jumped and turned away from the mirror. "Jack! This is the ladies' room, for God's sake. Get out of here before someone comes in and sues you for sexual harassment or invasion of privacy or something."

"No one can come in without mowing me down, and it's my restaurant. I'll show up any damned place I please. Now, tell me why your cozy table for two ended up being a table for five, one of whom is the wicked stepsister. I thought she was safely tucked away somewhere in the middle of the country, milking cows and scaring the natives."

Cat's smile was strained. "She just got back last week. Apparently life on a dairy farm wasn't as glamour-filled as she'd expected. She's moved back in with Larry and Susan, and is planning on getting her decorating business going again."

"That doesn't explain why she's here tonight. When you asked if I'd hold a table for you, you said you wanted a table for two.'' Jack crossed his arms over his chest and gave her a stern look. ''You didn't ask her along because you felt sorry for her, did you? Because I've got to tell you, the only thing feeling sorry for someone like that is going to get you is a kick in the teeth.''

Cat's fingers tightened on the soft leather of her small purse. ''Actually it was Luke's idea to invite her. Apparently he's hired her to do some work for him.'' She glanced up, saw Jack's look of surprise and looked away again, struggling to sound casual about the whole thing. ''He just bought an apartment complex that needs some spiffing up, I guess.''

''And he hired *Devon?*'' Jack asked.

''She's really a very good decorator,'' Cat offered weakly.

''Yeah, I bet Hannibal Lector could work wonders with fava beans, but I wouldn't hire him to cook dinner for me.''

Cat leaned back against the sink, feeling the tension drain away with her laughter. ''Devon's not into cannibalism.''

''Don't kid yourself,'' Jack said darkly. ''Women like that will eat their own young if it gets them what they want. What the hell was Quintain thinking?''

Cat shrugged and looked away. She wasn't sure she wanted to know what Luke had been thinking when he hired Devon. Worse, she was afraid she *did* know. She *knew* Luke wasn't emotionally attached to Devon, but that didn't mean he wasn't attracted to her. He'd wanted her before. Why wouldn't he want her now? She was pretty in that delicate, helpless blonde way that a lot of men seemed to like. Luke had obviously liked it enough to take her to bed. Cat was not unaware of her own attractiveness, but five minutes in her stepsister's company and she started to feel like an understudy for *Attack of the Fifty Foot Woman*. What had she been thinking of to put on heels? And what had made her think that the soft calf-length floral skirt and butter-yellow top looked pretty and summery? Devon's pink Capri pants and matching crop top worn with a white eyelet jacket were just so...so damned petite.

"I'm sorry about Keith bringing a date," she said, changing the subject. "When Luke suggested that Devon come along, I just couldn't face an entire evening as a threesome, so I called Keith and asked him to come along. When he said he had a date, I just didn't think."

Jack shrugged. "No big deal. It's not like we were dating. Hell, we haven't gotten together at all in almost a month. Maybe the novelty wore off." He caught the question in her eyes and smiled bitterly. "Being friends with a queer. Not many straight guys can handle that."

Cat shook her head. "I don't think Keith's like that."

"Maybe not." Jack shrugged again. "Hell, it's my own fault for living out the Hollywood cliché. I mean, gay guy falls in love with straight friend?" He rolled his eyes. "Please. Can you get any more predictable?" He uncrossed his arms and pointed at her. "And don't think you can distract me from the real reason we're locked in the ladies' room like something out of a bad independent film. What's going on with you and Quintain? And don't tell me 'nothing,'" he said, smiling grimly when Cat shut her mouth with an audible click.

"It's...complicated," Cat said, and then had to swallow an hysterical laugh. God, if that wasn't the understatement of the century. "Complicated" didn't even begin to cover it.

"Complicated how?" Jack asked, looking like he was willing to spend the rest of the night grilling her to get an answer. A knock on the door saved Cat from having to test her willpower.

"Jack?" The voice sounded tentative, a little uneasy. "Um...the kitchen is...really busy. Gail says we could really...um...we need you to...if you could..."

"I'll be right there," Jack said, and Cat could almost hear the sigh of relief from the other side of the door.

"What Gail probably said was that I should get my ass back to work." He scowled. "Sometimes, I think she forgets just who owns this place."

"She is your assistant and I suspect what she remembers is that you couldn't run this place without her," Cat reminded him.

"It may have been a mistake to tell her that," he muttered, as he straightened away from the door. He looked at Cat. "I don't care how complicated it is. If you need to talk to someone, you know I'm ready to listen."

Cat's throat immediately closed up and her eyes stung with emotion, but she managed to smile and nod. "Thanks. I do know that, but I'm okay. Really."

Jack looked unconvinced, but, to her relief, he nodded. She gave a shaky sigh of relief as the door closed behind him. Turning, she braced her hands on the edge of the sink. The woman in the mirror didn't look any more convinced than Jack had, which was kind of depressing. If she couldn't even talk herself into believing she was okay, who else was going to buy it?

Still, she couldn't hide here all night. Taking a deep breath, she straightened her shoulders and pushed open the door.

When Cat heard the bathroom door open behind her, she was too busy throwing her guts up to do more than moan, and even that was lost in a renewed bout of retching. She'd thought Luke was gone for the day. Bad as it was to start the morning off by tossing her cookies, she'd at least thought she could toss them in private. When she finished, she heard water running, and a moment later, Luke was crouched next to her.

"You done?" he asked, and for some stupid reason the matter-of-fact tone made her eyes sting. She blinked back tears and nodded.

"I think so." Her voice sounded raspy. Her throat felt raw, and her stomach was still twitchy, but she couldn't help but feel warmed by the concern in Luke's eyes, so different from his voice. It made her realize how long it had been since he really looked at her.

He helped her up and handed her a glass of water, waiting while she rinsed out her mouth. She felt parched and longed to gulp the whole glass down, but she didn't think her stomach would appreciate that. Instead she settled for a few tiny sips, letting the cool water trickle down her throat, grateful when her stomach didn't immediately rebel. Luke handed her a damp cloth, and she set the glass down on the counter, careful not to meet his eyes as she took the cloth from him.

"You're not coming down with the flu again, are you?"

That struck her as wildly funny. Her laugh was ragged and maybe just a little hysterical. This wasn't the way she'd planned to tell him. She'd planned soft lighting, a good meal, pleasant conversation and then gradually leading up to it. That plan had gone out the window when he invited Devon to join them for dinner last night, but maybe this was better. Maybe she'd just been fooling herself to think that there was a way to lead up to it, a way to wrap it all up in pretty ribbon.

"I guess you could say that, only instead of the forty-eight-hour flu, I've got the nine-month version."

Luke stared at her blankly, and she gave him a twisted little smile, her fingers knotting in the damp washcloth.

"I'm pregnant."

Chapter Fifteen

In the three days since she'd watched that little white stick change colors, Cat had pictured this moment at least fifty times. She'd imagined Luke angry—this hadn't been in the plan, after all. She'd pictured him denying the possibility, insisting the test was wrong. She'd imagined him simply passing out from the shock, and she'd indulged in a few wistful fantasies where the news that she was carrying his child had caused the blinding realization that he loved her more than life itself.

What she hadn't pictured was the way his expression iced over, eyes suddenly a pale, Arctic blue.

"If you think this is going to get you a bigger settlement, you can think again."

It was like taking a blow to the body. The impact went directly to her heart and Cat thought she actually stopped breathing for a moment. When she finally dragged in a breath, it burned her throat, as if the harsh words had actually left a taint in the air.

"What?" As responses went, it wasn't exactly original,

but the single word was all she could manage to force out.

"You heard me." Luke's upper lip curled. "Check the prenup. There's a clause in there that deals with this possibility. How stupid do you think I am?"

"Pretty damned stupid, apparently." The washcloth hit the sink with a muffled splat. Cat had a momentary wish that she could do the same with his head. Suddenly claustrophobic, she walked past him and into the bedroom. The drapes were still drawn, and she stalked over to the window to wrench them open. Sunshine spilled into the room. Talk about a situation that needed all the light it could get.

She turned to look at Luke, who had followed her out of the bathroom and was now standing in the middle of the bedroom floor, feet braced slightly apart, hands loose at his sides. A fighter's stance, she realized, and allowed herself a moment's fantasy of taking a swing at him. Let him bob and weave his way out of a solid punch to the jaw, she thought bitterly.

But that wasn't the way to go. Cat forced herself to take a deep, calming breath. Good as it would feel to pummel some sense into his thick skull, violence wasn't the answer. Not yet, anyway.

"You can't seriously think that I'd..." She had to stop and take another breath, striving for a calm center. "Do you honestly think I did this deliberately?"

"I don't know. Did you?" He was looking at her with the same cool speculation he might have given a business rival, weighing strengths and weaknesses, calculating motives.

"No, I didn't." Cat shoved her hair back from her face, wishing she'd had a chance to brush it, wishing she was wearing something besides a bright green sleep shirt, wishing she hadn't just spent the last ten minutes throwing up. It was hard to feel calm and in control when she looked like something the cat dragged in and felt even worse, but one of them had to stay rational, and it obviously wasn't going to be Luke. "You have to know that I would *never* do something like this deliberately. It was…when I realized I was…what had happened, I did some research online, and I think it probably happened because of the flu."

"Pregnancy as a virus?" Luke arched his brows, his mouth twisting in a nasty little smile. "It's an interesting theory, Cat, but I doubt it has AMA approval."

"Don't be an ass," she snapped. "I couldn't keep anything down for three days, including birth control pills. I didn't think about it while I was busy puking my guts up, but from what I've read, that was probably enough to throw my system off and make it possible for me to conceive. If you'd stop and think instead of acting like the wronged husband in a bad melodrama, you'd realize that I'd never do something like this deliberately."

Luke looked away from her, focusing on a thin crack in the wall above the windows. One of the hazards of living in earthquake country, those little stress fractures showing up, like some sort of cosmic nudge to remember that nothing was as solid as it seemed.

Pregnant. The word slid in under his guard, refusing to be ignored. Cat was carrying his baby. The thought just didn't compute. There was a mistake. The wrong rabbit had died, or the stick had changed colors when it shouldn't have. This wasn't part of the plan, had never been part of any plan. He'd decided a long time ago that he wasn't father material.

You decided you weren't husband material, either.

But that was different, dammit. The marriage was temporary, no matter how it felt sometimes. Kids were…hell, kids were forever, the ultimate in long-term commitment. The thought made him break out in a cold sweat.

"Luke, I know you're upset." Cat's voice was softer, almost pleading. "This isn't what either of us was planning, but now that it's happened, we need to deal with it."

"Do you plan on keeping it?" he asked abruptly, and she seemed to freeze for a moment.

"Are you asking if I've considered abortion?"

Luke nodded. It sounded painfully blunt when she said it, but it had to be considered.

"I thought about it." Cat shook her head slowly. "That's not what I want. I didn't plan this. I swear to you I didn't, but now that it's happened, I want this baby." She pressed one hand against her stomach, her expression gentling, warming. "It's already real to me."

Luke looked away. He didn't want it to be real. Didn't want any of it to be real. If he hadn't forgotten his briefcase, he would be at the office by now, blissfully ignorant of his impending fatherhood.

There was a waiting quality to the silence, but he didn't know what he was supposed to say. That he was happy about this? That he thought this was just great? That this changed everything, and now they were going to be one big happy family forever and ever? Well, life didn't work that way. There was no such thing as happily-ever-after.

"Luke?"

He looked at her. "I don't know what you want me to say," he said, and she closed her eyes. When she opened them again, he couldn't read her expression.

"Say you believe I didn't do this deliberately," she said quietly. "Tell me you know I wouldn't do that."

Luke hesitated and then nodded slowly. "I believe you."

"Thank you."

Silence stretched between them, thick and clumsy, until finally Cat looked at him, her eyes carefully empty of emotion.

"Didn't you have an appointment this morning?"

He didn't, but he nodded, glanced at his watch without seeing it and nodded again. "I should get going."

There were things he should say, things they needed to talk about, but the walls were suddenly closing in on him. It was hard to breathe, difficult to think. Without looking at her again, he turned and left.

Using a strip of cloth torn from an old T-shirt, Cat carefully tied a tomato branch to the wooden lattice that supported the plant. The distinctive sharp scent from the bruised leaves hung in the warm air. It was a smell she associated with summer, with green, growing things and the sweet-acid taste of a tomato pulled, sun-ripened and heavy, from the vine.

It was not yet midmorning, but the temperature was already creeping past eighty degrees. The weather reports were promising triple-digit temperatures in the valleys. The heat wave was in its fourth day, and her main job in the garden was careful watering and making sure there was plenty of mulch on the ground to keep the roots as cool as possible.

Sighing, she straightened and reached up to tug off the ratty straw hat she wore as protection against the sun. Sweat beaded on her forehead, and she wiped it away with the back of her wrist, leaving a streak of dirt above one eyebrow. She'd come out to the garden early, so she could work before the heat became unbearable, but *unbearable* was a relative term. It was already too warm, but it wasn't as bad as it would be later in the day.

Besides, it got her out of the house, away from Luke. Not that there was any need to work at avoiding Luke. He wasn't exactly seeking her out these days. Funny how her pregnancy had suddenly made him need to spend more time at the office. Her mouth twisted with bitter humor. It had been a week since she'd told him about the baby, and they hadn't exchanged any conversation more meaningful than ''Good morning'' and ''I'll be working late tonight.''

She kept thinking there were things that should be said, things they needed to talk about, but maybe not. Luke had made it clear that a baby wasn't in his plans, and it didn't look like he was interested in changing those plans. She wavered between thinking she shouldn't blame him for feeling the way he did and wanting to smack him with the nearest blunt object. This hadn't exactly been in *her* game plan, either, but she couldn't just close her eyes and pretend it wasn't happening.

She was waiting for Luke to say something, to ask what her plans were, to offer to help with the baby or to tell her that he wanted nothing to do with it. Did he plan on them spending the next four months in a state of semi-armed neutrality, then just ending their marriage with a quiet divorce? She would take her unborn child and go one way, and he would take his vineyard and go another?

Cat wasn't sure whether to blame the fact that her eyes were stinging on too much sunlight or an excess of hormones. She blinked rapidly to clear her vision and then wished she hadn't. Devon was coming down the back steps. Cat barely restrained an urge to drop to her hands and knees and scuttle behind a tomato plant. She didn't know if it had been blind luck or if Devon was no more

anxious to see her than she was to see Devon, but their
paths hadn't crossed since Devon moved back in with
Larry and Susan.

Apparently her luck had run out.

"Hi." Devon gave her a cheery wave as she crossed
the narrow strip of lawn. She was wearing a sleeveless
linen dress in a soft blue that made the most of her eyes.
Her legs were bare and lightly tanned, just enough to keep
her skin from looking like the underbelly of a fish. She
had on off-white sandals, and her toenails were painted a
pretty pale pink. Her light blond hair was artfully tousled,
and her makeup was perfect. She looked like something
out of a magazine article on how to look crisp and lovely
in the summer heat.

Cat thought about hating her, but it was too hot to expend the effort. Besides, what was the point? Her own
shorts, faded green camp shirt and battered leather sandals
put her so far out of Devon's league that it wasn't even
worth thinking about. Her hair was bundled up in a careless knot, and a quick coat of lip balm was the closest
thing to makeup her face had seen today. Jealousy would
be laughable.

"Can you *believe* this heat?" Devon stopped at the
edge of the redwood mulch Cat had spread between the
vegetable beds and fanned one hand in front of her face.

"It is warm," Cat agreed.

"I don't know how you can *stand* working outside in
this heat."

"Actually I was just about to call it quits." She waited
for Devon to tell her what she wanted. She couldn't imagine the other woman had sought her out just to comment
on the weather.

"You know a woman in *your* condition has to be extra
careful."

Cat had leaned over to pick up a bucket of weeds and plant trimmings for the compost pile, but, at Devon's comment, she straightened slowly, the bucket dangling loosely from her hand.

"My condition?"

"You know." Devon lowered her voice as if eavesdroppers might be lurking behind the chard. "The *baby*. Luke told me all about it."

Cat tightened her grip on the bucket handle until her knuckles ached. "Did he?" She thought she did a good job of keeping her voice neutral, but maybe not.

"Oh!" Devon pressed fingertips to her mouth, her blue eyes wide with distress. "Wasn't I supposed to know? Luke didn't say it was a *secret,* and I didn't think you'd mind if *I* knew. I mean we *are* family, more or less."

"More or less," Cat murmured. Luke had talked to Devon about the baby? He hadn't said a word to her about it, but he could talk to *Devon* about it?

"*Don't* be upset with him for talking to me, Cat. I dropped by the office this morning, and I could see that something was bothering him. I think he just needed *someone* to talk to. After all, this is hardly what he was *expecting.*" She reached out as if to put a consoling hand on Cat's forearm, saw the streaks of dirt there and drew her hand back without making contact.

"I'm not upset," Cat assured her. She might be ballistic once she'd had a chance to think about it, but she wasn't upset. Not yet, anyway.

"Good." Devon looked relieved; then she frowned a little, though not enough to invite wrinkles. "You know, Cat, if you thought that getting *pregnant* would be a good way to hold on to Luke, you just *don't* know him very well. I mean, *I* could have told you that would *never* work with him. You'll never trap a man like Luke *that* way."

"Really? Well, if I ever decide to try to trap him, I'll be sure to consult you first."

"You *are* upset." Devon's teeth worried her lower lip in a pretty display of concern. Cat wondered how she would look with a bucket of weeds and overripe tomatoes dumped over her head.

Or maybe she would save that treat for Luke.

Luke had spent most of the afternoon crawling around the half-finished shell of an office building in Van Nuys, listening to the forced good cheer of the current owner, who had run out of money and was desperate to unload the property.

With the temperature hovering around the one hundred degree mark, the San Fernando Valley was providing a pretty fair imitation of hell on earth. Heat, smog and traffic—nature's way of compensating for year-round sun, beaches and women in bikinis. By the time he'd finally managed to pry himself loose from Stu Luptmann's sales pitch, rush hour was in full swing and, as the perfect end to a long and tiring day, a tractor-trailer managed to jack-knife on the San Diego Freeway, bringing rush-hour traffic—not exactly rushing to start with—to a dead stop.

By the time he got home, he needed air-conditioning, an ice-cold beer, a cool shower and about twelve hours' sleep.

Luke pushed open the door, saw Cat standing next to the kitchen sink and, for just an instant, was tempted to duck back into the garage. Not that he was avoiding her. He was just…avoiding her. And, embarrassing as it was, he might have given in to the urge to hide in the garage until she left the kitchen if she hadn't turned her head and looked right at him. Trying to look as if he wasn't a yellow-bellied coward, Luke stepped into the kitchen.

"Hi."

"Hi." She smiled, but her eyes were guarded, watchful. "You look tired."

Wearing a pair of dark green shorts and a T-shirt the color of sunlight, she looked young and fresh, like she'd just stepped out of the shower. A week ago, he would have done his best to persuade her to get naked and wet again, and she probably would have taken him up on it. This week, he looked away, setting his briefcase on the counter.

"Long day." He ran his fingers through his hair. "Van Nuys was an oven. And then there was an accident on the San Diego. Traffic backed up for miles. Forty-five minutes of dodging idiots who apparently got their licenses out of a Cracker Jack box and you start to really appreciate the meaning of road rage."

Cat picked up her glass and offered it to him. "I made lemonade."

It wasn't beer, but it was cold and wet, and Luke drained the glass, tilting his head back to make sure he got every tart-sweet drop.

"Thanks. You may have saved my life."

"You're welcome." Cat took the glass from him, setting it on the counter with a little click. "I talked to Devon this morning."

Luke already had his hand on the refrigerator door. At her words, he hesitated, his grip tightening for an instant before he pulled the door open and took out the pitcher of lemonade and a bottle of Sierra Nevada.

"Yeah?" He poured fresh lemonade over the ice cubes already in her glass and set the pitcher on the counter before twisting the top off his beer. "She's staying with Larry and Susan, isn't she?"

"That's right." Cat leaned back against the counter,

bracing her hands on either side of her hips. Luke wasn't fooled by the relaxed pose or the casual tone. He was in trouble. The hell of it was, he couldn't even blame her. "She actually came looking for me this morning," she said, fixing him with a cool green look. "She wanted to tell me that I shouldn't have tried to trap you by getting pregnant."

He winced and offered up a weak defense. "I didn't say you'd tried to trap me."

"But you did tell her I was pregnant."

"Yeah." He pressed the cold bottle to his forehead, suddenly much too warm despite the air-conditioning. What could he say? He didn't know why, when Devon asked how Cat was, he'd found himself blurting out the news that she was pregnant. Maybe it was because he'd avoided talking about it with anyone—including Cat— and the words had just been waiting to pop out. "It just…slipped out. I'm sorry if you didn't want her to know."

"It isn't a secret," Cat said. "But Devon wasn't high on my list of people to tell about it, and I didn't particularly enjoy having her offer me advice on how *not* to trap you."

"I didn't tell her that," he said again, more firmly.

"I believe you." She sighed, and he could almost see the sharp edge of her temper drain away. "It's just…I wasn't really up for Devon's helpful advice."

She looked tired, Luke thought. It was the first time he'd let himself really look at her in a week, and he could see faint smudges under her eyes, as if she hadn't been sleeping well. And she was pale, with an almost translucent quality to her skin. She looked…fragile.

"You look tired," he said reluctantly. He didn't want to worry about her. He didn't want to…care.

"I guess I am. This heat is a little hard to take."

"You're not spending too much time working outside, are you? You shouldn't…with the…ah…" He gestured vaguely toward her stomach. "You should probably be taking it easy."

Cat didn't know whether to be annoyed or amused by the way he danced around the words *baby* and *pregnant* as if they were incendiary devices. Funny, that he could apparently tell Devon about the baby but couldn't even manage to get the word out in front of her.

"I'm not overdoing it. According to the book I bought, it's normal to be tired in the early stages of pregnancy."

"Okay." Luke nodded without looking at her, apparently fascinated by the label on the beer bottle.

Ah, the joys of overactive hormones, Cat thought, blinking against the sharp sting of tears. She wanted nothing more than to crawl into his arms and have him hold her and tell her that everything was going to be all right. Just as strong was the urge to bang his stupid head against the nearest wall and make him look at her, talk to her. So much for Naomi's pacifist upbringing, Cat thought ruefully. She drew a deep, calming breath and tried to find the quiet center that seemed so much harder to find lately.

"Luke, can't we…I mean, don't you think we should talk? About…everything?" She waved one hand in a vague gesture that she hoped would encompass their marriage, her pregnancy, the future.

Luke wanted very much to say no, he couldn't think of anything they needed to talk about, but he couldn't quite get the words out. No matter how hard he tried, he hadn't been able to convince himself that this…situation was not his problem. Pregnancy, babies—none of that had been part of his plans, but they hadn't been part of Cat's, either. He couldn't just dump the problem in her lap and walk away. On the other hand, he didn't have any idea what the hell to do with it, either.

Keith contemplated the lime, the salt and the shot glass, and tried to remember in what order they were supposed to be applied. Let's see, you sucked on the salt, bit the tequila and then drank the lime. No, that couldn't be right. You couldn't drink a lime, not without squeezing it first. Maybe suck the tequila, bite the lime and drink the... No, that wasn't going to work, either.

"Am I drunk?"

Luke had been contemplating his own drink, but, at Keith's question, he dragged his eyes up and studied his friend, squinting a little to compensate for the dim light in the bar.

"You're blurry around the edges," he said finally. "Either you're drunk or you're moving really fast."

"I'm not moving."

"Then you're drunk."

"Okay." Keith thought about that for a little while. "Maybe you should take my car keys."

"Why the hell would I want your car keys? I've already got my own keys, and I can only drive one car at a time."

"Good point." Keith nodded and then found it took a conscious effort to stop. "Don't let me drive, then."

"If you try to get behind the wheel, I'll knock you out," Luke promised.

"Thanks," Keith said with real gratitude.

Luke shrugged. "What are friends for?"

Keith started to nod and then changed his mind. He had visions of himself going through life nodding, like one of those dogs people put in their rear windows.

He'd definitely had too much to drink. Not that he should be surprised, really, because, when Luke had

called him, he'd specifically invited him to come get
drunk with him. Well, actually, what he'd said was, "I'm
going to get shit-faced. Want to join me?" And though
he wasn't much of a drinker, getting drunk had seemed
like a pretty decent idea. Better than sitting in his condo,
staring at a watercolor he was nearly sure he hated and
wondering what the hell was wrong with him that he suddenly had the hots for a chef who was ten years younger
than he was and, oh yeah, let's not forget the five-o'clock
shadow.

He tossed down the tequila, shuddered at the taste,
sucked on the lime and shuddered again. He really, really
hated tequila, but he had to admit that if your main purpose in life was to get shit-faced, it offered the shortest
route. So here he was, apparently in the midst of a major
sexual identity crisis, sitting in a dingy bar in a slightly
murky area of Pasadena with his best friend, who looked
about as miserable as he felt.

"Why are we here?"

Luke lifted his head slowly and gave him a bleak look.
"Cat's pregnant."

The flat, unemotional statement took a moment to sink
in. When it did, Keith's eyes widened and his breath
hissed out between his teeth. "Holy shit."

Luke nodded. That pretty much summed it up. He
dropped his gaze back down to his glass. He'd had a week
to think about it, but he wasn't sure he could add anything
to those two words. Must be one of the things a Harvard
law degree did for you, he thought. You didn't just learn
the big words but you learned how to sum things up.

"I take it this wasn't…planned," Keith asked, sounding more sober than he had a minute ago.

"No." Luke shook his head. "It was an accident." *A
huge train wreck of an accident.*

''What are you going to do?''

''Besides get drunk? I have no fucking idea.''

Luke thought about flagging down the waitress, a scrawny, bleached blonde who looked like she would rather be almost anywhere else, and ordering another drink, but it seemed like too much effort. He'd run like a damned rabbit when Cat suggested they should talk. He'd agreed that yes, they did need to talk, then made up a bogus excuse about already having plans to get together with Keith. He didn't think she'd believed him, but she'd either been too kind or too disgusted to call him on it. He wasn't sure if it was guilt over lying to her or some vague idea that drinking alone was a bad idea that had led him to call Keith from the car and invite him to this dive.

''Are you...? Is she going to...?''

''She wants to keep it,'' Luke said, guessing at the question Keith hadn't quite asked.

''She'll be a good mother,'' Keith said thoughtfully

Luke had a sudden image of Cat with a baby in her arms, her face soft with love. His baby. God. He tossed down the last of his drink and lifted his hand to signal the waitress.

''So how are you doing with this?''

''Okay.'' Luke shrugged. ''It wasn't in my game plan, but here it is.''

''Right.'' Keith rolled his empty shot glass between his palms, nodding when the waitress set down Luke's drink, and raised an eyebrow at him. ''So we're sitting here getting shit-faced because we're *celebrating?*''

Luke's fingers clenched around his glass—scotch, neat. He'd ordered Chivas but if this was Chivas, he would kiss the bartender's ass. On the other hand, in his current condition, it probably didn't much matter what he was drinking.

"Luke?" Keith arched one eyebrow. "Talk to me, buddy."

"Shit." Luke wiped one hand down his face. "I don't know what to do. What the fuck was I thinking of, marrying her?"

"You were thinking that you were going to beat your grandfather at his own game." Keith let the waitress take the empty shot glass and cupped one hand around the new glass she'd brought.

"Nick." Luke laughed raggedly. "He's sure as hell getting everything he wanted out of this, isn't he? This was exactly what he was after. A great-grandchild to carry on the Quintain name."

"Have you told him yet?"

"Hell, no." Luke shuddered at the thought. Nick would be delighted at this news.

"Kind of hard to keep it a secret," Keith commented.

No, a baby wasn't exactly the kind of thing you could hide. Luke took a swallow of scotch. It slid down his throat like liquid fire, but it couldn't touch the chill that had been building inside him this past week.

"You know, the prenup covers this." Keith sounded amazingly lawyerlike for a guy who'd downed several shots of tequila. "Whatever you do, you don't have any legal worries.

"Cat wouldn't use this to trap me." *Oh yeah, Quintain. Too little, too late. Why couldn't you have figured that out a week ago?* Luke scowled down at his drink. He hadn't done a lot of things that he was ashamed of, but his reaction when Cat had told him about the baby was certainly at the top of the list. Had he apologized for that, or had he just pretended it hadn't happened, the way he'd been trying to do with so many things lately?

"The prenup can go fuck itself," he muttered, tossing off the last of the scotch.

Keith frowned. "I'd have to see if there's a precedent for that."

Luke's half smile acknowledged the attempt at humor, but his expression didn't lighten. He signaled the waitress, and they sat in silence until she brought him another drink. Keith nodded when she looked at him. He hadn't finished the last drink, but he felt like he was going to need a couple more shots to get through the evening.

Fresh drinks were brought, and Keith contemplated the two shot glasses in front of him, while Luke stared grimly into his scotch for a moment before lifting the glass and downing half of it in a gulp. Oh yeah, life just didn't get much better than this, Keith thought. Luke was about to become a father whether he liked it or not, and he was...he was... He wasn't sure what he was. No, that wasn't true, dammit. He *knew* what he was. He fucking *knew*. He just didn't want to face it.

"I think I'm in love with Jack." In tequila *veritas*, Keith thought, downing the first shot and reaching for a lime wedge.

"Jack?" Luke frowned as if trying to place the name. The last drink seemed to have dulled a few important brain functions.

Too late to back out now. The closet door was wide-open.

"You know. Jack Reynolds. Cat's friend. Owns a restaurant?"

"Jack?" Luke's eyes widened as he made the connection. "Jack Reynolds? Cat's friend Jack? Owns a restaurant? *That* Jack?"

"Didn't I just say that?" Keith asked, aggrieved.

Luke thought about it, frowning a little as he made the connections. "Jack's a guy," he pointed out carefully.

Keith snorted. "Yeah, I kind of noticed that."

"You like women," Luke offered, just in case he'd forgotten.

"I always have but there's just something...I don't know...." Keith stopped and shook his head. "Hell, it's probably just a midlife crisis."

"At thirty-five?" Luke asked. "Aren't you too young for that?"

"Well, it all depends on how you define midlife." Keith picked up his shot glass and gestured toward Luke. "The average life expectancy for an American man is...what? Seventy-five, seventy-six, something like that? So half of that is—" He scrunched his face into a pained frown as he struggled to do the math through a tequila haze. "Something like thirty-seven or thirty-eight. So I'm really only a couple years ahead of schedule. Unless I die before I get to seventy-seven, in which case I might even be past midlife. I mean, I could get hit by a truck tomorrow, which would mean I was really due for a midlife crisis at seventeen."

Luke thought about it for a moment, decided it was much too complicated to deal with and returned to what he was fairly sure was the central point of the conversation. "Jack's a guy. You really think you're in love with him?"

"Yes. No. Maybe. Hell, I don't know. I like him. He's funny and he's smart. And every time I see him, I want to take a bite out of his ass."

"Yeah?" Luke considered that idea, nodded slowly. "He's got a nice ass," he admitted. "If you're into that sort of thing, which, as far as I know, you never have been." He peered at Keith suspiciously. "Have you?"

"No." Keith shook his head, but the movement made his stomach lurch, so he settled for a frown. "No. I've always been into women. I mean, I experimented some in college, but other than that—"

"Experimented?"

"You know, just a couple of guys, Saturday night, no dates, nothing else to do and you maybe—" He caught Luke's look of disbelief. "What?" he said defensively. "It was college. Everybody was experimenting. It didn't *mean* anything."

"I confined my experiments to the opposite sex," Luke said. He picked up his glass and tossed back the remaining scotch, then pointed the empty glass at Keith. "You, my friend, have obviously been so deep in the closet, you didn't even know it was there."

"Maybe." Keith stared broodingly into his glass.

"Maybe it's a temporary thing," Luke said, trying to cheer him up. "Maybe you've just been spending too much time at work. You need to get out more. Or it could be your pituitary."

"My what?"

"Your pituitary." It took a couple of tries for Luke to set his glass down. The table seemed to be shrinking.

"Do you even know what a pituitary is?"

"No, but my grandmother used to blame my pituitary for everything from insomnia to flatulence. I don't see why it couldn't shoulder the blame for this."

"I don't think pituitaries *have* shoulders."

"Whatever. Maybe you need more exercise."

"I tried that." Keith rolled the shot glass between his palms. "I started running. Got up at six o'clock every morning for two solid weeks, put on the shoes and hit the streets."

"And?" Luke prompted when he fell silent.

"I figure being gay has got to be easier than pounding the pavement at dawn."

Luke nodded, as if that made sense to him. "Gym. You need to join a gym. Lots of women in those little spandex things, and doing lots of sweating and grunting."

"I tried that, too. Even took out this aerobics instructor."

"Yeah?" Luke looked impressed. "An aerobics instructor went out with you?"

"Screw you. I'm having an epa...epiphany, and you're casting aster...aspersions on my manhood."

"Hey, I'm not the one who wants to take a bite out of another guy's ass." Luke shook his head. "Don't blame me if your manhood gets aspersed."

Keith nodded, struck by the truth of that. They sat in silence for a while.

"You okay with this?" Keith asked suddenly.

Luke peered at him owlishly. Maybe scotch on an empty stomach had not been the smartest thing he could have done. "Okay with what? You biting Jack's ass? Hell, it's *his* ass. You should talk to him about it."

"You okay with me maybe batting for the home team," Keith clarified.

Luke considered it, then shook his head very slowly, worried that any rapid movement might have dire consequences. "It's seriously weird, but, hey, you're already a lawyer. How much worse can it be if you're gay?"

Keith considered flipping him the bird, but he wasn't sure his coordination was up to the challenge. "Go to hell."

Luke's grin was lopsided. "Love you, too, buddy."

Keith shoved the remaining shot glass back so abruptly that tequila splashed over the side. His head was already buzzing, making it hard to think. "Jesus, Luke, I don't know what the hell I'm doing. I mean, this feels...real. I want to spend time with him, go out with him, walk on the beach, all that shit."

"You hate the beach," Luke pointed out.

"I know, but he likes it. He even offered to teach me to surf."

Luke considered that for a moment. "He ever seen you in swim trunks?" he asked. His doubtful tone startled a laugh out of Keith, a laugh that ended on a hiccup.

"Asshole."

"Just looking out for your interests, buddy," Luke assured him.

Chapter Sixteen

Somewhere in the back of Keith's mind, a little voice kept saying that this wasn't a good idea, that one o'clock in the morning was a very bad time to be pounding on someone's door. He ignored the voice in favor of knocking again, and nearly fell on his face when the door was abruptly jerked open.

"Keith! What the hell?" Jack grabbed his arm, steadying him as he wobbled in the doorway. "What's wrong?"

"Nothing." Keith thought about shaking his head, then thought better of it. Sudden movement seemed like a bad idea. "I wanted to see you."

"Jesus, you smell like you've been dipped in bourbon." Jack's nose wrinkled, but he pulled Keith inside and shut the door.

Keith had a bleary impression of furniture that looked as if it had been chosen more for comfort than style. A stack of books was piled next to an overstuffed chair that was upholstered in a subdued floral print, and a pair of battered running shoes lay under an end table that held a lamp, a remote control, sunglasses and a wadded-up sock.

It was the kind of room that invited you to kick off your shoes and be comfortable amid the clutter.

"Hey, anybody home?" Jack snapped his fingers in front of Keith's face.

Keith looked at him, puzzled. "You're home. Aren't you?" Was Jack drunk, too?

Jack laughed and shook his head. "Man, you *are* plastered."

"Yes." He was having a hard time with most things but he was sure of that much. He was definitely plastered. "Tequila."

"What?"

"Not bourbon. Tequila." He was here to get everything out in the open. He didn't want any misunderstandings. "Don't like bourbon." He frowned, thought about it, then admitted, "Don't like tequila, either."

"Bourbon, tequila—they smell a lot alike when I've been dragged out of bed at one o'clock in the morning."

"Did I wake you?"

"No, I always dress like this when I'm expecting guests."

Keith squinted at the gray boxers and ratty white T-shirt. "Really?"

Jack laughed again and shook his head. "You are totally wasted. Come on, let's get you sitting down before you fall down."

It was a good idea. Not that he was going to fall down. Well, he *probably* wasn't going to fall down. But sitting down was good. In fact, it was a wonderful idea, he decided when he felt the sofa come up under him. Jack eased him down, steadying him until he was safely seated and showed no signs of tipping over. When he started to straighten up, Keith grabbed his arm.

"Don't go."

"I was just going to get you a glass of water and some aspirin, try a kind of preemptive strike on the hangover you're going to have in the morning."

"My head's fine," Keith said, ignoring the swimming sensation and the way his eyes had a tendency to cross. "Want to talk. To you." It seemed important to add that. He didn't just want to talk. He wanted to talk to Jack. "To you. I want to talk to you."

"Sure. We'll talk." Jack's tone was soothing. He frowned suddenly. "You didn't drive over here, did you?"

"Cab."

"Good." Jack patted his knee. "Now let me get you some water and that aspirin."

"I don't get hangovers."

Jack grinned. "You just keep telling yourself that."

"I don't—" Keith struggled to focus his thoughts. God, why had he had so much to drink? Next time Luke called and wanted company to get drunk, he was going to hang up. He had things he wanted to say, important things, dammit, and his brain was stuck in Neutral.

"Look, whatever it is, it can wait until morning." Jack's expression was kind, a little amused. "You can crash here tonight, and we'll talk tomorrow."

Keith shook his head and then had to close his eyes when it threatened to roll off. He didn't want to wait until morning. If he waited until morning, he might remember all the reasons why this was bad idea, all the reasons why he didn't want to do…this.

He brought his hands up to cup Jack's face and saw his eyes widen in shock, and then Keith's mouth was on his and it was…different. He hadn't expected that. A mouth was a mouth and a kiss was a kiss, right? But Jack's mouth was wider than what he was accustomed to, and he'd never kissed anyone with five-o'clock shadow before. His hands dropped to Jack's shoulders, and the feel of muscle and bone was different, too. No delicate curves and soft, perfumed skin. Different, but not bad.

He'd wondered if he could do this, wondered if the differences would bother him, but this was okay. More than okay. It was good. Jack's mouth softened under his, and it was very good. Right. It felt right. And then Jack was pulling away, standing up and stepping back, out of reach.

''What the hell was that?''

Keith blinked up at him. ''It was a kiss.''

Jack stared at him, his blue eyes angry and...scared. ''I'm not going to be your walk on the wild side. You want to experiment with fucking a guy, go find someone else.''

''I'm not experimenting.'' Keith thought about standing up, but he was afraid he would end up falling on his face. ''I wanted to kiss you.''

Jack ran his fingers through his sun streaked hair, looking suddenly more tired than angry. ''You're drunk. You don't know what the hell you want.''

Keith started to argue, to tell him he knew *exactly* what he wanted for the first time in a long time, but Jack shook his head.

''Just shut up.'' He drew a deep breath, released it slowly. ''You're drunk. I'm tired. Let's just...let it go for now. Get some sleep. We can talk in the morning, or we can forget this ever happened.''

Keith opened his mouth, closed it again without speaking. He might be drunk, but he wasn't totally stupid. Jack wasn't going to believe anything he said tonight. Who could blame him?

Jack disappeared, reappearing with the promised bedding, a glass of water and a bottle of aspirin. Without looking at Keith, he dropped the pillow at one end of the sofa, and set the water and aspirin on the coffee table.

"The bathroom is down the hall and to the right. I'll leave the light on in case you need to find it in a hurry. Drink the water, take the aspirin and get some sleep. If you need anything, yell."

"I think I'm in love with you." He hadn't planned to say it, but the words just wouldn't be held back.

Jack hesitated for an instant and then shook his head. "Talk to me when you're sober. Get some sleep."

Keith watched him leave the room, then let his head fall back against the sofa. He'd just taken a major life-altering step. Jack didn't believe him, but he knew what he felt, and he was okay with it. More than okay. He'd admitted how he felt, said it out loud, and the world hadn't come to an end. Maybe Luke was right. Maybe he had been so far in the closet he hadn't even known it was there. Maybe there hadn't been a closet at all. Who cared? He'd outed himself to his best friend and told Jack how he felt, and it felt pretty damned good.

There were still things to be worked out. Even drunk and rapidly sinking toward unconsciousness, he knew that. Little details like whether or not Jack felt the same way he did, and what they were going to do about it if he did. But, what the hell, being gay or bi or whatever the hell he was had to be less painful than spending so much time at the gym.

There was nothing like sleeping in your clothes to make you wake up feeling like roadkill. Keith shoved the blanket away and swung his legs off the sofa. Sitting up, he scrubbed his hands over his face. A smarter man would have stripped down to his underwear, he thought, grimacing at the lived-in feel of his jeans and Polo shirt. Of course, a smarter man wouldn't have gotten drunk in the first place. At least he'd managed to kick off his shoes before he passed out.

Way to make a good impression, Lundquist. Show up at one o'clock in the morning, drunker than a waltzing pissant and smelling like you fell in a vat of José Cuervo, and declare your undying love for the guy. Oh yeah, it was hard to believe Jack hadn't just swooned with delight over that one.

He pushed himself to his feet, swaying a little once he got there. He hadn't lied when he said he didn't get hang-overs. Other than a mild headache and a mouth that tasted like something had died in it, the tequila had done no lasting damage, but sleeping on the too soft, too short sofa had left every muscle aching. He allowed himself a small groan as he made his way to the bathroom.

Ten minutes later, he followed his nose to find the kitchen. There was coffee. Good coffee, from the smell of it. Jack's kitchen was smaller than Keith would have expected, but then, since he had the restaurant to play in, he probably didn't need a huge kitchen at home. It was starkly modern, done in clean white and black, with splashes of red in the tile counter and the cushions on the bench seating in the breakfast nook. Pots of herbs lined the windowsill behind the sink, and the red-and-black-checkered curtains were pushed back to let the sun spill into the room.

Jack was standing at the counter. He was wearing a pair of faded jeans and a blue T-shirt, his feet bare and his hair tousled. Now that he'd admitted to himself how he felt, Keith wasn't caught off guard by the familiar little nudge of attraction he felt. It was okay to feel attracted if he was gay or bi or whatever he apparently was. But at the moment that attraction took a back seat in importance to the fact that Jack was pouring coffee into a thick white china mug. Keith swallowed a whimper at the smell of it.

"I heard you get up," Jack said, setting the coffee pot down and pushing the cup down the counter. "I wasn't sure if you'd be up for coffee."

"Please," Keith said fervently, lifting the cup and inhaling greedily. The scent helped clear the last of the cobwebs from his brain, and the first sip put him on the road to feeling like a functioning human being. He sighed as he lowered the cup. "You're a god."

"A demigod, maybe," Jack said, smiling a little. "How are you feeling?"

Keith rubbed his hand over his jaw. "Like I need a shave and some clean clothes. Other than that, not too bad." He caught the other man's look of disbelief and lifted one shoulder in a half shrug. "I told you, I don't get hangovers."

"Handy."

"I was the envy of all my frat brothers."

"I bet." Jack picked up his own cup and cradled it between his palm and chest. "In that case, I can make breakfast if you're hungry. I didn't want to cook anything, because I figured the smell would probably do you in. Unless you need to get going?" He arched his brows in question. "I can drive you to wherever you left your car."

"I don't have to rush anywhere. I didn't have any appointments this morning, and I called my secretary to let her know I wouldn't be in until this afternoon."

"In that case, I can make you one of my world-famous omelettes." Jack set his cup down and lifted a shallow skillet off one of the hooks next to the stove. "If you have any objection to mushrooms or ham, speak now or forever hold your peace."

So that was the way he planned to play things, Keith thought, watching him. Just pretend nothing had happened. He'd made that offer last night, said they could just forget the whole thing.

"There's some roasted asparagus in the fridge, and I've got some really incredible Muenster made by this couple in Sonoma County. They've been making artisan cheeses for the last five years or so, and they—"

Jack reached past him to open a drawer, and Keith wrapped his fingers around his wrist. The light patter of words dried up instantly. Jack froze for an instant and then tried to pull his hand back. Keith's grip tightened. He could feel Jack's pulse beating against his thumb.

"Don't do this," Jack said without lifting his eyes from their hands. "You were drunk. You said things you didn't mean. I get it."

"No, you don't." Keith reached across his own body to set his cup on the counter. "I *was* drunk but I didn't say anything I didn't mean."

Jack pulled his hand back, and this time Keith let him go. In the morning light, Jack's eyes were a pale, icy-blue.

"I told you last night, I'm not interested in helping you work through an early midlife crisis or expand your sexual horizons or whatever the hell you think you're doing. If you want to be able to say you've tried gay sex, find someone else."

Keith held on to his own temper. "I'm not having a midlife crisis, and I'm not looking to put a notch on my bedpost labeled 'gay sex.' I'm attracted to *you.*"

"Tell me something I don't know," Jack snapped. He crossed his arms over his chest and glared at Keith. "I probably figured that out before you did, but you made it damned clear you didn't want to do anything about it when you started avoiding me." His mouth twisted in a sneer. "You think you're so unique? Straight guy starts hanging out with gay guy. Makes him feel liberal all over. You tell yourself the fact that he's a fag doesn't matter. Hell, you're such a liberal guy, you don't even notice it, but you can't help but think about it a little. Just what *do* queers do in bed?"

"I haven't called you a fag or a queer. I haven't thought of you that way."

"No? Bet you haven't thought of yourself that way, either." Jack took a half step closer and jabbed Keith in the chest with one finger. "But you'd better think about it. Wake up and smell the mothballs, buddy, because if you're thinking about fucking a guy, you're about to open the closet door, and you may never get it closed again."

There was nothing loverlike about the grip Keith took on his wrist. "Don't talk to me like I'm an idiot. I'm thirty-five fucking years old. Career's going well. It's about time to find a nice girl, get married, buy a house, maybe think about having a kid or two, maybe retire young, learn to play golf. And then I suddenly find myself falling in love with someone who's not only ten years younger than I am but, oh yeah, did I forget to mention he's got five-o'clock shadow? Do you think this is a whim? Do you think I haven't given this a whole hell of a lot of thought? Give me a fucking break."

Jack stared at him, humor starting to edge out the temper in his eyes. "My father and my brother play golf."

"Then I'll never touch a golf club as long as I live," Keith promised without hesitation. "Just…give this a chance."

Jack looked at him, the brief flash of humor fading into somberness. "You say you've thought this out, but you can't possibly know what you're getting into. What about

your family? How are they going to react when you bring
your boyfriend home? What about your friends? Maybe
you think they're all cool about alternative lifestyles, and
maybe they are—as long as they don't have their noses
rubbed in it.''

Jack thrust one hand through his hair and shook his
head. ''Maybe you're thinking this is your life, that it's
no one else's business who you're tangling the sheets
with, but that's not the way it works. This is L.A., so it's
not as bad as it might be in a small town, but intolerance
is alive and well, even in the big city. And all that's even
before we get down to the nitty-gritty stuff between the
two of us. Had you ever even kissed another guy before
last night?'' He shook his head again. ''I don't think you
have any idea what you're getting into here. Trust me,
life's easier when you're heterosexual.''

Keith waited a moment to be sure he was done before
speaking. He ticked off the points on his fingers. ''My
family probably wouldn't notice if I brought home an
aardvark and announced that we were madly in love.
They're…well, *self-absorbed* is probably the kindest way
to put it. When I declined to join the family business, it
confirmed their long-held suspicions that I was alien
spawn. They wish me well, I wish them well, and we try
not to see each other more than once a year or so.''

He raised another finger. ''My friends and how they
might react. They'll learn to live with it or they won't. I
can't live my life based on what my friends are going to
think.''

A third finger. ''I think I can survive any intolerance
that comes my way. Remember, I'm a lawyer. I'm used
to being denigrated.''

He smiled a little at Jack's snort of laughter. ''Lastly,
I'm not…totally without experience in…this sort of

thing.'' To his annoyance, Keith felt his face heating and knew he was blushing. ''It was a long time ago, but...''

''Yeah?'' Jack was staring at him in fascination. ''How long ago?''

''College.'' Keith cleared his throat. ''It was just...I mean, it was nothing. I *thought* it was nothing. Just a couple of guys. A weekend, no dates. We fooled around a few times. I didn't think much of it afterward. I thought everyone did it.'' He caught Jack's look of disbelief and snapped defensively, ''It was college, okay? You're supposed to experiment.''

''I don't know how to break it to you—''

''Yeah, yeah. Luke already made it clear that maybe I overestimated the spirit of adventure of most college students.''

''You talked to *Luke* about this?'' Jack asked, startled.

''Last night, in between downing tequila shooters.'' It was Keith's turn to run his fingers through his hair. ''He said I was so deep in the closet, I didn't even know it was there. I don't know, maybe he's right. I just never gave it any thought.''

''You *told* Luke?'' Jack was having a hard time getting past that point.

''Yes.''

''What did he...I mean, how did he react?''

Keith looked at him and understood that there was a lot more to the question than what was on the surface. This wasn't just curiosity about how Luke had reacted to the news that his best friend was taking a sharp sexual left turn. What Jack really wanted to know was how Keith felt about telling Luke.

''He said it was weird, said I shouldn't let you see me in swim trunks and admitted that you had a great ass.''

"What?" Jack's mouth dropped open, and his eyes bulged a little.

Keith waited until he was starting to catch his breath before adding, "He said, if I wanted to bite your ass, I should ask you."

"You didn't really say you wanted to—" Jack flushed bright red and then shook his head, laughing a little. "Jesus, Keith, when you come out of the closet, you don't do it halfway."

"No point in doing it halfway." Taking a chance, Keith reached out and wrapped his fingers around Jack's wrist. A single step closed the distance between them. Jack's expression was wary, but he didn't pull away. Maybe, just maybe...

Last night, he'd been drunk and desperate to prove a point—to Jack and maybe to himself. This morning, he was sober, and he'd apparently come to terms with himself overnight. He could really savor the kiss this time around. The differences were still there—hard muscle instead of soft curves, aftershave instead of perfume—but it was good. The differences were good. Really, really good.

He'd half expected lights and sirens, bells and whistles, maybe a small earthquake, something to announce that Keith Richard Lundquist, Harvard grad, attorney-at-law, former straight guy, had just kissed someone who had that all-important Y chromosome, but nothing happened. The earth didn't shake, lightning didn't strike, no band of roving conservatives popped up to stone him. It just felt...right. Different, but right. Like something he could get used to. Something he *wanted* to get used to.

Jack drew back first. "Are you sure you know what you're doing?"

"No, but I figure I'll have fun finding out."

Jack leaned his forehead against Keith's, his laugh a little ragged around the edges. "I'm going to live to regret this, aren't I?"

"I hope not," Keith said fervently. "I hope not."

The bad thing about getting drunk—besides waking up with his cheek stuck to the leather upholstery of the sofa in his den, his mouth full of cotton and his head full of jungle drums—*besides* all that, the worst thing was that it was such an utter waste of time, money and mediocre scotch.

Luke shut down his e-mail program and leaned back in the desk chair, closing his eyes and rolling his head to work the lingering tension out of his neck. It was midafternoon, and liberal applications of coffee and aspirin had eliminated the worst of the hangover, but they hadn't done anything for the self-directed disgust he felt.

What the hell had he been thinking? That a few drinks would be enough to make him forget his impending fatherhood? Or that booze would somehow help him figure out what to do about the fact that his wife—his *temporary* wife—might be in love with him? All it had done was give him a hangover, make him oversleep so he missed his first appointment this morning and add to the creeping feeling that his life was spinning out of control. Ironic, really, when this marriage had been all about him keeping control. Keith was right about that—marrying Cat had been a way of thumbing his nose at his grandfather.

Keith. Now there was a new wrinkle in his already crumpled life. Luke nudged the desk chair around and frowned out the window at the hazy view of Los Angeles. Keith and Jack. Keith *with* Jack. Last night, cushioned by an ocean of scotch, the idea had seemed mildly bizarre. This afternoon, painfully sober, it seemed *incredibly* bizarre. He wondered if he should drum up some emotional reaction more than just thinking it was plain weird, but the thing was, Keith's love life hadn't really been any of his business before this. He didn't see any reason why that should change just because Keith was dating a guy.

It was going to be pretty peculiar if he and Jack started holding hands and acting like newlyweds, but he'd gotten used to stranger things. Hell, his housekeeper dressed like Vampirella. If he could get used to that, Keith and Jack making eyes at each other shouldn't be too hard to deal with. At least he liked Jack, which was more than he could say for a couple of his friends' wives.

Shaking his head, he tucked Keith's sudden team change away to think about later. Or not. Right now, he had his own problems to worry about. Cat had already left the house when he staggered out of the den this morning. He didn't know what she'd thought of the fact that he hadn't come home until two in the morning and had slept in the den. He'd tried telling himself that it was none of her business, that they had a business arrangement, not a real marriage, and he didn't owe her any explanations if he chose to stay out all night, but his conscience wasn't buying it.

The problem was, it didn't feel like a business arrangement. It felt like a marriage. And wasn't that the real reason he'd gone on a bender last night? Because he'd realized that his fake marriage was pretty damned real? Not just because of the baby, though, God knows, you didn't get much more real than that. No, even without the unexpected pregnancy, there were ties between the two of them. He hadn't just let Cat into his house and his bed, he'd let her into his life. She'd fired his housekeeper, stood up to his grandfather, argued with him over the relative merits of the Three Stooges and the Marx Brothers, and made him laugh more than anyone he'd ever known.

Luke realized his hands were clenched into fists and made a conscious effort to relax them. He hated feeling confused like this. When he'd decided to give in to his grandfather's blackmail, he'd had a relatively simple plan in mind: marry a woman Nick would despise and keep his own distance from her. He'd failed on both counts. Nick was halfway to liking Cat, though Luke still wasn't sure how that had come about, and he'd done a pisspoor job of keeping his own distance from her. If he'd wanted to keep his distance, he shouldn't have moved her into his bedroom or made it a point to introduce her to his friends and clients. Better still, he shouldn't have married her at all, because Cat wasn't the sort of woman you kept at a distance.

He would have been better off marrying Devon, he thought bitterly. She would have driven him crazy within a week of the wedding, but he'd expected that. Nothing about Cat was what he'd expected.

The discreet buzz of the intercom was a welcome interruption. Hopefully some terrible crisis had come up, something that would keep him occupied for the next decade or so. He hit the button.

"Ms. Kowalski is here, Mr. Quintain."

Devon? Luke stared at the intercom for a moment. Talk about speak of the devil....

"Send her in, Sharon."

Devon was wearing a powder-blue suit. The color looked good on her, and she wore it often. The narrow skirt was short enough to border on indecent exposure. The jacket was fitted, the neckline plunging just enough to hint at cleavage without being obvious about it. Sheer stockings and off-white pumps completed the outfit, which managed to look both professional and suggestive.

"I *hope* you don't mind me just *dropping* in like this," she said as she crossed the office toward him.

"If I minded, I wouldn't have told Sharon to send you in." She really was a very pretty woman, Luke decided, looking at her critically. Like the girl on an old-fashioned box of chocolates, she was all pale hair, blue eyes and soft skin. Dainty and feminine. Okay, she was also shallow and grasping and not particularly intelligent, but that made her predictable. There were no surprises with Devon, no hidden depths, no unexpected connections.

"I just wanted to come by and *tell* you again how much it *means* to me that you gave me this job."

"You're good at your job," he said, bypassing the emotional underpinnings and sticking with the simple truth.

"That means so *much* to me, Luke. To know that *you* think that." Tears shimmered in her eyes for a moment before she blinked them away. "I'm so *glad* you didn't hold a grudge. For the way I just left without a word, I mean. It was *terribly* unfair of me."

"You did leave a note," Luke reminded her.

Devon's mouth tightened for an instant, then relaxed into a sweet, wistful smile. "It's very kind of you to be so understanding, Luke, but I *know* I could have just *ruined* your life."

"It was damned inconvenient, but I don't think my life was on the verge of actual ruin. Can I get you a drink?"

Devon looked as if she might like to argue the issue of how close his life had been to ruin, then thought better of it. Her smile looked a little forced, but it stayed in place.

"Perrier, if you have it."

Luke remembered bringing Cat a glass of water that

first evening and the way her nose had wrinkled at the thought of sparkling water.

"Something funny about Perrier?" Devon asked, and he realized he'd been standing there smiling at nothing. He felt a quick surge of irritation that he couldn't seem to go even a few minutes without thinking about Cat.

"Not really. I was just thinking that Cat commented once that sparkling water tastes medicinal."

If Devon was irritated that he'd mentioned his wife, she was a good enough actress to hide it. "I'm not surprised." Her mouth pursed in a pretty little moue, her expression mildly indulgent as she shook her head. "Cat's a *sweet* girl but she's not exactly *sophisticated,* is she?"

"Have a seat," Luke said, ignoring the comment as he went to the built-in bar and took the familiar green bottle from the fridge. He got himself one while he was there. When he turned away from the bar, Devon had seated herself on the sofa, crossing one leg over the other. The position made her skirt inch even farther up her thigh. She had good legs, Luke thought as he walked across the room. But Cat had *incredible* legs—long and sleekly muscled, the kind of legs that made a man think all sort of things he— Dammit, he did *not* want to be thinking about Cat.

Irritation at himself made his smile warmer than it might otherwise have been as he carried the glasses across the room. "No ice, right?"

"How *sweet* of you to remember that."

When she took the glass from him, Devon made sure their fingers brushed, her eyes holding his for a moment in what she probably thought was a look filled with meaning. Luke kept his expression pleasantly bland. She patted the sofa next to her, giving him a playful look from under her lashes. Luke opted to sit on the coffee table so that

he faced her. It would have been smarter to opt for the
overstuffed chair that sat at right angles to the sofa. A
little extra distance would probably be a good thing. He
was fairly sure he knew what she wanted, and he didn't
want to encourage her.

Did he?

"I was really *worried* when I heard you'd married
Cat," she said, putting on a serious expression. "I'm not
saying a *word* against her, Luke. Really, I just love her
like a *sister*. But she's so young and *romantic*. And I was
worried that she might have *expectations*."

"Expectations?" Luke didn't think he'd ever met anyone who had fewer expectations than Cat. She seemed
willing to take life as it came—good, bad and indifferent.

"*You* know what I mean." Devon leaned forward
slightly, a position that gave him an up-close-and-personal
view of her cleavage.

As sales pitches went, it wasn't bad, he thought idly.
Not as good as Cat showing up in that coat, though. *That*
had certainly been a birthday present he wouldn't forget
any time soon. Luke realized where his mind had
drifted—again—and anger spiked in his veins. He wasn't
sure who he was angry at—Cat for refusing to stay banished or himself for not being able to keep her out of his
head. He had a beautiful, very willing woman all but offering herself on a platter, and all he could think about
was his wife. Not because of some vows he'd recited
without meaning them, but just because of who she was.
It was maddening.

"I worry about Cat," Devon was saying when he
dragged his attention back to her. "I'd just *hate* to see her
get hurt. But I have to admit, I was even *more* worried
about *you*."

"I can generally take care of myself." Luke took a sip

of his water and barely restrained a grimace as he set it aside. Cat was right, dammit, it did taste medicinal. As if it wasn't enough that she'd fired his housekeeper, now she was going to force him to find a new water.

As if she sensed that she didn't have his full attention, Devon leaned a little farther, reaching out to put one small hand on his knee. The water was forgotten as Luke stared at that hand. The light touch seemed to burn through the fabric of his pants. He wasn't sure what he was feeling. Anger, lust, guilt, maybe a touch of defiance. He lifted his eyes slowly, lingering on her chest, letting himself wonder what she had on under that trim little jacket.

"I would just hate for you to feel *obligated*," Devon was saying. "To Cat, I mean. I know a lot of men would feel that her being pregnant put some kind of *pressure* on them to take care of her."

Luke wondered if he should be insulted that she thought he was the kind of man who could casually walk away from his own child or congratulate her for knowing him so well. Because that was what he'd been thinking about doing, wasn't it? And he didn't have to feel guilty about it, did he? He hadn't planned this, hadn't wanted it. He would be a lousy father anyway, even if he did want to take on the task, which he didn't.

"It would be *such* a mistake to feel that way, Luke," Devon said earnestly. Her fingers flexed slightly, her hand creeping upward. "I know this is an *awkward* situation for you, and I just want you to know that I'm *here* for you."

Luke looked at that hand again, then lifted his eyes to her face. Her eyes were hungry. She wasn't particularly subtle, but he had to give her points for going after what she wanted.

As if from outside himself, he saw his hand come out,

fingers hooking in the neck of her jacket, tugging her closer until their knees were brushing. Devon's eyes widened, surprise edging out hunger for a moment.

"Are you offering to console me?" He hardly recognized his own voice. It sounded harsh and loud in his ears, but Devon didn't seem to hear anything wrong with it.

She licked her lips slowly. "If that's what you want."

What he really wanted was to feel in control of his life again. He didn't want to think or feel, or wonder just how he'd so completely lost control.

"Just as long as we both understand that this is nothing but a quick fuck," he said crudely.

No misunderstandings. No big green eyes giving him hopeful looks. Just two people having sex. A simple physical release, with no messy emotional entanglements.

Devon's expression was suddenly cool, a little calculating, her eyes hard and not nearly as pretty. She nodded. "I can live with that."

Without giving himself time to think about it, Luke tightened his grip on her jacket, bringing up his other hand to grasp it just above the row of tidy mother-of-pearl buttons. Devon's eyes widened as she realized what he was going to do, but she didn't say anything. Two quick yanks and the buttons were suddenly gone, one skittering across the table in a series of sharp little bounces.

Her breath caught in a ragged little gasp, arousal darkening her eyes and bringing quick, hectic color to her cheeks. Somewhere inside, Luke heard a warning voice, telling him this wasn't what he wanted, that it wasn't going to give him what he needed, but he ignored it. It was enough. He would make it enough.

Devon's fingers were busy with his shirt, buttons sliding free with almost magical speed. He felt a distant kind of interest in how quickly she managed it, in the ragged sound of her breathing. She reached for his belt buckle as he slid his hand inside the demibra that was all she had on under the jacket. She gasped and shuddered with arousal, while he tried not to notice that the weight and feel of her was all wrong. He didn't want to think about anything but this moment. He *wouldn't* think about anything—or anyone—else. This was what he wanted. And if it wasn't, then he would damn well make it what he wanted.

He stood, pulling Devon up with him, reaching for the waistband of her skirt while she slid his zipper down, the quiet rasp audible over the sound of her rapid breathing. Luke's fingers closed over the tab of her zipper. He was going to do this. He was not only going to do it, he was going to enjoy it. No reason why he shouldn't. It wasn't like he had any real commitments elsewhere.

He caught a flash of movement out of the corner of his eye and turned his head in time to see the office door swing the rest of the way open. Cat was already in mid-speech.

"Luke, I just wanted to—"

The words disappeared on a gasp. She stopped as abruptly as if she'd run into a wall, color draining from her face as she stared at the tableau in front of her. For a moment the silence in the room was so thick, he felt as if he could almost reach out and touch it. Then Devon giggled suddenly, a high girlish sound that tore through the quiet.

"Oh, my. Isn't this *awkward.*"

Chapter Seventeen

Luke had that feeling of standing outside himself again, seeing the scene the way Cat saw it. His shirt unbuttoned and hanging open, his belt undone, pants half-unzipped. And, of course, Devon's jacket was gone, leaving her essentially naked from the waist up, even the dubious covering of her lacy bra pushed aside to bare one breast completely.

There was no mistaking this for anything other than what it was. Another two minutes and he would have been caught literally with his pants down. He was vaguely grateful for being spared that ultimate cliché.

Cat's gaze lifted to his, and he forgot about his state of undress. He nearly flinched back from the pain in her eyes, the naked vulnerability. She stared at him for a long moment, her eyes empty of everything but that terrible hurt. He waited for the tears to start or the torrent of words, braced himself for the emotional scene that was sure to follow.

Cat turned and walked out without a word, closing the

door quietly behind her, leaving Luke staring at nothing, his mind a compete blank.

"Well, *that* was certainly a surprise."

With an effort, he dragged his eyes to Devon. She'd tucked herself back into her bra but hadn't made any effort to pull the ruined jacket into place. Her hair was tousled, and her face was still lightly flushed. Her mouth was curved in a smug little smile, and Luke was suddenly glad that at least he hadn't kissed her.

Oh yeah, like that makes everything okay. You stuck your hand in her bra, but you didn't kiss her, so everything is just fine.

He suddenly slammed back into his body, into the here and now, into the what-the-hell-have-I-done. His fingers were unsteady as he jerked his shirt closed and started buttoning it.

"Don't you want to finish what we started?" Devon asked, her lower lip thrust out in a pout.

Luke barely restrained a shudder. The thought was enough to bring on permanent impotence. "I have to go," was all he said.

Maybe she read something of his revulsion, because she abandoned the seductress mode for the concerned friend. "You know, Luke, maybe this is really for the *best*. Neither of us wanted to *hurt* Cat, but it's better that she finds out about us now rather than later."

"Us?" Luke paused in the midst of tucking his shirt into his pants and looked at her. "There is no 'us,' Devon. There has *never* has been an 'us.' This—" he gestured between them "—if we'd finished this, it would have been exactly what I said it would be—a quick fuck."

Devon's face tightened into something not at all pretty. "I suppose you're going to go after her now? Try to talk to her? You're wasting your time. She won't listen to you.''

''Yes, she will.'' Luke finished tucking in his shirt and buckled his belt with quick, jerky movements. He always kept extra clothes in the office, because he never knew when a site visit was going to involve getting dirty. A few quick strides and he had the closet door open and a shirt pulled off a hanger. ''Here. You can wear this for now.'' He handed it to Devon without looking at her. She was already half-forgotten. All he could think of was the look in Cat's eyes, the hurt he'd put there. ''Send me a bill for replacing the suit.''

''That's it?'' Anger gave a shrill edge to her voice. ''You're just going to shove me out the door?''

''You can stay as long as you like,'' he said absently. Keys, he needed his keys. He patted his pants pocket to confirm he had them.

''Fine,'' she snarled. ''Run off and apologize. I hope she spits in your eye. And when she does, don't come crawling back to me, because I won't be here.''

''Okay.'' Luke walked out, leaving Devon gaping after him.

On some level, Cat knew she couldn't really be as calm as she felt, so she took extra care driving home, checking traffic signals twice before going through them, watching carefully for stop signs, suicidal pedestrians and drivers talking on cell phones, and sticking strictly to the speed limit. She must have done all right, because she ended up parked in front of the garage, and both she and Ruthie seemed reasonably intact.

She shut off Ruthie's engine and got out of the car. That unnatural feeling of calm stayed with her. It was actually quite pleasant, she decided. Like being inside a glass bubble, cut off from the outside world. She hoped the feeling lasted a while.

The house was quiet. Merry had classes today, and this wasn't one of Consuela's days to come in. That was good. She didn't have to talk to anyone or explain anything. Cat went directly upstairs, taking her suitcase out of the hall closet before going into the bedroom. She hadn't given any conscious thought to what to do next, but leaving seemed like a good idea.

The black-leather-and-nylon Pullman was a battered veteran of more moves than she could remember. Naomi had bought it for her at a secondhand shop in Tennessee when she was five or six. It had been nearly as big as she was then and had held just about everything she owned. That wasn't the case anymore, she thought, as she opened the walk-in closet and began tugging garments off hangers. It would take more than one suitcase to hold her clothes, but she could get the necessities now and come back for the rest of her things later.

Or she could just leave everything. Her fingers tightened over the sleeve of a blouse. Naomi had liked to say that people were owned by their possessions, but that was only true if you let it happen. There wasn't anything here she had to have. She could just walk out and leave it all. But that seemed unnecessarily dramatic. She wasn't trying to make a statement. She was just…leaving.

The suitcase was almost full when Cat heard the door open downstairs. Her hands tightened over the stack of lacy underwear she'd been tucking in among her other clothing. She'd wondered if he would follow her or if he would stay at his office and…finish what he'd obviously started. She'd been hoping to leave without seeing him again, but maybe it was better this way. She wouldn't have to worry about what to say in a note, and they could just settle everything here and now. No loose ends to worry about later. Yes, this was better.

When Luke appeared in the bedroom doorway, Cat was just coming out of the bathroom. She'd loaded her toiletries into a tote bag, and she set it on the bed and frowned down into the still-open suitcase, wondering if she'd forgotten anything important.

"Very dramatic," Luke said dryly.

Cat glanced at him and then looked away. Her hairbrush. She didn't remember seeing it in the bathroom. Bottles rattled as she pulled open the tote and peered inside.

"As soon as I'm settled, I'll let you know where you can get in touch with me," she said, frowning a little as she looked around the bedroom. She'd used the brush this morning. Where had she put it?

"You're leaving? No discussion? Just walking out?" Luke sounded angry, which was interesting. Wasn't she the one who was supposed to be angry?

"I'll come back later for the rest of my things, or maybe Consuela could pack them up and you could send them to me." The dresser. She was almost positive she'd set her brush on top of the dresser.

"We have a contract. Remember? Stay married for a year. You get lots of money. I get my vineyards. Ring any bells?"

"Yes, of course." Brush in hand, Cat turned from the dresser and looked at him, surprised to find that it wasn't difficult at all. He was standing just inside the doorway, feet braced slightly apart, hands loose at his sides. His dark hair was rumpled, as if he'd run his fingers through it. Or as if someone else had. She looked away blindly, slamming the door on the images that brought to mind.

"Are you just going to break the contract?" Luke

asked, and the accusation in his voice helped reinforce that lovely wall that surrounded her. "I thought you agreed that saving the vineyard was important."

She carried the brush over to the bed and dropped it into the tote. "You and I both know that Nick isn't going to sell Maiden's Morning. Not now, probably not ever."

"And if he does?"

"Then I imagine you could buy it the same way anyone else could. You could have done that to begin with, if you hadn't wanted to beat him at his own game."

She sounded calm, a little distracted, as if only part of her attention was on the conversation. It threw Luke off balance. This wasn't what he'd expected. During the drive home, he'd prepared several different speeches, starting with justification and ending up with simple apology, because there was no justifying what she'd walked in on. He wasn't a hormone-raddled sixteen-year-old who couldn't keep his pants zipped. He was a married man, and the fact that their marriage was temporary didn't justify him screwing around with Devon.

Luke had pictured several different scenarios. Cat in tears. Cat screaming at him and maybe throwing small breakable objects in his direction. Cat refusing to speak to him. He'd considered them all, but he hadn't expected this—this calm woman who was snapping shut the latches on her suitcase and glancing around one last time as if this were a hotel room and she was checking to make sure she hadn't forgotten anything. He didn't know what to do, what to say. Worse, he wasn't sure she was even interested in listening.

"If you want, I'll tell Nick that moving out was my decision," she said. She picked up the tote and slid the strap over her shoulder, then reached for the handle of the suitcase with her other hand. "Or you can just let him think we're still living together. I don't see any reason why he should find out we aren't.''

She wasn't giving him anything to work with, nothing to push against. How could he explain when she hardly seemed to know he was there? How could he apologize when she didn't look at him?

"You don't have to do this," he said finally.

He saw her fingers tighten around the handle of the suitcase, the first sign of emotion he'd seen. "Yes, I think I do."

"Cat, what you saw—"

"Don't." The single word cut him off, sharp as a knife. For a split second he saw something wild and raw in her expression, a hurt so deep that it silenced him. An instant only, then it was gone, but he knew he wouldn't forget it or forget that he was the one who'd put that look in her eyes. "Don't," she said again, more quietly.

"Cat—"

"What are you going to say, Luke? Are you going to tell me it wasn't what it looked like?" Sarcasm edged her voice like a razor blade. "You and Devon were just playing doctor? You weren't really about to sleep with her?"

For one desperate moment, she half wanted him to deny it. Even if it was a lie, she wanted to hear him say it wasn't true, that it had all been a terrible misunderstanding and there really was some logical explanation why Devon had been half-naked in Luke's arms. She could learn to live with a lie. People did it all the time.

A muscle twitched in Luke's jaw, and his eyes had never looked colder or more distant.

"It was exactly what it looked like," he said finally, and Cat felt her calm facade start to crack, the words hitting it like fists. "But it didn't happen."

"Only because I showed up. You don't get points for

accidental fidelity.'' She tightened her fingers around the handle of the suitcase and moved past him to the door. ''I told you once that I don't share. I meant it.''

She was really going to walk out. So much for thinking she was in love with him, he thought bitterly. If she were, she wouldn't walk out so easily. She would be willing to listen to his explanation, never mind that he didn't *have* an explanation. Guilt and anger tangled in his gut. Anger surfaced first, and he spoke without giving himself time to think.

''If you walk out, all deals are off,'' he said harshly. ''I'll consider our contract broken, and you can kiss the settlement goodbye.''

Cat froze in the doorway, her back stiff. When she started to turn, he felt a sick kind of triumph. Money. It really was all about the money. He'd been a fool to think it was anything else. His sneer died half-formed when he saw Cat's face. Tears shimmered in her eyes, and her lower lip trembled.

''You never did get it, did you?'' Her voice was low, ragged with suppressed emotion, but it steadied, gained in volume, as she went on. ''I don't give a damn about your money. I never did. Do you know why I married you?'' Luke hoped it was a rhetorical question, because he couldn't think of an intelligent response. ''I married you because I was in love with you. Stupid as it sounds, I thought maybe, if we spent time together, you might come to feel something for me. I was wrong.'' She stopped and drew a shaky breath, released it slowly. A tear slid down her cheek, unnoticed. ''That's okay. I took a chance, and I lost. I can live with that.''

''Cat, I—'' He had no idea what he was going to say. That he hadn't meant to hurt her? That love hadn't been part of the bargain? He didn't know, but it didn't matter, because she didn't let him finish.

"What I can't live with is the idea that I fell in love with such a total jackass. Do you know what you can do with your contract and your settlement, Luke?" She took a half step closer, and Luke fought the urge to back up. Despite the tears, she looked mad enough to do bodily harm, and that suitcase was heavy enough to qualify as a lethal weapon. "You can take all of it, every clause and every dollar bill, and you can shove them up your ass."

Without waiting for a response, Cat spun on her heel and walked out. Luke stood where she'd left him, listening to the muffled clack of her sandals on the stairs and, a moment later, the quiet thud of the front door closing. It would have been better if she'd slammed it, he thought. There was something final about that quiet little click. Very final.

He stood there for a long time, listening to the emptiness all around him.

Chapter Eighteen

Luke had lived alone for a long time. When he started college, he'd bought a smallish condo on Sunset Boulevard, within tolerable driving distance of the UCLA campus. He'd paid for it with money from a trust fund his father had left him. It had been his first real-estate purchase, and when he sold it six years later, he got double what he paid for it. Even before that, when he was living with his parents, it had been almost like living alone. Between their skiing jaunts to Aspen, snorkeling trips to St. Thomas and shopping in New York or Paris, they were gone almost as much as they were home. And when they were in Los Angeles, the frenetic pace of their social life kept them out of the house most of the time.

Any way you figured it, he'd spent a good chunk of his life living by himself, and it had always suited him just fine. There was no one to answer to. He could come and go as he pleased without worrying about anyone else's plans. If he wanted to eat crackers in bed, there was no one to complain about the crumbs, and if wanted to paint the walls purple, he didn't have to justify it to someone else. Living alone was, as Martha Stewart might say, a good thing.

Or it had been.

Luke's fingers tightened on the steering wheel, and he scowled at the concrete wall of the parking structure. He'd lived in that house for almost a decade. Cat had lived there for eight months. Logic said that, when she left, the house should just go back to being *his* house again, but damned if she hadn't imprinted herself on it somehow. It didn't feel quiet and peaceful, it felt empty and full of echoes. And his office wasn't much better. Depending on his mood, he either remembered Cat showing up on his birthday wearing that long green coat and not much else, or he flashed on those few awful moments when she'd walked in on him and Devon in flagrante pretty-damned delicto. Either way, it didn't make for a relaxing workspace.

So in a few short months, she'd managed to pretty much ruin both his office and his house. Which was why he was sitting in his car staring at the wall of the damned parking structure, trying to figure out where he could go and *not* think about his wife.

He missed her, dammit. It had been three weeks, and he missed her like hell. He reached for the ignition key. He was also suffering from an acute—and deserved—guilty conscience. He'd behaved like the jackass she'd called him, starting with his reaction when she told him she was pregnant and culminating spectacularly in the scene with Devon. He owed Cat an apology—a really big one. She would probably throw it back in his face, but he owed her a chance to do that, too.

If he'd needed any proof of just how wrong he'd been, this morning he'd found her checkbook in her underwear drawer, empty now except for a pair of peach-colored panties tucked in a back corner and the leather checkbook. Flipping through the ledger, he'd found less than a dozen entries. If the last balance was accurate, Cat had barely touched the money that had been deposited in her account each month.

Standing in front of the dresser, he'd stared at the scrawled entries, thinking she had some of the worst handwriting he'd ever seen, thinking she'd left the checkbook behind deliberately, because it had never been about money for her. It had been about love. She'd loved him, and now she was somewhere in L.A., pregnant and alone, with nothing but that stupid little car that wheezed on steep hills and a suitcase full of clothes.

He'd been completely and totally in the wrong, and, if he'd had any doubts about it, no one else did. Even without knowing what had happened, no one seemed to have any trouble laying the blame on his doorstep. Merry sneered at him whenever their paths crossed. Consuela glared and muttered in Spanish. And his grandfather...his grandfather hadn't doubted for a minute that the breakup was his fault.

A week after Cat left, he'd gone to see Nick to tell him she was gone and more or less double-dog dare him to do his worst with Maiden's Morning. Nick had stared at him in obvious dismay.

"Catherine did what?"

"She moved out." Luke kept his voice casual. "I guess a year was too long to—"

"What the hell did you do?" Nick demanded.

"What did *I* do?" Luke's indignation was sharpened by the knowledge that his grandfather was absolutely right to assume his guilt. "What makes you think I did anything?"

Before Nick could respond, Luis brought coffee and a plate of cookies into the den.

"Arguing already?" He clucked his tongue in exasperation as he set the tray on the coffee table. "You two—you need a referee to keep peace between you." He handed the first cup to Nick. "I boxed up some of the cookies for you to take home to your wife," he told Luke. "She said peanut butter are her favorites."

"Might as well throw them to the hogs," Nick said, setting his cup down with a thud.

"We have no hogs," Luis reminded him calmly. "If you like, I can get some. I have a cousin in Corona. He has—"

"She's left him," Nick interrupted without apology. "Catherine's left him."

Luis stared at him, mouth open in shock, Luke's cup in one hand, the plate of cookies in the other. Luke waited for the inevitable questions and just as inevitable sympathy. If there was one thing he could count on, it was that Luis would take his side in any—

"What did you do?" Luis's dark eyes were fierce. "What did you say to her?"

Caught off guard, Luke gaped at him. "I... Why does everyone assume *I* did something?" he demanded.

"Because any idiot could see the girl was head over heels in love with you," Nick snapped.

"*Sí.*" Luis nodded vigorous agreement. Agitation thickened his accent and fractured his English. "She look at you in *such* a way, and I think to myself, you are very lucky."

"It wasn't real," Luke protested. "It was... You both knew why I married her." *Jesus, had everyone but him known that Cat was in love with him?* He paced to the empty fireplace and back, tension coiling in the pit of his stomach. He glared at his grandfather. "You're the one who pushed me into this."

"Ha." Nick bristled with irritation. "Don't you lay this at my door. You got engaged to the stepsister because you knew I despised her, but you married Catherine because you *wanted* to marry her."

"I didn't *want* to marry anyone," Luke said, his voice hoarse with the need to shout. "I got married because you were going to sell Maiden's Morning if I didn't." He jabbed a finger in Nick's direction. "You're the one who set this in motion."

Nick shoved himself to his feet, and the two of them faced each other across the length of the coffee table. The air crackled with tension. Luis stood, arms crossed on his chest, and watched the show. "Even if I'd sold the vineyard, you could have bought the damned thing from me if you wanted to," Nick said.

Luke barely restrained the urge to pull his own hair out by the roots. *God, had everyone thought of that but him?* It was so obvious, but he'd been so damned focused on beating Nick at his own game that he hadn't even looked at alternatives.

"What happened with Catherine?" Nick demanded. "Are you going to be able to patch things up?"

Luke shrugged, hoping he didn't look as sullen as he felt. Nothing in his life was going the way it was supposed to, and the most disgusting thing about it was that he didn't have anyone to blame but himself. He damned well wasn't going to tell his grandfather why Cat had left. He wasn't proud of what had happened—what had *almost* happened—with Devon.

"What are you going to do about Maiden's Morning?" he asked.

Nick glared at him. "You can have the damned place.

Now, are you going to tell me what happened with Catherine?''

Luke waited to see if the top of his head was going to stay in place before attempting a reply. After all the manipulation, blackmailing him into marriage—and yes, dammit, maybe he *could* have bought the damned place himself but it had still been blackmail—after all that, Nick was just going to *hand* him the deed?

For some reason, he flashed on the look in Cat's eyes when she'd walked into the office and seen him with Devon. She'd been so hurt, and though he knew it was unreasonable, a part of him felt that at least some of the blame for that hurt could be laid at Nick's door. If he hadn't tried to play God with someone else's life...Jesus, he was about to become a *father* because of Nick's damned meddling. Never mind that his own pigheaded determination to best the old man had contributed to what had happened. Nick had set the whole thing in motion.

''I want the paperwork on my desk tomorrow,'' he said, then turned and walked out, ignoring Nick's furious demand that he return and Luis's exasperated comment that the two of them were worse than goats.

Almost three weeks later, Maiden's Morning was his, lock, stock and oak barrels. Luke hadn't talked to his grandfather again. He knew he would eventually. He was angry at the old man, but he would get over it. In the meantime, it wouldn't hurt Nick to stew in his own juices a bit. He almost wished he'd told Nick about the baby. Let him wonder if his meddling was going to cost him the great-grandchild he'd been so bound and determined to have.

Luke stopped at a red light and realized that he was only a few blocks from Keith's condo. He'd been driving on autopilot, reluctant to go home to an empty house. He flipped on his turn signal. If Keith hadn't eaten yet, maybe they could have dinner. They hadn't gotten together since the night they both got drunk, the night before he'd done such a good job of blowing his life apart. Keith didn't even know yet that Cat had walked out.

"I know."

"You do?" Luke looked at his friend in surprise. Keith already knew Cat had left him? "How?"

The two of them were in Keith's living room, which was decorated in a sort of Danish-modern-meets-real-life motif. Pale wood and clean lines were blurred by a scattering of *Sports Illustrated* issues, two pairs of running shoes under one of the chairs, a basketball on one end of the sofa and, for some unknown reason, a tower of copper pans that leaned drunkenly against the fireplace. Luke couldn't remember ever seeing the place so untidy and wondered vaguely what had happened to Keith's maid service.

"Cat told me she'd moved out," Keith said, and Luke's already minor interest in his friend's housekeeping arrangements vanished instantly.

"She told you?" he repeated blankly. "When?"

Keith shifted uneasily on the sofa, as if the pale linen upholstery had suddenly sprouted tacks. "Actually, it was…um…the day she left."

"She came to see *you?*" Luke tried and failed to think of a reason why Cat would go to Keith. Unless she was worried about his threat to nullify their contract if she walked out. She hadn't seemed to care about that, but maybe she'd changed her mind.

"Did she want to know if walking out would break the contract?"

"The contract?" Keith looked blank for a moment and

then shook his head. "You're the only one who cares about that contract, Luke. I don't think Cat ever cared about the money."

He sounded faintly disgusted, and Luke felt himself flush. "The whole arrangement was about money," he snapped. "Settlements? Large dollar figures? Ring any bells?"

"Cat complaining it was too much money? You threatening to double the settlement? Ring any bells?" Keith asked with heavy sarcasm. "If you'd been paying any attention, you'd have figured out it wasn't the money from the beginning."

Luke opened his mouth to protest, then shut it again without speaking. Keith was right. He'd seen exactly what he wanted to see and had missed the obvious.

"Okay, so why did Cat come to see you?"

"She didn't." Keith leaned back, one ankle braced on the opposite knee. "She came to see Jack, and I happened to be there. She was very upset."

"Yeah, I'm not surprised." Luke looked away. "Did she tell you what happened?"

"Just that you'd both realized what a mistake it had been to get married, and that she was sure you and Nick would work things out about the vineyard."

Luke nodded, relieved that she hadn't told Keith about walking in on him with Devon. It hadn't been one of his better moments.

"I don't think I've ever seen anyone cry that hard," Keith said, and Luke's relief was immediately swamped by guilt. The thought of Cat in tears was like acid in his gut.

"It was my fault," he said abruptly. "All of it was my fault."

"I figured it was," Keith said, nodding.

"What is it with everyone?" Luke asked, aggrieved. "Do I have a sign on my forehead that says I Screwed Up?"

"No, but you do have one that says I'm A Prickly Bastard, And I'm Too Stupid To See What's In Front Of My Nose."

Luke glared at him and then gave up. How the hell could he defend himself? He'd been wrong all the way down the line. From the moment he accepted Cat's crazy suggestion that he should marry her right through to letting her walk out the door without getting down on his knees and offering her the groveled apology she deserved, he'd been wrong about everything.

"Fuck you," he said finally. As comebacks went, it was pretty weak, and he wasn't surprised when Keith grinned.

"Yeah, I love you, too, buddy."

Luke let his head fall back against the chair. God, he was tired. He hadn't had a decent night's sleep in three weeks. The damned bed was too big, too empty, just like the house. Just like his life.

"Do you know where she's staying?" The phone number she'd left wasn't her stepfather's, not that he could imagine her moving back there while Devon was in residence.

Keith looked surprised. "She hasn't gotten in touch?"

"She called and left a message, gave me a phone number. No address."

"Did you try calling her?"

"No. I need to see her. I need to tell her I'm sorry."

"About what?"

"None of your damned business." Luke lifted his head to glare at his friend. "So do you know where she's staying?"

"Yes." He continued before Luke had a chance to feel relieved. "But I'm not going to give you her address."

"What?" Shocked, Luke stared at him.

Keith shrugged. "I'm sorry, Luke, but if she wanted you to have her address, she'd give it to you."

"You're *my* lawyer, dammit."

"I'm not acting as Cat's lawyer," Keith snapped. His foot hit the floor with a thud, and he leaned forward, eyes dark with temper. "I'm acting as her friend." He stabbed one finger in Luke's direction. "I don't know what the hell you did, but I don't *ever* want to see anyone cry like that again, especially not Cat. If you'd been standing in front of me, I'd have punched you in the nose. And you're damned lucky Jack couldn't get his hands on you."

"I want to apologize to her, dammit."

"Do it over the phone."

Luke was just debating the satisfaction to be gained from beating his best friend to a pulp when they both heard the sound of a key in the front door. Keith stiffened as if he'd been hit with a cattle prod, his eyes going wild and panicky.

"Lucy, I'm home." The thud of the door shutting punctuated a very bad Cuban accent. "Gail is handling the early setup. I told her I'd be back by eight to take care of the—"

Jack's voice trailed off as he walked into the living room and saw Luke.

Keith stood up. "We've got company."

We? Luke thought. *There's a "we"?*

"So I see." Jack's tone was less than welcoming. His smile was blade sharp. "You ought to be more careful who you open the door to, Keith. I've got standards about that sort of thing."

He had standards? Luke looked around the living room,

really paying attention to what he was seeing. Two pairs
of shoes. And the damned pans. Not exactly Keith's style,
not to mention that, in all the years he'd known him, he'd
never known Keith to be anything but a neatnick.

Holy shit, they'd moved in together.

"You're living together?" Feeling at a disadvantage
seated, he stood up and looked from Keith to Jack, then
back again. "He moved in here?"

"Yeah." Keith flushed and tilted his chin. "Is that a
problem?"

"A problem?" Luke blinked. Was it a problem that his
best friend was sleeping with a guy? That he was sleeping
with Jack in particular? Or that Jack was obviously a total
slob?

"It's kind of sudden, isn't it? I mean, you just decided
you—" He waved vaguely between Keith and Jack. It
seemed tactless to say that, less than a month ago, Keith
had been, as far as he knew, a heterohappy kind of guy,
but the change was startling enough to warrant at least a
mention. "And now you're living together?"

"Life's short," Keith said, shrugging. "We decided to
take a chance. If it doesn't work out…well, at least we
gave it a shot."

Luke didn't know whether he should admire his
friend's guts or suggest therapy. He settled for something
more conventional. "I hope it works out."

"Thanks." That was Keith. Jack gave him a grudging
nod and looked marginally less hostile.

"Now, are you going to tell me where Cat is?" Luke's
focus shifted back to what really mattered.

"No," Jack said instantly.

"I need to talk to her."

"Why?" If Jack had suffered any temporary softening

of hostility, he'd recovered from it. He came forward, his expression sharp with anger.

"I want to make sure she's all right, dammit," Luke snapped. "She hasn't picked up the rest of her things. That damned car isn't much more than a tuna can on wheels, and she's pregnant. I think that's reason enough to worry."

"You should have thought of that sooner," Jack said coldly. "If she wanted to see you, she'd call."

Luke ignored him, focusing his attention on Keith. "You're not going to tell me where she is?"

Keith looked regretful but shook his head. "I can't. I can tell you that she's okay, though."

Later he would be relieved to know that, Luke thought distantly. He would be glad to know that Cat was safe and well. He would probably even be grateful she had friends she could count on, even if one of them was supposed to be *his* best friend. He might even appreciate that Keith was doing the right thing, keeping Cat's confidence like this. He would see that this was a good thing, an admirable thing.

Maybe later, when he'd gotten past the urge to bounce someone's head off the nearest wall.

Knowing that anything he said was likely to be something he would later regret, he turned and walked out.

Worried, Keith watched him leave. He'd never seen Luke look so…empty.

"Well, wasn't that cozy?" Jack commented when the door had closed behind Luke.

"He looks like hell," Keith said, wondering if he should go after him.

"I can't think of anyone who deserves it more."

"Maybe," Keith admitted reluctantly. He'd known Luke too long to have any illusions about him. Cat hadn't said anything about what had happened to make her leave, but he didn't doubt it was Luke's fault. "I still don't like seeing him that way."

"That's okay," Jack said with a grin. "I enjoyed it enough for both of us."

The cheerful heartlessness startled a laugh out of him. He'd lived alone since moving out of his parents' house, and he'd expected it to be difficult to get used to sharing his space with someone, but so far it had been a nearly painless transition.

It was ironic that the breakup of his friend's marriage had been the catalyst for him suggesting that Jack move in with him. Jack had insisted that Cat stay with him, but his apartment only had one bedroom. After a week of sleeping on the sofa, Jack hadn't offered more than a token protest when Keith mentioned that his condo had two bedrooms and Jack was welcome to one of them.

Neither of them had mentioned making the arrangement permanent, but more and more of Jack's things migrated from Santa Monica to Beverly Hills on an almost daily basis, and it was already difficult to imagine living alone again. Officially Jack was staying in the extra bedroom, but his clutter spread outward like an invasionary force, and he'd yet to spend a night in the spare room. Keith was faintly astonished to find that he really liked sharing his life with someone—with Jack.

It wasn't all sweetness and light. Considering the fact that his staff referred to him as the neatness Nazi in the kitchen, he was a total slob in the rest of his life. He was also a bed hog, and it had taken all of Keith's legal skills to negotiate possession of the remote control, but those were minor annoyances. He liked having someone to talk to in the morning, liked listening to Jack plan the daily menus for the restaurant, even if he had proven resistant to Keith's suggestion to add s'mores and SPAM to the selection.

They suited each other more than he would have believed possible, and he couldn't help but feel a little guilty that things were falling into place for him just when Luke's marriage was falling apart.

"Hey." Jack slung an arm around his neck and dragged him into a quick, hard kiss. "No brooding allowed. I was going to drag you off to a movie, but we're a little short on time for that now, so just because I'm a really nice guy, I'll cook you dinner." He waggled his eyebrows. "If you're a very good boy, I'll let you mince the garlic."

"Oh, goody. Just what I dreamed of during all those years at law school." Keith was smiling as he followed Jack into the kitchen.

Cat slid Ruthie into a parking place near the restaurant and shut off the engine. She let her head fall back against the seat. This was one of those days when she was pretty sure she should have stayed in bed. Morning sickness, dry crackers and discovering an infestation of aphids on the broccoli seedlings she was nursing along until the weather cooled off enough for them to go in the garden had just been the start of her day.

For three weeks and two days, she'd managed to avoid Devon, and then, this morning, when she was already feeling like a limp dishrag, there Devon had been in all her perky blond prettiness, wearing a white suit, jacket open to reveal a pale blue silk shell, her pale hair a cap of artfully tousled curls, her makeup perfect, and not a speck of dust on her white sling-back pumps.

One glance was all it had taken. Cat was suddenly painfully conscious of her hair bundled in a careless knot on top of her head and the fact that she was wearing not a speck of makeup. Her baggy denim cutoffs, bleach-splotched T-shirt and scuffed clogs weren't exactly a fashion statement, even if they were perfectly appropriate for pulling weeds and harvesting vegetables.

Her imagination presented her with a cruelly accurate comparison of the two of them, and for one thoroughly maudlin moment she thought she could hardly blame Luke for wanting Devon. Then Devon saw her. She hesitated, as if thinking about coming over, then settled for a small, pitying smile, and Cat felt a flash of white-hot anger that had her clenching her fingers around Ruthie's steering wheel hard enough that the plastic made little creaking noises.

Devon was pretty, but she had the depth of a mud puddle, and if Luke was stupid enough to prefer her, then he deserved what he got. Teeth clenched against the urge to get out of the car and throw Devon into the compost pile, she watched the other woman get in her car—a boring little pseudo-sports car, Cat noted with a sneer—and drove off.

Four hours later, the memory was still enough to make Cat grit her teeth. She pushed open Ruthie's door and got out. Naomi would tell her that she had to let go of the anger. She would say that anger was a poison and urge her to meditate until she'd purged it from her system.

It had been three weeks and two days since she'd walked into Luke's office and caught him with his pants practically down around his ankles. Three weeks and two days, and the memory of it was still a huge aching hole in the pit of her stomach. The frozen calm she'd felt at first had dissolved by the time she got to Jack's apartment, and she'd cried until she couldn't cry anymore. Since then, she'd alternated between a sort of numb emptiness—Luke was gone from her life—and an anger like nothing she'd ever felt before—how *stupid* could he be? In between, she dealt with morning sickness and tried to figure out what the hell she was going to do now.

She'd thought vaguely about what she was going to do if, at the end of the year, Luke still wanted to end their marriage, but none of those tentative plans had included a baby. Now, here she was, pregnant, alone and without a clue.

"Should have taken the damned checkbook," she muttered as she opened the back of the car. In the first flush of hurt and anger, she'd deliberately left the checkbook behind, telling herself she didn't need any of Luke's money. "Pride goeth before a fall."

Cat dragged a bright orange hand truck out and then loaded the first carefully packed box of vegetables onto it. Leaving the checkbook had been a noble gesture but not the brightest thing she'd ever done, she thought. Now that she was about to become a parent, she was really going to have to cultivate practicality over grand gestures.

She shut the hatchback and set her foot against the bottom of the hand truck, tilting it back until it was balanced over the wheels. It wasn't that she was in danger of starving, and thanks to Jack, she had a place to live. At first she'd worried about putting him out of his own apartment, but it was pretty obvious that neither he nor Keith had any problem sharing Keith's condo, so maybe something good had come out of this mess.

Still, she was going to have to do some serious thinking about the future. Stupid as it had been to leave the checkbook behind, she couldn't bring herself to ask Luke for it. He was so obsessed with the idea that she'd married him for his money. If she asked for the stupid checkbook, it was just going to confirm his suspicions. Not that she could entirely blame him, she admitted reluctantly. That *had* been the deal, complete with contracts. It wasn't his fault that she'd had something else in mind. Now, thanks to her pride, she was broke and pregnant—damn near a walking cliché.

Cat pulled open the door of Jack's Place, propping it open with her foot while she pushed the hand truck through. The lunch crowd was gone, and it would be another two hours before the restaurant opened for dinner. Jack referred to this time of day as the lull between battles, cleaning up after lunch and starting preparations for the dinner crowd. The dining area was quiet, tables empty and waiting. The kitchen would be in a subdued bustle, gradually building up to an organized frenzy as the door opened and customers began to arrive.

Cat had barely made it through the door when Jack appeared, taking the hand truck from her with a frown. "I told you to let me know when you got here and I'd unload this stuff for you."

"I'm pregnant, Jack, not paralyzed. They both begin with the letter *p,* but one has more syllables than the other."

"You shouldn't be lifting heavy boxes."

"Pregnancy, not a hernia." She patted him on the cheek, grinning when he scowled at her. "You really need to brush up on your medical terms."

"Smartass," he muttered.

"Thanks. I love you, too." Cat trailed after him as he pushed the cart into the kitchen. It was kind of sweet, really, the way he'd gone all overprotective male on her the minute he found out she was pregnant. "Wait until you see the corn. It's incredible, and the yellow plum tomatoes are producing like crazy, so I brought some extra of those."

Jack was stacking the boxes on the stainless steel

counter as she spoke. Cat had to admit that she wasn't sorry to leave the job to him. Hot pinchers couldn't have pulled the admission out of her, but she was feeling just a little fragile these days.

Jack rattled off a few instructions to the kitchen staff, then wrapped his fingers around Cat's upper arm and tugged her out of the kitchen, into the relative privacy of the empty dining room.

"Are you all right? And don't give me any crap about pregnancy not being an illness," he added, cutting her off.

"I'm fine." He looked doubtful, and she tried again. "I'm really fine, Jack."

"Well, you look like hell,' he said bluntly.

"Thanks. You don't know how reassuring that is." She reached up to run her fingers through her hair. "I'm a little tired, that's all. It's perfectly normal."

"You're not working tonight."

She'd already anticipated that argument. "Are you firing me?"

"I'm trying to give you the night off," he said through gritted teeth.

"Thanks, but no thanks." Cat grabbed hold of his hand, squeezing affectionately. "Jack, you've got to stop this. You're the one who insisted that I come to work for you. If I'm going to work for you, you've got to treat me like you would any other employee. I'm *fine*. I'm a little tired, but I really am okay. I need a job, and if you're not going to let me do this one, I'll find something else."

"You don't need a job," he protested. "You can stay at my place as long as you want, and if you need more money than what you make with the garden, I can help you, at least until you've had a chance to look around and figure out what you want to do. Believe me, I can afford to semisupport you for a few months."

Cat restrained the urge to roll her eyes. This wasn't the first time they'd had this argument, and she was fairly sure it wouldn't be the last. She'd known it was a mistake to let him talk her into working for him, but he'd been so insistent, and she had to admit that she hadn't really been excited by the idea of trying to find a job.

Jack must have seen the exasperation she was trying to hide, because he threw up his hands in frustration. "Fine. You're tough. I get it."

Cat laughed and patted his arm. "You're cute when you're frustrated."

"And you're stubborn as a mule."

Traffic noise rushed into the room as the front door opened. They both turned as someone walked in, a tall figure silhouetted against the bright sunlight outside for a moment before the door closed behind him.

"Sorry, we're closed," Jack said. "We open for dinner at—" He broke off, his expression hardening when he saw who it was. "We reserve the right to refuse service to anyone, Quintain."

Luke barely glanced at him, and Cat felt seared by the intensity of his look. "I want to talk to you."

"*She* doesn't want to talk to *you.*" Jack shifted subtly, putting himself between them.

"Jack." Cat spoke softly. "It's okay."

"You don't have to talk to him."

"I know, but I want to." Not quite true, she admitted to herself. What she really wanted was to dive through the nearest door and run like hell. She'd assumed that she and Luke would eventually talk, but she hadn't expected it to be here and now. But there was no good reason to refuse to talk to him.

Jack looked like he really wanted to argue, but instead he nodded abruptly. "I'll be in the kitchen if you need me." He gave Luke a hard, warning look before pushing through the swinging door, leaving the two of them alone.

Chapter Nineteen

Luke had already admitted to himself that he missed her, but he hadn't realized how much until he saw her again. It was like that scene in *The Wizard of Oz* where Dorothy opens the door of the farmhouse and suddenly there's color everywhere. His eyes drank her in. She was wearing a camp shirt the color of ripe peaches, and trim black jeans that made the most of those long legs. A pair of dull gold clips pulled her coppery hair back from her face.

She looked tired, he thought. Pale, and a little fragile, as if she hadn't been sleeping well.

"How have you been?" Cat asked, breaking the tense silence and making Luke realize that he'd been staring at her. He forced himself to look away, trying to act as if he wasn't thinking about throwing her over his shoulder and carrying her off.

"Fine. You?"

"Good. I've been good." She slid her hands into the back pockets of her jeans, and Luke tried not to notice the soft thrust of her breasts. "I've been busy," she added. "With the garden and…things."

Trying to put her life back together. Trying not to think about him.

"I guess this is a busy time of year in the garden," Luke said.

"Pretty busy."

God, he looked incredible. He must have come from the office. He was wearing gray slacks, and a light blue shirt with the collar unbuttoned and the sleeves rolled up his forearms. He would have been wearing a tie, and she didn't have to close her eyes to picture him tugging it off, long fingers impatient with the knot. His hair was a little untidy, as if he'd run his fingers through it, or maybe he'd had the car window down.

Looking at him was both pleasure and pain. She'd missed him so much. Over the last three weeks, the pain had gone from acute to a sort of dull ache. Seeing him like this meant she was going to have to start all over again, convincing herself that she'd done the right thing, the *only* thing she could have done, ignoring the part of her that wanted to pretend the scene in his office had been a figment of her imagination.

Remembering that, she suddenly wanted to get this over with.

"You wanted to talk to me?"

"You...forgot this."

He held out her checkbook, and Cat flushed, hesitating a moment before sliding one hand out of her pocket to take it from him. She was sure he knew that she hadn't forgotten it, that she'd left it behind deliberately. It was kind of him to offer her that pretense.

"Thanks." She turned the butter-soft leather over in her hands, head down to watch the aimless movement. "How did you know where I was?"

"Would you believe I hired a private detective?" His voice held rueful amusement.

"You're kidding." Cat's head came up, and she stared at him in disbelief.

"No. I figured that was the fastest way to track you down. It didn't take her long to find you."

"Well, I wasn't exactly trying to hide," she pointed out. "I gave you a phone number. Why didn't you just call?"

"I did. A couple of times, and got an answering machine."

"You could have left a message."

"I wasn't sure you'd call me back."

Cat started to say that of course she'd have called him back, and then hesitated, not sure it was true. She hunched one shoulder in a half shrug and tightened her grip on the checkbook. "Thanks for bringing this to me."

"Well, whatever else happens, you earned that money."

She startled herself by laughing, a short sharp sound that held real amusement. "Oh yeah, living in the lap of luxury for eight months. I really deserve pay for pain and suffering."

Luke smiled a little. "Yeah, well, you had to put up with me."

"True." She shot him a teasing look from under her lashes. "Now *that* was *real* torture."

He grinned. "Cruel and unusual punishment?"

"Time for hazard pay."

The laughter faded abruptly, and they looked away from each other. Luke could hear voices and the occasional clatter of pans coming from the kitchen, but the sounds somehow added to the feeling of isolation.

"You don't have to worry about the contract," he said

abruptly. "I won't try to break it." His mouth kicked up at one corner. "I don't think my lawyer would let me, even if I wanted to."

Cat laughed softly. "Keith's been great. You...um... you know that he and Jack are...uh..."

He came to her rescue. "Yes, I know that they're... uh..." She laughed again, and he felt the tightness in his chest ease. Things couldn't be hopeless if she could laugh like that, could they? "From the looks of it, if Keith doesn't end up killing him because he's a slob, they may do okay together."

"Tidiness isn't one of Jack's better qualities."

"I told Nick that you left," he said abruptly.

She looked up at him, her eyes dark with worry. "How did it go?"

He shrugged. "Okay, I guess. He signed Maiden's Morning over to me last week."

"Oh, that's wonderful." Cat's smile was warm with relief. "I knew he'd be reasonable about it."

"I'm not sure reasonable is the word I'd use," Luke said dryly. "We're sort of not speaking at the moment."

She clicked her tongue and shook her head in exasperation. "Honestly, Luke, someone should bang your heads together. What is it with the two of you?"

"I don't know." He hunched one shoulder defensively. "We're too much alike, maybe."

"Both pigheaded."

"Goats," he said. "Luis says we're both goats."

"The goats I've known have been very intelligent," she said dryly.

"Ouch." He flinched. "Guess that puts me in my place."

"It wouldn't if the two of you would just *talk* to each other. Nick's not getting any younger, you know. How are you going to feel if something happens to him while the two of you are in the midst of one of your snits?''

"Snits?" Luke was torn between amusement and annoyance. He had good reason to be pissed at the old man, though it didn't seem nearly as important as it had a few days ago. She had a way of putting things in perspective, of putting his whole damned life in perspective.

"Come home, Cat." He hadn't meant to say it, hadn't intended to ask her. He hadn't even let himself think about the possibility, but the words were suddenly there, and he didn't take them back.

He heard her breath catch a little, and her eyes went big and dark. For just a moment, he thought he saw longing there, and he thought maybe... But then she was shaking her head.

"I don't think that would be a good idea, Luke."

"I didn't sleep with Devon." The words came out stark, half defensive, half pleading.

Cat paled, her expression closing up, closing him out. Her voice was tight, as if she had to force the words out. "No, but if I hadn't walked in, you would have."

He wanted to deny it, but it would have been a lie. The whole scene with Devon had the hazy darkness of a bad dream. He remembered a vague feeling that he had to prove something to himself—or maybe to Cat. It didn't make any sense now, hadn't made sense then, but he knew he would have gone through with it.

"I don't give a damn about Devon," he said at last.

Cat's mouth twisted in a sad half smile. "I know."

Had he really thought that would make it any better? Luke wondered. Like meaningless sex with another woman was somehow less of a betrayal?

Cat sighed and reached out to pat his arm, soothing him. "You don't need to worry about me, Luke. I'm going to be fine. And you don't have to worry about the baby, either. I've seen a doctor, and she says I'm healthy as a horse. I...we never really talked about it, so I don't know if you want to be...involved at all. I know this wasn't what you had planned.''

"It wasn't what you had planned, either.''

"No, it wasn't.'' Her smile was rueful, a little self-mocking. "But here I am and I...I really want this baby, Luke.'' She put one hand on her still-flat stomach, and this time her smile was soft and warm. "Now that it's happened, I really do want it.'' Her hand fell to her side again, and her tone became brisk, businesslike. "Anyway, I don't want you to feel obligated. Jack has already agreed to be my childbirth coach. I'm staying at his place now, and since it looks like him living with Keith might be a permanent arrangement, I may just stay there.'' She lifted the checkbook a little sheepishly. "I can afford it now.''

Listening to her, Luke felt as if he was being hollowed out, as if each word was taking away a vital part of him. She was telling him—politely, kindly—that she didn't need him, that she would manage just fine without him. And she would. She would build a life without him, a life for her and the baby. She wouldn't ask him for anything, wouldn't expect anything from him. And that was pretty damned depressing. When had he become the sort of man that a woman would expect to walk away from his own child?

"Cat, I—"

Whatever he'd planned to say, it was drowned out by a sudden rush of noise as the kitchen door swung open. A short, swarthy man stalked out, waving his arms and talking rapidly—and loudly—in French. Jack followed hot on his heels.

"No one wants to eat pumpkin pie in September, Armand."

"How do you know?" Armand turned and jabbed one finger in Jack's direction. "You know nothing. I make a pumpkin pie light as a feather. Put it on the menu and people will order it."

"I don't care if the damned thing is so light it has to be tied to the table. Americans aren't going to order pumpkin pie in September. You're the dessert chef, not the owner. *I*—" Jack's thumb hooked back at his own chest "—am the owner. *I* decide what goes on the menu."

Armand's dark eyes flashed, and his chest swelled with indignation. He opened his mouth, the words *I quit* hovering almost visibly on the air, but Jack spoke first.

"We'll put the damned pie on the menu. If people order it, fine. If they don't, then I don't want to hear another complaint out of you for the next six months. Not about the ovens, not about not being able to get pickled pokeberries for some damned dessert you think will take L.A. by storm. No threats to go back to Provence, no bitching about the smog and the traffic." He glared at the other man for a moment. "Do we have a deal?"

"Of course." Armand gave a regal nod and started back to the kitchen. "They will love my pie. *You* will feel like a fool. And I will complain about the ovens, the smog and the traffic, but not about pickled pokeberries, which are something I do not believe exists."

He disappeared through the swinging door, leaving a dead silence behind him. Jack huffed out a breath and shoved his fingers through his hair, making it stand up in dirty-blond waves. He gave Cat an apologetic look.

"Sorry about that. Just a small culinary crisis."

"Pickled pokeberries?" She arched her brows, mouth tilting in a smile.

Jack laughed and shook his head. "I don't remember what the hell he was complaining about last week. Some ingredient he can't get here that proves America is a culinary backwater." He looked from her to Luke and back again. "Everything okay?"

"Just fine." Cat's smile was a little too bright, and the glance she flicked at Luke didn't quite land on him. "Actually, Luke was just about to leave."

It was news to him, but Luke didn't argue. He wasn't sure what he'd had in mind when he came here this afternoon. He'd wanted to make sure Cat was okay. At least that was what he'd told himself, but he'd needed—wanted—something else. He'd wanted her to come home, dammit. He'd wanted her to come back and fill up all the empty places in his life. And she might do it, but not unless he was willing to give something in return.

"I should get back to the office," he said, glancing at his watch. "Sharon was putting together some paperwork for me to sign."

"It was nice to see you," Cat said in a flat little voice, polite, as if he were a casual acquaintance.

"You, too." Luke thought about offering his hand, decided that would be just too surreal and settled for a smile. "I'll be in touch."

Cat returned the smile, but her eyes said she didn't believe him, that she wouldn't be surprised if she never saw him again. He wanted to argue with that look, wanted to tell her that he...that he what? That he wanted her? She knew that already. That he loved her?

Love? Jesus, where had that come from?

An hour later, Luke was staring blankly at the contract in front of him. Sharon was waiting on the other side of the desk, too polite—and too well paid—to mention that it was getting late and if he would just sign the contract, they could both go home. She risked a discreet glance at her watch and resigned herself to dealing with the worst of rush-hour traffic.

"What do you get for a woman to tell her you love her?" The abrupt question startled her, and it took her a moment to register the content of it.

"Excuse me?"

"Not jewelry," Luke said impatiently, as if she'd suggested it. "She doesn't care about jewelry. She doesn't wear perfume."

"Are you... Is this something for your wife?" she asked carefully. The atmosphere in the office was friendly and informal, but Luke had never invited any inquiry into his private life. She had guessed something was wrong in his marriage only from his increasingly surly moods and the fact that his wife hadn't called or come by in almost a month.

"Of course it's for my wife," he snapped, glaring at her. "I want to get her something special. Is that so unusual?"

Sharon valued her job too much to give him the unvarnished truth, so she settled for a noncommittal little *hmm*. He looked a little desperate, she decided. It was a surprisingly good look for him and she couldn't help but think it was a pity his wife wasn't there to see it.

"Does she have any hobbies or interests? Maybe she collects something?"

"Books. She has more damned books than a library." Luke shoved his chair back from the desk and stood up. "I could buy her a bookstore, but that doesn't seem... She gardens. Vegetables, mostly. Grows tons of them."

"Maybe a plant or a tool," Sharon suggested helpfully.

"Compost," Luke said, snapping his fingers.

"Compost?"

"Rotted plants and manure and stuff. Sounds worse than it is."

"I know what compost is," Sharon said. She had a small rose garden of her own. She looked doubtful. "I could order some bags of compost, if you'd like."

"Not bags. She doesn't like the bagged stuff." Luke tapped his fingers on the desk, frowning as he tried to remember a months old conversation he hadn't really been paying attention to at the time. "Mushroom compost," he said suddenly. "That's what it was. Find me some mushroom compost and order a lot of it. I don't know how much. I want it delivered as soon as possible." He glanced at the clock on his desk and frowned in irritation. "Probably too late tonight, but see if you can get them to deliver it tomorrow morning. I don't care what it costs. Double, triple, whatever. How expensive can a bunch of dirt be, anyway? I'll get you the address."

He gave her an impatient look, as if wondering why she was still standing there, and Sharon hurried out of the room, back to her own desk to search out mushroom compost.

There was nothing like spending half an hour hanging over the toilet, throwing your guts up, to start your day off right, Cat thought. God, what sadistic wit had said that pregnancy made a woman glow? The pale, hollow-eyed creature who looked back at her from the mirror had about as much glow as a mud puddle. Even her hair looked dull.

The fact that she'd cried herself to sleep the night before probably didn't help, and she promised herself that it was the last time she would indulge in that particular bit of stupidity. She hadn't realized how much she'd been clinging to the idea that Luke was secretly madly in love with her until he came to the restaurant yesterday, when it had been so very clear that he wasn't madly in love with her, secretly or otherwise. In *like* with her, maybe, but not in love.

A guilty conscience had brought him to see her. Guilt over the scene with Devon, guilt over the baby, maybe guilt about marrying her in the first place. She was fairly sure she would eventually be glad that he'd gone to the trouble of finding her. She would appreciate that he'd cared enough to want to apologize and to check up on her. The pragmatic side of her admitted to being grateful to get the stinking checkbook, even as the hormone-crazed emotional side of her longed to burn it and send him the ashes.

Hopefully, in another three or four weeks, her heart would stop feeling as if it had been ripped from her chest again. And that thought was so maudlin that she felt mildly disgusted with herself.

Splashing water on her face helped, and a quick swipe of mascara and a dusting of blusher improved her reflection to the point where she was fairly sure she wouldn't frighten any small children she happened to encounter. She tried out a few smiles in the mirror, but a stiff baring of teeth was the best she could manage, so she gave up and went into the bedroom to get dressed.

It was still Jack's bedroom, even though she'd been sleeping there for almost a month. Jack had cleared out most of the closet and drawer space for her, but she continued to live out of her suitcase. As she pulled out jeans and a T-shirt, Cat wondered if maybe she hadn't unpacked because, subconsciously, she'd been thinking she would be going home soon. Home to Luke.

Time to put aside that particular fantasy, she told herself briskly. She had tonight off, so she would spend it unpacking, settling in. It was time to face the fact that this *was* home. She wasn't sure where she would end up eventually, but for now, anyway, this was where she was hanging her hat.

Twenty minutes later, she had Ruthie pointing east, a plastic baggie of saltines and a bottle of 7UP in the passenger seat. What would Naomi have to say about this whole situation? Her mother had always said it was important to detach with love, but Naomi had always made it a point to be the one doing the detaching. What if you were the detachee? Had Naomi ever thought about the people she was leaving behind with each of their moves? Had she thought about her daughter when she left to explore her spiritual side? Or was detaching with love a euphemism for "forget as soon as they're out of sight"?

Sighing, Cat decided it was a waste of time to wonder. Naomi was gone, off getting her spirit enlightened. Her own marriage was, for all intents and purposes, over. Luke had said he would be in touch, and she believed him. His conscience would dictate that he make sure she was all right, but having him check on her health wasn't exactly the fulfillment of her dreams.

She patted her stomach. "Looks like it's going to be just you and me, kid." And that wasn't so bad, she told herself, as she flipped on the turn signal to exit the freeway.

Luke had said he wouldn't try to break the contract, which meant that, in a few months, she could be a wealthy woman. Her first instinct was to refuse the money, but she was a soon-to-be-single mother, and she had to put practicality ahead of pride. That money would mean she and her child would never have to worry again. She could buy a house—something modest in a nice neighborhood. She could afford private schools when the time came. It meant security, which hadn't been a driving priority in her life up until now, but a single parent couldn't afford to—

What the hell? Cat stomped on the brake so suddenly that Ruthie's rear end fishtailed before the little car shuddered to a halt. In front of Larry's house, where there had always been something that passed for a yard of sorts, there was now a huge mound of dirt. More than six feet high at the peak, and spreading out from there to take up more than half the yard. She knew it was more than six feet high because Luke was standing in front of it. Luke, who she'd just resigned herself to not seeing much of. Luke, who had turned and was looking at her with an expression that mixed embarrassment, guilt and a peculiar kind of defiance.

Feeling as if she might be stepping into the Twilight Zone, Cat shut off Ruthie's engine and got out of the car. Larry and Susan were standing next to Luke, contemplating the pile of dirt. They turned when she shut the door. Larry gave her a welcoming smile.

"Isn't this interesting, Cat? Luke says it's mushroom compost. Rotted horse manure, if I recall from my reading. And he actually *paid* for it. You know, maybe I was going the wrong direction with my worm project. I was thinking of selling the worms, but maybe I should have been thinking about marketing the castings. Of course, I'd have to do some calculations to see how many worms it would take to produce a cubic yard of castings, but I really think—"

"Good idea," Susan said, taking his arm. "Let's go find a calculator." She cast Cat a speaking look and rolled her eyes toward Luke. "I think Cat and Luke want to talk."

"Yes, of course." Larry patted his pockets, apparently hoping to find a calculator lurking in one. "I'd need to stack the boxes, I think, and I can't remember which variety of worm produces the most—''

He was still muttering as Susan led him around the mound of dirt—mushroom compost—and into the house.

Cat looked from Luke to the compost and back again. Maybe pregnancy had drained away some brain cells, because for the life of her, she couldn't figure out why Luke would have bought enough mushroom compost to mulch half of Los Angeles.

"I wanted them to deliver it around back," he said abruptly. "But they couldn't get the truck back there, so they dumped it all here. I thought maybe I could move it with a wheelbarrow, but it was pretty obvious that I wouldn't live long enough to do it that way.''

"No, probably not," Cat murmured, taking in his disheveled condition. He was wearing jeans and what had probably been a white T-shirt. It was now a sort of tweedy brown, with occasional free-form streaks of black. His face was flushed, either with heat and exertion or with embarrassment, she couldn't be sure which, and his hair was rumpled and liberally dusted with dirt.

"Maybe I shouldn't have ordered so much of it."

"Well, that depends on what you had in mind," she said cautiously.

"This is the stuff you like to use in your garden, right? That stuff you put on the ground to keep the moisture in and do…things?''

"Mulch?"

"Yeah, mulch. You said you liked to use mushroom compost.''

Cat looked at the mound behind him and mentally spread it over her garden beds. With luck, she might still be able to see the top of the cornstalks. Maybe. She had to bite her lips to hold back a semihysterical giggle.

"It's very... Thank you. It's... Why did you buy me compost, Luke?"

"It's an apology." He thrust his fingers through his hair, raining dust onto his shoulders. "And a bribe, I guess."

"An apology for what and a bribe for what?" Cat moved close enough to reach out and take a handful of soil. She could almost feel the life-giving potential of it.

"An apology for being such a jackass." Luke looked at her, then looked away. "The thing with Devon...it... there's no excuse for it."

Cat tossed the compost back on the heap and dusted her hands together, careful not to look at him. "No, there isn't."

"I'm not making excuses," he said doggedly. "I'm apologizing. And I'm apologizing for the way I acted when you told me about the baby. I was wrong to accuse you of trying to get more money. I knew...I always knew it wasn't about the money for you. It was just safer to believe it was."

"Safer?" Cat looked at him, her head tilted as she tried to read his expression. "Safer than what?"

"Than believing you loved me," he said starkly. "I'm...not good at emotions. Not that kind of emotion, anyway. My parents were...well, *dysfunctional* is an understatement. My mother treated infidelity like it was an indoor sport and she was going for the gold, and my father was so obsessed with her that he pretended he didn't see what was going on, even when she brought her lovers home with her." His bleak expression made Cat want to put her arms around him, hold him until the hurt went away. "I'm not using that as an excuse. I'm just telling you so you can maybe understand why I wouldn't be exactly thrilled with the idea of falling in love."

Falling in love? Him? Cat's heart was suddenly thudding against her breastbone.

"I married you because I wanted to get you in bed," he said bluntly.

Cat flushed but met his eyes calmly. "I pretty much figured that out."

"I figured the arrangement would work out pretty well for both of us. I'd get the vineyard, you'd get a lot of money, and we'd spend a year having really hot sex." His mouth curved in a rueful smile. "I just didn't figure on liking you so damned much."

"Sorry," Cat said flippantly. Something was uncurling in the pit of her stomach, something warm and soft and…hopeful.

"I started to think maybe we wouldn't end things at the end of the year. Maybe you'd just hang around a while longer, until we got tired of each other."

"Quite the romantic, aren't you?"

"No, but I thought it was realistic." As if he couldn't help himself, Luke reached out to finger a copper-colored curl that had escaped from the loose knot on top of her head. "I was still thinking of us being long-term bed partners more than anything else. Sort of an affair that happened to come with a marriage license. And then you told me you were pregnant."

"I told you it didn't have to change things between us," Cat reminded him. She turned her head, felt the slight tug on her hair before he released her and let his hand drop to his side.

"Yes but a baby changes everything, whether you want it to or not. Talk about the ultimate in long-term commitment." He met her eyes directly. "I was scared to death. What the hell did I know about being a father? You said I didn't have to take responsibility, but what kind of a man was I if I could walk away from my own child? I'd always despised my father for being weak, for letting my mother humiliate him, and I'd despised them both for being such pisspoor parents but here I was, contemplating abandoning my own child. And you.''

"I'm not a child, Luke. You don't have to worry about abandoning me. I can take care of myself.''

"I know you can.'' His mouth twisted in a self-mocking little smile. "The truth is, you're actually a lot older than I am, Cat. A lot older and more mature, and you can take care of yourself better than I could ever hope to. To be honest, it's a little intimidating. If you were just a little more helpless, I could have told myself I *had* to take care of you, and then I wouldn't have had to face the fact that I flat didn't want you to go.''

"Loving someone isn't a bad thing.''

"It can be.'' Luke shoved his hands in his pockets. He looked at the compost, sighed, then looked back at her again. "I want you to come home, Cat. I want you to live with me. You and the baby. I don't have any idea what kind of a father I'll be, but I figure you'll be a good enough mother to make up for my failings.''

Cat wanted to shout "yes.'' She wanted to leap into his arms, throw herself into happily-ever-after, but she didn't ever want to hurt as much as she'd hurt these past few weeks.

"What happens if you start to panic again?'' She worked hard to keep her tone neutral. "I... Seeing you with Devon was...'' She stopped, shook her head. "I don't think I can do that again.''

"You won't have to.'' Luke took his hands out of his pockets, risked reaching for her. The feel of his fingers gripping hers made Cat shiver, pushed back the cold little knot of fear in her chest. "I may be a jackass, but I do learn from my mistakes. I can't make any guarantees for the future, but I want this. I want you, and I want the baby, even if it scares me to death. Come home, Cat. The house is empty without you. Merry threw a red sock in with my underwear and everything's pink now. Consuela mutters under her breath in Spanish every time she sees me. I think she's putting a curse on me. Keith thinks I'm a jerk. My grandfather told me I was a fool, and Luis just looks disgusted with me.''

"So you want me to move back in because everyone else thinks I should?" Cat was starting to believe it. Starting to believe this was really happening.

"No, I want you to move back in because I love you." Luke tugged her closer, and she let him, let him draw close enough to feel the heat of his body along the length of hers. He smelled of sweat and earth and sunshine. She reached up to wipe her finger across a streak of dirt on his cheekbone.

"So the compost is a bribe?"

"Absolutely. If you'll come home, I'll move the whole damn pile myself, one shovelful at a time."

Her smile was a little shaky, but there was no mistaking the love in her eyes. "I can think of better things for you to do with your time."

"*Home Before Dark* is a beautiful novel, tender and wise.
Susan Wiggs writes with bright assurance, humor and
compassion about sisters, children and the sweet
and heartbreaking trials of life—about how much
better it is to go through them together."

—Luanne Rice

SUSAN WIGGS

Though she's seen the world through her camera lens, Jessie Ryder has
never traveled far enough to escape the painful moment she gave her baby
daughter away. Now, sixteen years later, she's decided to seek out Lila,
even if it means she has to upset the world of Lila's adoptive mother...
her very own sister, Luz.

As Jessie and Luz examine the true meaning of love, loyalty and family,
they are drawn into an emotional tug-of-war filled with moments of
unexpected humor, surprising sweetness and unbearable sadness.
But as the pain, regrets and mistakes of the past slowly rise to the surface,
a new picture emerges—a picture filled with hope and promise and
the redeeming power of the human heart.

HOME BEFORE DARK

"With its lively prose, well-developed conflict and passionate
characters, this enjoyable, poignant tale is certain to enchant."
—*Publishers Weekly* on *Halfway to Heaven* (starred review)

On sale April 2003 wherever hardcovers are sold!

MIRA®

*Introducing an incredible new voice
in romantic suspense*

LAURIE BRETON
FINAL
EXIT

Ten years ago tragedy tore them apart....

But when FBI Special Agent Carolyn Monahan walks back into
the life of Homicide Lieutenant Conor Rafferty, the sizzle
is undeniable. They are back together, albeit reluctantly,
to find the serial killer who is terrorizing Boston.

As the pressure builds to solve the murders, so does the attraction
between Caro and Rafferty. But the question remains:
Who will get to Caro first—the killer or the cop?

Available the first week of April 2003 wherever paperbacks are sold!

MIRA®

Dallas Schulze

66791	LOVING JESSIE	___ $6.50 U.S.	___ $7.99 CAN.
66553	SLEEPING BEAUTY	___ $5.99 U.S.	___ $6.99 CAN.
66464	THE MARRIAGE	___ $5.99 U.S.	___ $6.99 CAN.
66295	THE VOW	___ $5.50 U.S.	___ $6.50 CAN.
66290	HOME TO EDEN	___ $5.99 U.S.	___ $6.99 CAN.

(limited quantities available)

TOTAL AMOUNT $_____
POSTAGE & HANDLING $_____
($1.00 for one book; 50¢ for each additional)
APPLICABLE TAXES* $_____
TOTAL PAYABLE $_____
(check or money order—please do not send cash)

To order, complete this form and send it, along with a check
or money order for the total above, payable to MIRA Books®,
to: **In the U.S.:** 3010 Walden Avenue, P.O. Box 9077, Buffalo,
NY 14269-9077; **In Canada:** P.O. Box 636, Fort Erie, Ontario,
L2A 5X3.

Name:_____
Address:_____ City:_____
State/Prov.:_____ Zip/Postal Code:_____
Account Number (if applicable):_____
075 CSAS

*New York residents remit applicable sales taxes.
 Canadian residents remit applicable
 GST and provincial taxes.

MIRA®

Visit us at www.mirabooks.com   MDS0403BL